Dear Mr. Brody

A.M. JOHNSON

Cover Design: Enchanting Romance Designs
Illustrated Cover Design: Murphy Rae
Cover Illustration: Ashley Quick
Editing: Elaine York, Allusion Publishing
www.allusionpublishing.com
Proofreading: Kathleen, Payne Proofing
Formatting: Elaine York, Allusion Publishing
www.allusionpublishing.com

Dear Mr. Brody

"Dreams do come true,
if only we wish hard enough.
You can have anything in life
if you will sacrifice everything else for it."
— J.M. Barrie, *Peter Pan*

To those who are caught between
different worlds of wanting,
I see you.
Your love is real.

For
Kristy and Cornelia and Anna
Because you're my ride or die.

Note from the Author

One of the characters has a history of being assaulted.
The assault is only spoken about on page briefly,
no graphic depictions are written.

Prologue

DONOVAN

I wanted to believe her tears, but all I saw behind her eyes was a washed-out version of who we once were. Hiding behind my job, her hiding behind friends, we'd found excuses. Too tired to touch, too busy to look, and all we'd had left were wasted pieces of memories—her tan skin on the day we met, and the river water in my shoes. I'd tossed my sneakers down a well because she'd made a joke about how they'd squeaked as I walked. I'd left them behind where countless wishes sank into oblivion, and I'd forgotten, under her gaze, the things about myself that had scared me.

"It isn't what you think," I tried as Elaine's hands fisted in her lap. "Lanie... please. Listen, I—"

"I know what I saw," she said, sounding resigned.

"You have no fucking clue what you're talking about. Mara is a client, for Christ's sake."

I'd taken an author I'd been chasing since I'd started at Lowe Literary two years ago to Sal's for lunch yesterday. Sal's was a diner a few blocks away from my office in downtown Atlanta. It was one of my favorite places, and I used to meet my wife there all the time. If I had seen Lanie walk in I would've introduced her to Mara and had her join us, but instead of being rational, which wasn't a surprise, she'd made an assumption. She'd seen a woman, leaning in, sitting beside me, her hand on my shoulder. It didn't mean anything. Mara was an author I wanted to sign, there was nothing more to it. Instead of confronting me, Lanie blindly pulled the pin from a grenade and ripped our marriage apart.

Maybe now I could tell her the truth.

The truth I'd kept hidden all these years because once I'd met Lanie it didn't matter anymore. I had her. I'd always had her. I'd pushed these pieces of myself aside every day, but in the end, it didn't save us. She'd made sure of that when she'd slept with one of her yoga students last night. My anger surfaced as I stared at my wife, a spiteful barb loaded on my tongue, but I remembered Anne was a room away, sleeping, unaware her whole castle was about to crumble. My ten-year-old daughter, our daughter, was everything. My bright spot on the worst of nights.

"Elaine..." I choked on her name. "It doesn't matter what I say, does it? You've made up your mind." She sat in silence, her lashes wet. "I'd never..." My words stuck in my throat. "I'd never do that to you, to Anne. But you did..."

She raised her eyes and I saw the first flash of worry.

"I... Oh God, what have I done?" she asked, tears leaking down her cheeks.

A tired breath left my lungs, and I raked my fingers through my hair. "What you wanted to do, what you always do. Act impulsively, consequences be damned."

Despite the mood, she huffed out a laugh. "Self-sabotage."

Her lips trembled and I wanted to tell her she fucked up, make her remember, remember us, remember the first time we'd met that day at the river when we were young and stupid. Life was simple back then, music on the car stereo, summer breaks, rafting on Saturdays, her in a see-through yellow bikini. Melted Popsicles, and the cherry flavor of her lips as we kissed under the tree behind her parents' house.

"Why didn't you talk to me, Lanie?"

"I don't know," she said and wiped at her cheeks. "I saw her sitting next to you, her hand on you, it looked... intimate. And things between us haven't been right for a while, Van. We don't... talk. It made sense to me... seeing you there with her. I was upset and he was there for me. I made a mistake."

"I've known you since we were sixteen years old, and you what? Decided our marriage wasn't worth a simple conversation?" I stood from the bed and ran a hand over my face. "You fucked a random yoga student because you *thought* I was cheating on you?"

Her eyes fell to her lap. "I felt relief... when I was with him."

"What?" The heaviness in my chest unbearable.

The green color of her eyes dulled as she held my stare. "You've always held back with me. I feel it, Van. Right here." She rubbed her fist against her breastbone. "Something has always been between us, and I don't know, I thought maybe you'd finally found what you were looking for. You seemed comfortable with her."

"I thought maybe you'd finally found what you were looking for."

Lanie had been enough for me. But knowing she could sense this gap between us all this time, guilt filled my stomach with lead. I couldn't help the curiosity I had about men. Or the way my body reacted without my permission when I looked at a good-looking guy. Since I was a pre-teen, popping boners for no good reason, I'd wondered what it would be like to kiss a guy, and I'd thought about girls with equal curiosity. When I'd met Elaine, everything had seemed to click into place. We'd stayed together through high school, and even managed to make it through college and graduate school. We got married when we got pregnant with Anne at twenty-three and my attraction to men never went away, but it wasn't like I didn't notice other women too. It didn't matter. It was human to look, and I loved Lanie. I loved what we had and never wanted more. But I'd never shared that part of myself, that question I had about my sexuality, and I should have. Maybe if I had been open with her she wouldn't have felt like something was off between us. It was too late now.

"I think I want a divorce," she said, and a wash of surrender poured over me.

It should've gutted me, but I'd be naïve to think this was the first time she'd thought about separating. I sat down across from her on the mattress, her eyes tracking me like she was afraid I'd shatter. She seemed different to me now. Her long, dark hair was pulled into a messy bun. Dressed in workout clothes as always, she looked the same but didn't. Like a painting that had faded over time, she had become a part of my history, my future unknown.

"What about Anne?" I asked. It wouldn't have been like her to turn this into some ugly custody thing. But I had to be sure.

"She needs us both. She needs you."

"I don't want to hate you." It wasn't a total lie. I didn't hate her. I was hurt.

One choice, and she'd changed the course of our lives. For better or for worse, I had no idea. She leaned over, placing her fragile-looking hand on my knee.

"We've been friends for half of our lives, we can't hate each other," she said, the soft smile on her lips faded. "Do you... hate me, though?"

The word yes tripped over itself inside my brain, but I shook my head. "You're not the only one to blame, Lanie. It takes two people to have a strong marriage, I know I've made mistakes."

"And there really isn't anyone else?" she asked, and hell, I wanted to tell her then. Maybe if I said it out loud it would be real, not just a concept I'd wrestled with all my life. "For a minute I thought you were into the blonde agent you work with."

"Claire?" A real laugh escaped from my aching chest. "Hard pass. She's Satan in heels. Not my type."

"Maybe Anders is more your type?" she teased, making my pulse jump, wondering if maybe she'd figured it out.

Anders Lowe owned Lowe Literary. I envied my boss sometimes. He happened to be openly bisexual and was engaged to a man. I couldn't lie to myself and pretend I didn't find him attractive. It was another secret I kept in a vault, buried where I couldn't evaluate it too much. But as she looked at me, waiting for an answer, that secret stabbed me in the ribs as I tried to breathe.

"There's never been anybody else for me, Lanie. Only you. Stop trying to be the victim, you're the one who fucked around."

"Van, I'm so —"

"I don't want an apology." I didn't want to fight. Exhaustion weighed on my shoulders as I stood and turned down the sheets. I could feel her eyes on me as I lifted my shirt over my head and took off my watch, setting it on the side table like I did every night. Anxious, I didn't think I'd be able to sleep. "I'm going to take shower."

"Okay."

"I think I should sleep in the guest room, until we figure shit out."

"Okay."

"We should tell Anne tomorrow, maybe let her school counselor know as well."

"Okay."

"Okay?" I asked, and she blinked a few times before fresh tears appeared on her cheeks.

"I don't know what else to say. This is really happening. We're getting a divorce."

It would be easy to walk over to her, to take her into my arms and kiss her, ask her if we could do couples therapy, and hope maybe one day I'd forgive her. But the thought of a fresh start released the tight knots in my shoulders. Lanie and I hadn't been happy for a long time. I couldn't remember the last time we'd gone out together without Anne, or talked about something other than bills, and work, or argued over whose turn it was to do the dishes. We didn't find ways to touch each other like we used to. We didn't stay up late tangled inside one another, fucking and talking about dreams and hope and us. Her infidelity was the wakeup call, the key to something we'd shoved neatly behind a closed door. We'd changed, we'd become different people. I was thirty-three years old and had no idea who I was anymore, who she was. How was it possible to know everything about a person, and yet they were still a stranger?

"I think... I think it's a good thing. For both of us. For Anne."

"I think so too," she said, a sad smile rising at the corner of her lips.

I waited for the fear, the uncertainty to overwhelm me, but the possibility of finally getting to know the person I'd locked away all these years made everything seem less tragic. For the first time in over a decade I had a chance to be on my own, to discover who I was without her.

Chapter 1

DONOVAN

Six Months Later

A nervous excitement coursed through me, my hands shaking as I packed my laptop into my bag. Glancing at the clock, I had about an hour before my class started. *My class.* I smiled and all the nervous energy lifted. I'd gotten a second job, part time as an adjunct professor at a small state college teaching an introductory creative writing class in the evening. After my divorce finalized a couple of months ago, I wanted to do something for myself. I'd always wanted to be a teacher. I loved writing, and being an agent was amazing, but I was tired of always feeling like a salesman. I wanted to be a part of the process, I wanted to help people create. But getting pregnant with Anne as fast as Lanie and I had, I hadn't had the option of being picky. With my lack of experience, I would have had a better chance of getting struck by lightning than finding a spot as an English professor at any of the local colleges. I'd tried to look in my field of study for a job, and the only thing I'd found was an entry-level editor job at Bartley Press. It hadn't been exactly what I'd wanted, but it had paid the bills. I'd worked my way up and found I didn't hate being a copy editor. I'd worked there for eight years before Anders recruited me to work at his agency. The money sounded amazing, and I'd loved the idea of working with authors one on one.

Since my divorce, something had shifted. I moved out of the home I'd built with my ex-wife and moved into my small, three-bedroom house in Decatur, a suburb east of Atlanta. Anne was with me two nights a week and every other weekend, but my loneliness, when she wasn't there, was bone deep. Nights were the worst. I couldn't sleep, my mind would race, and I'd wonder about Anne, wonder if she'd brushed her teeth, if Lanie had remembered to read her our bedtime stories. It didn't matter that there were always sixty minutes in every hour, in the darkness of night, time was infinite. A loop that never ended, and I needed something to fill all those seconds of worry and doubt. I'd found this part-time job through an old colleague at Bartley, and I snagged it. Winchester State College wasn't a prestigious school, and the pay was nothing compared to what I made with Lowe, but it was something to do. Something to stop myself from overthinking every choice I'd made. To stop myself from sinking into depression. It would be too easy to allow the dark, the night, to swallow me whole.

I ran a hand through my hair and laughed at myself. Fuck, I was being overdramatic.

"Something funny?" Anders stood inside the doorway of my office.

The stern set of his shoulder belied the humor in his tone.

"Nah... just thinking." I checked my watch. "I better head out if I'm going to make it on time."

"I wanted to remind you about Wilder's release party tomorrow, he'll never let me live it down if I don't invite everyone."

"If Lanie is okay to watch Anne I can be there." He seemed relieved. I wished I could say the same. I hadn't been out to a club since college. "Why is he having it at a night club?"

Anders quirked his brow and shook his head. "I stopped asking him about his choices a long time ago. I love the guy, but he is hands down the most unpredictable author I have on my client list."

"And the most lucrative," I reminded him. Wilder was quirky, but I guess it didn't matter when he was one of the top-grossing authors Lowe Literary represented.

"Touché..." He leaned against the doorjamb, stuffing his hands in his pockets. He seemed anxious, his eyes avoiding mine. "I know we already talked about this but... this professor job, it's not something you'll eventually want to do full time, right?"

"I'm not going anywhere, I promise. This is... I'm not sure how to explain it. I need something that's just mine. That wasn't a part of my life when I was with Lanie."

"That makes sense." He relaxed a little and gave me a small, sympathetic smile. "You're a great agent, I don't want to lose you."

I laughed and his smile widened. "Trust me, I couldn't afford the gas it would take to drive to WSC with what they're paying me."

"Is it terrible I'm glad the salary isn't comparable?"

His chuckle was warm, and it lightened his mood even more. Anders was a hard ass when he wanted to be, but once you got to know him, once he trusted you and let you in, you'd never find someone more loyal.

"Maybe I'll find the next Kurt Vonnegut in my class."

He scoffed, arrogant as hell. "I highly doubt it. Let me know when you get sick of reading mediocre poems about adolescent loves lost, and kids looking for an easy A. Maybe I'll give you a raise."

"Hey, you never know," I said, and he moved aside as I stepped out into the hall.

"Just don't tell them you're a literary agent, you'll have a bunch of want-to-be Wilder Welles blowing up your inbox."

"When did you get so cynical? Please tell me so I can skip that part of my thirties."

He smirked as we rounded the corner to the lobby. Kris, his assistant, was on the phone. Her brows creased as she frowned. "I'll tell him," she said. "He's in meetings for the rest of the afternoon, but I'll let him know you called." Kris exhaled, a tired smile forming on her lips as she hung up the phone. "Ready for your first day, Van?"

"Don't encourage him." Anders lips twitched, fighting a smile. "It's almost like you want him to leave."

"I liked it much better when you weren't a smart ass," she said. "But I suppose I have your fiancé to thank for that."

"He has helped me reach my full potential." Anders clapped me on the shoulder. "Seriously, though, good luck today."

"Thanks... I'm going to need it."

"Nonsense," Kris chided, clucking her tongue like a mother hen even though she was my age. "You'll knock 'em dead."

God, hopefully not of boredom.

I ignored the anxiety fluttering around in my stomach as I turned to leave. On the way to my car, the late August heat made the fabric of my dress shirt stick to me like a second skin. I rolled my sleeves to my elbows, but it did little to help. Once I was in my car, I cranked up the AC, hoping this job would be the thing I needed to move on, and not a giant mistake.

A few students were already in their seats when I walked into the classroom. I probably should have nodded my head or something, but I walked past them without an acknowledgement, far too anxious to even manage a smile.

Not very friendly, professor.

The room wasn't as small as I thought it would be. Six long tables divided the room and could seat five students. The odd number of seats per row niggled at my already amped-up brain. What if there was only one seat left, and two students wanted to sit together on the same row? What if there was only one seat, and it was in the middle? Who the hell would want that seat? Not me, and Jesus Christ, I needed to calm down. I told myself to take a deep breath and set my laptop bag under my desk. A little less frazzled, I unzipped the bag and pulled out what I needed. I could hear the classroom door opening and closing, the whispered conversations hummed around me. I kept busy fiddling with the papers I'd set out, and took my time, breathing, counting backward from one hundred in my head. Counting was a tool I used. It soothed me. Numbers never changed. I hadn't been this nervous in a while, and as I connected the wire from the overhead projector to my laptop, I internally laughed at myself. Most people considered me laidback, and for the most part I was, but every now and then, all the worry and insecurities I figured we all had to fight every day would stage a coup.

The time on my watch warned me I couldn't delay any longer, and I inhaled deeply one last time as I raised my eyes and met the class.

"Good evening, everyone, I'll try to make introductions as painless as possible." Soft laughter sifted through the air, and I gained the confidence I needed to continue. I swept my gaze around the room, not lingering on one student for too long as I spoke. "I probably shouldn't tell you this, but this is my first teaching job, so go easy on me." A blonde girl in the front row blushed when my eyes landed on her, and I averted my gaze. Shit, I was awkward. "My name is Donovan Brody, and I'll try to remember all of your names, but I can't promise anything."

One of the students near the back of the classroom raised his hand with a smirk. My heart rattled out a few unsteady beats as I braced myself for a smart-ass comment.

"Yes... Mr.—"

"Mills, sir. Parker Mills."

His eyes, though I couldn't decipher the shade from where I stood, twinkled with mischief. His features were classically handsome. A strong jaw, a sharp nose, full lips, and why the hell was I looking at his lips?

He ran a hand over his short, dirty blond hair, his smirk turning into a lopsided smile before I looked away. "Can we call you Donovan?"

Shit.

Could they?

I racked my brain, trying to remember if any of my professors were okay with being called by their first names and came up blank. Parker chuckled at my hesitation and my face heated.

"I think Mr. Brody would be most appropriate."

He tapped his pencil to his bottom lip. "Noted."

I should have moved on. I had an entire speech prepared about my history with Bartley Press, and how writing was my passion, but for some damn reason I went off script. "How about we all take a second to get to know each other. Tell us your name, and something about yourself you'd like to share. Starting with you, Mr. Mills."

The guy sitting next to him stifled a laugh, but I ignored it. Putting students on the spot hadn't been my intention, these icebreaker tactics were my least favorite when I was in school. But writing was personal, and if I wanted them to create together, we had to get comfortable with each other.

"As you already know, my name's Parker Mills, but call me Parker or Park, it doesn't matter to me. I served four years in the Air Force. I'm getting a late start at college, but I'm grateful to be here."

"Thank you for your service," I said, and he lowered his eyes, rubbing the back of his neck as he nodded, his humility surprised me. "And how about you?" I asked his friend.

"Name's Marcos Basulto, I'm a design major, but this idiot made me take this class with him." He elbowed Parker and he winced.

"Oh?"

"Yeah, but I needed the extra humanities credit so..."

Marcos waved his hand dramatically for me to move on, and I noticed his nails were painted bright pink. It stood out against his tan skin, but the color suited him.

"Well, Mr. Basulto, I hope this class won't be a waste of your time." I hadn't meant to sound as harsh as I had, so I added, "I'm glad you're here."

It took about fifteen minutes for the whole class to introduce themselves. The majority of the twenty-three students were here for the humanities credits, only a handful wanted to be actual writers. It disappointed me what Anders had said might've been right, that most of these kids would write bullshit, looking for an easy A. My hopes had been high, but I refused to lower the bar. If they wanted an A, they would have to earn it.

"Let's get started," I said, and Marcos raised his hand.

"What about you?" he asked, speaking before I had a chance to address him. "Aren't you going to tell us some random facts about yourself? I mean, it's only fair."

A quiet wave of smiles and laughter streamed through the room again, but Parker kept his eyes glued to the desk, slumping down in his chair as his friend beamed. Apparently making people uncomfortable was something he did for sport.

"You're right, Mr. Basulto. It's only fair." I leaned against the desk. "I worked as a copy editor for most of my career until I started two years ago at Lowe Literary as an agent, helping writers to get published, and managing their careers. But I've always wanted to teach, so here I am."

A young woman near the back shoved her hand in the air. "Do you work with famous authors?"

"Sometimes... and no, I'm not at liberty to discuss which authors I represent." I smiled as I picked up the course syllabus from my desk and started to pass them out. "Though this is a writing class, I'll be requiring you to read three books over the semester." A collective groan echoed throughout the class, and I tried not to laugh. "Come on now, three books in fifteen weeks isn't a lot to ask."

I made my way up the aisle, giving each student at the end of a row a few handouts to pass down, when I reached Parker, he thanked me and grinned. This close it was easier to decipher the light sapphire color of his eyes. A familiar twinge warmed my stomach and I looked away. Swallowing, I found my voice as I made my way back to my desk. "It's important, as a writer, to never stop reading, expanding your vocabulary. You may choose whatever three novels you like, but they must be fiction, and they must not all be in the same genre."

A student from the second row, Gerald if I remembered correctly, asked, "What's a genre?"

I had to stop myself from cringing.

Was he kidding?

"It's a type of book." Another student answered for me.

"That's correct," I said. "Fiction is a genre, but within fiction there are other genres." He chewed his lip as he furiously wrote down what I was saying. "Young adult, mystery, women's fiction, historical fiction... For the purposes of this class, I would like you to try and pick at least one classic."

"Classic, like Hemingway?" Parker asked.

Though it shouldn't have mattered to me, I wondered why he'd taken this class. Why he'd forced his friend to take it with him? Did he want to be a writer, or was he here for a quick three credits like most of his classmates?

"Sure... Bronte, Fitzgerald, or even Salinger are acceptable. There's this marvelous thing called a library if you find you're having trouble picking a book."

"Ha-ha." He smirked again, and I found myself smiling as well. "I hear Google is great too."

"Indeed, Mr. Mills. It is." I held onto his gaze longer than I should have, and a wide smile spread across his lips.

I couldn't tell if this guy was a class clown or not, but despite his sarcasm, he seemed like he wanted to be here, unlike his friend who looked half asleep at his side. As I spoke, I raised my voice and Marcos jumped. "Now, for your first assignment."

Another chorus of groans.

This was going to be a long semester.

Chapter 2

PARKER

"Why are you so annoying?" I asked as Marcos hovered over my shoulder, his hand on the arm of my desk chair. "Seriously, man. If you want me to go to that club with you tonight, you have to let me finish this essay."

"You've been working on this forever, *mijo*. Mr. Brody asked for a get-to-know-you essay, not an autobiography." He fiddled with the small blue feather earring dangling from his earlobe.

"Nice feather."

"What do you think? I bought it today," he said, and I shrugged, the motion earning me a slap to the back of the head.

"Ow... I'm sorry. It's kind of flashy." I had to press my lips together to stop myself from smiling.

"Thank you."

"That wasn't a compliment."

"That's why I know it's perfect. You have terrible taste." Marcos grinned and dropped his eyes to the document on my screen.

I attempted to close it before he could get a good look at what I'd written, but he reached over me with his long-ass arm and snatched it right off the desk.

"Asshole, you're going to break it."

He swiped a handful of his wavy dark hair from his forehead as he sat down on my bed. "Why so secretive?"

"Give me my laptop, shithead. Don't make me kick your skinny ass."

He ignored me like I figured he would, reading my damn essay like he had some sort of best-friend-roommate right to invade my privacy. To be fair, there wasn't much we kept from each other. I'd never hidden anything from him before, and I wasn't sure why I thought I needed to now. But the smirk on his face while he read my essay had me feeling queasy. If he thought it was crap, my friend who'd always had my back, my ride or die, what the hell would my professor think? Marcos and I had been friends since our first day of basic training in San Antonio when we'd both puked up our guts after running miles in the mid-summer heat. It had been a relief to know I hadn't been the only one struggling that day. By some sheer magic, we'd both gotten through training and had been stationed at MacDill Air Force Base, in Florida, after graduation. Those four years could stay in the past as far as I was concerned. If it hadn't been for Marcos, I'm not sure I would've made it. Like ashes scattered in the wind, without him I would have been lost. For four years I'd forced myself to stay in a closet I never wanted, and every now and then, I worried some of that darkness would never fade.

"This is good," he said, surprise coloring his tone. "I guess that public affairs job was useful after all."

"I basically wrote propaganda for the Air Force, Marcos." I rubbed my palm over my short hair, a familiar knot twisting inside my stomach. "This class... it's different. I want to write stuff I'm proud of, stuff for me."

"It wasn't propaganda."

"Close enough." I stood, not wanting to go down this road. When I was enlisted, it had been my job to make the Air Force look good regardless of the truth. Some days being in the service had been everything I'd thought it would be, and other days I'd rather not revisit. "Give it back."

Marcos sighed and handed me my laptop. "I think the essay is good, I mean, I'm no expert, but it's missing something."

"Oh yeah, what's that?"

Sensing my mood, Marcos did what he did best. Made me laugh. "In the hopes and dreams portion..." He tapped a finger against his lips. "You forgot to add how bad you want to fuck our new teacher."

"Christ... get out of here with that bullshit." I laughed and set my laptop on my desk, opening it before I sat down again.

"Whatever, *mijo*. Don't act like you weren't flirting with him yesterday. *Can we call you Donovan*?" He mocked. "You might as well have gotten on your knees for him right then and there, it was that obvious."

"Fuck off." I tried to sound pissed but my widening smile gave me away. "He's hot, I couldn't help myself."

"You never could," he said, his smirk a reminder of how well this asshole knew me.

"Do you think Mr. Brody even realizes how sexy he is?"

He had a quiet confidence, but there was something timid about him. Something nervous behind those wolfish gray eyes of his.

"Probably. And I'd bet money he's straight and married to some perfect-looking woman and has perfectly boring sex. A man that gorgeous has to have flaws. It's the way the universe balances shit."

"You're probably right," I said, and he hummed his acknowledgement. "I bet he has a big dick, though."

"You wish." Laughing, he flopped backward onto my mattress. "Speaking of big dicks... Tam's going to be at the club tonight."

Tam worked with Marcos at an upscale clothing boutique near Piedmont Park. He wasn't one-hundred-percent my type. I liked my guys to be a little less fragile. Tam was elegant with long legs and pretty lips. His ass was nice, though. I was a sucker for a bubble butt. And it wasn't a secret he'd be down to mess around. He flirted with me relentlessly whenever we all got together.

"Yeah?"

"Yup, you should go. You never go out anymore. Always sitting around reading, you need to get a life."

"I guess I could tear myself away from this essay for a few hours."

Marcos sat up and smiled. *"Thank God...* you take this school shit way too seriously."

"It's kind of important if we ever want to have real careers."

He stood and sauntered toward my bedroom door with purpose. "We're just starting our junior year. It's okay to have a little fun, Park... we can worry about real life later. You haven't hooked up with anyone in a while. And one-on-one time with yourself in the shower doesn't count. Be ready by ten. And that's not a suggestion, it's an order."

I huffed out a laugh as he left. I wasn't much of a hookup kind of guy, it reminded me too much of all the sloppy, under-the-radar shit I had to pull while enlisted. Nothing ever felt real then, it had to be quick blow jobs in bar bathrooms or fucking in a back seat of a car like a teenager, hoping to God no one would find out. I wasn't into that anymore. I wanted something solid, something I didn't have to hide. Being out in the military wasn't impossible, but I'd learned the hard way it was easier if I kept my head down. There were some memories not worth dredging up, and as if the bruises and the cracked ribs had never healed, I struggled to take a deep breath. I'd never change my choice to join, my choice to stay. I'd joined to make my dad happy, even though he'd passed away of a heart attack when I was ten, enlisting was something I had to do for him. I'd idolized my father and the stories he'd told me about serving his country. When he'd died, I'd promised myself I would make him proud. On some of my hardest nights, I'd lie awake, wondering if my father would accept me as a gay man. When I'd come out to my mom, I was only fourteen, and she'd told me he'd love me no matter who I was attracted to. My sister Mandi was six years older than me and had gotten to spend more time with him, and she agreed with Mom. She'd said my dad thought the world of me, and there wasn't anything that would've changed how much he'd loved me. I'd like to believe that was true, that he was up in heaven smiling down on me.

I swiped my finger over the touchpad of my laptop and the screen came to life, my essay staring back at me. Reading over it again, I deleted at least half of it. Marcos could make fun of me all he wanted, tell me it was only an essay, but I'd written enough half-truths to last me a lifetime. I couldn't do it anymore.

"In fifteen-hundred words tell me who you are, tell me the story of your life. It doesn't have to be perfect, but it does have to be honest. Real words matter."

Mr. Brody's challenge sat heavy on my shoulders. Without knowing it, he'd given me the courage to write what I wanted. What I needed.

Real words. The real me.

Humid air thick with sweat surrounded us as we made our way toward the bar. The Masquerade wasn't the biggest or the best gay club in Atlanta, but it had amazing music on Tuesday nights according to my best friend and perpetual thorn in my side. The place was decently sized with three bars, a large, circular one in the back, and two smaller ones on each side of the open industrial space. Exposed ventilation and metal beams decorated the high ceilings, and the bright multicolored lights bounced off the concrete walls and floors creating a dizzying effect on the dance floor. The sea of bodies moved to the beat of the bass, pushing us down stream toward the back of the club. Hands and fingers brushed against my bare arms, setting off an explosion of goosebumps across my skin.

"What about that guy?" Marcos hollered back at me once we'd found our way out of the crowd. "The one with the goth vibe."

"The guy in the leather Speedo?" Laughing, I shook my head. "He has a nice body, I guess, but he looks like he's in his forties?"

"Nothing wrong with a silver fox."

"I'm not drunk enough for forties or leather." We'd been here for about an hour, giving the buzz of my first few drinks time to wear off while we'd danced. "I think I'll pass."

"It's not always about you... I was looking for me." He bumped me with his hip, and I chuckled. "You really think he's that old?"

"At least."

"Fuck, I don't think I care... look at his abs." Marcos licked his lips, subtle as ever, and the guy smiled at him. "Oh shit, he saw me."

"He could probably feel your boner from across the room."

Marcos flipped me off, and I followed behind him, wishing I had half his confidence sometimes. I was nervous about meeting up with Tam tonight. It had been forever since I'd had any interest in dating. But Marcos wasn't afraid of anything. He wore what he wanted. Fucked who he wanted, and never apologized for any of it. Like me, he'd hidden his sexuality while he was enlisted. He could say it hadn't affected him, he liked to pretend everything was butterflies and cupcakes for the most part, but when we'd gotten out two years ago, and he'd decided to move back home with me to Atlanta, a switch had flipped inside him. Maybe he wanted to make up for lost time, and hell, maybe it was time I did too.

Once we found our way to the bar, I ordered our drinks. I took a sip of my vodka tonic and scanned the dance floor. "I wonder where Tam is."

"He said he'd be here thirty minutes ago."

"Maybe he changed his mind?"

"That guy has the biggest hard-on for you, I doubt it." He pulled out his phone. "I'll text him."

"Don't make me look desperate. If he doesn't show, it is what it is. There are a few guys here I wouldn't mind hanging out with tonight."

"Oh yeah, show me one," he said, calling my bluff.

He rested his hand on his cocked hip, and if it wasn't for the red harness and white skinny jeans he had on, I'd say he looked almost maternal.

"The bartender for one."

"Ew, no, everyone fucks the bartender."

"That's a stereotype," I argued. "Don't be a dick."

"I veto the bartender. Moving on... what about..." He glanced over my shoulder as said slutty bartender smiled at me. "*Holy shit.*"

26

"What?"

Marcos's eyes were wide as he lifted his glass to his lips and took a sip. "Mr. Brody."

I exhaled, annoyed. "Marcos... you have to stop with that shit, it's not—"

"No, Mr. Brody is here. In this club. Right fucking now."

"What?" I turned my head, following his line of sight and froze. Mr. Brody tipped his head back and laughed. His dark, almost black hair looked blue under the lights. "Um..."

"I know."

"Oh, my shit... is that Wilder Welles?"

"Who?"

"Holy fuck, it is."

"Park, I don't know who this Wilder whoever the hell is, and I don't care. Our hot as sin professor is standing less than a hundred yards away. In a gay club." He knocked on my forehead with his knuckles. "Gay... Club."

I shoved his hand away and laughed. "Wilder Welles... he's one of my favorite authors, and he's famous as fuck, dumbass."

"Yeah... still don't care." He grabbed the sleeve of my shirt. "Let's go say hi."

"Marcos, come on... we shouldn't—"

"We should and we shall."

When I didn't budge, he groaned.

"It's not a good idea. We should give Mr. Brody some privacy, isn't there some code of conduct about fraternizing with your teacher?"

Marcos stared at me, his face expressionless. "Who cares about codes and rules? We don't subscribe to any of that shit anymore, my friend. And if the man wanted privacy, he wouldn't be out at a club."

"Fair, but it feels rude. He's with a huge group of people. And just because he's out with friends, doesn't mean he wants to be bothered." I drained my drink in one gulp and set it on the bar. "Besides, Tam is probably up front looking for us."

"Fine..." Marcos finished his drink and lifted his hand, grabbing the bartender's attention. "If you want to suck your whole life, I can't stop you."

I gave him a cheesy grin. "I'm pretty good at sucking."

"Ew... I need to find my silver fox anyway. I'm in desperate need of some maturity."

Marcos was a lot to handle sometimes, and living with the guy, I questioned my sanity. But he was the levity I needed, and I was his gravity. We balanced each other. I draped my arm around his shoulder, and he turned to look at me. "Thanks for dragging me out tonight."

"Kicking and screaming," he teased and ordered another round of drinks. "Can we get four shots of whiskey."

"Whiskey?" I asked.

"Why not?" He shrugged off my arm. "Liquid courage."

"For what?"

"See, that's the fun part," he said. "I don't know."

The bartender poured our shots, not spilling a drop. He winked at me as he slid them across the counter. "Enjoy."

Marcos rolled his eyes and picked up his glass. "Here's to leather Speedos and hot teachers."

"And slutty bartenders," I added.

"I guess I can drink to that."

We tossed back both of our shots in less than a minute, and as the warmth of the alcohol crawled through me, though I'd never admit it to Marcos, I might've snuck another look at Mr. Brody.

Chapter 3

DONOVAN

Overwhelmed. The word circled around my brain as I tried to soak everything in. The club pulsed around me, the lights, the music, the people, all of it too much to process. I couldn't decide if I was turned on or terrified. I drank in all the half-naked bodies, the men dancing with men, the kissing in dark corners. Picturing myself out on the dance floor, hands, and skin, and sweat, I couldn't breathe. I wanted it but had no idea how or where to start. It was comfortable here, with a gin and tonic as my shield, standing by the table Lowe Literary had reserved for the party. The alcohol warmed me from the inside out and made it easier for me to smile back at the men who'd pass by me on their way to the bar.

"You're a popular attraction tonight," Wilder said out of breath, grabbing a bottle of water off the table. "Half of the guys I invited have asked me if you're single."

My face heated and I took a deep sip of my drink. Wilder unscrewed the cap on his bottle and stared at me.

"What?" I asked. "You're serious?"

"Oh no... you're one of those guys," he said, lifting the bottle to his lips.

Intimidated, I avoided his scrutinizing gaze. Wilder was a beautiful man, tall and lean, with thick, curly brown hair that never knew which way it wanted to lay. I had to admit I liked the way he wore make-up sometimes. Tonight, he had a dark shade of blue shadow on his eyes. His skin dewy with sweat, glistened like the sequined letters on his shirt. *Gay As Fuck.* I loved that he wore his eccentricity like a crown. He was also very married.

"I have no idea what you're talking about."

Wilder raised a skeptical brow and leaned his hip against the table. "You have no idea how attractive you are. My husband is the same way. Y'all walk around looking like gods, giving all the gays a heart attack, and you don't even know it." He nodded his head toward the dance floor where Jax, his husband, was dancing with two women I didn't recognize. "I mean, look at him, it's unfair, if I'm being honest."

Jax was tall with blond hair and big blue eyes. He had a smile that could light an entire room, and it didn't help that the guy was built with muscle I could only dream about. I looked nothing like him. "Your husband is a gladiator."

"I know, right?" He grinned and poked me in the chest. "You may not be a gladiator, but you could get any guy in this club if you wanted to. I mean, at least the single ones. All of this..." He waved his hand at me. "Wasted on a straight man."

"Who said I was straight?" I asked, and he blinked at me a few times. A speechless Wilder was unheard of, and it took me a second to realize what I'd admitted to. I blamed the gin. "I mean... I'm not sure?"

"Is that a question?" His smile widened and he leaned in closer, entirely too excited.

I cleared my throat, my nerves itching at the back of my neck, I tried to rub them away with the palm of my hand. I'd never told anyone about my attraction to men. But as I looked around, this need inside me bloomed. I wanted to experience all of this, to feel free to do what I wanted, to say out loud what I never could before. "I've always been attracted to men, but I guess I never had a chance to do anything about it."

"You're in the right place, then," he said. "Or when you're ready, you could download the Pegasus app. It used to be my favorite. All kinds of guys to choose from."

"Is that a dating app?"

"Sure," he said, his lips spreading into a knowing smile before taking another swig of water.

"Wilder..."

"Ugh... fine, it's kind of a hook-up app, but you can find guys who aren't just down to fuck. Make an anonymous account and have a look. No one has to know." He gently shoved my arm. "Live a little. Explore. It's fun."

"Maybe I will... Thanks."

"Of course." He waved at Jax, and his husband smiled back at him.

"You know... I've never told anyone before."

He held his hand to his chest. "Aw... I'm honored to be your fairy gay godmother. You're like my very own bi Frodo looking for his Sam."

I laughed and set my empty glass on the table. "Anders told me you have an unhealthy obsession with *Lord of the Rings*."

"Anders is an asshole."

"Why am I an asshole this time?" Anders asked as he walked past Wilder and handed me another drink. "I saw you needed a refill."

"Thanks," I said.

"It's in your nature, babe. You can't help yourself." Wilder kissed him on the temple. "I'm going to dance with my husband and celebrate the fact I wrote another fabulous book."

Anders laughed. "So humble."

"I do try," Wilder said with a sly grin before walking, with his head held high, to the dance floor.

"He's not really that conceited, you know," Anders said, setting his drink on the table. "All that attitude, it's a defense mechanism."

"You think so?"

"I've known him a long time. He's happy tonight. His book is published. He can breathe. You should see him when he's behind on his deadline and hasn't showered in a week. He's not so arrogant, then."

I laughed, unable to picture him not being elegant at all times.

"How are you doing?" he asked. "You've been hiding out over here all night."

"I'm absorbing... everything."

He chuckled. "The club scene can be a lot to take in. Not really my thing. I'm glad you came out, though, since Claire couldn't be bothered."

"Not surprising," I said. "She's not very social."

"Understatement of the year," he said, shaking his head with a laugh.

It was rare, getting to hang out with Anders outside of the office. Though I considered him a friend, he tried to be as professional as possible at work. He talked about his life, and his fiancé popped in all the time for a visit, but it was nice to see this casual side to him.

"You're not an asshole, by the way," I said over the rim of my glass. "Wilder was mad that you called his love for *Lord of the Rings* obsessive."

"I'm simply an asshole who speaks the truth."

A few people from the party started to crowd around the table. Some of them I recognized as Anders's clients, and a handful from Bartley Press, but for the most part, I'd never seen half these people before. Ethan eventually made his way over from the dance floor, his hair sticking to his forehead with sweat as Anders leaned down to kiss him. I didn't mean to stare, but it was impossible not to. A mixture of envy and wonder swirled through my veins, the gin lighting it on fire. Ethan pulled away, his face flush as he pressed another kiss to Anders's jaw.

Feeling like an intruder, I moved my attention to take another look around the club and almost dropped my drink. "Oh my God."

"What is it?' Ethan asked, and I quickly stepped partially behind Anders.

"I think I saw one of my students."

Ethan exhaled a laugh. "Shit, you scared me, I thought it was something serious."

"It is serious. I've never felt this old in my life."

"Welcome to the club." Anders patted my back. "Just wait till you're thirty-nine and you're staring forty in the face."

"Shit, I hope he didn't see me."

I chanced another glance at the dance floor to be sure and found Parker Mills and his friend Marcos from my creative writing class grinding against each other under the strobe lights. Curiosity winning over caution, I stared longer than I should have. Parker pulled Marcos toward him, a salacious smile on his full lips as his hand slid down to Marcos's ass. A knot formed in my throat, and I found it difficult to swallow. Were they together? It dawned on me I shouldn't care. My students' relationships were not my business.

"Which one is he?" Ethan asked.

"Two of them, actually." I nodded to where they were both dancing.

"The guy in the red harness is a student?" Anders sounded incredulous.

"Yeah, and the guy he's dancing with is a student as well."

"Damn," Ethan said. "I could not be a teacher."

"Should I be concerned?" Anders asked with a smile, draping his arm around Ethan's waist.

Ethan grinned up at him and whispered something in his ear I couldn't hear. By the look on my boss's face, I didn't think it was something I'd want to know anyway. Luckily, when I turned around, Parker and Marcos weren't there any longer, or at least I couldn't see them anymore. Just in case, I decided to leave and avoid an awkward run-in if possible. It was late enough, I needed to head home anyway. Lanie had to be at the yoga studio early tomorrow, and I'd promised to take Anne to school if she watched her tonight. We'd planned for her to drop Anne off at seven in the morning, and even though I'd only had a few drinks, I was old enough to know I'd regret it tomorrow.

"I think I'm going to head home. I have an early morning."

"I thought the office was closed tomorrow," Ethan said.

"It is, but I have to take my daughter to school, and I have a lesson to plan for tomorrow night."

"You're not driving, right? You have a ride?" Anders asked, pulling out his phone. "I can call for one."

"No, I didn't drive, and I can grab a Lyft. Don't worry about it."

"I insist." Anders's fingers tapped across the screen of his cell before I could argue. "Looks like they're about five minutes out."

"Thanks, I appreciate it."

I said my goodbyes to Ethan and Anders, asking them to tell Wilder thank you for the invite, and headed toward the front door. A guy with dark hair and a nice smile caught my eye as I passed the bar. His light brown eyes met mine, and my mouth went dry. My heart wild in my chest, I slowed as he stood. Did I have the courage to talk to him? Each one of my breaths was thick with anticipation as he moved closer, and I took a step toward him. I was in my head, going over what the hell I would even say to him. A simple hi could work, or hello. As I was trying to build up the courage and untie my tongue, someone knocked into my right side. A splash of liquid rained down on my shoes and wet the bottom of my jeans.

"Shit, I'm—" he stuttered as I grabbed him by the arms, hoping to stop us both from falling onto the sticky floor. Parker Mills stared at me, his blue eyes wide, his cheeks filling with color. The guy I'd wanted to talk to completely forgotten. "Fuck... I mean, I'm sorry. I wasn't paying attention."

"It's okay," I said, shocked and fumbling for words, I realized I was still holding on to him for dear life. This close I could smell his soap and sweat. The thick muscle of his arms warm under my palms. I dropped my hands immediately. "It's not a big deal."

"I think I ruined your shoes," he said, placing his half-empty glass on one of the nearby tables.

"I never liked these shoes anyway."

His laugh was nervous. "I should watch where I'm going."

He sounded a little drunk, and it made me smile for some reason.

"Shit happens," I said again without thinking and exhaled. "I was just leaving, actually... my ride is probably waiting outside."

"Oh."

"I was here for a work thing," I blurted, and his lips twitched as he nodded. "A release party... For a client."

"Cool... I'm here for the alcohol and the men." His smirk was unapologetic, and I huffed out a laugh.

"This is awkward, isn't it?" I asked.

"Only a little."

He rubbed the back of his neck, and his shirt lifted, exposing a small sliver of skin. I turned and looked toward the door. "I should probably..."

"Yeah... You wouldn't want to miss your ride home," he said, and his light eyes came alive with the same playful spark I'd noticed the other day in class. Parker smiled as he took a step backward, his cotton shirt stretching across his broad chest as he shoved his hands in the back pocket of his jeans. "See you tomorrow, Mr. Brody."

As I predicted, the minute my alarm had gone off, I regretted every last sip of gin I'd had last night. I sat on the edge of my bed, my face in my hands, groaning at the sunlight like I was seventy-three instead of thirty-three. My throat was raw as I tried to swallow past the sour taste in my mouth. I had a half an hour before Anne was supposed to be here, and all I wanted was a shower and a cup of coffee. I stood and my head throbbed as I walked to the bathroom. My body wasn't built for late nights and booze anymore. And I hadn't even gotten drunk. I wished I'd gotten drunk, maybe then I would've blacked out and forgotten about the uncomfortable run-in with my student. I scrubbed a palm down my face, scratching at the stubble on my chin, and turned on the hot water. Giving it time to heat up, I brushed my teeth and stripped out of my sweats. Once I was in the shower, I let the water pour over me, supporting my weight with my hands against the tile, and closed my eyes.

I thought about last night, about the guy I hadn't gotten a chance to talk to. Would I have woken up alone if we'd actually met? I wiped the water from my eyes and laughed at my overactive and sex-deprived imagination. Of course, I would've woken up alone. It would've been a miracle if I'd even managed to get through a conversation with him, let alone go home with a stranger. I wasn't a one-night-stand kind of guy. Or at least I didn't think I was. I hadn't ever dated anyone besides my ex-wife, and that was over a decade ago. I had no idea how to be single. The Internet freaked me out, but in some ways, it seemed less aggressive than the club scene. At least online, I could take a chance without revealing who I was like Wilder had suggested. I could ease myself back onto the market. Jesus, it wasn't like I was a piece of real estate. Thoroughly discouraged with myself, I quickly cleaned up, shaved, and got ready for the day, tabling my bi-curiosity and dating life for more important topics, like what Anne would want on her waffles this time.

I'd barely switched on the griddle when my doorbell rang. Lanie didn't wait for me to answer the door, most likely knowing I'd unlocked it for her like I usually did when she dropped off Anne. Some people might've thought it was weird that my ex-wife and I got along as well as we did, but we'd both wanted to be a united front for Anne. Giving her as much normalcy as possible. Our relationship wasn't hostile, and after seeing some of my friends and their bitter divorces, I was grateful Lanie and I weren't at each other's throats.

"Dad," Anne squealed, running toward me with her arms open. Her dark blue backpack almost bounced off her shoulders as she threw herself at me.

"Hey, little monster, I missed you." I picked her up and squeezed her until she growled. When she was a baby, she used to snore loud enough we never needed the baby monitor to tell if she'd stopped breathing. I started calling her little monster because she'd sounded like a bear. It stuck. "You ready to make waffles?"

"Hey." Lanie smiled and leaned in to kiss me on the cheek. As I set Anne onto her feet, she handed me a small bag of strawberries. "Here, I grabbed these at the market yesterday, they looked too good to pass up."

"Thanks," I said, setting them on the kitchen counter.

"You don't have to work today?" Lanie asked, her gaze roaming over my cotton t-shirt and jeans.

"Anders figured we'd all be hungover after last night." I chuckled. "But I'm grateful for the time off, I can get ahead on my lessons for class."

"How was it last night? Did you have fun?" she asked, and like so many times, I toyed with the idea of telling her I wanted to try dating men.

But I chickened out.

She'd been my best friend for so long, I missed having someone to talk to, someone to tell everything to without fear of judgment. But now I wasn't sure what she would think. Besides, this wasn't one of those topics you dropped in casual conversations.

"Yeah. It was good."

"Good," she said, looking down at her watch, distracted. "I need to get going."

She reached for a hug, but it was empty. I didn't love Lanie anymore, at least not romantically, and sure, we got along well enough, but there was this loneliness I couldn't explain. It settled in my stomach like a brick whenever we had these fill-in-the-blank moments.

"Bye, baby," she said and kissed Anne on the top of her head. "We can get smoothies after school, okay?"

"Sure, Mom." Anne was busy dividing the strawberries into two equal piles on one of the plates I'd set out earlier.

Lanie pulled her bag up higher onto her shoulder, giving me a small smile before she turned to leave. Six months later, and it still felt odd watching her go.

"Can we have powdered sugar?" Anne asked, once her mom was out of sight. "Mom said powdered sugar is bad for me, but I think it tastes good, so I don't care."

Laughing, I pulled the powdered sugar from the cupboard along with the waffle mix. "Sure, kiddo. But she's right. Too much sugar can be unhealthy. But every once in a while, it's nice to have a treat."

She scrunched up her nose. "I guess."

"Will you grab the syrup while I mix the batter?"

"Yes." She hopped down from her stool, her long braid bouncing as she skipped toward the pantry. If only waffles made everyone that happy. "Mom told me you

41

went dancing with friends. How come you never dance with me?"

"You never ask," I said, smiling at the irritated crease between her brows. "I'm kidding, little monster, I'll dance with you whenever you want."

I took the syrup from her hand and placed it on the counter before twirling her in a circle. The long blouse she had on billowed around her waist and she giggled.

"This isn't how you dance, Dad."

"No?"

"You're supposed to shake your booty," she said, and I choked back a laugh. "What? That's what Jess says."

"And who is this Jess?"

"A girl in my class."

"Ah..." I grabbed the eggs from the fridge. "She sounds pretty smart."

"She's popular." Anne dug out the measuring cup from the drawer and filled it with water. This was our routine, and as I watched her, I wished it was something I could do every morning with her. "And she has gel nails."

"Gel nails?" I asked, cracking an egg and plopping it into the bowl.

"It's polish, but it doesn't come off easy like the stuff Mom makes me wear." She flipped her braid over her shoulder, and rolled her pale gray eyes, eyes she'd gotten from me. "It's organic."

Organic nail polish?

Lanie was over the top when it came to chemicals and nutrition. A kid should get to be a kid sometimes, eat processed corn syrup, and drink water from the tap. But

I'd never undermine her mother. Lanie only had Anne's best interest at heart.

"Hey... nothing wrong with organic. Your generation will be the healthiest and live the longest."

"If we have a planet to live on."

"Now *you* sound like your mom," I said, and she giggled again as she poured the water into the bowl.

Anne continued to be a chatterbox all through breakfast and on the way to school. It was too quiet when I walked back through my front door and surveyed the mess we'd left behind on the counter, though. Sighing, I dropped my keys in the bowl on the sideboard table and got to work cleaning my kitchen. It was after ten by the time I finished up and sat down at my desk to start on the lesson for tonight, hoping to finish a few more so I wouldn't get behind. Taking on two jobs and being a single parent, I might've bitten off more than I could chew.

My phone chirped with a notification, and when I opened the screen, I laughed. Wilder had invited me to join Pegasus.

Me: You're a very persistent fairy gay godmother.

Wilder: Hey, I'm head recruiter, I have to keep my numbers up.

Me: Well, in that case...

Wilder: Let me know if you need help deciding if someone is a serial killer. I have very good intuition.

Me: Thanks?

Wilder: Anytime.

I opened the app with a stupid smile on my face. But as my thumb hovered over the create account icon, my hands started to shake.

Was I really doing this?

"Screw it. Why not."

I pulled my bottom lip through my teeth and clicked the link.

Chapter 4

PARKER

With a hangover from hell, I had a hard time keeping my eyes open. It was barely ten in the morning, and the wall clock in the study room seemed to tick louder than usual. I'd started working as a tutor at Pride House, a shelter for homeless LGBTQ youth, when I'd moved back to Atlanta two years ago. I'd sort of fallen into the role of unofficial counselor for a few of the residents, as well, which on most days I loved, but today I couldn't seem to keep focus. Denny, one of my regulars, grumbled and scratched out the last sentence he'd written with his eraser. While most seventeen-year-old kids worried about who to ask to their senior prom, Denny had to worry if he had enough money to eat. He was rough around the edges, scarred from his time on the streets, and locked up tighter than Fort Knox. Running an aggravated hand through his short, blue hair, he slapped the pencil down on the table. The loud smack resonated through my head like shrapnel. Fucking Marcos and his whiskey. I should have known better not to go out when I had to work the next morning.

"I hate this shit." Denny shoved his paper to the side, knocking his pencil to the tile floor. "Why can't I just work full time at the shop, man. Why do I need some stupid diploma anyway?"

"Because it's required to become a mechanic."

He leaned back in his chair and pulled at the piercing in his bottom lip with his teeth. He'd been homeless since his parents had thrown him out at fourteen. His offense—kissing a boy in the backyard. He'd told us, when he'd started coming to Pride House six months ago, it had been his choice to leave. He'd said his parents had given him an ultimatum. Change or get out. My gut, already uneasy from last night's poor decisions, churned as I thought about how scared and alone he must feel every fucking day. I got lucky in the parent department and getting to work with these kids reminded me of that fact every day.

"You think you'll be happy working the register, that's fine, nothing wrong with that, but you want to get your hands dirty, am I right?"

"I wanna fix cars, why do I gotta know how to write an essay?" He leaned down and grabbed his pencil. "I ain't smart enough for this bullshit."

"Hey... look at me." He kept his head down, carrying the weight of every last insecurity the world had given him on his shoulders. "You're smart... there's no way you would've made it on your own for the last two years without being smart. This stuff…" I tapped my finger on the piece of notebook paper in front of him. "It's important, Denny. Knowledge is a weapon… a tool, yeah?"

"Yeah."

"You need tools to survive, weapons to protect yourself," I said, and he nodded. "You're not stupid, you're learning. There's a difference."

"Why do you like writing so much?" he asked, drumming his fingers against the edge of the table.

"It helps me clear my head, I guess."

"Heavy…" He gave me a small smile and sat up. "I like reading sometimes. Graphic novels and comics."

"I used to read *The Sandman* series when I was a kid."

"No shit, Gaiman is legit."

I reached into my backpack and grabbed my well-worn copy of *The Lost Boys*. "Have you ever read Pen Aster?" I held out the book and he stared at it. "It's not a graphic novel, but if you love Gaiman, you have to read this."

"Never heard of it."

"This is hands down one of my favorite books of all time. It has killer LGBTQ rep, and the writer is gay too. Check it out…"

Denny hesitated, his eyes taking in the pale purple and blue cover. "It's your favorite?"

Nodding, I set the book in front of him, hoping he'd pick it up. Trust was hard to come by with these kids, and

I wanted him to know I was someone he could count on. Maybe giving him a piece of myself, something I loved, would let him know he mattered to someone.

"It's a queer retelling of *Peter Pan*."

"No way," he said, and I smiled when he finally opened the cover.

"The author created his own world but kept a lot of the original elements. It's phenomenal."

Denny turned the book over, whispering the words as he read the synopsis. "Pan falls in love with one of the lost boys?"

Biting back a smirk, I shrugged. "I know nothing."

"Is King Juno supposed to be Captain Hook?"

"Yeah, and Wendy is a villain."

"Fuck... this sounds awesome."

The excitement in his voice was palpable.

"It's yours."

Denny's smile fell as he set the book on the table. "Nah... it's your favorite. I ain't gonna do that."

"I can buy another one." Which was true, it wasn't like the book was out of print. I'd had this copy since I was seventeen. And sure, it was sentimental. It was the first book I'd read that had characters I could relate to as a gay teen. But if it gave him the same peace it had given me, I wanted him to have it. "Take it... seriously. I want you to have it."

He swallowed as he picked at the corner of his essay, tearing off a small piece. "What do you want in return?"

"Nothing."

"There's always something, man." He could barely look me in the eyes, and it broke my fucking heart.

Thinking about some of the shit this kid must have gone through, the way people had hurt him, manipulated him while he was most vulnerable, made me want to punch something.

"Denny... I don't expect anything from you. Not one damn thing. This book is yours, okay?"

"Yeah, alright..." His fingers trembled as he picked up the book. "Thanks... I mean, yeah... that's cool. I'll read it."

"Cool."

Denny put the book in his bag, and while he grabbed the pencil from the floor, I fought to contain my smile. Maybe it wasn't that big of a deal, but it sure as hell felt like a win to me. I cleared my throat and rapped my knuckles on the desk once he was settled and back in his chair. "Should we finish this damn essay so we can grab some cookies from the kitchen?"

"Hell yes."

"Alright... then show me what you got."

I quietly slid into my seat next to Marcos near the back of the room, thankful Mr. Brody had his back to the class while he scribbled what I assumed was our next assignment onto the white board.

"You're late," Marcos whispered. "You missed it."

"Missed what?" I asked and opened my notebook. "Did you take notes?"

Marcos reared his head, his nostrils flaring like I'd just shit in his lap.

"Um... of course not." He leaned closer and lowered his voice. "When I walked in, Mr. Brody stared at me, and I swear to God, you should have seen his face... it was like I stole his ice cream cone or some shit. I think he was disappointed you weren't with me."

"This again? I should have never told you I talked to him at the club last night." I ignored him and flipped past my math notes to find a clean page to write on.

"Listen...okay, you weren't here, you didn't see his face. I'm telling you—"

"Welcome to class, Mr. Mills. I'm sure you and Mr. Basulto have a lot to catch up on, but I'd appreciate it if you both could wait until after my class." Mr. Brody set his dry-erase marker down on his desk, his piercing gaze sending a flash of heat to my neck and face.

Shit.

"Yes, sir. My apologies."

Marcos chuckled, and I gave him my shut-the-fuck-up-or-I-will-end-you look. It only made his immature ass laugh harder.

"I want to thank everyone for getting their essays in on time," Mr. Brody continued, no trace of the adorably nervous smile I'd been treated to last night.

Running into him had been awkward, but considering the obscene amount of alcohol I'd consumed, I thought I'd handled myself well enough. Too bad I hadn't been able to muster up some of that control when Tam asked to suck me off. He'd shared a ride with us, and instead of going back to his own place, he wound up in my bed. Not one of my finer moments. He'd left right after we hooked

50

up, and when I'd woken up this morning, I'd almost thought I might've had some weird, drunk, sex dream. But Marcos had been sure to remind me I had him to thank for my "good time."

I was too busy worrying I'd made a huge mistake fucking around with one of Marcos's co-workers, I missed it when Mr. Brody called my name.

"Park," Marcos hissed. "Wake up, *mijo*. He's talking to you."

I lifted my eyes from my notebook and met Mr. Brody's expectant stare.

"Could you repeat the question?"

Hell, had he even asked me a question, his quiet laugh had me thinking maybe not?

Before he could speak, a girl in the front raised her hand.

"Yes, Ms. Williams?"

"I'm not very good at free writing..."

"What did he say?" I whispered to Marcos while Mr. Brody discussed the merits of free writing.

"He asked if you could tell the class the definition of free writing." Marcos flicked his gaze to the front of the room before he whispered, "And you literally said nothing."

"It's your fault, I'm still hungover from last night. Never again, Basulto."

"Whatever, you enjoyed yourself... according to Tam, a couple of times, actually." He smirked and I dropped my face into my hand. "Don't worry, he said it was casual... Though, I think you should text him for a re-do. You get cranky when you haven't gotten any."

"I hate you."

He squeezed my thigh under the table and kissed my cheek. "I love you too, *mijo*."

A quiet laugh escaped my chest, and as I turned to face the front of the class, I caught Mr. Brody staring at us. Two or three seconds passed before he lowered his eyes and cleared his throat, shuffling a few papers on his desk. Feeling like a dick for disrupting his class again, I focused on my notes and tried not to engage with Marcos about his ridiculous hot-for-teacher theories, and by the end of the hour, I'd wished I'd never asked him to take the class with me in the first place.

"That's it for today," Mr. Brody announced, and laughed when practically everyone jumped up, eager to leave. "Don't forget," he said, raising his voice over the rustling of backpacks and whizzing zippers. "You need to choose a book to read before our next class... That's Monday, guys," he added when no one seemed to be paying attention.

"Want me to grab some take-out on my way home?" Marcos asked as he slipped the strap of his bag over his shoulder. "I was thinking about that amazing tikka masala we had last week."

"Sure." I shoved my notebook into my backpack. "Make sure you order extra bread this time."

"So needy." He grinned as he brushed past me. "See you at the apartment."

I pulled my bag onto my shoulders and was about to follow him out when Mr. Brody approached me. "May I speak to you before you go?"

"Uh... sure, I have a second." Anxiety kicked off the drum in my chest. "I'll see you at home, Marcos."

His brows raised all the way to his hairline, but miraculously, he didn't say anything stupid. "See you later."

Mr. Brody nodded and smiled at the rest of the students as they cleared out. Once the room emptied, we both tried to talk at the same time.

"I wanted to—"

"Sorry I was—"

Laughing, I rubbed the top of my head, nervous as hell.

"What were you going to say?" he asked first, his smile less confident than a moment before.

Under the bright light of the classroom, his eyes were less gray and more of a silvery blue. Distracted, it took me a second to remember what I'd wanted to say. "Umm... I'm sorry for being late... and disrupting the class. Marcos struggles with a filter sometimes."

"Don't worry about it, I probably shouldn't have called you out in front of everyone." He huffed out a laugh. "I never thought I'd be one of those teachers."

"We were being rude. You were in the right."

"Water under the bridge," he said, an anxious edge to his tone. "I actually wanted to discuss your essay."

"Oh, okay... did I do it wrong?"

"No... not at all, Par..." He caught himself before he said my name, and I smiled when he exhaled a flustered breath. "Mr. Mills, it was excellent."

"Excellent?" I asked, realizing how much I'd needed his approval.

Not his necessarily. But someone besides Marcos to tell me I could do this. That writing didn't have to be lies. That my truths mattered.

Real words matter.

"Truly. I know good writing when I read it. It's kind of my job."

Maybe I was high on his praise, because even though I shouldn't have, I loved the easy, almost arrogant smirk on his lips.

"Wow... uh..." I laughed at the irony of my inability, in that moment, to articulate a sentence. I shoved my hands in the back pockets of my jeans and bit the corner of my bottom lip trying to collect my thoughts. "I wanted to say something more eloquent than a simple thanks, but I think I'm in shock."

"Thanks, works just fine," he said, and the silence stretched between us again. "You're a communications major?"

"Yeah, for now. It's kind of what I did for the Air Force. I worked in Public Affairs."

"Ever thought about majoring in creative writing?"

Every day.

"Not really," I lied. "Starving artist isn't really my goal."

"You're talented, Mr. Mills. I think it's something you should at least consider."

"Maybe... you know you can call me Parker. The Mr. Mills thing is kind of stuffy."

"It's stuffy?" he asked, and I noticed he'd shaved today. His jaw line was unfuckingreal.

"Definitely," I said. "You might get more engagement in class if... I don't know... maybe you relaxed a little."

"Thanks for the tip." A pale pink filled his cheeks and he glanced at his watch. "Well, I should let you get going..."

"Yeah... you too."

Neither one of us made the first move to leave, and the same weighted static from last night surrounded our clumsy goodbye.

"About last night..." I started to say, but he cut me off with the wave of his hand.

"It's not my business what you and your boyfriend do outside of class, Mr. Mills."

"Boyfriend? Last time I checked I was single."

"I thought..." His eyes drifted to the seat Marcos had been sitting in earlier.

"Marcos and I are just friends who unfortunately live together."

He raked a hand through his dark hair, the thick strands falling back over his brow shadowed his eyes as he laughed. "I saw you dancing together last night, and I assumed he—"

"You saw us dancing together?" I asked, unable to hide the humor in my tone. "And you didn't join us?"

Three soft laugh lines appeared at the corner of each of his eyes as his crooked smile spread across his face.

"And this is why I'll never call you Parker."

Chapter 5

DONOVAN

*P*reoccupied with the manuscript I'd been working through, I hadn't realized how late it had gotten. I had to pick up Anne at six from Lanie's yoga studio, and it was already four-thirty, giving me less than forty minutes to finish up. I rushed through reading the last pages, deciding the book would be a hard sell in a young adult market, and hoped maybe with a few changes it would be more appropriate. I attached it to an email and sent it off to Kris, asking if she wouldn't mind setting up a meeting with the author for tomorrow. Even though she was Anders's assistant she helped me out every once in a while. Since I'd taken on this other job, I had a feeling I might need my own assistant at some point. I was only one week in, and I already had too much on my plate. How the hell did all the other professors teach more than one class? There was no way they read all the papers they assigned. I barely had the time to finish grading all the essays from Monday, and I already had students submitting the essay I'd assigned yesterday. Whatever happened to good old procrastination? When I was in college, I waited until the last minute to turn in my work. It was a motivation technique. Stress-induced writing was always my best. These students were overachievers. One student, in particular, came to mind.

Parker Mills.

I'd read his first essay at least five times. It was only three pages long, and sure it hadn't been filled with lyrical metaphors, but he'd painted such an honest, clear, and vivid picture of his life. I envied him in some ways. His talent. His confidence on and off the page. I was ten years older than him, but in fifteen-hundred words he'd already lived more of a life than I ever had. It wasn't professional to show favoritism, but the truth was, I couldn't wait for him to send in the new assignment. I might've double-checked my WSC email account once or twice or twelve times this afternoon to check if he'd sent it in yet. Which I thought was a perfectly acceptable professor thing to do. But to stop myself from checking again, I shutdown my laptop and started to pack up my things.

"Serrano is booked for tomorrow at nine," Kris said as she walked into my office.

"Wow. That was fast."

Her pink-painted lips broke into a wide grin. "I'm that good, Van."

"I'd say so." I laughed as I stood. "How much would it take to steal you away from Anders?"

She pursed her lips and leaned a hip against the doorjamb, tucking a piece of her hair behind her ear. "Aw... you're sweet. You know you can't afford me."

Cracking up, I slipped my bag over my shoulder. "Honest and loyal, two very admirable qualities."

She lifted her hand to her mouth and whispered, "For Christ's sake, don't say it so loud. Next thing you know, Claire will be asking me for favors too."

"Well, I'm thankful for the help."

"Pfft... I don't mind. I know how busy y'all get, and most of the time I'm bored gossiping on the phone with my neighbor from across the street..." Her eager eyes found mine. "Who is newly single, by the way. Cute girl, works at the library."

Once my divorce had become official, Kris had decided to play matchmaker.

"Thanks, but—"

"She's nothing like Lanie, not that Lanie was bad, but Beth is more studious. Bookish. She's kind of a wallflower, though. Shy, but I think y'all would get on well."

"I appreciate it, but I'm not interested in dating right now." Not women, at least, but I kept that distinction to myself. "I'm finding my bearings. I'm not quite there yet."

"Let me know if you change your mind," she said, but knowing Kris, this wouldn't be the last time she'd try to set me up with someone. "Oh, I almost forgot. Anders asked that you check in before you leave."

"Sure... Anything I should know before I go in?" I asked.

"He's in a mood."

"Great." I stepped out into the hall and stared down at his closed office door. "When you say mood..."

"Oh, you know, the usual..." She patted me on the shoulder. "The world just won't spin fast enough for that man." I didn't necessarily agree with her assessment. Anders was usually an even-keel kind of guy, if he was pissed off about something it had to be bad. "Don't say I didn't warn you."

"Thanks," I said, and she snorted at my sarcasm as I knocked on his door.

"Come on in."

Anders was behind his desk, his blond hair disheveled, his shirt sleeves rolled up to his elbows. Photos and what looked like color swatches were strewn across his desk.

"Uh... what's happening in here?" I asked and couldn't help my small smile when he grumbled something incoherent under his breath.

This was a man who had all of his shit in order. Seeing him all over the place was kind of amusing.

"I'm glad you find this funny, Van."

"I'm sorry," I said, holding my hands up in surrender and trying like hell to hold back my laughter. "What's going on?"

"My mother... she's driving me crazy with all of this." He waved both of his hands dramatically and slumped backward in his chair. "She wants me to get a wedding planner."

"Oh God."

"I know." He exhaled a noisy breath. "Ethan wants to get married on the bank of a river, not at some fucking bullshit hotel, with a color theme and dinner menu."

The f-bomb was enough evidence he'd started to spiral, the man never swore at work.

"Have you talked to her?" He immediately glared at me. "Okay..." I said, dragging the word out. "Apparently, that was a dumb question." I approached his desk slowly, taking in all the pictures of flower arrangements and color palettes. I picked up a square piece of fabric, the shade somewhere between pink and red.

"Watermelon," he said. "Which I didn't even know was a fucking color."

"Two f-bombs in five minutes, I may have to call your mom and tell her she's ruined the only boss I ever loved."

His head tipped back as he laughed. "By all means, I won't stop you."

"You want my advice..."

"Absolutely."

"Get married however and whenever you want. This is for you and Ethan, no one else. She'll understand."

"That's what Ethan said. You're both right... I only have to figure out a way to let her down easy."

"You're a literary agent, crushing unreasonable expectations is what you do."

"You're right," he said again and pinched the bridge of his nose. "Sorry, I shouldn't have exploded on you like that, this isn't your problem."

"Anders, we're friends... I'm here for all the groomzilla meltdowns you can throw at me."

"Thanks..." he said, his smile almost reaching his eyes. "I think I needed to hear it from someone other than Ethan. I can be biased when it comes to my mom."

"I have older siblings who would say the same thing about me. I'm the baby of the family, and I let my mom get away with murder."

He chuckled. "I'm glad you can empathize."

"Kris said you wanted to see me before I left?"

"Yes, I apologize. I got sidetracked for a moment... I was curious what you thought about Serrano's manuscript. I think it might be too gritty."

"I agree, I had Kris set up an appointment with him for tomorrow, I'll see if he's willing to tone down some of the language and sex."

"Sounds good."

"Was that it?" I asked and he nodded.

"Yeah..." He scanned the mess on his desk. "And maybe I needed someone to throw me a rope."

"Glad to be of service."

I was only about fifteen minutes behind by the time I left the office, and I was almost to my exit on the interstate when my phone vibrated in the center console. Figuring it was Lanie asking how much longer I'd be, I ignored it until I was parked out front of the studio. I swiped my thumb across the screen ready to text her to let her know I'd arrived and to bring Anne out, when I noticed the notification from the Pegasus app. After I'd created my account the other night, I'd gotten a few messages, mostly from guys looking for more than what I was ready for. My hope for the app being a successful way to meet

61

men died when I'd gotten a dick pic this morning. Was that what was expected? If so, I was screwed. There was no way I was okay with sending random guys pictures of my genitalia. I planned to ignore the current message, not wanting to be traumatized yet again, but the guy's username caught my eye. I couldn't be sure, but I hoped it was a reference to one of my favorite books. The same book I'd referenced in my username. I clicked open the message and was relieved there wasn't a picture waiting for me.

@TheLOstBOy: Like the handle, you into Aster?

Excitement flooded my pulse, warming my stomach as I stared down at the screen. Pen Aster's retelling of *Peter Pan* had been iconic when I was in middle school. It was the first book I'd ever read with gay characters, and it had made all the questions I had about my sexuality seem less isolating. As much as I'd liked girls, I'd wanted to be Pan and fall in love with a lost boy too.

Several replies went through my head. Should I text something about the book? Something flirty? Or would that be considered too forward? I mean, I wasn't about to send a dick pic. Maybe a simple yes would suffice. *Fuck.* Why was I making this more difficult than it needed to be. Trying not to overthink, I chose to follow his lead.

@MeAndMyShadow33: Who isn't?

I pressed send and switched out of the app, sending Lanie a quick text. Not even a minute later, he sent another message.

@TheLOstBOy: Most straight guys? And radicalized conservatives.

A laugh snuck past my lips; curious, I clicked on his profile. He was from Atlanta, too, and like me, hadn't given his name. I liked the idea of being able to walk away without anyone knowing who I was in case it didn't go like I'd wanted it to. Maybe he felt the same way. His interests were very simple and to the point. *Into books and bottoms.* I definitely loved books but was utterly clueless about what I wanted or liked when it came to sex with men. Top or bottom, I wouldn't be able to be casual about fucking someone. As much as I wanted to explore, I also had to trust the person in order to be vulnerable like that. My mind spinning with possibilities, I flipped to his profile photo. He'd only uploaded one picture, an obligatory ab shot. I had to say his six-pack was as intimidating as it was sexy. His muscles were etched to perfection, a deep V cut along his hips and disappeared below the waistline of his low-riding pants. I pinned my bottom lip between my teeth and zoomed in to get a better look, my throat dry as I stared at the dark smattering of trimmed hair, peeking out just above his buckle.

The car door opened, and I practically threw my phone into the center console, grateful when the screen had gone black. No reason my ten-year-old daughter needed to see her father drooling over a half-naked stranger.

"Daddy!" Anne hopped into the back seat. "I was waiting forever."

"Sorry, little monster. I got stuck at work." I lowered the passenger side window and Lanie leaned down, resting her elbows on the frame. "Hey, traffic was—"

"It's fine. Jules started the class for me. I should head in, though." She turned and smiled at Anne as she buckled in. "Bye, baby, see you tomorrow."

"Bye, Mom."

Lanie walked away with another small wave as I backed out of the parking spot. "Want to go to Sal's for dinner?"

"Yeah!"

A smile stretched across my face, and for the first time in six months, it didn't hurt to drive away.

"One more, Dad." Anne yawned as I leaned over and kissed her on her forehead. Her eyes heavy with sleep, she blinked up at me as I stood. "Tell me the story about the toad and the chicken. That one is the best."

"How about I save that one for this weekend? It's late."

"No, it's not," she protested as she fought to keep her eyes open.

"It's time for bed, Anne." She didn't argue, her eyes slowly closing. "Love you, sweet girl."

I switched off the overhead light, and the glow-in-the-dark stars illuminated on her ceiling.

"Love you, too," she said and turned onto her side, pulling the blanket all the way up to her chin.

I left her door open a crack and headed to the kitchen

to grab a beer. It was only eight, and I'd been on the go all evening. I wanted to unwind a little before I started grading essays. The light in my office was already on, and I groaned like an old man as I sat down at my desk. I pulled my phone from my pocket before taking a swig from the bottle. I was tempted to text that guy again, but worried I'd let too much time lapse and he'd moved on. I wasn't sure how great I was at navigating all of this. I set my beer down and opened the app. For a solid five minutes, I argued with myself on whether or not I should text him and decided I had too much work to do to worry about it right then. I opened up my email, instead, and like I'd figured, I already had about seven essays submitted. I scrolled down, not even trying to pretend like I wasn't looking for Parker's name and grinned when I found it.

FROM: Parker.Mills@WSC.mail.edu
TO: Donovan.Brody@WSC.mail.edu
Date: Aug 26 7:16 PM
SUBJECT: ASSIGNMENT 2

Dear Mr. Brody,
I attached my essay. Not sure if I did it right. It's probably shorter than you wanted it, but once I got going, it all sort of fell out onto the paper. In my defense, it felt like much more than a paragraph while I was writing.
I decided I'm a fan of free association.
Your "excellent" student,
Parker~

His sign off made me chuckle, and I opened the attachment, my impatient finger tapping on the desk while I waited for it to load.

Sweat finds its way down the middle of my back, and I don't want to stop the dream, the sound, and the wave as it crashes into me. His hands are rough. Warm and heavy, and I'm falling for him. I feel the sand scratch at my knees, and I close my eyes, absorb it all, feel the humid air on my skin, the sky as it falls. Feel it like I did that night, loving the taste of salt on my tongue. The air is heavy with it, and it bites at my cheeks as the sand fills my hands. He won't stop until the sand consumes me. Until all I feel is the wet truth on my skin, until every touch meets its perfect mark, until I'm broken open for him. His words, a comfort, tell me I'm enough, that I'm not sick, that I never deserved to bleed. And with every hard breath, I won't stop dreaming, feeling, and I think this is how I will find the end, find my freedom. This man. I didn't know. I didn't know. Turns me to dust.

Jesus Christ.

One paragraph and he'd annihilated me.

Fighting the arousal his words had conjured, I pressed the heel of my palm into my groin. This was too personal, read too real. Images I shouldn't have had popped up inside my head like little bolts of lightning, spreading heat throughout my entire body.

Shit.

I swallowed and closed out of the email, telling myself the reaction I'd had was evidence of his talent and nothing more. Needing something to divert my attention from the very well written, and rather erotic paragraph,

I picked up my phone and clicked open the Pegasus app. I scrolled to the conversation I'd had earlier and typed out a fashionably late reply, dispelling all thoughts about students and their borderline inappropriate words.

@MeAndMyShadow33: Did you think Pan would end up with Silas?

I didn't expect an answer right away, so when the app pinged again, I was relieved.

@TheLOstBOy: Not at first. You?

@MeAndMyShadow33: They had too much stacked against them.

@TheLOstBOy: That's what made the story great. When they finally get together you know they fucking earned it.

@MeAndMyShadow33: Love isn't easy, is it?

@TheLOstBOy: Is that what you're looking for?

@MeAndMyShadow33: I'm not sure what I'm looking for.

@TheLOstBOy: Looks like we have a lot in common.

@MeAndMyShadow33: Is this when you send me a freaky picture of your junk?

@TheLOstBOy: *cringe* Hell no. Just like Pan... you have to earn it.

Chapter 6

PARKER

I had about an hour's worth of math homework to finish, but instead of being responsible, I was stretched out on my bed, fucking around on a dating app. It was rare to find anything more than an opportunity to hook up on Pegasus, and maybe that's all this guy wanted, but I had to admit I was intrigued. *The Lost Boys* was more of a cult classic, it wasn't a popular book, by any means, unless you were a book junkie, queer or not. Avoiding the tedium of statistics, I'd hopped onto the app, not really thinking I'd find anyone interesting to help me procrastinate. I'd scrolled through the new local members list and was beyond stoked when I'd come across his username. Peter Pan's shadow showed up in most adaptations of the original story. The guy very well could've been referencing any one of them, but I'd taken a chance, and I was glad I did. Unfortunately, there wasn't much on his profile, and if I banked on my past experience, the odds were he'd end up being an asshole. I checked out his info again anyway while I waited, or rather hoped for a response to my last message.

His profile picture was a grainy shot of a shadow on a white wall, which heightened my interest. It stood out in a sea of abs and skin. I wanted to know if he'd taken the picture himself, or if he'd found it online somewhere. His bio was about as informative as his picture. He was thirty-three, lived in the Atlanta area, and identified as bi-sexual/questioning. The questioning part made me hesitate. I wasn't one to jump to conclusions, but I'd served enough time in the closet, and had no intention of going back in. I scrolled down to his interests and laughed out loud. *Introverted bookish waffle aficionado.* I checked the time, and it'd been ten minutes since I'd sent my last message. Bummed, I tossed my phone onto the mattress, and with a loud, pathetic sigh, dragged my laptop onto my thighs. I'd gotten through maybe four problems when Marcos let himself into my room.

"God... you're doing homework again, aren't you?" He scratched at his bare stomach as he walked across my room without invitation and plopped down onto my bed. "I'm bored. Entertain me."

"Let me get this shit done first." I shoved his hip with my foot.

"Hey... that kind of hurt, dick."

Marcos flicked my big toe with his finger.

"I feel like I have to tell you this at least twice a day. The more you bother me, the longer it will take," I said and smiled when he tried to flick my toe even harder. "I swear, you're like a little kid sometimes."

"I'm young at heart. When you're old with saggy balls, you'll be grateful for my immature spirit." He pulled off my sock and threw it at me. "Gross, you need a pedicure..." His eyes widened as I lifted my sock from my chest and started to put it back on. "What are you doing tomorrow morning?"

"Not getting a pedicure." I laughed when he narrowed his eyes. "I have to work, and then I have my stats class."

"I told you not to take Friday classes."

"I want to graduate sometime this century."

"You know... every once in a while, I think about quitting," he said, lowering his eyes to his lap. He fidgeted with the string on his sweatpants and exhaled a heavy breath. "I'm never going to graduate... I should have picked a different major. Something to fall back on."

"Come on, man, you can't quit. You've already put in the work. You'd be good at anything you decided on."

"I like retail," he said. "I like clothes. I can't get a degree in shopping."

"Shopping, no... but business, yes. Open your own shop. Or be a designer like you've always wanted. Marcos, there's tons of shit you could do. You should talk to an academic advisor if you're worried."

He chewed on his thumbnail, my least favorite of his nervous habits. I lightly pushed him with my foot again and he dropped his hand. "Sorry, I know, it's gross, blah blah blah... it's how I cope, deal with it."

"Chew away, but don't lecture me about pedicures..."

I smiled when he rolled his eyes.

"I'll talk to an advisor... and I will *never* stop lecturing you about pedicures. No guy wants to feel your nasty, calloused feet on their ass when they're fucking you."

"Good thing I'd rather top."

Marcos scooted off the bed and stood, his hands on his hips. "You're missing out... that's all I'm going to say."

With Marcos it was never "that's all I'm going to say." He could nag a motherfucker until the sun came up.

"Can I do my homework now?"

"I'll allow it. I'll be out in the living room, not being a boring ass bitch."

I laughed hard enough my stomach ached as he shut my bedroom door. Christ, he was something else. A lot of our friends said we were like an old married couple. And I supposed they were right. But even if I was into him like that, I'd never do anything about it. We would probably end up killing each other if we were a real couple, and then I'd be out one hell of a best friend.

Totally distracted, I couldn't seem to get through the last few problems on my homework. I hadn't been blessed by the math gods like my older sister had. She loved math so much she'd decided to teach it. Too bad she lived in Arkansas. I grabbed my phone, hoping she might still be awake, and smiled at the message I'd missed.

@MeAndMyShadow33: Thank God. The unsolicited dick pics are a little unnerving.

@TheLOstBOy: But the solicited ones are okay?

@MeAndMyShadow33: I'm not sure. I've never asked for one.

@TheLOstBOy: Does anyone ever ask for one?

@MeAndMyShadow33: Good point. Maybe some guys? But I'm not that kind of guy.

@TheLOstBOy: No? What kind of guy are you?

Waiting for his answer, I pressed my lips together, my pulse thrumming a beat or two faster than normal. I didn't usually get excited about chatting with guys on here. It was too impersonal. But this guy, he'd made me want to dig deeper.

@MeAndMyShadow33: The truth is, I have no idea. I've never done this before.

@TheLOstBOy: You'll have to be more specific. Define "this."

@MeAndMyShadow33: I've never used a dating app.

That was vague.

@TheLOstBOy: You'd rather meet guys at a bar or something?

@MeAndMyShadow33: I've never been with a guy before.

@TheLOstBOy: Ever?

@MeAndMyShadow33: Never.

Well, fuck. As curious as I was about this guy, I wasn't down with being an experiment. He was probably married looking to satisfy some unfulfilled need he'd had his whole life but never wanted to admit. Textbook closet case. No, thanks.

@TheLOstBOy: Bummer. I'm not into closeted guys though.

@MeAndMyShadow33: Who said I was closeted?

@TheLOstBOy: You've never been with a guy and you're thirty-three. What's stopped you, then?

It was probably rude as fuck of me to ask. But I had no desire to pursue something with no ending in sight. I wasn't trying to get married or anything, but I'd like an actual relationship. A person I could trust and be with without all the games and noise.

@MeAndMyShadow33: I've never had the chance. Got married to my high school girlfriend.

@TheLOstBOy: Ahh. You're married. I figured. Not interested in being anyone's dirty secret. Thanks for the chat, though.

I was pissed at myself for falling for the bullshit. Instead of wasting my time, I should've been on the phone with my sister getting help with this stats nightmare. I closed out of the app and called her. She answered after two rings, her voice scratchy with sleep.

"Oh man, did I wake you up?"

"It's okay... Jones was a terror today. I fell asleep on the couch. I swear, I love my kid, but he runs me ragged."

"Aren't two-year-old's known for being terrible?" I asked and laughed when she groaned.

"If I had only known...."

"You love that kid."

"I do..." she said. "But what's going on with you? Everything okay?"

She yawned again and I regretted calling. My sister worked her ass off, and basically raised her son by herself, with her husband Brett always away on business. I'd never liked the guy. He had never said it outright, his homophobia was more passive aggressive. He'd referred to my sexuality as a lifestyle choice and would say shit about nature versus nurture. Basically, implying that because my dad had died, and I'd been raised by my mom and my older sister, I was somehow less masculine than him. Never mind the fact that I served my goddamn country for four years while he played golf with his country club dudebros. Of course, he'd never said any of it in front of Mandi. But, unfortunately, because of him, my sister and I had become more distant over the years. She thought the guy shit stars out of his ass. I couldn't be the one to ruin her happily ever after. She'd done too much for me. I missed my sister, but it was probably a good thing she lived in another state.

"Ordinal and nominal... qualitative and quantitative... I'm lost. This stats class sucks."

Her giggle made me smile, making me miss her even more. "I got you, little brother."

Mandi saved my ass yet again. After only twenty minutes, I already had a better grasp on the concepts, and was able to work through two of the problems with her. I almost asked her to help me with the last two, but it was late for her, and I didn't want to be the reason she was tired in the morning.

"Thanks, again," I said. "And I'm sorry I woke you up for this."

"No, you're not." She laughed. "Call me anytime, Park. You know I'm here for you. Always."

"Love you."

"You, too," she said, and the call disconnected.

Looking at my phone, I had a message from Pegasus, but I didn't pay it any mind. I shut my laptop and got out of bed. Stretching my tired muscles, I debated on going to the gym. It was late enough, I could tell myself I didn't have to go. Plus, Marcos would most likely give me a ration of shit if I ignored him much longer. But I was irrationally irritable, and I didn't know why. I'd gotten most of my work done like I'd wanted, but I couldn't seem to shake my grouchy mood. I wanted to blame the stats class, but I had to admit, I was let down the guy I'd chatted with had turned out to be a bust. Restless, I grabbed my phone off the bed and my keys from my nightstand, deciding the gym was my best option for blowing off some steam. I'd made it halfway to my bedroom door before my phone vibrated in my hand. Taking a quick look, my stomach dropped when I saw I had an email from Mr. Brody.

The essay I'd sent him was the most personal thing I'd ever written. I almost didn't turn it in. But he'd asked for real words, and when I'd sat down to write, I couldn't change the path my mind had wanted to take. I'd written about this random guy I'd let fuck me one night under a pier at the beach when I'd lived in Florida. He hadn't meant anything to me, but what had happened that night had meant everything. That night I'd taken back what had been beaten out of me. The man had been a stranger, but I'd given him all my secrets, and he'd given me back my pride. My confidence. It had been the night I'd stopped being a victim and had become a survivor.

Swallowing past the ache in my throat, I opened the email.

FROM: Donovan.Brody@WSC.mail.edu
TO: Parker.Mills@WSC.mail.edu
Date: Aug 26 9:58 PM
SUBJECT: RE: ASSIGNMENT 2

Mr. Mills,
"Excellent" work.
P.S. I did dock a few points for not meeting the word requirement. To be fair.
Donovan Brody
English Department
Winchester State College

Something excited and nervous fluttered in my stomach, my grin unwilling to subside as I typed out my response.

FROM: Parker.Mills@WSC.mail.edu
TO: Donovan.Brody@WSC.mail.edu
Date: Aug 26 10:05 PM
SUBJECT: RE: ASSIGNMENT 2

Mr. Brody,
If you want, I could write more over the weekend and send it? Technically I have until Monday.
Thanks,
Parker
P.S. FYI... it's perfectly acceptable to address me as Parker via email. All my other professors do... unless you like being stuffy.

I hit send and winced, overanalyzing the stuffy comment. I'd teased him about it before, but having it written down, without a tone of voice for reference, it almost seemed disrespectful. I hit refresh about twenty times until finally my inbox lit up with another email.

FROM: Donovan.Brody@WSC.mail.edu
TO: Parker.Mills@WSC.mail.edu
Date: Aug 26 10:20 PM
SUBJECT: RE: ASSIGNMENT 2

Mr. Mills,

You are welcome to write more. I'd actually love to read anything you might want to send my way. As I've mentioned before, your talent exceeds any expectation I might've had for a student taking this introductory class. I maintain that your ability would be wasted in your current course of study and ask that you might speak with your academic advisor. Not all writers are "starving artists." You're a writer, Parker. Your voice is genuine. I hope you'll consider my suggestion with an open mind and be willing to accept how much more you're capable of.

Donovan Brody
English Department
Winchester State College

I read the email twice, standing in the middle of my room, silent and still. Hadn't I told Marcos he should do whatever he wanted to? Failure was something I didn't allow myself. Something I feared. It's why I'd joined the Air Force. *Make Dad proud.* It's part of why I'd stayed in the closet for those four years. *Don't be a disappointment.* It's why I chose communications instead of creative writing. *Steady income, easy life.* Steady and easy didn't seem as appealing to me anymore. My mom and sister were always supportive, but this was different. Support was great, but having a person believe in me, believe I was more than those safe expectations I'd set, it untwisted those knots inside me that I'd been holding on to. It made me want to start writing and never stop, to somehow live between my words and bones, somewhere between reality and fiction, to pour myself out onto the page and discover what I was truly capable of. My chest tight, I read it again for the third time and laughed when I realized he'd called me Parker.

Feeling triumphant, I figured he could have the last word, and tried to close out of my email. But the Pegasus chat notification popped up again, and I accidently opened it. Cursing under my breath, I was ready to block the fucker, when one word caught my eye.

Divorce.

@MeAndMyShadow33: I'm divorced. Sorry for the misunderstanding.

@TheLOstBOy: Probably should have let you explain.

@TheLOstBOy: These apps can make a man cynical.

@MeAndMyShadow33: I assure you. I'm divorced. And though I've never had a chance to act on it, I have always been aware of my attraction for men since I was a teenager.

@TheLOstBOy: And now you get to test the waters. It's like reading your favorite book and getting to experience everything for the first time. I'm kind of jealous.

@MeAndMyShadow33: I'm nervous as hell.

@TheLOstBOy: What are you nervous about?

@MeAndMyShadow33: I was with my ex since I was in high school. The dating game has changed.

@TheLOstBOy: And the gender... at least, for you.

@MeAndMyShadow33: And sex. I have no clue what I'm doing.

@TheLOstBOy: You'll have to find someone you trust to help you with your water wings.

@MeAndMyShadow33: Is that some type of euphemism?

@TheLOstBOy: Ha! No. You're testing the waters, remember? Water wings... You know those little plastic things kids have to wear on their arms when they're learning to swim. It made sense in my head.

@MeAndMyShadow33: It makes sense. Apparently, I'm more tired than I thought I was. I'm not usually up this late.

@TheLOstBOy: Late? I thought you said you were 33 not 80.

@MeAndMyShadow33: Ten-thirty is late when you have two jobs.

@TheLOstBOy: And now I feel like a dick.

@MeAndMyShadow33: Don't, it was funny.

@MeAndMyShadow33: How old are you? If you don't mind me asking, your profile doesn't say.

@TheLOstBOy: 23 but I'll be 24 on September 1st.

@MeAndMyShadow33: Shit. Now I feel old.

@TheLOstBOy: Age is only a number, baby.

@MeAndMyShadow33: Baby? I don't think we're there yet.

@TheLOstBOy: You realize I'm going to call you baby from now on.

@MeAndMyShadow33: I could block you.

@TheLOstBOy: Yeah, but you won't

@MeAndMyShadow33: No?

@TheLOstBOy: Nope...

@MeAndMyShadow33: Why's that?

@TheLOstBOy: You need those water wings.

@MeAndMyShadow33: You want to be my water wings?

@TheLOstBOy: I thought you'd never ask.

Chapter 7

DONOVAN

"I can't believe you've never been in here." My sister Olive, also known as Olivia, but only if you wanted her to hate you, smiled at the lady across the counter as she grabbed a bag of fresh bagels. "I worry about you, Van. Living alone in that house, eating take-out every night."

"Hey now... I'm living my best single dad life, okay?" I smirked, reaching in the refrigerator case and grabbing some lox and cream cheese. "Besides, I think you might've forgotten how pathetic you were when you divorced Jonathan."

"That was three years ago, and I handled it with grace. Thank you very much." She flipped her long, black hair over her shoulder. "We didn't have a kid to worry about though. You do."

"I have a kid? I had no idea," I said, sarcastic as hell. "You know, ever since you and Owen turned forty, you think you know everything."

"You sound like a moody teen right now... in case you can't hear yourself." She laughed when I pushed the cart a little faster leaving her behind. "See. You're a child, Van," she said, raising her voice embarrassingly loud, drawing the attention of everyone at the meat counter.

God, my sister was a shit sometimes. I was the baby of the family, born six years after my twin siblings. We'd been raised in an especially typical mac and cheese American family. My mom stayed home while Dad worked at Emory as a mathematics professor. There was never a reason for it, but Owen and Olive had always tried to parent me, a hobby they hadn't yet given up. Which I found comical, seeing how neither of them had very stable lives. Olive was a therapist who was hung up on her emotionally abusive, toxic ex-husband, and I was pretty sure she still slept with the asshole. And Owen couldn't hold down a stable relationship if he tried. Not that he wanted to. The perpetual bachelor. He was too busy trying to be the king of the marketing firm he worked at. Classic workaholic. Honestly, I was the only normal one in the family.

"Why do you do that?" I asked as she sidled in next to me. "I already have two parents who ride my ass enough, I don't need you or Owen making it worse."

"Mom and Dad do not ride your ass. You're their favorite." She threw a bag of chips into the cart, and I reached in and put it back on the shelf.

"Hey, those are for Anne," she said and placed them back in the cart.

"Lanie doesn't want her eating certain types of oils." I debated if I should buy the chips or not, but after the look of annoyance Olive shot my way, I decided it wasn't worth the fight. "I know it sounds ridiculous but—"

"Good, because for fuck's sake, Anne's ten. The pre-teen years are all about junk food. Or did you forget after eating couscous for over a decade?" Her familiar gray eyes found mine. "I'm sorry... I shouldn't say anything."

"But you do."

"Come on, do you really care what kind of oil Anne has?"

I exhaled a long sigh and leaned against the cart. "No... but I want to co-parent the best we can. And I'm being respectful."

"Which I can appreciate. But your opinions matter too." She wrapped her arm around me and squeezed once before letting go. "Don't be a doormat... that's my job."

"Jonathan again?"

"I'm such an idiot." If my sister was the type to cry, I imagined her eyes would have welled up with tears by the way her face paled. "He's engaged."

"Again?"

Groaning, she grabbed two more bags of chips, and I had to stifle my laugh. Not only was she a doormat, but she was also an emotional eater.

"Yeah... again. But I don't want to talk about it."

Of course not.

"Okay... but I would like you to remember this next time you start butting into my life." I grinned and her lips perked up at the corners. "Thanks for helping me with dinner tonight. I'm nervous for Mom and Dad to see the place."

"I can't believe it's taken this long for them to wheedle their way in.... you know Mom will probably walk around and straighten all your picture frames," she said as we made our way to the checkout stands. "And Dad will dote on Anne while passive-aggressively chastising Owen and me for not giving him any grandkids."

"Which Owen won't even hear because he'll be on the phone *with the office*." Laughing, I shook my head. "We're such a cliché dysfunctional family."

"Right?" she asked, grinning from ear to ear.

"You look so much like Mom when you smile."

"God, don't say that. Have you seen the grays in my hair?"

"Mom's beautiful, and so are you."

Which was true, at least in my opinion. With their delicate features, long, dark hair, and fair skin, they both resembled Snow White. Thinking about the fictional princess led to a thought about *The Lost Boys* which made me think about the guy I'd been talking to on Pegasus the other night. Truthfully, I hadn't stopped thinking about him since our conversation the other day, and with it being my weekend with Anne, and having my family over for dinner tonight, I hadn't had a chance to message him again. Not like he'd messaged me either. I wasn't sure of the protocol when it came to the amount of time I was supposed to wait before reaching out to him again, and if I asked my sister, it would open up a dialogue I did not want to have in the checkout line at a farmer's market. The way the conversation had ended with him, it seemed as though he'd left the ball in my court.

Olive scrolled through her phone while we waited, and I used the moment to check my messages, as well, hoping maybe he'd reached out, and I didn't have to. I pulled my phone from my back pocket and opened the app, disappointed when there were no new messages waiting. I read over our conversation again, smiling at his "water wings" comment. I should've cared more about our age difference, but in the grand scheme of things, nine years wasn't that bad. He was an adult. But then again, when I was in my second year of college, he was the same age as my daughter. *Shit*. Maybe nine years was too much.

"What's that face?" Olive asked and I quickly closed out of the app.

My heartbeat trampled all over itself, like I'd been caught trying to shoplift a Kit Kat bar.

"Nothing." I tried to casually slip my phone into my back pocket, but like the cadaver dog that she was, Olive smelled blood.

Her lips parted in a slow grin. "Nothing... I don't think so."

Thankfully, the line moved, distracting her, but I knew it would only offer me a brief reprieve. I could tell her it was something about Lanie, but I didn't want her thinking I was at my ex-wife's beck and call. But then there was this itch, this need I had to tell her, to tell someone in my family the feelings I'd been hiding all this time. I hoped they'd all accept me and my sexuality, but the not knowing made it difficult to keep my imagination in check, to keep all the what ifs from getting out of control. What if they disowned me? What if they thought I was bad for Anne? What if I had to give up this side of myself in order to have my family? All these things I never had to think about when I was with Lanie. Even when she'd pissed off my sister, or offended my mom, they still accepted us. Accepted her. Would they be okay with me bringing a man home?

"There it is again," Olive said, pointing an accusatory finger in my direction. "That face. Are you worried about leaving Anne with Owen? Because I would be."

Laughing, I started to load the groceries onto the stand. "Owen is capable of watching Anne for an hour while I shop."

"Only because Anne is self-sufficient." She raised her eyebrows in a way that suggested there was no room to argue. "Besides... we're getting off track. The face, Van... What's going on?"

I smiled at the cashier as I stepped forward, and pushed the cart toward the bagging area, efficiently ignoring my sister entirely. I thought I might've been in the clear when she hadn't mentioned anything again, but as soon as the bags were in the car, and we were on the road, she made it apparent she was not going to drop it.

"You're hiding something. And I'm freaking out a little, because I'm terrified you're going to tell me you're getting back with Lanie. And I can't, Van. I can't with that chick."

Gripping the steering wheel tighter than necessary, I grit my teeth. "Jesus Christ, Olive. Can you let it go? I'm allowed to have a private life."

She turned in her seat and I exhaled, waiting for the inevitable guilt trip she was about to throw down.

"You *are* hiding something... I can't believe you're getting back with Lanie. She's too controlling, if you ask me, and she cheated on you the first chance she got. I swear to God if –"

"Holy shit, will you calm down. I'm not getting back with Lanie."

"You're not?"

"No.... I'm..." A burning ache threatened to close my throat, fear's firm grip attempting to render me silent.

"What?" she asked, and I could hear the genuine concern in her tone. "If it's not Lanie, then... shit, you're okay, right? You don't have cancer or something terrible like that because if you die, I—"

A wild, anxious laugh pushed its way past the lump in my throat. "No... I'm not dying, Liv... I'm bisexual."

"W-what?"

I glanced at her for a second, taking my eyes off the road. She didn't seem disgusted. Or angry. Shocked was more like it.

"I mean... at least, I think I am."

"Have you ever—"

"Been with a guy? No. I've only been with Lanie... but..." I stared straight ahead. Mostly to make sure we didn't rear end anyone, but also because I couldn't look at her. My nerves were too raw for anything other than an accepting expression. "I've always been attracted to guys. I've known since middle school, but once I met Lanie, I didn't think it mattered anymore."

"Of course, it matters." she said, speaking softly. Olive had put on her therapist hat, and it made me smile. "God, Van. You've been carrying this around that long?"

"It's not like it was a burden. I was happy with Lanie... until I wasn't." The trees whistled by, creating a long stretch of calming green as the silence settled inside the car. I let a few minutes pass, let Olive digest what I'd told her before I spoke again. "If I met a woman tomorrow and she was amazing, I wouldn't hesitate to date her. I haven't been living a lie or anything. I like women. But I'm attracted to men too. And I want to explore that even if it scares the shit out of me."

"What are you scared about?"

"Everything. Being judged, losing Mom and Dad, not knowing how to navigate the whole dating scene." I huffed out a laugh. "I set up a profile on a gay dating app."

"Shut up, you did not," she gasped, pushing my shoulder hard enough I swerved.

"You're going to get us killed."

"Have you met anyone yet?"

I didn't want to say yes. But I needed all the help I could get.

"Yeah... but it's very new, and he's very young and I'm not sure it will turn into anything more than chatting."

"How young?"

"He'll be twenty-four on Wednesday, actually."

"My baby brother is a bisexual cougar." she teased, and the last bit of anxiety I had lifted. "Wow."

"You're okay with all of this?"

"Why wouldn't I be? And don't worry about Owen, he won't care at all. Shane is gay."

"His roommate?" I asked. "Since when?"

"Since always..."

"Huh... Owen never tells me anything anymore," I said, feeling more relieved by the minute. "What about our parents? Do you think they'll freak out?"

"I've never heard them say anything homophobic." She turned to look out the window. "But you never know with them... they still love me, and I'm a hot mess. So that's a good sign. Besides, being bisexual isn't a bad thing, you can't help who you're attracted to."

"I know that... and you're not a hot mess, by the way," I assured her as I turned into my driveway. "But you're right... they've always been supportive. I don't know. I guess we'll see."

"Are you going to tell them tonight?" she asked, and I turned off the engine.

Maybe I should rip the Band-Aid off, quick and easy. The thought didn't sit right, though. It shouldn't have to be this big announcement over steak and mashed potatoes. I'd tell them when I actually started dating a guy.

"Nah... I'm not ready yet."

"Can I tell Owen?"

"Fuck, no." She laughed at my outburst. "You're such an ass."

"Yeah... but you love me," she said and opened the car door.

Dinner with the family had gone about as well as it always

did. My brother actually only took three phone calls, and Olive only had three glasses of wine. All in all, I'd call it a success. The mess in my kitchen, though, not fun. Anne was on the couch watching *Twister* for the thousandth time. She wanted to be a storm chaser when she grew up. And the president. And a veterinarian. I had to have done something right as a parent, at least she had goals.

I'd finished putting dinner away and had started on the dishes when my phone vibrated against the countertop. I held up my hands over the sink as I looked for the towel that should've been on the handle of the oven, but it never seemed to be there when I needed it.

"Anne," I called out. The kitchen was open to the living room, and despite the volume on the television I knew she could hear me. "Can you grab a towel from the basket in the laundry room, please?"

"In a minute, Dad. They're about to launch Dorothy into the tornado."

"Now, Anne. You can press pause you know."

She grumbled but did as I asked, huffing the whole way to the laundry room. I chuckled, shaking some of the water off of my fingers while I waited. I supposed I could have waited to check my phone until after I was finished cleaning, but I couldn't deny the jump in my pulse thinking it might be a message from him. Him. Jesus, I didn't even know his name. This online dating thing was weird as fuck.

"Here ya go." Anne basically threw the towel at me and ran back into the living room, dive bombing onto the couch.

"It's almost time to brush your teeth, kid."

"Dad," she whined. "It's Saturday."

"I'll let you stay up till nine, but then it's time to get ready for bed."

"Nine-thirty?" She bargained.

"Nine-fifteen." I wiped my hands dry and picked up my phone. "Deal?"

"Ugh... fine."

"Thanks, little monster," I said and unlocked my screen, my smile widening when I saw the Pegasus message icon.

@TheLOstBOy: You ready to swim?

It was only four words, but hell, my pulse picked up its pace, making my stomach feel light.

@MeAndMyShadow33: I think I've always been ready.

@TheLOstBOy: Good, because I have a lesson planned.

@MeAndMyShadow33: You planned a lesson?

@TheLOstBOy: Sort of... humor me...

@MeAndMyShadow33: You've got my attention.

@TheLOstBOy: First, we should establish a few boundaries.

@MeAndMyShadow33: I agree.

@TheLOstBOy: Good. I'll go first. Are you looking for sex, or to start a relationship?

@MeAndMyShadow33: Definitely not looking for a one-night stand, but I'm not looking to get serious either. At least not right now.

@TheLOstBOy: Same.

@MeAndMyShadow33: What about personal information?

@TheLOstBOy: Good question. I think staying anonymous will make it easier for us to walk away if shit isn't working. But I would like to call you something other than "the dating app guy."

@MeAndMyShadow33: How about we use middle names?

@TheLOstBOy: I'm down with that.

@MeAndMyShadow33: Then, it's nice to meet you...

@TheLOstBOy: Michael. And you're...

@MeAndMyShadow33: James.

@TheLOstBOy: Wow... we're generic.

@MeAndMyShadow33: Or traditional.

@TheLOstBOy: There's nothing traditional about any of this.

@MeAndMyShadow33: Definitely not.

@TheLOstBOy: Ready for Lesson 1?

@MeAndMyShadow33: You don't waste any time, do you?

@TheLOstBOy: I find it's easier to learn to swim if you just jump in.

@MeAndMyShadow33: Baptism by fire?

@TheLOstBOy: Exactly... Lesson 1: Likes and Dislikes.

@MeAndMyShadow33: As in, I like extra cheese on my pizza and hate mushrooms?

@TheLOstBOy: Sure. Or if you're feeling more open-minded, you could get more personal.

@MeAndMyShadow33: Personal how?

@TheLOstBOy: As in, I like giving head better than receiving.

"Christ." I choked on a laugh, and quickly glanced up from my phone to check on Anne, like somehow, she might've been privy to my conversation, which was asinine. She hadn't even moved an inch.

Thank God for disaster films.

Chapter 8

PARKER

Two very slow minutes ticked by, and I worried I might've spooked the poor guy when he hadn't replied. He had zero experience with dudes, and here I was already talking about blowjobs.

@TheLOstBOy: Did I freak you out?

@MeAndMyShadow33: Not really. Just took me by surprise, and now I'm trying to think of something more "personal" to share.

@TheLOstBOy: Only share what you're comfortable with. Full disclosure... I was kind of messing with you. Testing your boundaries.

@MeAndMyShadow33: So you don't prefer giving head, then?

@TheLOstBOy: No, that was true. I love sucking dick.

@MeAndMyShadow33: Interesting...

@TheLOstBOy: Yeah?

@MeAndMyShadow33: I'm curious if I will too.

This guy. His inexperience shouldn't have turned me on, but apparently my body did not agree. I shifted, sitting up against the headboard, and adjusted myself. I liked the idea of being his first. Obviously, he'd been with a woman before, but I liked the idea of being the first man he ever tasted, touched—fucked. Hell. I didn't even know what the guy looked like. He could be some greasy, sixty-year-old pervert who liked to get his rocks off by fucking with guys on the Internet. But that image didn't ring true either. I had no way of actually knowing, but James seemed genuine to me.

@TheLOstBOy: You might not like it at first. Or ever. And that's okay, there's always someone like me who would rather do it anyway.

@MeAndMyShadow33: What if I'm not any good at it?

@TheLOstBOy: Meh. Even bad head is good head.

@TheLOstBOy: The more you practice, the better you'll get.

@MeAndMyShadow33: That sounds like a line to me.

@TheLOstBOy: I mean... I'm only trying to speak the truth.

@MeAndMyShadow33: I'm standing in the middle of my kitchen cracking up.

@TheLOstBOy: Is that a bad or a good thing?

@MeAndMyShadow33: Good. You make me laugh.

@MeAndMyShadow33: I haven't laughed this much in a long time.

@TheLOstBOy: Humor is one of my many talents.

@MeAndMyShadow33: He's funny... definitely patient... not opposed to blow jobs, I mean, what else is there, really?

@TheLOstBOy: Ass play.

@MeAndMyShadow33: Jesus.

@TheLOstBOy: Too soon?

@MeAndMyShadow33: A little.

@TheLOstBOy: I'll save it for lesson number 3.

@MeAndMyShadow33: What the hell is lesson 2 about?

The doorbell rang and I jumped up when I checked the time. "Shit."

@TheLOstBOy: Don't worry. We're not there yet. I should probably know your favorite color and how you take your coffee before we start talking about frotting.

@MeAndMyShadow33: Purple... With cream and two sugars. Now what the hell is frotting?

@TheLOstBOy: Eager to learn. I like it. But I'm afraid, young Grasshopper, you'll have to wait. I'm about to head out with some friends.

@MeAndMyShadow33: Way to leave a guy hanging...

I grinned as I typed out my next message.

@TheLOstBOy: Look it up online, it can be your homework assignment.

@MeAndMyShadow33: That sounds like a bad idea.

@TheLOstBOy: Or a great one. I'll be around later if you have any questions.

@MeAndMyShadow33: Have fun tonight.

@TheLOstBOy: Probably not as much as you're about to have. You're welcome.

Reluctantly, I slid my phone into the pocket of my gym shorts and grabbed my wallet and keys. I didn't know what it said about me that I wanted to sit in my room on a Saturday night, chatting with a total stranger about sex rather than go to the bar with my buddies where I might meet someone to have actual sex with.

"Let's go, *mijo*." Marcos hollered and knocked on my door. "Put your dick away. Alex and Davis are here."

Davis and Alex were a couple we'd met during Pride Week our first year at WSC. They'd been together forever, and I envied what they had. The stability. The love they had for each other. I wanted that. I was tired of the scene. I wanted something comfortable, someone I could sit with in bed, both of us reading, the silence a companion, not a third party, and without saying a word I'd know how much he cared about me. It was probably corny or sentimental, but that sounded a whole hell of a lot better than waking up to randoms for the rest of my life.

I checked myself over in the mirror, deciding I looked good enough for a shitty pool hall where I would most definitely not be finding my perfect man. Slipping my hat on backward, I was ready to go.

Marcos almost had a panic attack when I opened the door. "No... Not happening. Go change." He grabbed my shoulders and tried to spin me around. I overpowered him and he gave up with a groan.

"You're wearing jeans and a tank top, how is what I'm wearing any worse?"

"This *tank top*," he said, using finger quotes. "Was designed by Patrice Nichols."

"An overpriced tank top is still just a tank top." I smirked when he threw up his hands. "Someone's feeling extra tonight."

"You look like a frat boy."

"Then I'll blend in well." I teased and pushed past him. "Hey, Alex, Davis. Sorry if I held up the party."

"No worries, man. And for what it's worth..." Davis grinned. "You look good to me."

"Whatever... This look is giving me stank ass sweaty sac vibes. If that's the look you're going for, have at it." Marcos shook his head, and I coughed to cover my laugh. "When you go home alone tonight, I'll be sure to tell you I told you so."

"I don't doubt it."

"Can we go?" Alex asked. "I want to get a table before the place gets packed."

Davis took Alex's hand and headed for the front door, leaving Marcos to glare at me one last time. He mumbled something in Spanish under his breath, and fuck, it took everything I had not to snap back with some smart-ass comment about the manufactured, well-placed holes in his jeans. But I liked my balls too much to risk them.

The bar was filled to capacity in less than an hour. I didn't understand the appeal. The cheap beer they offered was pretty decent, and there were enough pool tables, most people were able to get in a few games, but it smelled like stale cigarettes and bad cologne. The floor was always sticky, and the vinyl booths had duct tape holding them together. The best thing about the place was the old jukebox in the backroom where people could dance. We'd gotten here early enough, we'd been able to grab one of the rare tall tables in the corner near the bar. Bored, I'd had more beer than I should have. My stomach was warm, and my head was heavy on my shoulders. Some 80's song I recognized played loudly through the overhead speakers, and I chuckled to myself when the lead sang about liking older girls. Evidently, I did, too, but not girls. Guys. Older guys. But not like grandpa old or anything.

"You've reached the talk-to-yourself-out-loud level of drunk, and it's not even midnight, Park. How is that even possible?" Marcos asked, gulping down his own beer as beads of sweat gathered along his hair line from dancing.

"What did I say?"

"Something about liking older men," he said and set his empty glass on the table. "Come dance with me. Alex and Davis are being all coupley, and I swear this is the straightest bar ever created. Why the hell do we come here again?"

"Easy buzz?"

He hummed, his gaze snagging on a good-looking blond guy as he walked by. The dude was ripped, wearing jeans that left little to the imagination.

"Goddamn." Marcos started to follow him, and I grabbed his arm.

"Nope, that man is straight as hell."

"Maybe not," he said and frowned as we both watched the guy stick his tongue down some woman's throat. "That's depressing." He pulled out a stool and sat down, stealing my glass of beer.

"By all means, what's mine is yours."

"Thanks," he said, breathless, as he lowered the glass from his lips. "Who's the older guy you like?"

"It's nothing." I usually told Marcos everything, even though he was the biggest pain in my ass. For the most part, his heart was always in the right place. But I wasn't ready for him to deconstruct every detail of what I had going with James. "Haven't heard from Tam since the other night," I said in an attempt to divert his attention.

"I thought you didn't want to hear from him?" He pulled Chapstick from his pocket and swiped it over his lips, leaving behind a glossy pink hue. "He did mention the other day that he had a good time. But got the impression it was a one-night thing."

"It was."

"And just so you know, I'm not stupid or drunk enough to not notice you changed the subject. You're not very subtle." He poked me in the chest. "Spill it, Mills."

"Promise you won't judge me?"

"I'll do no such thing." He shoved my knee with his hand, his smile as saccharine as ever. "Did you go and find yourself a daddy?"

"He's only thirty-three."

"Well, that's boring. Where did you meet him?"

"Pegasus."

"No, you did not." He closed his eyes and shook his head. "Park. That place is a breeding ground for catfish."

"He seems nice."

Marcos raised his hand, holding up two fingers, he'd grabbed the waitress's attention. "I need more beer for this conversation."

"His name is James—well, that's his middle name. We decided to keep it anonymous."

"Red flag number one, continue."

Exhaling an exasperated laugh, I searched the room for our friends, who maybe could offer me some kind of buffer, but came up empty. "You're going to ruin it."

He sat up and took a deep breath as he rolled his shoulders.

"I'll be quiet."

"No, you won't."

"I will. I promise. Continue." He brought his fingers to his lips and pretended to zip them shut.

"I'm anonymous on Pegasus, too, by the way. It's better that way. Makes for a less awkward exit when things don't pan out." Marcos, as promised, didn't comment. "The story is he's divorced. Was married to the same woman his whole life. And he's ready to explore his attraction to men."

"Wait, he—"

"You promised to keep your mouth shut," I said and smiled when he rolled his eyes.

"May I ask a question?" He spoke slowly, his aggravation apparent in the tight set of his jaw.

This was awesome.

"You may."

"And you're going to be, what, his guinea pig?" All traces of humor evaporated from his face. Shit, I was in for it now. "I know I'm a nag, and half the time I do it to get a rise out of you, but Park... this could end like Florida and—"

"Stop," I said and stood abruptly. "I'm not fucking naïve. I know how to protect myself."

"Okay," he breathed, looking around the room. A few people had started to stare at us, and I couldn't give a shit less. "Sit down, alright. I'm sorry."

My jaw pulsed as I sat down, my heart banging around in its cage like it wanted to escape this conversation as much as I did.

"I'm not a victim."

"I know. I'm sorry."

"Then, stop treating me like one."

His dark eyes searched my face, and once my breathing evened out, he spoke again. "I love you like a brother," he said and leaned toward me, his hand covering mine. "I know you're not a victim. But I also know how fucked up you were... after what happened to you. We kept our heads down, *mijo*, for far too long. I don't ever want that for you again."

"I can't let that one moment define me. I got my ass kicked. I was a dumb kid who trusted the wrong person." Marcos gave my hand a squeeze before he lowered his own to his lap. "I won't ever let that happen again."

"And if you meet this James guy, you'll do it in public?"

"Of course. Again, I'm not an idiot."

Marcos had been there for me when I'd been left for dead, when I'd healed, when I'd thought fear was all I'd ever know. It's what he did. He showed up when I needed him to, and I had no doubt he'd do it again. But more than anything, I needed him to trust me.

The waitress, already knowing our order from earlier, dropped off two more beers. Grateful for the interruption, I gave her a smile and she blushed. "If y'all need anything else let me know," she said. "I'll be around."

She walked off and I watched as she swayed her hips, her ass practically hanging out of her short shorts. "Nope... still does nothing for me."

Marcos laughed a little and it broke the tension. I stared at my best friend, my chest about five times lighter than it was two minutes ago. "James is into *The Lost Boys*."

"Yeah?" He let out a resigned breath, a silent white flag of surrender. "That's like your soulmate shit, right?"

"Pretty fucking close."

Marcos glanced toward the back room. "You want to dance?"

"Sure," I said, even though it was the last thing I felt like doing. "Let's finish these beers and find Alex and Davis. They're probably the only gays on the dance floor."

"I'm never coming here again." He cringed and the look on his face made me smile.

He was so over the top. But it was exactly how I liked him.

"You said that when we came here last Saturday."

"I mean it this time," he said. "This place is a dump."

"I told you it wasn't worth dressing up for... It never is."

"Whatever... hurry up. The quicker you finish your beer, the faster we'll get on the dance floor, and hopefully get the hell out of here before I start finding frat boys attractive."

"Aren't they, though?"

He tilted his head, checking out a decent-looking jock over by the pool table. Who like me, was dressed in gym shorts and a t-shirt.

"Only when they're naked."

Chapter 9

DONOVAN

I rolled onto my right side, staring at nothing in particular. The pale blue light from the clock on my nightstand was the only light in the room. I punched my pillow a few times, trying to get comfortable, and kicked off the covers, only to pull them back up again when the slight chill of the room pricked at my skin, causing the hair on the back of my neck and arms to rise. The bed was too soft and too firm at the same time. I moved to the left side of the mattress, but it didn't help the restlessness taking root inside my limbs. Scooting back to the right side, I squeezed my eyes shut. I counted to one hundred, then counted backward, my traitorous brain fighting against my efforts. I opened my eyes, and unsuccessfully, tried not to check the time again. It was a little after one in the morning, and clearly my brain did not give a shit that I had to get up early and be a parent. Instead, it had reverted to my horny teenage years. I couldn't stop thinking about the *homework* Michael had given me. After I'd put Anne to bed for the night and graded a few papers, I'd done a quick internet search for the term frotting like he'd suggested. I hadn't dared to look at the video that had popped up, but the definition alone had made me hard, had burned into my synapses, and for the rest of the night it was all I'd been able to think about. Images I'd conjured up on my own hadn't been enough to sate my curiosity. Swearing quietly, I fell onto my back and fixed my eyes on the ceiling.

I'd been in this uncomfortable state of arousal for hours, and debated texting Michael liked he'd said I could, but what the fuck would I say? *"Wow, that looks like fun, maybe we should get together and jack each other off sometime?"* I wasn't that sleazy or desperate, and not to mention, I didn't think we were at the meeting-in-person stage yet, no matter how impulsive I wanted to be. I sat up and threw the covers to the side feeling overheated, my phone staring back at me from the nightstand.

"Christ," I grumbled as I got out of bed and trudged off to the bathroom.

I hadn't bothered to turn on the light, and after I'd splashed cold water on my face, I examined my reflection in the mirror. My hair was damp from where I'd slicked it back with wet hands, and the lack of light muted my features. Standing in only a pair of dark blue boxer briefs, I almost didn't recognize myself. My eyes were too vivid, too awake. I exhaled and rested my hands on the counter, lowering my head, I took a deep breath. After a minute, I gave up the struggle to control my racing thoughts and walked into the bedroom. I grabbed my phone off the nightstand, and even though Anne was all the way on the other side of the house, sound asleep, I locked my door.

Once I was in bed, sitting up against my pillows, I opened up my previous search. It wasn't a big deal, guys watched porn all the time. At least that's what I told myself as I clicked on one of the videos. The volume was low, but I could hear the deep, masculine moans of the men on my screen. My hand trailed down my chest and over the lightly etched ridges of my stomach muscles, my breath catching in my throat as I palmed my growing erection over the cotton of my underwear. Feeling guilty, I quickly glanced at my bedroom door, double-checking it was locked.

God, was this pathetic?

My head fell back, and I knocked it against the headboard.

Yes... One-hundred percent pathetic.

My eyes dropped to the screen, and I paused the video. Exhaling a frustrated breath, I reached over to set my phone on the nightstand, and it vibrated in my hand. It was almost one-thirty, and in my current state I didn't think it was smart to reply, but his name popping up on my screen was the first bit of relief I'd had all night.

@TheLOstBOy: Did you do your homework?

@MeAndMyShadow33: I did.

I should have tried to play it cool, maybe wait a few minutes to answer, but I was too riled up for games.

@TheLOstBOy: And...

@MeAndMyShadow33: And now I can't sleep.

@TheLOstBOy: Too weird?

@MeAndMyShadow33: No, not weird.

@MeAndMyShadow33: It turned me on.

I'd hit send before I changed my mind. I shouldn't be embarrassed. Sex was sex, right? But I'd only ever had sexual experiences with Lanie. Michael was a stranger, this idea floating somewhere in the unknown, and I feared his judgment. I didn't want to say the wrong thing, or sound perverted or naïve. Hiding behind the façade of anonymity didn't stop me from being me. I was still this awkward-ass guy who'd floundered his way through his sexuality and was finally coming into his own at the ripe old age of thirty-three. I wanted to be enough for myself, and for him.

@TheLOstBOy: Yeah?

@MeAndMyShadow33: Yeah.

@TheLOstBOy: And now you can't sleep?

@MeAndMyShadow33: Pretty much.

@TheLOstBOy: Because you're turned on? Right now?

@MeAndMyShadow33: Right now.

An agonizing minute passed before he responded, giving me enough time to want to wish back the words I'd sent.

@TheLOstBOy: We should do something about that...

@MeAndMyShadow33: Now?

@TheLOstBOy: Don't worry I don't mean face to face. Not yet.

Not yet.

@TheLOstBOy: But if I was there... there's lots of ways I could help you sleep.

The images from the video flooded my rushing pulse, spreading heat over every inch of my skin. I ached for some type of release, my fingers moving swiftly across the screen, driven purely by need. My rational brain could deal with any regrets later.

@MeAndMyShadow33: How would you help me sleep?

@TheLOstBOy: It depends on what you want.

@MeAndMyShadow33: You.

Everything.

@TheLOstBOy: I'm assuming we're undressed in this little scenario.

Dying inside, my face flushed. I'd never done this kind of stuff with my ex. Dirty talk was definitely not my forte. But I couldn't say I wasn't intrigued on how this would go. Laughing at myself, I winced as I typed.

@MeAndMyShadow33: I'm already in my underwear.

@TheLOstBOy: That makes it easy. Not to leave you hanging, I get undressed too and...

@MeAndMyShadow33: Get in bed with me?

@TheLOstBOy: Thanks, I'd love to.

Smiling, I relaxed some.

@MeAndMyShadow33: What would you do next?

@TheLOstBOy: I run my hand across your chest, and you pull me in. I have to straddle your thighs to kiss you. I start with your lips and work my way down your jaw to your neck.

Feeling unsure of myself, I typed without thinking.

@MeAndMyShadow33: I want you to touch me.

@TheLOstBOy: I'm here for whatever you want. This is all for you.

His assurance lifted away my hesitation, and with one hand, I pulled down my briefs. A rough, uneven breath parted my lips as I stroked myself, circling the head of my cock with the pad of my thumb. I shuddered, closing my eyes for a few seconds, and pretended it was his hand, his heat surrounding me, his tight grip drawing me closer to the line I'd been dying to cross.

@MeAndMyShadow33: This feels too real.

@TheLOstBOy: Please tell me you're touching yourself right now.

Swallowing my self-doubt, I told him the truth.

@MeAndMyShadow33: I am.

@TheLOstBOy: Fuck, me too.

My entire body burned with need, knowing I'd made him just as hot as he'd made me.

@MeAndMyShadow33: I wish you were here. I wish I could feel you.

My head tipped back as I cupped my balls, wishing it was his mouth, his fingers, anything besides my own hand. I was wound up, my cheeks and neck blazing with a mixture of arousal and uncertainty. I wanted to come. I wanted to be like the men in that video, lying side by side, my hips aligned with Michael's while he jacked us at the same time.

@TheLOstBOy: I'm here, James. You're so close, so fucking hard for me. Can you feel me, feel how hard I am for you?

"Yes," I grunted, my climax already trying to surface.

I forced myself to slow down, my hand finding a lazy rhythm, up and down the steeled length of my shaft. I wanted to draw this out, I wanted to see how far I'd let myself go.

@MeAndMyShadow33: I feel you.

@TheLOstBOy: Yeah... what am I doing?

@MeAndMyShadow33: Stroking me.

@TheLOstBOy: Fast or slow.

@MeAndMyShadow33: Slow.

@TheLOstBOy: I want to taste you. Fuck, I bet you taste good.

God.

@TheLOstBOy: I lean down for a taste, but it's not enough. I love the way the head of your cock stretches my lips, the weight of it on my tongue. I want to feel you in my throat, suck and swallow you until you're shaking. I want your fingers in my hair, James. Use my mouth, make yourself come.

I was lost in this fantasy, to this faceless man. My

legs spread open, I imagined him kneeling between them. Imagined my fist in his hair as I raised my hips and fucked my hand until I couldn't hold back any longer, until my climax barreled through me. I clenched my jaw to subdue my loud groan, shooting my load all over my chest and stomach. A calm sleepiness loosened every muscle in my body with every heavy breath I pulled into my lungs. It took a minute for the initial high to start to fade and for me to realize I'd dropped my phone. Feeling lightheaded, I reached for it and unlocked the screen.

"Holy shit."

He'd sent a picture of his incredible, chiseled chest and stomach covered in his come. It was the sexiest thing I'd ever seen. I thought about taking a picture of my own mess and almost chickened out. But I had nothing to lose at this point, and admittedly, I wanted him to have it, wanted him to have this piece of me, this first. I snapped a shot, exactly like his, and after I sent it, I went to the bathroom to clean up. It only took me a few minutes, but by the time I crawled back into bed, all the post-orgasmic adrenaline had dissipated, and my exhaustion hit me like a truck. My insecurities made me reluctant to open our message thread, to see the proof of what had happened. Half smiling, half cringing, I lay back on my pillow and swiped my thumb across the screen.

@TheLOstBOy: If I was there, I'd lick you clean.

Jesus.

@MeAndMyShadow33: I think I could enjoy watching you do that.

@TheLOstBOy: I thought you might've fallen asleep.

@MeAndMyShadow33: Had to clean up.

@TheLOstBOy: See, it's too bad I wasn't there to help.

I laugh quietly as I turned onto my side and typed.

@MeAndMyShadow33: Maybe next time.

@TheLOstBOy: Maybe. You're okay, though? Handling your first guy-on-guy sext fest without any regrets?

@MeAndMyShadow33: Only one.

@TheLOstBOy: Uh-oh....

@MeAndMyShadow33: I wish I knew what you looked like. It would've made your visualization exercise more realistic.

@TheLOstBOy: We skipped over lesson 1 and went straight to lesson 2 didn't we?

@MeAndMyShadow33: We can always circle back. Are you tall? Short? Dark hair? I can tell by your picture you're very into fitness. Very sexy, by the way.

@TheLOstBOy: Thanks for the compliment. It's

not like I send pics of my spunk-covered abs to just anyone.

@MeAndMyShadow33: I feel special.

@TheLOstBOy: I think I might frame the picture you sent.

@MeAndMyShadow33: Very funny.

@TheLOstBOy: You are right, though. I'm pretty into fitness. Not like a narcissist, douchebag, gym rat or anything. But I work out and eat right. I'm tall... six-foot-one, dirty blond hair, blue eyes. I'm as generic as my middle name.

@MeAndMyShadow33: Then, I guess my type must be generic.

@TheLOstBOy: *blushes*

@MeAndMyShadow33: That was corny, wasn't it?

@TheLOstBOy: It's late. I'll allow it.

@MeAndMyShadow33: I should let you get to sleep.

@TheLOstBOy: Nope. You owe me some personal details.

@MeAndMyShadow33: I'm six-foot-three. Dark hair. Light eyes. Mostly gray, but depends on what I'm wearing. You already know my favorite color and how I take my coffee. What about you?

@TheLOstBOy: Gray and with as much sugar and cream as it takes to make it not taste like coffee.

@MeAndMyShadow33: Gray is your favorite color?

@TheLOstBOy: No, but since you were corny earlier, I thought I'd be too.

@TheLOstBOy: Green is my favorite. Especially after it rains. When the trees and grass sing.

@MeAndMyShadow33: Very poetic for two in the morning.

@TheLOstBOy: You should hear me when I'm well rested. I'm a real Robert Frost.

@MeAndMyShadow33: I'll let you get some rest, then.

@TheLOstBOy: Think you'll be able to sleep now?

@MeAndMyShadow33: Like the dead.

My heart stammered, not truly wanting to say good night, but knowing I needed to. Before I sent another message, I stared at the picture he'd sent with a crooked smile on my face.

> **@MeAndMyShadow33**: Talk to you soon?

> **@TheLOstBOy**: Like I said before, I'm here for whatever you want.

> **@TheLOstBOy**: This is all for you.

Chapter 10

PARKER

Since it was my birthday, I'd left work around two. I'd gone out for a late lunch with my mom and had shown up a little early for class. The room was quiet when I walked in, only a few students had already arrived. Mr. Brody raised his gaze and gave me a small smile as I slid into my seat. I grinned back, loving how easily the man blushed. He was dressed in charcoal gray slacks today, and a dark blue button down with the sleeves rolled up to his elbows. His inky hair fell over his right brow as he lowered his steel-colored eyes to his laptop. It was an absolute crime for a man to be that hot and adorably clueless at the same time. His shyness made me think of James and how much he'd opened up to me this past Saturday. I hadn't thought anything would happen when I texted him after I'd gotten home from the bar that night. I thought he'd be asleep and had been pleasantly surprised by how the night unfolded. But between work and school, we hadn't had the chance to text as much as I would have liked. Our conversations were never too personal, and most always sexual. We had a repeat of Saturday night again on Monday. Two days had passed, and I was already craving more.

Like an addict, I pulled my phone from my backpack. Swiping my thumb over the screen to check the time, I smiled. Class didn't start for another ten minutes. And instead of using my time wisely to go over the flash fiction story Mr. Brody had asked us to write last class, I opened up the Pegasus app.

> **@TheLOstBOy:** Can't stop thinking about Monday night.

I looked over my shoulder as the classroom door opened and a few more students filed in. I set my phone on the desk and reached into my bag for my notebook. My fiction piece wasn't my best work. Telling an entire story in less than fifteen-hundred words was damn near impossible, but I wanted to impress Mr. Brody, prove to him my first two assignments weren't a fluke. I pulled out the paper and started to read over what I'd written when my phone vibrated loudly on the desk. The girl in the row in front of me turned in her seat with a judgmental raise of her brow.

"Sorry," I whispered, giving her an apologetic smile, as I checked my messages.

> **@MeAndMyShadow33:** You're all I think about.

@MeAndMyShadow33: Happy Birthday, Michael.

He remembered.

A stranger should not have had the power to make me smile like this, to make my stomach drop like I was a kid all over again, riding my bike with my arms stretched out to my sides, coasting down the giant hill behind my mom's house. Lust had turned me into an adrenaline junkie again.

@TheLOstBOy: Thanks… I don't feel any older.

@MeAndMyShadow33: That starts after you turn thirty.

I laughed quietly as I typed out another response.

@TheLOstBOy: I have a few things I need to do but was hoping you'd be around later.

I pressed send and lifted my gaze briefly, checking for Marcos, and my gaze snagged on Mr. Brody's radiant smile. Unrestrained and candid, it opened him up, relaxed his entire posture. It was one of those smiles that would have knocked me on my ass if it had been directed my way. His eyes were glued to the phone in his hand, and it made me curious who might've been on the receiving end of that perfect smile.

"Quit staring at the teach like that, it's fucking creepy," Marcos said as he sat down next to me.

"But look at that smile."

To my chagrin, when we both looked toward the front of the classroom the moment had passed. Mr.

Brody's brows were pinched together as his thumbs tapped against the screen of his phone.

"He looks the same to me." Marcos leaned back in his chair. "You finish his assignment?"

"Yeah," I said as another notification from Pegasus came through. "You?"

Marcos started rambling about not having enough time, and something about a customer at the boutique, and like an asshole, I checked my message instead of paying attention to him.

> **@MeAndMyShadow33**: I'm having dinner with a friend, but the rest of my night is yours.

Dinner with a friend.

I had no claim on him, no right to feel possessive. James was free to have dinner with whomever the hell he wanted. And wasn't I literally just crushing on my professor. But the idea of someone else getting to spend one-on-one time with him made me realize how much I wanted that too. I wanted more than a quick release, more than dirty talk in the dark cover of night. I wanted to know him, to touch his actual skin. A shadowy shot of his come covered abs wasn't enough for me. His middle name wasn't enough. I wanted first names and real lips. Fingers and hot hands. I wanted more than his favorite color. I wanted history and details, to know what he looked like when he smiled. It had only been a week, but I was ready to meet in person, and hell, I hoped he was too.

> **@TheLOstBOy**: Text me when you get home. There's been a change in my lesson plan.

"Oh my God, you're not even listening to me." Marcos' sharp elbow dug into my rib cage.

"Ow, what the fuck?" I hissed under my breath, and he snickered. "Glad you think it's funny I might have a cracked rib."

"And I'm supposed to be the drama queen." He rolled his eyes as I rubbed my side. "Tam and a couple of friends from work want to go out for drinks tonight. Do you think you could pry yourself from your precious phone for a few hours?"

"I can't tonight."

"It's your birthday."

"Exactly, it's *my* day, and I don't feel like getting wasted."

"Why? Got a hot date with your hand again?" he asked, and if we weren't in a classroom filled with people, I might've tackled his smug, smiling ass. "Don't look at me like that, *mijo*. It's not my fault the walls in our apartment are thin."

"I have homework, dipshit." Irritated by how close he'd come to the truth, I flipped my hat backward on my head, keeping my eyes trained toward the front of the class.

"Oh... I didn't get the memo. We're calling it homework now?" He dropped his voice as Mr. Brody called the class to attention. "Okay then, I have homework, too, but I'll do mine in the shower before I head out for drinks."

I raised my fist to my mouth to cover my laugh. Only Marcos could have me pissed one second and laughing the next.

"Pay attention," I said. "You might learn something."

Marcos hummed under his breath but kept his comments and attitude to himself.

"I have exciting news," Mr. Brody said as he walked over to his desk and held up a book for the class to see. It was a copy of *The Street Vendor's Son,* by Wilder Welles. "We have a special guest speaker coming today, he's running late, but should be here soon."

"Holy fuck," I whispered. "Remember that author from the club the other night?"

"Yeah." Marcos couldn't have looked less enthused.

"That's the guest speaker."

"I should have skipped class."

"You could always leave."

"I think I'll stay. Watching you fan girl should be interesting." An evil glint flickered in his eyes. "I promise not to embarrass you too much."

"Marcos, I swear you better—"

The classroom door opened, and I forgot what I was about to say as Wilder fucking Welles strolled past me. Mr. Brody smiled at him as he made his way down the aisle to the front of the room.

"I'm sorry I'm so late." Wilder huffed, as he set his bag on Mr. Brody's desk. "I had to drop Sam with Jax."

"Not a problem. I'm glad you could make it." Mr. Brody gave him a few seconds to settle in before he introduced him. "Class, I'd like you to give Mr. Welles a warm welcome. He's taken time out of his busy writing schedule and from his family to be here this evening."

Wilder's face turned beet red as he swallowed and gave a reluctant wave. "Thank you."

"Mr. Welles is a—"

"Christ, Van. Call me Wilder. I'm not that old yet."

Marcos quietly laughed as he leaned toward me. "I don't care if he kicks you out of this class, I dare you to call him Van." I shook my head and strained to hear Mr. Brody. "Just once, it's all I'm asking."

"Shut the hell up so I can listen."

"...is a *New York Times* Best Selling Author. His debut novel, *Love Always, Wild* topped the charts its first week, his second book is being adapted into a television series as we speak, and he just released a new book last Tuesday."

"I sound busy," Wilder teased. "I swear... Most of my time is spent sitting around a coffee shop staring at a blank screen, second-guessing myself, and growling at unsuspecting customers who happen to walk by during one of my many panic attacks. I promise my life isn't glamorous." He reached into the pocket of his jeans and pulled out a few Cheerios. Laughing, he threw them in a wastebasket near Mr. Brody's desk. "My daughter Sam loves these."

Daughter? He seemed way too young to have a kid. Dressed in tight black jeans and an expensive-looking, oversized shirt, he could've passed for a freshman.

"I ran into Wilder yesterday at the agency and asked if he would mind going over his writing process with us. He graciously accepted, and hopefully if there's enough time, we'll get to torture him with questions."

"Shit, should I be scared?" he asked, and Mr. Brody's eyes filled with mirth as the class laughed. "I probably shouldn't swear either."

"We're adults," someone in the front row said. "Swear all you want."

"Thank you, Ms. Billings." Mr. Brody chuckled. "The floor is yours, Wilder. But please try and keep the profanity to a minimum. I'd like to keep my job."

Wilder pushed his heavy curls from his forehead, and with an anxious smile he told us about what he called his "writing journey." He talked about how he'd met his husband Jax in college, and how his relationship with him had paved the way for his first book. Hearing his story, learning about how he'd started, it was like Wilder had opened up this private door and asked us to climb inside his heart.

"Writing stories is giving life to your dreams," he said, and the room was silent, breathless as he continued. "Van can teach you about the eight elements of fiction, teach you the definition of a metaphor, but your process is something that belongs only to you. Your words and how you choose to sew them together isn't something that can be taught." Wilder ran his hand through his hair again and leaned against the desk. "I hope that's okay to say, Van... no offense."

"None taken." Mr. Brody waved him off with a smile from where he stood in the corner of the room.

I kept my gaze on him as Wilder continued, watching as he stared at the author with what could only be described as awe. It made me want to ask him why he hadn't written a book. Why he'd chosen to sell them, instead.

"I'll go ahead and take some questions before you get sick of the sound of my voice." Wilder glanced around the classroom, his smile dimming when no one raised their hand.

"I have a question," I blurted, and Marcos nearly choked on his laugh.

Wilder's dark eyes held mine, and it was the first time I noticed he had on eyeliner. Intimidated as fuck under the weight of his stare, my words caught in my throat, and I stuttered. I was sure Marcos would never let me live this moment down.

"D-did... you ever worry about hiding your sexuality in order to sell books?"

"I've always been open about who I am, but my parents wanted me to use a pen name. Asked me to not write the book at all, actually." Wilder laughed without humor. "And there was this brief but big moment where I hesitated... when I thought maybe they were right. I thought maybe I couldn't have both. I couldn't be out and proud and have my dream. But then I realized writing was like love. I didn't get to choose. I couldn't stop writing any more than I could stop loving men, and eventually said fuck it and published anyway."

Almost all the students applauded except for the two guys at the end of our row. Indignant, they sat with their arms crossed, with disgusted looks on their faces. The world could evolve, and time would continue to push its way forward, but no matter how far we'd come, there'd always be a select few ready to drag us back fifty goddamn years.

Once the applause died down, Wilder answered a few more questions before it was time to go. Mr. Brody thanked him again as everyone started to pack up. "Don't worry about sending your flash fiction stories into me until Friday. Any submission received after that will not be graded."

Marcos stood and lugged his bag over his shoulder. "You're really going to stay home tonight?"

"I've got a history quiz to study for, stats to do, and I think I'm going to rewrite this story," I said, slipping it into my notebook as I stood.

"Shit... I forgot about the history quiz." He clapped me on the arm. "You're the murderer of dreams."

"Me?" I asked and zipped up my backpack. "I didn't make you take history."

"No, you made me take this fucking class. Which eats up a lot of my social time."

The classroom emptied around us as I pulled my bag onto my shoulders. "Then, drop it. You still have time."

"Mr. Mills, do you have a moment?" Mr. Brody asked, his expectant gray eyes a much better visual than my best friend's stupid smirk.

"Of course."

Marcos squeezed past me. "Try not to drool on the cute author."

Mortified, I made my way down the aisle, hoping Mr. Brody and Wilder hadn't heard his commentary.

"What's up?" I asked.

"I was hoping to receive your fiction piece. I'm surprised you haven't turned it in yet."

"Uh..." I pushed my hands into my back pockets, and in my peripheral, I saw Wilder set down his phone on the desk. One of my idols stood less than ten feet away from me, and Mr. Brody wanted to talk about my amateur fiction piece? "I... I finished it, but it sucks. I'm rewriting it tonight."

"I want to read both, then."

"That sort of defeats the purpose," I said, and holy shit, Wilder laughed.

"How so?" Mr. Brody seemed genuinely confused.

"The first one is garbage, and I'd rather you not read it, hence the whole reason I'm rewriting it in the first place."

"Mr. Mills—"

"Parker," I reminded him, and his smile mirrored mine.

My gaze flicked between his eyes and his mouth, lingering on the curve of his bottom lip as the seconds ticked by. One, two long breaths passed between us before he spoke again.

"Send me both. I want to see your progression."

"Do the other students have to write two papers?" I asked, knowing this was my choice, but wanting to tease him anyway.

He made it too easy.

"You can turn in what you have," he said, his tone professional and even. "I'm not requiring you to—"

"Got it... I'll send both."

"Good. I'm eager to see what you came up with." He turned to look at Wilder. "This is the student I was telling you about the other day. Parker Mills."

To my utter horror and thrill, Wilder walked toward me. "It's nice to put a face to the name." He held out his hand and I stared at it, totally starstruck. "I think he might be in shock."

"Oh shit... I'm sorry." I took his hand, probably more aggressive than was socially acceptable. "You're Wilder Welles."

He smiled at Mr. Brody. "God, he's cute."

I let go of his hand and rubbed the back of my neck. "I'm overwhelmed, I guess. I've never met an author before. Your work is... inspiring."

"Thank you," he said, the tops of his cheeks dusting with a pale shade of pink. "I'm lucky I get to do what I love."

Mr. Brody picked up a booklet from his desk and handed it to me. Bright purple and gold script unraveled across the page. "Did you know the school has a literary magazine?"

"No. I had no idea," I said, skimming through the pages.

"They take submissions every quarter. I think you should enter."

"I don't know."

"Think about it, look over the content, and then make a decision. The deadline is a month from now. You have time."

"Trust me. Van is an agent..." Wilder laughed as he spoke. "If he didn't think you were talented, he wouldn't even bother."

"Yeah... okay. I'll look at it." I rolled up the magazine and tucked it in the side pocket of my backpack, knowing I wouldn't submit anything, at least not anytime soon.

My work was private. I wasn't ready to share it with the entire school. "Thanks."

"And I'm a professor before I'm an agent when it comes to my students. It's my job to help you grow."

"I stand by my previous statement." Wilder grinned, setting a stubborn hand on his hip. "You can water a plant all fucking day, but if it has weak roots, it's gonna rot."

"Am I the one with weak roots in this scenario?" I asked and they both laughed.

"Definitely not." Mr. Brody nodded toward the classroom door. "We can talk more about this after you've thought it over."

"It was nice to meet you," I said, and managed to shake Wilder's hand like a normal human being this time.

"Likewise."

"Don't forget, you have till Friday to turn in the assignment. Don't rush it." Mr. Brody gave me another one of his lopsided grins. "I want both drafts, Parker."

I nodded and bit the corner of my lip, trying like hell not to smile when he'd said my name.

"Talk to you on Monday, Mr. Brody."

Chapter 11

DONOVAN

"You didn't have to buy me dinner," Wilder said as he pulled out a chair on the other side of the table. "I'm not opposed to bribes from most people, but I would've spoken to your class either way."

"I appreciate it, this is my way of saying thank you. I hope Jax doesn't mind."

Wilder's head lilted back as he laughed. "Jax is probably grateful to have a night to himself without me buzzing around making him crazy. Believe it or not, I'm a lot to handle."

From what I'd heard from Anders, and from my own interactions with Wilder, I could understand how his strong personality might not be for everyone. He took a look around the restaurant, and I followed his gaze, taking in the wide-open floor plan. Steel beams and exposed brick created a minimalist atmosphere. The brewery opened a few weeks ago and had gotten rave reviews. With his overgrown shaggy hair, and trendy clothes, Wilder fit in with the young-looking crowd even though he was older than me. I, on the other hand, stood out like a sore thumb. In slacks and a button down, I was the most overdressed person in the place. As if the universe wanted to pour salt in my wound, a group of what looked like college-aged kids walked in the front door.

"I shouldn't have picked a place so close to campus," I said with a resigned exhale and lifted my menu.

"I think... yeah... isn't that guy in your class?" Wilder asked and my stomach fell about three stories.

Marcos Basulto stood near the hostess stand chatting with the small group that had just walked in a minute ago. I did a quick sweep, looking for Parker, and a weird sensation hit my stomach when I realized he wasn't there. I swallowed, assuming it was unease, dealing with students outside of the classroom wasn't something I'd prepared for or wanted. When my gaze found its way back to Marcos, a slow smile spread across his face as he waved his polished fingers at me.

"Oh fuck," I said, sinking a little lower in my chair. "Yeah, he's in my class."

"I think he's coming over here."

"Shit. What should I do?"

Wilder laughed and wrinkled his nose. "I don't know... say hi? What's the big deal?"

"Hey, Mr. B." Marcos smiled down at me with pink-painted lips. "Small world."

"Mr. Basulto, it's... good to see you."

"Don't worry," he said with a quick flourish of his hand. "I won't hover, just had to stop by so I could brag to Parker that I saw you. He'll be so disappointed."

Heat crawled up my neck and pooled in my cheeks. "Ah..."

"I love your shoes," Wilder cut in, saving me from the strained conversation. "Bella Lou?"

"The one and only." Marcos took a step back, the awkward moment on pause as we all stared at his feet. He had on dangerous-looking green heels at least three-inches tall. I would've broken my neck trying to stand, let alone walk in those things. But Marcos jutted his hip, and pointed to his toe, his tight jeans and high heels accentuating his long legs. "I got them for fifty-percent off."

"No shit? How?" Wilder asked.

"I work there."

"You work at Bella Lou Boutique?" Wilder gawked at me, but I had no clue what the hell they were talking about. "I'm insanely jealous. I never go in because I can't justify the price."

"I thought you were like a famous, bestselling author?" Marcos asked.

"Not that famous." Wilder grimaced. "But fifty-percent off, I can handle that."

"Come in anytime." Marcos glanced toward the front. "I'll let you guys do your thing. Good to see you, Mr. B."

"You too," I said. "Enjoy your evening."

Enjoy your evening. Jesus, was I fifty?

Marcos nodded, a smirk forming on his lips. "Sure thing, I'll tell Park you said hi."

"God, that was weird, right?" I asked once Marcos was out of ear shot.

"He seemed harmless, but Parker's trouble."

"How do you mean?"

Wilder flipped over his menu. "Have you looked at him?"

"Just because he's attractive does not mean he's trouble."

"The guy is sex, Van." He set down his menu. "He reminds me of Jax. All that muscle, the blue eyes... the blond hair... plus, he has a crush on you."

I brushed him off with a laugh and shook my head. "He's a flirt... but a crush? Not likely."

"Okay," he said, his flippant tone accompanied by a smirk. "If you say so."

A waiter walked up to the table before I had a chance to argue.

"Welcome to Hemingway's. What can I get you two?" We both ordered the seasonal craft beer with a burger and fries. The waiter scratched everything onto his pad before scooping up our menus with an overzealous smile. "I'll be right back with your beers."

Once he walked away, I steered our conversation away from Wilder's theories. It didn't matter how attractive Parker was or if he had a crush on me or not. I was his teacher. I couldn't think of him like that. He was a smart kid, with a bright future in writing. End of story.

"I met someone on the app you told me about."

"Really?" Wilder leaned his elbow on the table and rested his chin in the palm of his hand. "And... how did it go?"

"We haven't met in person yet. But he seems great."

Great was an understatement. Every day I had to stop myself from texting him as much as I wanted. Our relationship, which was a generous word for what we had, was physical. But underneath the surface of it all, there was so much possibility. He cared, and it showed in the way he let me cross boundaries in my own time. He could've moved on to a guy with experience, but he'd chosen me. He wanted me.

"Great? I'm going to need more details than that."

"There's not a lot to tell," I said. "We're both anonymous. We haven't talked much about our real lives."

"You don't know what he looks like?"

"No, but I have seen his abs a few times."

The waiter chose that moment to drop off our drinks and I avoided his eyes.

Wilder leaned in and lowered his voice as the waiter moved on to the next table. "Did he send you a dick pic?"

"God... no."

"What? Dick pics can be fun."

Not as fun as sexting. But I kept that nugget of information to myself.

"I'm sure they can be, but I don't know, shouldn't I wait to meet him in person first?" I asked and lifted my pint glass to my lips. The sour citrus flavor of the beer exploded across my taste buds. "But I'm not sure how soon we should meet."

"I say the sooner you meet the better. That way if he's a troll, you can move on. Also, send a dick pic if you want... there are no rules, Van."

"Yeah... okay."

"Oh, I wanted to tell you, my assistant... totally hot and single."

"Andrew?"

"Yup." He grinned and took a sip of his beer. "And he's bi."

"Huh... he seems kind of cold, though."

"Don't be mean... He's just quiet. He's got the whole tall, dark, and mysterious thing going for him." Wilder set his beer down and pulled out his phone. "If you want, I'll give you his number."

"What? No... I... I like this guy I'm talking to. I want to see how it goes."

It might've been naïve for me to think Michael wasn't seeing other people, but I'd already given him one of my firsts. I wanted to give him more. If he turned out to be the good guy I'd hoped for, I'd give him everything.

I set my keys and wallet on the kitchen counter and started to unbutton my shirt. It was later than I had anticipated, but once I'd started talking about Wilder's new book and market strategy, we'd lost track of time. Marcos and his friends had already left by the time we finished up, sparing me from an uncomfortable goodbye. In my laundry room, I slipped out of my shirt and grabbed my phone out of my pants pocket before throwing everything I had on into the washing machine. I'd meant to start a small load this morning but hadn't gotten around to it. I shut the lid and pressed start, the low hum of the machine gave me an odd, domestic satisfaction. Naked, I walked back to my bathroom and turned on the shower. After I'd left the restaurant, I'd sent Michael a text telling him I was on my way home, but when I opened the message thread, there was no reply.

I stared at my reflection as an explicit idea crossed my mind. The thought alone had me half hard already. Stroking a hand down the length of my cock, my heart hammered in my chest. Emboldened by all the dirty things Michael had said to me on Monday night, I lifted my phone, angling it in a way I was able to hide my face, and snapped a few pictures. I scrolled through the shots and swallowed, my eagerness facing off with my indecision. Each picture offered a full view of my body from my chest down to my feet against the tile floor. The head of my dick was on full display with my fingers firmly gripped around my shaft. I deleted all but one, and my hand shook as I attached it to a message.

> **@MeAndMyShadow33**: I can't believe I'm sending you this. But after Monday I think you earned it.

I hit send, and an immediate wave of nausea crashed around in the pit of my stomach. Leaving my phone on the counter, I got in the shower, too anxious to wait for a reply. I took my time, letting the hot water untie my nerves, and by the time I was finished, the whole room was covered in a blanket of humidity. I definitely did not look at my phone while I dried off, or after I'd gotten dressed, and not once or twice while I brushed my teeth. The damn thing sat on the counter, a beacon of vulnerability. Michael had made all the first moves. He'd set and pushed the boundaries. What if I fucked up? What if I'd pushed one step too far and made a fool of myself?

After a good five-minute panic attack, I picked up my phone and headed into my room. In bed, I glared at the black screen, willing myself to unlock it. Worst case he blocked me. It had only been a week. It wasn't like I couldn't try again or meet someone else. I could chalk up these past seven days as experience gained and move on. I held on to my false bravado and swiped a thumb across the screen.

@TheLOstBOy: Fuck, you're perfect.

I read his message with a surprising ache in my throat, my bottom lip trapped between my teeth, containing my overwhelming smile.

@MeAndMyShadow33: I'm still in shock I actually sent it.

@MeAndMyShadow33: I thought you might block me.

@TheLOstBOy: Hell no. Look what you do to me.

A picture came through, and holy shit, he was stunning.

He must've been in bed. The angle of his shot was different, but showed every single line, every sculpted muscle of his chest and stomach, beyond the soft looking patch of hair down to his thick cock, the tip glistening with pre-come. My mouth watered, dying to know what it would be like to have him, to run my tongue along the veins, to have his hand on the back of my neck while I tasted him for the first time.

@MeAndMyShadow33: You give me confidence I've never had before.

Another picture loaded. This one a blurry shot of his hand grasping the base of his dick.

@MeAndMyShadow33: I wish that was my hand. I wish I could touch you.

@TheLOstBOy: You can. All you have to do is ask.

I wasn't sure if he meant for real, or if we were playing the game again. Either way I was okay with it. If I wanted to do this, if I wanted to dive into my sexuality, I had to be the one to take the leap.

@MeAndMyShadow33: I want you.

@TheLOstBOy: You have me.

Reaching under the wide waistband of my briefs, I shuddered at the heat of my fingers over my sensitive skin and snapped another shot for him.

@MeAndMyShadow33: I want you in my bed. Your hands on my body. Not pictures. I want you. I want the real thing.

@TheLOstBOy: When?

@MeAndMyShadow33: Does Friday work?

The beat of my heart pulsed frantic and wild in my chest, stealing my breath as I waited for his answer.

@TheLOstBOy: Two days feels like forever.

God, it did. But I had Anne tomorrow. I'd made plans to check her out early from school and take her to the zoo. Owen had gotten tickets from one of his clients and asked if he could take us. He never had time for shit like this, and I wasn't about to cancel our plans no matter how hard up I was for sex.

@MeAndMyShadow33: I have a crazy week planned, but my Friday belongs to you.

@TheLOstBOy: I work during the day, but I'm all yours after six.

@MeAndMyShadow33: Where should we meet?

@TheLOstBOy: Someplace public. No offense. It's safer that way for both of us.

@MeAndMyShadow33: None taken. I agree.

@MeAndMyShadow33: We could meet for drinks? There's a pub close to my house, or if you know of a good place...

@TheLOstBOy: A pub sounds chill.

@MeAndMyShadow33: Let's meet around eight at the Brick Store Pub.

It took him a couple of minutes to reply, and for a second, I thought he might've changed his mind.

@TheLOstBOy: In Decatur?

@MeAndMyShadow33: Yeah, is that too far?

@TheLOstBOy: Not at all. I looked it up, the place looks cool.

@MeAndMyShadow33: Friday then...

@TheLOstBOy: Shit just got real, didn't it?

@MeAndMyShadow33: If you change your mind, I'll understand.

@TheLOstBOy: I won't change my mind.

@MeAndMyShadow33: I'm nervous.

@TheLOstBOy: I'll be gentle.

@MeAndMyShadow33: What if I don't want you to be...

@TheLOstBOy: Is it Friday yet?

I laughed out loud.

@MeAndMyShadow33: Two days.

@TheLOstBOy: I can't wait.

I'd waited over fifteen years for this. Waited and wondered and wanted. And in two days, I'd finally get to meet the truth inside me, because of him, in two days my entire life was about to change.

Chapter 12

PARKER

Sweaty and overheated, I opened one bleary eye to glare at my open blinds. The sun poured in, baking my sheets, and I internally cursed Marcos for being such a cheap ass. He never kept the air conditioner below seventy-six. Kicking off the blanket, I sat up and almost had a stroke when I found said roommate sitting on the edge of my bed staring at me.

"Jesus, Marcos. What the hell are you doing?"

He picked at his nails, calm as a cucumber. "You overslept."

"Shit, what time is it?" I asked as I jumped out of bed, tripping over my sneakers, and nearly falling on my ass.

"Ten."

"Fuck." I grabbed the shorts I'd worn yesterday and pulled them on. "I'm so late."

147

"I know," he said, and the slight touch of glee in his tone pissed me off. "Did you pass out in a post, self-induced orgasmic coma and forget to set your alarm?"

"Why you're so interested in my masturbation routines is beyond me. It's weird, bro..."

"I'm weird?"

"Yeah... this isn't news," I said, digging through my dresser drawer and pulling out a t-shirt.

It was wrinkled and on the smaller side, but I hadn't had time to do my wash all week. Maybe if I hadn't been thinking with my dick every night, I might've been able to get some laundry done. I was up late again last night, chatting with James, more like getting off with James, but I wasn't complaining. I'd have all the time in the world to get to know him after Friday.

"Why were you watching me sleep like a stalker?" I slipped my shirt over my head and grabbed a hat from the top of my desk.

"I wasn't watching you. I was waiting."

I looked over my shoulder and furrowed my brow. "Waiting for what? To scare me to death?"

"I figured you'd feel my presence and wake up... and you did."

I laughed and he shrugged as I picked up my keys and wallet from the nightstand. "Your presence, huh? You should have woken me up, you knew I was late."

"I'm not your babysitter, *mijo*. Or your momma."

He followed me into the hall and all the way to the bathroom. "I need to take a piss."

"So?"

"Get out," I said, but of course he stood in the doorway like an asshole.

"Not like I haven't seen your dick before."

"I thought we'd agreed to never talk about that night." I unzipped my shorts thinking he'd turn around or leave. He strummed his fingers on the doorjamb, instead.

"Believe me, that night has been violently scrubbed from my brain."

"It wasn't that bad."

"Walking in on you getting plowed is always a bad thing." The soft line between his eyes deepened, his face contorting like he'd swallowed spoiled milk. "I really need a new best friend. I think we've crossed one too many lines, Park."

I rolled my eyes and took a leak with my unwanted audience hovering in the doorway. "Why are you following me around like a lost kitten?" I asked as I finished up and washed my hands.

"Guess who I saw last night?"

I stared at his reflection in the mirror, twisting off the cap to the toothpaste. He was shirtless, wearing thin pajama shorts that did nothing to hide his junk. His hair was messy, sticking up on one side, and the mascara from the previous night had created heavy gray smudges under his eyes. He looked hungover as fuck.

"Based on your appearance, I'm afraid to ask." I smiled around my toothbrush when he flipped me off.

"My appearance?" He bumped me with his hip, making room for himself at the sink, and leaned against the counter to get a closer look at his face in the mirror.

He wiped a thumb under his eye and removed some of the dark make-up. "Honey, I can smell the spunk on you. You better do more than brush your teeth, or all the boys at Pride House will be scandalized."

My smile withered and I spit my mouthful of toothpaste into the sink. "I do not smell like spunk."

"Hmm... okay. You're delusional... but okay." He shrugged, and I snatched his cologne from the medicine cabinet.

"Don't you dare, that's expensive." He tried to grab it out of my hand, but I held it over his head like I was a twelve-year-old boy fighting with his brother for the "good" game controller.

"But I don't want to smell like jizz all day," I whined, an evil grin stretching across my face as I threatened to spray his precious perfume. However, unlike my roommate, I wasn't a dick. After a minute, I set the bottle on the countertop and picked up my deodorant, instead.

"You're disgusting. And quite frankly it's alarming..." he said, waving his hand in front of my face. "You sit in your room all night jacking off like some hard-up, pimply teenager. You need real dick, man."

"Friday."

"What?" he asked, caught off guard, and I pushed by him.

"I'm meeting James on Friday," I repeated. "The guy from Pegasus."

Back in my room, I pocketed my phone and slid my backpack over my shoulders.

"Some place public, I hope?"

"Yeah, a pub in Decatur," I assured him, and he crinkled his nose. "Hell... Marcos. Don't worry, I'll give you the address and let you know I'm alive periodically throughout the night. Unless I'm too busy, like you said... getting real dick."

Marcos's teasing smile sobered. "You act like I'm crazy for being worried."

"You act like I've... *you've* never hooked up with a guy from an app before."

"Point made, but I—"

"I haven't forgotten what happened..." We stared at each other for a few seconds, and he crossed his arms. "I know how to be careful."

"What's the name of the pub?"

"Brick Store."

"How will you know it's him?" he asked. "Will you bring a copy of your favorite book like that movie... shit, what's it called?"

"Fuck if I know."

"*You've Got Mail*," he said as he snapped his fingers.

"Never heard of it." I made a move to pass him, and he blocked me.

"What's the plan, then? Do you know what he looks like now?"

"No... We agreed to text each other when we got there and send a picture of what we're wearing."

"Why not send a picture of your face?" he asked.

"It kills the suspense." I smirked and he dropped his arms to his side.

"That's dumb."

I laughed and tried to step past him, but he wouldn't budge. "I've got to go, Marcos. I'm already forty-five minutes late."

His lips parted into a slow grin. "You never answered my question, though."

Exhaling an annoyed breath, my head tipped back, and I stared at the ceiling. "What question?"

"Guess who I saw last night?"

"Will you move so I can go to work if I let you tell me?"

"Yes." His crooked smile was anything but humble.

"Fine... I'll play. Who did you see last night?"

"Oh... I never thought you'd ask," he said with a shimmy of his hips. "None other than the hottie creative writing professor you think about when you're jacking off with your little friend from Pegasus."

If it wasn't for my curiosity about Mr. Brody, I wouldn't have continued the conversation. "Where?"

"Hemingway's."

"That hipster restaurant?"

"Yeah, he was there with your author crush." Marcos gazed at me, waiting for a reaction I refused to give him.

"Cool, can I go now?" I asked with as much nonchalance as I could muster.

Was I curious about Mr. Brody? Absolutely. Did I think he was one of the most attractive men I'd ever seen? Definitely. But it was of no consequence. He was a hot guy, who happened to teach something I loved and nothing more. I was invested in James. Our chemistry was undeniable, and I couldn't wait to find out if it would translate beyond the screen. I wanted to know him. Unravel him. Mr. Brody was fun to flirt with, but he was my professor, unattainable, and there were some boundaries that couldn't be crossed.

"You're jealous. I can tell."

"Yup. I'm dying inside," I deadpanned and he visibly deflated.

"Go to work, asshole."

"Bye, baby." I puckered my lips and blew him a kiss as I walked backward out of the room. "See you tonight."

"If you're lucky," he called out, and I laughed as I closed the front door.

By the time I got to work, I was well over an hour late. I set my bag at the desk I used in the main office and headed back to check in with my manager. Rachel was a chill chick, and I didn't think she'd be too pissed since I was always on time, but when I found her at her desk, with a glower on her face, I stopped short. Her usual friendly smile was nowhere to be found. Her russet eyes, tired, stared absently at the screen of her computer.

"I'm sorry... I know I'm—"

"I don't care," she said in an uncharacteristic snappy tone. "You missed the morning meeting. Everyone is flipping out."

"Because I was late?"

She shot me a glare that silently said, "No, dumbass."

"They're restructuring Pride House."

That didn't sound good. And by the sullen look on most of the staff when I'd walked in, it sounded downright devastating.

"Is that code for shutting down or something?"

She huffed out a humorless laugh. "Or something."

"Hey, Park." One of the residents gave me a sad smile as he walked toward the kitchen.

"Hey, Jake."

Rachel wiped her eyes with one hand, while handing me a slip of paper with the other. Her tears stained her dark cheeks, and it was surreal, watching her cry. She was always happy.

"What's this?" I asked, my chest suddenly tight.

"The director's new plan... he's retiring." She exhaled a wet breath and leaned back in her chair. "He sold Pride House to a non-profit out of Florida, and they want to make it a national company."

This was huge, but I didn't understand why she thought it was a bad thing. "Doesn't that mean we'll get more money to help the residents?"

"Sure, but at what cost? This is a home, not a business."

"But there could be more homes... across the country. Rach, this is great news."

She sniffed, pulling a few tissues from the box on her desk. "You weren't at the meeting. It feels like too much. I'm afraid the mission will get lost."

"I hear that. But think about how many more kids Pride House could help if it was nationwide." I sat down in the chair across from her. "Change is scary, but I think this could be great for these kids."

"You think so? What if the new director is a shithead? They didn't even ask me if I wanted the job."

I tilted my head and raised my brows. "Come on... like you'd want that job. You hate being the manager."

Rachel cared more about the kids and less about the administration side of things.

"Yeah... but this new company doesn't know that. They're bringing in one of their own, and he's bringing some staff as well. What if he comes in here and thinks he can just change everything?"

"Then, we'll show him how it is." I grinned, and she finally smiled. "He'll figure out his place."

"I hope so. Silver lining, with the expansion, each director will have an entire region they're responsible for. Maybe he won't be around much."

"Way to be positive." I chuckled. "Or... maybe he's awesome and we'll be lucky to have him."

She pulled on the end of her braid, a habit she had when she was stuck in her head.

"I don't know... he'll be here in a month. I guess we'll find out, then."

I read over the letter, impressed with the new guy's experience. "Shit. He's been all over the world."

"He sounds too good to be true, if you ask me. And he's only been with this non-profit for a few months." She leaned over the desk and pointed at his picture. "He looks arrogant, right?"

He was handsome as hell, but I kept that thought to myself. He seemed weathered, like his skin had seen too much sun. But it was his bright blue eyes that softened the rugged edges of his appearance.

"I mean... he's kind of hot."

She playfully ripped the paper from my hand, a laugh bubbling past her lips. "You're such a whore. If this Chance guy was a woman, would you be so relaxed? I swear, y'all men stick together."

"Is that his name? I didn't finish reading because some out-of-control *woman* stole the paper out of my hand."

"Yeah... Chance Davenport. Snooty name, arrogant face." Rachel closed her eyes and rubbed her forehead. "Why is he bringing staff? What if he goes on a firing spree? We're all fucked."

"Shit. I didn't think about that. You think he'll fire us?"

"I don't know."

"I'd like to see him try. This is our place, Rach. It'll be alright." It had to be. "I know what will make us feel better," I said, holding out my hand as I stood. She laced her fingers through mine, and I smiled when she gave in. "Coffee."

"Cup and Quill?" she asked.

"Sounds good to me. It's the closest place."

We walked into the hall, and one of the kids cooed when they saw we were holding hands.

"Simmer down, Makayla," I said in a teasing tone, and they giggled.

Makayla was one of the youngest residents. They moved in about two months ago after being removed from an abusive situation. They had come out as transgender to their mom, and she'd flipped out. When Makayla arrived at Pride House, they didn't speak for almost two weeks. Now they were one of the most vocal and fun residents we had in the home.

"I thought you liked boys?" Makayla asked.

"I only have eyes for Rachel," I said, and she dropped my hand.

"Good Lord, when the new director gets here, he'll end up firing your inappropriate behind." Rachel shooed Makayla out of the hall. "Shouldn't you be in the study room?"

"That's where I'm going," they said and stuck their tongue out as Rachel turned the corner.

"Hey... I saw that," I warned and laughed when Makayla stuck their tongue out at me as well.

Rachel was right. Pride House was a home. A home where family was found and made. A home where there was acceptance and love and safety. It was a privilege to work here, a privilege to be in these kids' lives, and as I watched Makayla walk down the hall, I understood why Rachel was afraid of this big change headed our way. This wasn't just a job for her. This was her home. Her family, and it was mine too. This new guy, he had big shoes to fill.

Chapter 13

DONOVAN

"*A*nne... Don't get too far ahead," I called out as she disappeared into a large crowd of people. Swearing under my breath, I took off at a jog after her. A glimpse of her dark head of hair had me sucking in a deep breath of relief, but it wasn't until I heard my brother's low chuckle that I realized how panicked I'd gotten.

"You're worse than Mom," he said, popping a piece of caramel corn into his mouth.

"You're not funny," I said as Anne came into full view.

I slowed my pace, relaxing and let her jump onto the bench by one of the river exhibits. Her fingers tapped fast and furious against the glass to get an otter's attention as it swam by.

"See... look, she's fine." Owen's blasé tone pissed me off. "She's right there. It's not like she's two anymore,

Vannie. Anne is capable of walking a few feet ahead of you without coming to any great peril."

"Don't call me Vannie." I ignored his smirk and walked ahead of him, making a beeline for my daughter. "Hey, little monster, what did I say to you about a hundred times already today?" A mom with her two kids smiled at me, a knowing glint in her eyes. I kneeled to Anne's level. "This place is big, you could get lost, or worse... Just stick close, okay?"

"Yeah, okay." Her gray eyes widened as my brother approached. "Can I have some popcorn, Uncle Owen?"

"Sure thing, kid." He grinned and handed her his half-eaten bag. "I'm stuffed."

"Thanks!"

She wasted no time shoveling her face with the sticky treat, and as much as I wanted to throttle my brother for being a condescending prick sometimes, his love for my daughter softened my anger.

"Are you going to pay for her cavities to get filled?" I asked, half joking, half serious.

"I can afford it." Owen's mop of brown hair fell over his forehead, and he swept it to the side with his fingers. "Why so prickly?"

"I'm not prickly, I'm a parent." I swatted his hand away as he tried to press his finger into my cheek. "Until you have kids of your own, don't give me shit."

"Ouch." His playful smile fell, and he turned away toward the glass. "Something's up, you being oversensitive proves my point."

"Because you know me so well."

"I do."

"Says the guy who's never around."

Owen's gaze swung back in my direction, assessing me with his shrewd, all-knowing goddamn eyes. I could say what I wanted about him not being around, and as much as I hated it, he did know me better than most people.

"You know how busy I am," he said. "I have a lot going on."

"You and me both," I muttered, and the weight of his stare became almost unbearable.

Anne jumped down from the bench and crouched lower to the ground. "I think that's a baby... aww, how cute."

She glanced over her shoulder, and I gave her a tight smile. "So cute, honey."

"What do you have going on? Is it Lanie?" he asked in a whisper.

I shook my head, wanting to tell him about my plans for tomorrow, and dreading his judgment at the same time. The group of people surrounding us dispersed, and I exhaled, bracing for the inevitable. I couldn't not tell him. He'd never let up if I didn't.

"I'm meeting someone I met on a dating app tomorrow night," I said and winced when he punched me in the shoulder.

"Yeah?" His smile was infectious. "Look at you, little brother... getting back on the horse. What's her name?"

"Michael," I said, keeping my eyes fixed on the glass in front of us.

Several seconds passed in silence, and the longer it dragged on, the harder it was for me to take a breath. Anne was completely enthralled, unaware of the drama unfolding behind her. After a full minute passed without a word from my big brother, I gave in and looked at him. Unable to read his impassive expression, I spoke first.

"Owen... I—"

"Does Olive know already?"

I scratched the nape of my neck. "She does."

He took a deep breath, the tension between us as thick as the mid-day humidity.

"Mom and Dad?"

"I haven't said anything to them yet."

His gray eyes found mine. "Good... I wouldn't. It would crush Mom."

"Jesus, Owen... I didn't think you'd care so much. Olive said Shane is gay. You're okay with a gay roommate, but not a gay brother?"

"So, you're gay, then?" he asked, and by the look on his face you'd think I'd told him I had three months to live.

"Would that be a problem for you?"

Owen ran a hand through his hair and shook his head. "No... I guess not."

"That doesn't sound very convincing."

"Van... I... I'm... Shane and—"

"I'm not gay," I interrupted him, worried he'd say something I couldn't forgive. Not wanting my private life on display, I kept my voice low as a family of five walked up to the exhibit. "I'm bi..."

He nodded and shoved his hand in the pocket of his shorts.

"You really think it would crush Mom?" I asked and the pain that flashed across my brother's eyes cut straight into my chest as he shrugged.

"I don't know," he said. "But would you want to risk it? Disappointing her and Dad... it would hurt, Van... if they didn't support you, it would hurt to know they weren't the parents you thought they were."

"Can we see the elephant?" Anne asked. "It's right over there."

She pointed toward the back of the zoo, and it pulled my attention away from my brother's despondent stare.

"Yeah, let's go," I said, desperate for a reprieve from the conversation, and took her hand in mine.

Owen followed us, keeping a few steps behind. His reaction surprised and rattled me. I'd hoped he'd accept it, hoped my mom and dad would too. The confidence Olive had given me paled with every sideways glance my brother gave me throughout the rest of the afternoon. Torn between anger and confusion, I didn't bring it up again until we were getting ready to leave. With Anne buckled into the back seat of my car, I shut her door.

"Thanks for today," I said, and Owen gave me a half-hearted smile.

"It was fun... I miss spending time with her."

He waved at Anne, and she pressed her lips against the window and puffed out her cheeks. Owen laughed, and the sound of it made a home in my chest.

"Are we okay? I can't change who I am." My voice broke and he hauled me into a hug.

"Fuck... I'm sorry..." He cleared his throat as he pulled away. "It took me by surprise. You and Lanie... I never thought—"

"It's new for me, too," I admitted. "Tomorrow night is a first for me."

"Michael..."

"That's his middle name." I laughed and rubbed my forehead. "Shit, Owen, I don't even know what the guy looks like. I met him on this app called Pegasus."

"I've heard of it," he said, his lips twitching up at the corners. "I don't need to tell you to be careful, right?"

"No, *Dad*... I think I can handle myself."

He punched me in the shoulder again, an incredulous smile spreading across his face. "This is... I mean... have you always known... I mean, before Lanie?"

"Yeah... but tomorrow will be the first time I've ever done anything about it," I said, and Anne knocked on the window. I held up my finger and she rolled her eyes. "I better get her some food before she turns into a Gremlin."

"Forget what I said earlier... about Mom and Dad."

"Too late."

"I'm serious," he said. "I think I was shocked... maybe projecting a little."

"Projecting?"

He waved me off. "Whatever, I was being a dick. Don't worry about it. Mom and Dad love us..."

"I mean... yeah. I hope so."

His Adam's apple bobbed as he swallowed. "They do. They have to, right?"

"We're good, then?"

"Solid." He pulled me in for another hug. Squeezing me tighter than before, he clapped me on the back. "Let me know how it goes."

"You really want to know?" I asked and he laughed.

"My brother is about to embark into the wild world of bachelorhood, of course I want to fucking know... it should be comical, if nothing else."

"Thanks," I said, and he chuckled as I climbed into the front seat of my car.

When I pulled away, he waved one last time, and any trepidation I'd had about his acceptance of my sexuality faded with his wide smile. Perhaps I should've been anxious about what my parents might think, but it wasn't enough for me to hide who I was or what I wanted. If I was a disappointment to them strictly based on who I happened to fall in love with or who I was attracted to, then maybe I didn't need their acceptance anyway.

After I dropped Anne at school the next morning, the rest of the day dragged. I'd spent the majority of my day zoning out at work, mindlessly rereading manuscripts as I thought about everything that might happen tonight. For the most part, I'd been able to harness my nerves, but as I pulled into a parking spot behind the brewery, every apprehensive thought I'd tried to keep at bay came rushing forward. I lowered the stereo as my car came to a stop. My head ached with anxiety and what ifs. I smoothed a hand down my chest as I looked into the rearview mirror. God, what was I doing? I'd tried to talk myself out of showing up tonight about a thousand times. Each excuse I'd come up with more creative than the last. What if I wasn't what he expected? What if my experience, or lack thereof, turned out to be too much of a burden for him? What if he was a serial killer who collected skin, and was obsessed with lotion and wells? I fell back in my seat and laughed at myself. Swiping my thumb across the screen of my phone, I opened the message he'd sent me earlier. It was a snapshot of him from the neck down. I'd sent him something similar before I left my house. We'd agreed to send the pictures as a way for us to recognize the other by what we'd chosen to wear. He had on a dark blue shirt that hugged his broad chest and biceps, and a pair of worn jeans. I stared down at the gray button down I'd chosen, hoping it wasn't too much. Part of me wondered if we should have sent pictures of our faces as a last-minute, get-out-of-jail-free card. The other, more insecure side knew, if we had, and he was as good looking as I'd imagined him to be, the likelihood of me chickening out at the last second would have been exponentially higher. I counted backward from fifty before I typed out a quick message.

@MeAndMyShadow33: Just got here.

I cut the engine and got out of the car after a few minutes with no reply. Assuming he was on his way, and not standing me up, I headed inside. The place bustled with laughter and energy as I walked in. I did a quick scan of the room, looking for a guy in a navy-blue t-shirt, and came up empty.

"How many?" the hostess asked as I stepped forward.

"Two, but my... friend isn't here yet."

"No problem. You can wait at the bar if you want..." I looked over her shoulder. There were only a few empty seats available, none of which were seated together. "Or I have a booth open."

"A booth would be great. Thanks."

She grabbed two menus, and I followed her through the busy restaurant. The atmosphere was warm with brick-covered walls. Light-colored wood trimmed a wide staircase that led to a second floor toward the back of the open room, and with a large, iron chandelier hanging from the high ceiling, the place had an old saloon vibe. We stopped at a booth next to the bar, and I took the seat facing the front door.

"Is this okay?" she asked, and I smiled.

"It's perfect."

As she walked back to the front, I looked over the menu she'd left behind. The words swam on the page as I stared at it, too nervous to remember how to read, apparently. I checked my messages again to no avail. He hadn't replied. After a few minutes, a waiter had stopped by the table, asking if I wanted a drink, and I'd ordered a beer. I figured if Michael never showed up, the alcohol would be a nice bandage for my ego. I picked at the damp, wrinkled label on the bottle, checking the door occasionally, and by occasionally, I meant every five goddamn seconds. My dry mouth found no relief from the cold beverage, and the more I checked the door, the more I started to second-guess everything. I ran my hand through my hair, the questions in my head firing in rapid succession. What if I'd pushed myself into this? What if we should have waited to meet? What if I was being catfished? What if he was scared too? What if he walked in and saw me and walked out before I had a chance to notice?

Fuck.

This was a mistake.

I shouldn't have come.

"Mr. Brody?"

My head snapped up at the familiar voice, and my heart plummeted into my stomach. Having a student here was the last thing I needed.

"P-Parker? Hi... H-hello."

"Hey." He ran a hand over his short hair, his cheeks turning a deep shade of pink as his lips parted with a crooked smile.

"Are you here with friends?" I asked, trying to be polite as I looked around him toward the front door.

"Nah..." Without asking, he slid into the seat across from me. "I'm meeting someone."

"Oh... That's—"

Right then, a few obvious things clicked into place, and I'd forgotten what I was about to say.

His shirt. His jeans. Those fucking arms.

Parker's smile widened as my eyes fell to his navy-blue shirt, the fabric stretching across the expansive muscles of his chest and shoulders. Images of his skin assaulted me, every dip and dent of his abs flickered like a perverted slide show. These things I shouldn't be privy to. Not him. Not Parker. Holy fucking God, I'd sent my student a picture of my dick. Heat crawled up my neck, burning my face as everything hit me at once. I thought about leaving. I should stand up. I should get the hell out of here right now. I thought about walking through the front door and never looking back, but my legs wouldn't move. All the things we'd shared...

"Breathe," he said and reached for my hand across the table.

I moved it quickly to my lap and shook my head. Swallowing down all my regret, I attempted to put on a professional front to save us both from this nightmare.

"I had no idea," I said, finding my voice. "You have to know that?"

He sat back, his crystal blue gaze penetrating right through me. "Neither did I."

I wanted to believe him. But in some desperate attempt to salvage my pride, I snapped back. "Are you sure about that?"

"How the fuck would I have known it was you?" he asked, his smile long gone.

I scrubbed a palm down my face. "I'm sorry. I didn't mean to—"

"Accuse me of catfishing a professor?" he asked, and I flinched at the word professor. "I'm just as shocked as you are... trust me." His smile resurfaced, and I hated myself for noticing the dimple in his left cheek, or how handsome he looked at that very moment. "This doesn't have to be a bad thing, Mr.—"

"God. Stop... don't call me that."

"What would you prefer I call you, then? James? Donovan..." He smirked and my stomach flipped. "Van?"

My name in his low, gruff whisper sent an electrical pulse down my spine. Every dirty word he'd sent sounded off in my head in that same deep timbre, and Jesus Christ, it turned me on. I gripped the edge of the table. This was wrong on so many levels.

"This can't happen."

"It already happened," he said matter of fact. "Might as well enjoy ourselves."

He reached for my beer from across the table, and I clenched my jaw, watching in a mix of shock and fascination as he lifted the bottle to his full lips. Lips I'd never get to taste.

"I need to go."

"No one's stopping you, Donovan." He took another long sip of my beer, his smile confident as he called my bluff.

"You don't get it..."

"Then, explain it to me," he said and set my empty bottle on the table. "Because I don't see a problem. We're attracted to each other. So what?"

"You're my student," I hissed as quietly as possible. "You're twenty-three years old, for Christ's sake."

"My age didn't bother you when you came all over your chest the other night. And I'm twenty-four, remember..."

"Parker," I warned, my face on fire. "I didn't know who you were."

"I'm glad it's you." He rolled his bottom lip through his teeth, and I had to forcefully lift my gaze to his eyes.

Which, if I were being honest with myself, wasn't any better. They were too genuine. Too vulnerable. "I think maybe... maybe... I hoped for you all along."

"Shit." I exhaled a shaky breath, my chest too tight for how wild my heart needed to beat. "We can't... I... I have to go." I slid out of the booth, and Parker didn't try to stop me, but something in his bottomless blue stare asked me, begged me to stay. I pulled my wallet from my back pocket and set a twenty on the table. "I'm sorry."

"I'm not."

We watched each other for a few agonizing seconds, everything that could've been rained down on me, pinning me to the wood floor. He was this beautiful thing, smart, and everything I'd imagined, everything I could ever want.

"Van, I—"

"Goodbye, Parker."

Those two words shouldn't have stung as much they did, but before I could fuck up any more than I already had, I turned and left him behind.

Chapter 14

PARKER

Goodbye, Parker.

Goodbye.

Good... bye...

Stunned, I gave myself one full minute to process the clusterfuck that was my life to make sure I wasn't in some weird-as-hell, blue balls, sex dream. The noise in the room seemed to swallow me whole as I turned to watch Donovan Brody walk through the restaurant toward the front door.

You're my student.

It was hard to concentrate, all the reasons I wanted to chase him were the same reasons he'd push me away. James and Van were one person. He was my professor. That alone should have been enough for me to want to heed his warning.

This can't happen.

If anything happened between us, and if somehow the college found out, I assumed he could lose his job. We'd have to hide, and that's not something I'd ever wanted to do again. At least that's the standard I'd set for myself the day I was discharged from the Air Force. I'd spent too much time living in some twisted, fake reality, too afraid to be myself, to live my life.

You're a writer, Parker.

You give me confidence I've never had before.

But this was different. I wasn't stepping back into the dark closet I'd left behind. Keeping a relationship on the downlow for a few months was a hell of a lot better than what I'd put myself through for those four years. Maybe if he was some random guy, it wouldn't be worth it. But something tugged inside my stomach as my pulse quickened, and I knew I couldn't let him walk away.

Donovan disappeared through the door like the sun dipping below the horizon, and I had no idea when I'd be awake again to see it rise, to see him like I had through the anonymous conversations. When he'd shown me his truth. When there had been no wall built out of words like *this can't happen.* And *you're my student.* There had been other words. Words that were ladders, words that jumbled up inside my chest and made me push out of the booth.

Your voice is genuine.

I want you. I want the real thing.

I didn't take time to assess the situation, or worry about the consequences, as I made my way to the front door. Brushing past a couple of waiters, I didn't even apologize. The evening air did little to cool my overheated skin once I was outside. At first, I didn't immediately see him and thought I'd missed my chance, but as I looked to the right, I caught a glimpse of his gray shirt as he turned down the alley toward the back parking lot.

"Shit."

I took off jogging after him. He'd opened his car door by the time I'd made it around the corner.

"Donovan," I called out and he froze. "Wait a second."

I slowed my pace, catching my breath as I approached him. Close enough, I could smell his cologne and something else, something earthy and sweet like lavender. The scent calmed me.

He closed the door but kept his eyes straight ahead.

"Hey... look at me."

He shook his head, his shoulders falling.

"Please, Van... I need you to."

"It's done, Parker." He slowly turned to face me with weary eyes.

His hair was messy, like he'd taken out his frustration on the dark strands. A few stray pieces had fallen over his forehead, and like it was a normal everyday thing to touch him, I lifted a hand and brushed them away.

His breath hitched and he took a step backward. "Park..."

His sleeves were rolled up to his elbows, his jeans hugging his thighs. Donovan was the picture of perfection. His sharp jawline pulsed under the short, dark stubble that dusted his flawless skin. The stormy gray color of his eyes darkened as he stared back at me. The desire was there, the need I'd tapped into over the past week when we'd interacted online. He wanted me.

"It doesn't have to be done," I said, keeping my tone as even as possible.

"You're my student."

"Yeah, I know... you keep saying that." I smiled, quiet and easy, but it hadn't changed the strict edge to his posture. "And I get it. It's against the rules, but Van—"

"This is my job... my life. I can't just do whatever the fuck I want because it feels good."

I risked taking a step closer and he swallowed as my eyes fell to his mouth. I should've listened to him, respected his concerns, but his tongue darted across his bottom lip, and I swear the phantom touch of it tingled across my lips.

"And what do we do on Monday?" I asked. "Look at each other from across the classroom and pretend we haven't said the things we have... pretend I'm not dying to know what you taste like?"

"That's exactly what we're going to do," he said, his face flushing a deep crimson. "There isn't any other alternative."

"I could drop the class."

"No... that's not an option." He shook his hands at his sides, and I wondered if he was fighting himself, wondered if he wanted to reach out and touch me as much as I wanted to touch him "This is why we can't do this. I can't expect you to upend your life because of me. It's an abuse of power, Parker. It's unethical. You can't do that... You're too good of a writer to quit."

I couldn't stop myself from smiling at his compliment, or how his voice had softened when he'd said it. "It's an introductory class... I could take it again next semester with a different—"

"No." He shook his head, his tone taking back it's hard line. "Absolutely not."

"I'm an adult the last time I checked. I can do what I want. And I want you."

I drew in a breath and moved in even closer, crowding him in, leaving only a few inches between us. Donovan's hands lifted, and for a moment I thought he would push me away, but his fingers curled into the fabric of my t-shirt instead.

"I can't do this."

"Then, don't." I held his stare for one... two... three seconds. "If you don't want this, then let go."

His grip tightened as his pupils dilated, his chest rising and falling, his hesitation and want warring inside the silver ring of his irises. Static buzzed along my limbs, waiting for him to make a move, aching for it.

"Parker," he whispered my name, but all I heard was his submission.

I leaned in, and the invisible barrier he'd tried to maintain snapped as his mouth plunged into mine with violent precision. My hand found the back of his neck, using the heat of his skin as an anchor. The burn of his stubble etched its way across my lips, my chin. He released his hold on my t-shirt, and the palm of his hand made its way up my chest to the side of my neck. His thumb rested on my pulse point, my frantic heartbeat giving away how gone I was for this, for his kiss. My tongue slid into his mouth, grazing his tongue, and when he moaned, I pushed in deeper, tasting him like I'd wanted to since that first day of class. He was sweet and pliable, with a hint of beer lingering on his lips. I should've slowed down, taken a breath, taken a second to savor this, but I was afraid, any minute, he'd remember all the reasons why we shouldn't do this, and reality would come crashing down on both of us.

His thumb grazed the length of my jaw as he tilted his head, taking more as I pushed him against the car. Panting, he gasped as I pressed my hips into his. My fingers twisted in his hair as the evidence of his arousal pressed along the length of my hard dick. There was no question of whether he wanted this, no more hesitation as his hands fell to my ass, grabbing and grinding his body against me.

"Fuck," he whispered against my ear as I bit his jaw and sucked on his neck.

His skin was salty, the thin mist of sweat heavy on my tongue as I licked the hollow below his Adam's apple. I wanted more. I wanted to bury my nose in his groin, inhale his musky scent, taste the first drops of pre-come as they leaked from his slit. Intoxicated by the thought, I forgot myself, and lowered my hand to the bulge in his jeans. I forgot we were standing in the middle of a parking lot, forgot that he could come to his senses, and I'd never get a chance to be with him like this ever again. But his forehead fell to my shoulder, his hands grasping at the sides of my shirt as he moaned and pushed his erection into the palm of my hand. The evening sun had set, casting us both in the muted light of the streetlamps like we were the only two people left in the city, even if that was far from the truth, this was private. It was for us. For him.

Donovan shuddered against me as I worked my hand up and down, taking his mouth with mine, his teeth sinking into my bottom lip as he hissed out a low groan.

"Come home with me," I whispered, and immediately wished I hadn't said a fucking word.

He pulled away, leaving a cold space between us.

"Home with you?" he asked and laughed without humor. His chin was red from my five-o'clock shadow, his lips swollen. A faint purple bruise had started to form low on his neck, and I would have reached out, dusted my thumb across the mark, but the shame in his eyes stopped me. "Where you live with another one of my students..."

"Marcos wouldn't—"

"It doesn't matter. Jesus Christ... what did I do?"

Risking ruining everything, I grasped his chin, gently urging him to look at me. It took him a second to yield, but his conflicted gaze eventually found mine.

"You did what you wanted. You didn't do anything wrong."

"It's wrong... if you were anyone else, it wouldn't be an issue. But we shouldn't have, *I* shouldn't have—"

"Stop, alright... Fuck, forget about all that shit for two seconds. Tell me how you *feel*, how it felt..." I smiled when he bit his lip. His hot breath fanned over the tip of my thumb as I brushed it along the curve of his mouth. "Kissing a man... Kissing me."

He raised a hand and trailed it across the arch of my cheek, the small touch writing a blazing line of heat down my spine.

"It was..." he took a breath, his eyes closing as his hand settled on my neck. "Nothing has ever felt this right." His dark lashes slowly parted again, and he watched me for what seemed like an infinite number of minutes, hours, hell if I knew, all I wanted was to kiss him again. "I don't know what to do."

Never taking my eyes off his, I brought our lips together. Cautious and slightly timid, he kissed me back. This kiss wasn't like the last, desperate, and clinging like the storm of indecision might rip us apart. This kiss was a hint of maybe, an exploration of what could be. It wasn't frantic and hopeless. It was *trust me*, as my tongue dove into his mouth, it was *let it happen*, as his finger curled through the belt loop in my jeans, it was *I want to show you everything*, as I sucked on his bottom lip.

Donovan kissed the corner of my mouth, my cheek, before resting his forehead against my brow. "I need to think."

"Thinking sounds pretty awful."

His chuckle resonated inside my chest.

"I can't believe it was you," he whispered, cupping my face in his hands. A pink shadow made its way up his neck to his cheeks. "But as much as I want to say I wish it wasn't, I can't. I fucking can't, and it's killing me."

"After December, it will be a moot point."

"We don't know that. I never planned on dating a student, so I'm not one-hundred percent sure of the policy."

"You want to date me?" I teased, my smirk growing the deeper he blushed.

"I didn't say that, Mr. Mills."

"Fuck, that turns me on." I pressed our hips together and his hands fell to my waist. His body responded and I grinned, loving the effect I had on him.

"Yeah?" he asked, his smile vulnerable as he leaned in and brushed his lips over mine.

Caught in the moment, it took longer than it should have for us to realize we had an audience.

Someone cleared their throat, and Donovan's body went rigid.

"I... uh... just need to get by."

"Oh God... Sorry." Instead of pushing me away, he pulled me close, hiding my profile against his neck.

"Don't be..." The woman's voice held a hint of humor. "I'm sorry to interrupt."

As she walked past us, he released his death grip on my waist. She got into the car behind Van's, and I could've sworn he'd held his breath until she'd pulled out of the parking lot.

"Not everyone knows you're my teacher," I said, and he exhaled a sigh.

"This is why we shouldn't do this."

Shouldn't. Not can't.

I grabbed onto the word like a lifeline.

"We can figure it out." Not giving him any room to argue, I said, "Not everything has to be decided this very second. Enjoy the kiss, Van. Enjoy this."

I ghosted a finger under the waistline of his jeans, teasing his hot skin, and he grabbed my wrist.

"Not here."

"Where, then?"

"Not yet," he breathed into the crook of my neck. The soft pressure of his lips tickled my skin. "If we're going to do this... I want to do it right." I laughed and he pulled back, his brows furrowed. "What?"

"You do want to date me."

"Yeah." His laugh was quiet and soft like his smile. "I guess I do."

Chapter 15

DONOVAN

*P*arker pulled into my driveway, and I turned to look at him through my driver-side window. Every ethical bone in my body told me this was reckless, told me I shouldn't risk it, shouldn't risk losing my job at Winchester, possibly even at Lowe. What would Anders think? It was a stretch, and my brain tended to jump from zero to sixty, but what if we got caught, and there was some kind of scandal, would he fire me for bringing a bad reputation to the agency? Jesus, I'd jumped right into a worst-case scenario. WSC was a mediocre school, and Parker was an adult. Maybe in hindsight the word scandal was a bit overdramatic. Either way, it was definitely a good thing we'd agreed that it was best to have dinner at my place and not in public. At least not until we figured out boundaries, and how this thing between us would work.

On the way to my house, my ten-minute drive had been plagued with conflicting thoughts. I hadn't given myself a chance to properly think about everything. His kiss, his touch had made me want to be impulsive, and the whole way home I'd hoped Parker hadn't thought I expected anything from him. We needed to talk. Just talk, I told myself as thoughts of his hands in my hair, his hard body pressed against me, his confident lips claiming my mouth, invaded my brain. I'd never kissed like that before. Kissed like a fire consumed oxygen and it burned through me, scorching any misgivings I might've had about him, about us. He was twenty-four, and it wasn't like I'd lured him unsuspectingly to my house with promises of good grades for sexual favors. This thing between us, this unlikely coincidence, it snuck up on us, or maybe it had been there all along, but it happened. Parker walked around the hood of his car, his shoulders loose, his confident blue eyes meeting mine as one of the most handsome smiles I'd ever seen broke across his face, and I shelved any remaining trepidation I had for the moment.

"Were you thinking again?" he asked as I stepped out of the car.

"It's not a bad thing." I shut the door and approached him. His grin even wider than before. "One of us has to have a clear head."

"And I don't?" he asked, reaching for my hand. He threaded his fingers through mine, and I nervously glanced around the cul-de-sac. It wasn't like I spoke to my neighbors very often, or that they would even know who he was, but the fear was there. The guilt. "Hey, it's okay. We don't have to do this... I can go. No questions asked."

"No," I said, refusing to succumb to my doubts. This wasn't some forbidden thing. This wasn't wrong. We were adults, the rest of it was semantics, shit I would have to figure out later. Not now. Not with the heat of his skin against mine. Not when my pulse shouted stay, stay, stay. "I want you here."

He raised my hand to his lips and brushed a kiss across my knuckles, sending a shivery heat over my skin. "Good because I'm hungry... and you did promise me food."

"I did."

Laughing, I invited him inside, and he released my hand as we walked up the small path to the front door. I'd be lying if I said I didn't miss the touch. His rough skin was different from Lanie's. The callouses on his palm were satisfying in a way soft skin could never be. It scratched at something inside me, made me want to keep touching, keep feeling everything he had to offer.

Once we were inside, I dropped my keys on the sideboard table and flipped on the living room lights. "This is nice," he said, running a hand over the back of the couch. "Remind me never to invite you to my shitty apartment again."

"It can't be any worse than the place I had in college."

My comment was another reminder of our age difference. Nine years in the grand scheme of things wasn't a big deal. Parker was obviously mature and had a plan for his life. But he was at the beginning of everything. The starting line. I was a divorced thirty-three-year-old with a kid he didn't even know about yet. Not a very tempting prospect for a guy with his entire adult life ahead of him.

"Van," he said, pulling me from my thoughts. "You're doing the thinking thing again."

"It was nothing, just..." I huffed out a laugh. "Overthinking."

"About?"

I walked past him and into the kitchen. Switching on the light, I avoided his eyes.

"We don't know each other very well."

"Isn't that why you date someone, to get to know them. See if they're worth pursuing?"

"Exactly," I said, finally raising my gaze. His brows were pulled into a tight line. "What if they're not worth it? Or there's dealbreakers?"

"Like?"

"Answer the question."

"Then, you move on." He shrugged. "Not every date will end with a picket fence and a dog named Chuck."

Smiling, I leaned against the kitchen counter. "A dog named Chuck. That's very specific."

"Maybe I've thought about it... what settling down would look like." He moved toward me, or more like prowled, and my pulse took notice, sprinting as he placed his hands against the counter on either side of me. "My only dealbreaker... must love dogs."

My eyes dipped to his mouth as my fingers found his waist. He was solid, and I craved the heaviness of his weight. "What kind of dog?"

"An Irish setter." He leaned in and kissed the corner of my mouth. "But that's not the point, is it? You're worth pursuing, Van. Even if you don't think so."

My lips parted on an exhale, and he took advantage of the moment, sliding his mouth over mine. He tasted like mint, and I wondered if maybe he'd chewed a piece of gum on his way here. It was sweet and tentative the way his tongue fell into a rhythm with mine. Too soon he pulled away, his gaze serious as he dragged his thumb across my bottom lip.

"This doesn't have to be complicated. I want to know you, see where this goes." His smile was quiet. "I'm not ready for Chuck yet."

"I have a daughter. Is that a dealbreaker?"

"You have a daughter?" he asked, and I nodded once, waiting for him to put some distance between us. He didn't move. "How old?"

"Ten."

He rubbed a hand over his hair. "Ten... you were only—"

"Twenty-three when she was born... it feels like a lifetime ago," I said. "My life is complicated, Parker. A kid. An ex-wife. I'm your teacher, for hell's sake. It's a lot."

"Like Pan and Silas from *The Lost Boys*," he said, his thoughtful expression melting into a small smile. "We have a lot stacked against us."

"This isn't a queer fairytale."

"No, it's not, but I happen to know this really awesome professor who once said, *'some of the best stories are the ones we can relate to.'*"

"I never said that."

"I know." He grinned, his eyes gleaming with humor. "It was Mr. Douglas. I had him for English 101 last semester. But he isn't as sexy as you are, terrible teeth."

My shoulders shook as I laughed. "I don't think I've met him yet."

"You're not missing anything." Parker pressed his chest against me. "One step at a time, okay? We should at least have dinner before we plan our nuptials."

"Ha-ha."

"I'm pretty funny when I want to be."

I grazed the back of my hand along the coarse, stubbled line of his jaw. "And you're okay with me having a kid?"

"Like I said... one step at a time."

"Yeah." I swallowed and nodded again. "I can handle that."

"What's your daughter's name?"

"Anne."

"Too bad Chuck isn't more gender neutral..."

I kissed him with a smile on my lips, and my empty stomach filled with butterflies. His taste of mint enveloped me, muting any memories I'd had of cherry Popsicles, summer sun, and riverbanks. It became a part of me, the two pieces of myself finally merging into one.

Parker sat next to me on the couch, coughing as he set his beer on the coffee table next to the empty box of pizza. "Wait," he managed to say, tucking his leg underneath his thigh. "Your ex cheated on you with one of her yoga students?"

"They were together until about a month ago... evidently it wasn't as random as I'd thought."

"She was fucking around for a while, then?" he asked, and I wanted to smile at his irritation. It was almost protective.

"No, but when she saw me with my client, she assumed I was cheating. I guess it was enough for her to finally act on her feelings for him."

"Shit."

"Yeah... shit." I finished my beer and set it on the side table. "It seemed impulsive to me at the time. How could she throw away everything for some random guy? Turns out he wasn't that random."

"You guys are still close?" he asked, picking up my hand. He turned it over in his lap, tracing the lines of my palm with his finger. "For Anne?"

"We want to do what's best for her, but Lanie was... is a huge part of my life. It's different now, but it's better this way. We weren't invested anymore. Our relationship had run its course way before she cheated."

"Does she know you're bisexual?"

"No, but I told my sister and my brother."

"Were they okay with it?"

"They were. My brother thinks my parents won't be as accepting, but I don't know. They've always been supportive, it's hard to say how they will react." I squeezed his hand. "What about you? Are you out to your parents?"

Parker's gaze was distant, his posture smaller than it had been two seconds ago.

"My mom was good about it, my sister too." He swallowed; his voice hoarse as he spoke. "I never got to tell my dad. He passed away when I was ten from a heart attack."

"I'm sorry. I can't imagine what it would have been like, losing a parent that young."

"I would think losing a parent at any age would suck," he said. "It was hard, but we got through it. We moved a lot because he was in the Air Force. He was stationed here in Georgia when he died, and the hardest part was how final it all felt. When he died, our lives kind of stopped and became static." He exhaled and let go of my hand. "I joined for him, you know. The Air Force. I wanted him to be proud of me."

"I'm sure wherever he is, he's more than proud."

"I'd like to think so," he said with a hesitant smile.

"You should write about him."

"I have." He bit the inside of his cheek, like he had something to say, but wasn't sure if he should or wanted to. "I mean... I can show you what I have sometime... if you want."

"I'd love to read it."

The television was on in the background, playing some old comedy from the nineties. The volume, a low hum, did nothing to break the charged silence between us. I wanted to kiss him, to bring back the mischievous spark in his eyes, but I wasn't sure if he'd want me to, or if he was stuck in his head, remembering things much bigger than anything I'd lived through. He wet his lips, and his bright blue eyes darkened like they had back at the restaurant. Clumsy and unsure, I leaned in quicker than I'd anticipated, and he chuckled as our mouths collided.

"Easy... like this..."

He pressed a slow, soft kiss to my upper lip, to the corner of my mouth, making a lazy circuit from my chin, along my jaw, and back again. My hands framed his face as he sucked on my bottom lip, his fingers in my hair held me steady. I inhaled his spicy, soapy scent, pulling it into my lungs, my heart thumping loudly in my chest as he moved with easy grace and straddled my legs. My hands shook as I snuck them under the hem of his t-shirt, remembering the images he'd sent me on the app. I traced the lines of his muscles, his skin prickling under my fingertips. The heat of his flesh soaked into my right palm as I flattened it against the ridges of his abs. He lifted up onto his knees and reached behind his neck, pulling his shirt off in one swift movement. I gripped his hips, my gaze roaming over every inch of exposed, golden skin. Quiet, he watched me explore the dips and valleys of muscle, each breath shorter than the last as I skimmed my lips over the carved curve of his hip, to his belly button, to the dark blond hair that disappeared below his jeans. My curiosity and fear were both fighting for the number one spot in my head as I stared at the bulge in his jeans.

Firm fingers ran through my hair, tipping my head back, a crooked smile appeared on his full lips. "You can touch me if you want to... or not." He lowered his big body, pinning me to the couch, and rolled his hips. "Or this is fine too." He kissed me, his tongue diving into my mouth until I moaned. "This is enough. We don't have to do anything else."

I didn't know what to say. I wanted to do everything and nothing at all. I wanted to stare at him all night, kiss him until my lips were properly chafed from the stubble on his sharp jaw. I wanted to feel his calloused hands on my dick. I wanted to taste him. Need scrambled and jumbled all my rational thoughts, but the burning blush on my cheeks spoke of my inexperience, and I had to count to ten before I could find my voice.

"I'm nervous," I admitted. He started to climb off my lap, but I grabbed his hips and pulled him closer. "Stay... this is... this is good. Just..." I sucked in a breath as he moved against me, grinding his hips, stoking the fire, the ache that threatened to consume me. "Fuck... just... Just kiss me."

Parker didn't think twice, his hand wrapping around the back of my neck as his lips caught mine with a bruising kiss. I couldn't touch him enough. My hands skated over his broad shoulders, my fingers clinging to his back, the muscles like granite as I lifted my hips to meet his, over and over again.

Panting, my head fell back into the couch. "Park... I..." I was about thirty seconds away from coming in my pants, my balls tight, all the friction too much to take. "Shit... wait."

He lowered his nose into the crook of my neck, his breath harsh and out of control. Smiling against my skin, he said, "Why did you stop?"

"You know why."

He leaned back and grinned at me. "I don't think I've come in my pants since I was like sixteen."

"I didn't come in my pants." I pinched his ass and he jumped.

Laughing, he started to unbutton my shirt. "You could always come in my mouth."

"Wasn't frotting supposed to be my first lesson?" My bold question wasn't enough to hide the slight tremor in my voice as he unfastened the last button.

He pushed open my shirt, running a hand down the center of my chest. Parker had seen my chest in photos, but having him here, staring down at me like a sculpted statue of a god come alive, my inadequacies threatened to drown me.

"Christ... you're even better in person." He flicked his thumb over my nipple, smiling when I hissed. "I didn't think it was possible to say the word frotting and sound cute at the same time. You proved me wrong."

"Cute?"

"Fucking adorable."

He kissed me again until I begged him for more, until I whispered his name, overwhelmed as his fingers worked open the fly of my jeans. I lifted my hips and shoved my jeans and briefs down as much as I could,

Parker's lips never leaving mine. His hot, rough hand gripped the base of my dick, and I bit his lip. He grunted, his hold only getting tighter as his tongue plunged into my mouth. I fumbled with the button and zipper on his jeans, taking longer than I would have liked. But it was worth the effort. I'd never looked at another man's dick like this, and definitely not this close. Thick and not too long, the pink head touched his stomach. My mouth watered, and if I was brave enough, I might've leaned down and tasted him. But all I had the courage to do was touch him. I ran my thumb through the moisture leaking from his slit and down his crown to his shaft. He was foreign and decadent.

"Fuck, do that again," he said, raising his hand to his mouth, he spit into his palm.

I did as he asked, watching as he lowered his hand and wrapped it around me. Slick with saliva, he pumped his fist up and down my length. My fingers curled around his cock, working him in fast, needy strokes, his deep moan resonating inside my chest. He grabbed my wrist, and at first, I thought he was about to put on the brakes.

"Why did you—"

But he took us both in one of his large hands, silencing me with his mouth. Skin on skin, our cocks aligned, smooth and hard, sliding and rubbing together inside his vise-like grip. The friction was beyond anything I'd ever felt before, and there was no way I would last more than a few minutes. Our tongues, urgent and insistent, tangled together, our teeth crashing and biting as we both climbed higher and higher, desperate to reach the peak.

"Ah... God... oh fuck—"

Gritting my teeth, my hands held the back of his neck, my forehead pressed against his as my orgasm ripped through me, spilling over his fingers. Parker wasn't far behind, the sound he made, this low, rumbled growl, branded itself in my brain as his release coated his stomach and my chest. We didn't speak, our heads still together, both of us breathing, chests heaving with our eyes closed. I didn't think I'd feel emotional about it, about getting off with a guy, but for some damn reason my throat felt thick, and I had to pull away.

"Everything alright?" he asked.

"Yeah... you?"

He chuckled and rubbed his sticky hand through the mess on my chest. "I think I'm doing okay."

It was hard not to smile, the intimacy of the moment passed, taking the heavy feeling inside my chest with it.

"Should we clean up?"

"Might be a good plan..." he said, a smirk lighting his eyes. "But I've got to say, I kind of like the idea of you being covered in my spunk."

"Like a dog pissing on a hydrant?"

"When you say it like that, it sounds gross."

I laughed, and he was all smiles as he placed a chaste kiss to my lips. I stood and tucked myself into my briefs and zipped up my jeans, the evidence of what had happened already drying on my skin. Parker used the guest bathroom to clean up while I used mine. By the time I finished, I found Parker standing, fully dressed, washing our dinner dishes.

"You don't have to do that," I said.

He set a plate into the drying rack. "I don't mind."

Parker dried his hands with a towel and hung it on my stove. It all felt too familiar again, and the awkward feeling I'd had earlier resurfaced.

"You're freaking out. I can tell," he said, slowly approaching me.

"No... I'm good. I promise."

He draped his arms around my waist. "You're not a very good liar, Mr. Brody."

"Honestly, tonight was... emotional for me," I said, and he pulled me closer. "That sounds ridiculous, but it's the truth."

"It's not ridiculous. Tonight was a first. Firsts are always emotional."

I kissed him in the middle of my kitchen, the frenetic energy from before had become more sedate. I wanted to ask him to stay, to sleep in my bed, to give me another first. But I wanted him to leave, too, wanted to have the rest of the night to remember, to process, to fight through the inevitable self-doubt in private. It turned out I didn't have a choice.

"Shit... I don't want to leave, but I have to go," he said, brushing my hair off my brow. "I've got to work in the morning. The kids hate it when I'm late."

He'd told me earlier he worked as a tutor at Pride House. Just another thing that made it impossible for me to tell myself I shouldn't be with him.

"I understand."

"I shouldn't have started something, knowing I had to—"

"Parker... It's okay. Maybe next time you can stay later... if that's something you'd want."

"It's something I want."

His lips were soft against mine as he kissed me, and as much as I wished he could stay longer, the prospect of *next time* made it easier for me to watch him leave.

I walked him to the front door, and after we exchanged our cell phone numbers, he kissed me on the forehead with a promise to text me once he was off work tomorrow. I shut the door behind him and leaned against it, staring at the couch. The night filtered through my brain, and I saw us there, lips and skin and heat. Everything too fast. I thought about the things we still had to say, the ground rules we never set, but before my panic could set in, my phone vibrated on the coffee table. I walked over and picked it up, smiling when I saw the Pegasus notification.

> **@TheLOstBOy:** I kissed you, knowing the flavor of your ruin.

> **@MeAndMyShadow33:** Did you write that?

> **@TheLOstBOy:** I did, just now, sitting at the stop sign.

> **@MeAndMyShadow33:** Knowing the flavor of your ruin.

> **@MeAndMyShadow33:** That's dark.

@TheLOstBOy: That's one way to look at it.

@MeAndMyShadow33: And the other?

@TheLOstBOy: Ruin can mean change. For the better or for the worse.

@MeAndMyShadow33: Am I your ruin?

@TheLOstBOy: I don't know yet, but after tonight, I sure as fuck hope so.

Chapter 16

PARKER

A bright crack of lightning lit up the sky as I ran toward the front door of my apartment. By the time I made it inside, I was drenched from head to toe, even my socks squished inside my shoes.

"Goddammit. It's a fucking disaster out there," I said, and set my backpack down onto the floor.

"Shh, I'm watching a movie."

Marcos was spread out on the couch, rolled up in a big fuzzy blanket with wadded-up tissues strewn all around him. Several empty mugs and a couple of bowls littered the surface of the coffee table.

"Aren't you supposed to be at work?" I asked.

"I'm sick, asshole." He was congested enough that his speech sounded almost slurred, making it hard to take his attitude seriously. "I have a fever and I hate the world, and men, and possibly you too... depending on a few things."

"Oh yeah? What's that?"

"Will you make me a cup of tea and a bowl of that Lipton noodle stuff I like?" He stuck out his bottom lip, pouting like a five-year-old. "I think I'm dying."

"You're not dying." I rolled my eyes as I kicked off my soggy shoes.

"Gross, go put those in your room. I can smell your feet from here."

"I doubt you could smell your own shit right now. You sound awful, by the way." I removed my socks and walked over to the laundry closet between the living room and the kitchen.

"I feel like death."

I pulled off my shirt and threw it into the washer with my socks. "I'm about to start a load, got anything you need me to throw in?"

He raised his arm and weakly pointed toward his bedroom door. "My basket is in there."

Marcos's room was surprisingly spotless for once, except for the old vintage vanity table he had in the corner. It was covered with make-up, jewelry, and some sort of lacy shit I'd never seen him wear. He had pictures and postcards pinned on the wall with silver star-shaped tacks, framed by a white string of Christmas lights. I loved the lived-in quality of his room, it was such a contrast to mine. All I needed were the basic necessities, nothing special. I had a couple of framed pictures on my desk of my mom and my sister's family, but the rest of it was cast in a monochromatic shade of gray—a blank slate. My most prized possession was my large bookshelf, and the books it held the only real bit of personality I'd added to my room. I liked my space to feel quiet, but I had to admit, even after two years, it didn't feel like a home.

"What the hell? When was the last time you did laundry?" I asked as I hauled his clothes basket from his room. The thing weighed a ton.

"Two weeks ago."

"I don't even have two weeks' worth of clothes," I said, shoving everything into the washer and pressing the start button.

"Yes, you do... but you choose to look like a homeless gym rat half the time. You're hopeless. If it wasn't for your abs, you'd always be single, hiding in the corner, reading a book with a finger up your ass, trying to remember what real sex used to feel like."

"Wow..."

"I only speak the truth."

"You're speaking man-flu." I plopped down into the recliner and kicked a few of his snotty tissues toward the coffee table. "This is next-level disgusting, but I'll give you a pass since you're being so nice to me today.

"My bones hurt," he whined. "What about my tea and soup?"

"I don't know," I said, fighting my smile. "I have a busy day planned, reading... and pegging my prostate."

Marcos's laugh turned into a coughing fit, and for the first time since I'd gotten home, I started to worry.

"Shit, you need to see a doctor, man. What if you have pneumonia or something?" I leaned over and touched his forehead with the back of my hand. "Marcos, you're burning up."

"I know... I need tea and soup."

"No, dumbass, you need meds and a medical professional. Come on."

I stood but he waved me off. "It's raining."

"I'm sure the doctor's office is open even when it rains."

"And I'm in the middle of this movie."

"*Hocus Pocus?* You've seen this a billion times. Up... let's go. I'll carry you if I have to."

He stared at the television and fucking ignored me.

"Marcos, stop being a toddler. What if it's serious?"

He groaned and burrowed deeper into his blanket. "Go away."

"Not happening," I said, and blocked the view of the television. "I'm not messing around. I will put you over my shoulder."

"Move your wide ass, this is the best part."

He glared at me, calling my bluff. My best friend and I didn't have much in common, beside our ability to be stubborn to a fault. I stepped toward him, and he held up his hands.

"Don't you dare, Par—"

I reached down and tried to scoop my arms underneath him. He wasn't a big guy by any means, but he sure as shit wasn't as light as a feather. It wasn't easy with him fighting against me, and it didn't help that I couldn't stop laughing, but eventually I was able to lift him.

"Are you fucking crazy? Put me down." His laugh sounded more like wheezing as I tried to get a better hold on him. "If you drop me, Parker... So help me God..."

"Stop squirming, then."

"I'm not playing. Put me down."

"Go to the doctor."

"Jesus, fine..." He stopped fighting, going completely limp in my arms. "Now put me down, before I pop a boner. All this aggression. I can't be held responsible for what my body likes."

I dropped him onto the couch like his body had burst into flames. "I can't believe you just said that to me."

A shit-eating grin spread across his lips as he readjusted his blanket cocoon. "I like to be manhandled. Don't kink shame me."

"Are you going to let me take you to the doctor's or not?"

"Ugh... I hate you," he said as he kicked off his blanket. Clad in only a pair of pale blue boy-short underwear, he brushed past me, clipping me in the shoulder. "When we get back, you're making me that fucking tea."

There was nothing worse than being stuck in a waiting room at an urgent care. A bicyclist who'd probably seen better days sat across from me in her rust-stained shirt, dried blood on her chin and neck. Little kids with runny noses ran up and down the hall, screeching, while their parents fucked around on their phones. But the biggest drama queen happened to be sitting next to me, moaning like a sick cat.

"Marcos," I said under my breath. "People are staring at you."

"They're probably staring at the bite mark on your neck." He spoke loud enough the receptionist could probably hear him. The bicyclist lowered her eyes when I caught her staring at me. "Did you think I wouldn't notice?"

"Could you not—"

"You dragged me here, I might as well have fun with it." He waved, wiggling his fingers at the guy sitting across from him. "He's cute."

"And married to the chick sitting next to him." I shifted in my seat with a tight smile on my face as the guy scowled at us. "Please stop being you for like five seconds."

"Tell me about your date with the app guy, and I promise I won't make a scene."

He drew an invisible halo around his head with a finger.

"There's nothing angelic about you, my friend."

He reached up and touched the mark Van had left behind. "Hooking up on a first date... didn't your momma teach you to be a lady?"

We had the entire attention of the doctor's office by this point, and I actually contemplated waiting in the car. I hadn't had a chance to text Van yet, and after everything that had happened last night, I didn't want him thinking I'd blown him off. But the rain hadn't let up, and if I left, Marcos would follow. Pain in the ass or not, he needed to be here.

"You got home late... I'm assuming it went well?"

"It did."

"What did he look like?" Marcos asked, lowering his voice this time. "I'm guessing by the bite mark he wasn't a total troll?"

I'd never kept anything from my best friend. He was more like a brother to me. If I lied to him, he'd see right through me. Van hadn't seemed too thrilled about Marcos knowing about us, and even though Marcos would take this secret to his grave for me, I needed more clarification from Van before I said anything.

"Definitely not a troll."

"Details, please, I could be dead by tomorrow."

I decided I'd skate as close to the truth as possible. Lies by omission were the easiest to forgive, right?

"Dark hair, light eyes..." Those light eyes were my favorite thing about him. The color of rain and storm clouds, and as deep as an ocean when he came. "He has a nice smile."

"A nice smile?" He hummed and turned to face me. "You're being vague."

"I'm not," I said, trying to think of a detail I could give him that wouldn't give anything away. Van hadn't ever mentioned his daughter in class. "He has a kid."

"Umm... what?" He rubbed his temples with his fingers. "I'm sorry, I think I just had one of those fever-induced hallucinations, because it sounded like you said he has a kid."

I exhaled a long sigh, and flipped my hat backward, settling in for the lecture.

"He has a ten-year-old daughter."

"Nope... veto, veto, veto."

"Veto? Since when do you get to veto who I date?"

"We're best friends, it's implied."

"I like kids."

"Sure, you do," he said, his tone laced thick with sarcasm. "And tomorrow, I'll magically wake up and start wearing basketball shorts every day."

"I like kids, Marcos. I work with kids. I might even want to have my own kids one day."

"*One day* being the key words in this little horror show." He stared at me, waiting for an explanation I didn't have.

It scared me that Van had a kid. I'd never been in a serious relationship. Never dated a guy for more than a few months. I was only twenty-four, kids weren't on my radar yet. But I liked him. I couldn't explain it, and it sounded far-fetched in my head even thinking about it, but there was something pulling at me from the inside. And I had no words for it, but it was the same feeling I'd had when he'd walked away from me last night at the brewery. Like a tether ready to snap, I had to hold on to it. I had to let it take me where it wanted me to go.

"I like him, Marcos."

"You sure that's not your dick talking?"

I didn't dare glance around the room. My cheeks on fire, I shook my head. "No... this is different." Shrugging, I pulled at the frayed piece of fabric on the chair. "The kid thing, yeah, I get it. It's big. But we've only hung out once. I want a chance to see where it goes before jumping ship. Who knows, she could be sweet as hell."

"Or the spawn of Satan, but no big deal." He exhaled and dropped the attitude. "You like him?"

"I do."

"Just promise me you won't do that people-pleaser bullshit you pull." His brown eyes lost their edge as he spoke. "If it's too much... walk away, alright?"

"Yeah... okay."

He turned in his chair, seemingly satisfied for the moment, but I should have known better.

"Did you guys fuck?"

The cyclist dropped her phone.

"Jesus," I said in a gruff whisper and sank even lower in my chair, like somehow, I could find a hole in the floor to fall into. "Can we not talk about that here?"

"What? You don't want to tell me how big—"

"Marcos Basulto?" A lady in scrubs called out, holding open the office door with her foot, and if I could, I would have hugged her. Employee of the fucking month right there.

"This conversation isn't over," he said as he stood, and even with a fever he walked away like he was on a runway in heels.

Once he was behind the office door, I pulled out my phone and found a missed message from my mom about mowing her lawn tomorrow. I sent off a quick reply before scrolling through my contacts for Van's number.

Me: I'm thinking of sending you a present.

I opened my email and attached the two documents I'd saved to the cloud today while I was at work. I'd never shown anyone what I'd written about my dad. When Van had said he wanted to read it, I didn't know in what capacity. Was it as a teacher or... Shit, I didn't know what to call him. Boyfriend seemed too official. Either way, I hesitated to press send. This wasn't an assignment, and yet I feared his critical review. These were profound pieces of my life, my father—my memories. Writing them had been hard enough, sharing them terrified me. I deleted the email and then opened a new one. I did this a few times, my anxiety preventing me from pressing send. I was about to delete it all over again when a text notification came through.

Van: Is it NSFW?

Me: Are you working?

Van: I'm grading papers in my home office. Does that count?

Me: It doesn't. But unfortunately, it's not a dick pic.

The three dots popped up at the bottom of my screen, and the smile on my face would have made Marcos nauseous.

Van: The real thing is better anyway.

Me: I think this is where I'm supposed to say something humble, but my dick is pretty awesome.

Me: Are you blushing?

Van: See for yourself.

He sent a selfie and I laughed. His cheeks were, in fact, pink, and I wanted to kiss the shy smile on his lips.

Me: If I wasn't stuck at the Urgent Care with Marcos, I'd invite myself over.

Van: Is everything okay?

Me: He has the man flu, or pneumonia. I'm not sure yet.

Van: That sucks, I'm sorry.

Me: He's a miserable prick when he's sick. Would I be a terrible friend if I left him to fend for himself?

Van: I wouldn't say terrible, but...

Me: You're supposed to convince me to come over, not be my moral compass.

Van: I'm not sure how accurate my moral compass is these days.

Me: Are you having regrets?

Van: No and yes. But that's my own battle. It has nothing to do with you. I don't regret you, Parker. Just the circumstances.

I lost nothing if we got caught, but Van, he had everything to lose.

> **Me: I feel selfish for wanting you. For asking you to risk your job for me.**

Expecting a text and not a call, it startled me when my phone rang in my hand. Van's name, in bright blue, lit my screen.

"Hi."

"You're not selfish," he said, and fuck, I loved the quiet, low rasp of his voice. "I want this as much as you do."

"It's three months until the semester is over," I reminded him. "I can handle three months of take-out if every date ends like last night."

His chuckle was soft and warm, and I wanted to wrap myself in it. In him.

"We can go out on dates, but probably not near campus. Atlanta is a pretty big city."

"When do I get to see you again?" I asked, not giving a shit if I sounded needy.

"Is tomorrow too soon? "

"Hell no. If my stupid ass roommate wasn't dying of the flu, I'd be there right now."

"You think he'll feel better tomorrow?"

"Probably not. But I can only handle so much."

His laugh scratched through the speaker. "When are you going to tell me about this present you have for me?"

"Oh... that." I stood and headed to a quiet corner of the waiting room, hiding by a giant fish tank. "Were you serious about reading the stuff about my dad?"

"I'm serious about anything you write."

"I don't think I want a critique on this. It's too personal."

"That's understandable, and you don't have to send it if—"

"I'll send it." I leaned my back against the wall, wishing it was Sunday already. "What time tomorrow?"

"Does six work for you?" he asked.

"I'll see you at six."

"Park?"

"Yeah?"

"Don't send it if it's too hard."

"I want to."

"Then, I'm looking forward to reading it."

We said goodbye, and as I opened my email again, I thought about all the risks Van had to take for us to be together. If I wanted more than what I'd had in the past, if I wanted a chance at a real relationship, I could risk this. I could let someone in. He understood what it meant to give yourself to the page, and these memories, these words, were part of me. If I couldn't trust him with that, then I shouldn't trust him at all.

Chapter 17

DONOVAN

The pat of butter sizzled in the hot pan, my damp hair falling into my eyes as I bent down to grab a pot for the pasta. I filled it with water and set it on the stove to boil while I finished chopping the mushrooms. I didn't even know if Parker liked mushrooms. For all I knew, he could be allergic to them. I exhaled, edgy and anxious, my hands shaking as I picked up the knife. I thought I wouldn't be this wound up after the other night. Mutual orgasms should have been enough of an ice breaker, but evidently, the more I liked a person, the more my mind found ways to make me nervous. I'd spent most of my day trying to catch up on work. I had two manuscripts I needed to finish, and a few more papers to grade, but my eyes kept drifting to my damn couch. From my office, I had a straight view through the living room. My mind kept recalling every sound he'd made, every touch, every kiss, and I'd end up reading the same page over and over again. I wondered if it had been enough for him. Or if he'd want more tonight. I was ready for more. All these thoughts had inevitably ruined my ability to focus. Instead of doing what I was supposed to, I'd opened the files he'd sent me last night and reread the stories he'd written about his father for a third time.

Parker had a brilliant mind. His writing voice mature beyond his years. I'd considered sending his stories to Anders, but I needed his permission first. His prose was vivid and alive, every sentence a reel of film rolling across the page. His life, in his words, played out like one of those old family home movies, steeped in sepia-colored tones, where everything seemed slightly out of focus and sped up, and as I'd read, my eyes and chest burned with a sentiment that only the past could create. By giving me those stories, he'd opened a window, lifted the shade, and let me in. I might not know what food Parker preferred, but I'd felt his pain, his loss, the pieces of his past. It wasn't all of him, but it was enough to know I'd made the right choice by taking a chance on this. On us.

Distracted by my thoughts again, the butter started to smoke.

"Shit."

I removed the pan from the heat, setting it in the sink. The stench of burnt butter filled the room and I cracked open the window, hopefully saving my ears from the smoke detector in the living room. After a few minutes, the room cleared out, but as I turned on the water to wash the pan, it splashed back, splattering brown grease onto my shirt. I tried to clean it off with a dish rag, but it only made it worse. Pissed at myself, I turned off both burners, and left the mess in the kitchen. I walked back to my bedroom to change, and with the way my night had been going, I thought it might be better if we went out for dinner, instead. And because I couldn't catch a break, the doorbell rang after I'd barely taken off my shirt. I checked the clock on my nightstand realizing how far behind I'd gotten. It was almost six o'clock and I was half-dressed, and nowhere near ready for Parker to be here. I hadn't even finished cutting all the vegetables for the sauce I'd planned on making. The bell rang again as I opened my closet door and grabbed the first shirt I could find. Pulling it over my head, I made my way to the front of the house. I ran my hands through my hair, hoping it wasn't a mess, and took a deep breath before I unlocked and opened the door.

"Thank God, I didn't think you were home," Lanie said, sounding as frazzled as she looked. She released Anne's hand, and my daughter took off toward the kitchen without saying hello. "I tried calling you a thousand times."

"You did?" I asked, looking over Lanie's shoulder, my anxiety and confusion tangled in my stomach.

Parker would be here any second.

"My mom was supposed to watch Anne for me tonight." She walked past me without invitation, and I shut the door. "But she and my dad got food poisoning and I have to work."

"What's that smell?" Anne asked, holding her nose. "It smells like burnt popcorn."

"Close... I burned butter."

"You're making dinner?" Lanie reached across the counter and picked up a mushroom, popping it into her mouth. "Is Olive coming over?"

"What?"

"It's Sunday, doesn't she try to con you into making her dinner on Sunday nights?" She smiled and ate another one of my fucking mushrooms.

"Lanie, why are you here?"

Her brows knitted together, my tone sharper than she was used to hearing. But she couldn't just barge into my house whenever she pleased, with this air of familiarity like she still had some right to my life and my damn food.

"I told you I have to work. I have two classes tonight. One at seven and another at nine."

"Since when?" The palms of my hands were sweaty, and I wiped them off on my jeans as I checked the time again.

"I picked it up, the money is too good not to."

"Can we have waffles for dinner?" Anne climbed onto a barstool, sending a dubious stare at the cutting board filled with various types of vegetables.

Waffles...

Holy shit.

"Lanie, I..." This wasn't happening. Anne couldn't be here. "I can't..."

What the hell was I supposed to tell her? My head ached as I stared at my daughter, her dark pigtails swaying as she hummed to herself, lining up the mushrooms in neat, orderly rows.

"I tried to call, Van. What's the big deal? I can pick her up in the morning for school if it's such a hassle."

"My daughter is not a hassle," I snapped.

"Our daughter." Lanie scowled at me. "Why are you being difficult?"

"I'm not."

"You are... I'm sorry if I'm disrupting whatever plans you had for tonight, but I had no other choice." Lanie walked over to Anne and kissed her on the cheek. "I have to go, baby. I'll see you tomorrow."

She pulled her keys out of her shorts, and I pinched the bridge of my nose, the trapped feeling in my chest smothering me.

"Do you need me to get her in the morning or not?"

Maybe I had time to call him. Even if he was on his way, he'd understand.

"I can take her."

Lanie narrowed her green eyes. "Thanks for the help."

I followed her to the door feeling like an asshole. I would spend every damn second with my daughter if I could. And Lanie knew that.

"Hey," I said, and she turned to face me. "Don't act like I don't want her around. I'm always here for her. You caught me by surprise."

"What do you want me to say? I tried to call."

I reached around her to open the door. "I'm sorry I snapped at you."

"I'm sorry, too," she said, and it sounded sincere. "I was stressed. I didn't think you would mind."

"I don't mind. But—"

The doorbell rang and my stomach dropped.

Lanie cocked her head when I didn't move. I was frozen in place, wishing I could throw up, or better yet, disappear.

"Are you going to answer that?"

I nodded, my tongue like sandpaper in my mouth as I opened the door. Parker smiled at me, and for a second, I forgot I was in the middle of a panic attack. God, he looked good. He had on a tight white t-shirt that stretched over his wide chest, and dark-fitted jeans. His cheeks were sun-kissed like he'd been outside all day, and he'd gotten his hair cut since the other night. The sides had been cleaned up, but he'd left what little length he had on the top. If I could have, I would have kissed him right there on my front porch, rubbed my fingers over the shaved sides of his head. But his eyes widened, his smile faltering as Lanie came up beside me.

"Hey," I said and let out a shaky breath. "I, uh—"

"Hi there." Lanie waved at him, totally oblivious. For someone who practiced energy work, she sure couldn't read a room. "I was on my way out." She glanced at me and back at Parker, when neither of us said anything, she laughed. "Well, aren't you going to introduce me to your friend?"

Parker's Adam's apple bobbed in his throat as I tried to speak past my fat tongue. "Sorry... um... this—"

"Parker." He fixed his smile. "It's nice to meet you..."

"Lanie... the ex-wife." She fucking giggled. I guess I wasn't the only one here who found Parker attractive. "Do you work with Van?"

He said yes at the same time I said no. Lanie's flirty smile faltered.

"I should say I'm hoping to work with him." Parker chuckled and rubbed the back of his neck. "I'm a writer."

It wasn't a complete fabrication.

"One of the best writers I've ever read," I said, finally finding the courage to speak as I held his stare. "I think he could have an amazing career ahead of him."

"I didn't mean to ruin your dinner plans... I'm sorry," she said. "It was nice to meet you, Parker. But I have to run. Thanks again, Van. You're a lifesaver."

Parker stepped to the side as she moved past him, and instead of inviting him in, I looked over my shoulder. Anne hadn't moved an inch.

"Shit, I'm so sorry," I said and shut the door behind me. I watched as Lanie backed out of my driveway and pulled away. "She literally just showed up."

Parker ran his thumb over my lips, moving closer he spoke in a low voice I felt down to my toes. "It's okay... she's gone now."

With Anne only a few feet away inside, I should have stopped him. But my heart was all over the place, the adrenaline in my system overriding my common sense. He cupped the back of my neck, his firm fingers releasing all my anxiety as his lips tasted mine. I fisted my hand in his t-shirt, closing the space between us, and he backed me into the door, smiling against my mouth when I groaned.

"Hi," he whispered before pulling my bottom lip through his teeth. "As much as I love a good public display of affection, are you going to invite me in sometime tonight?"

I rested my forehead against his. "My daughter is here."

"No shit?" He dropped his hands from my waist and nearly fell off the porch as he tried to put as much space between us as possible.

"Lanie tried to call me, but I was in the shower, and I didn't check my phone." I raked a hand through my hair. "She has to work, and her parents are sick. I didn't know what to do, and I wanted to call you, but—"

"Breathe," he said, his lips lifting into a lopsided smile. "It's not the end of the world."

"You're right... We can have dinner another time."

But now that he was here, I didn't want him to leave. Why did my life have to be this goddamn complicated?

"Oh... sure, yeah... another time," he said, shoving his hands into his back pockets.

"Wait... do you want to stay?"

"Why would I want to leave?" he asked, his smile playful. "I'm capable of keeping my hands to myself long enough to have dinner with you and your daughter. I'm not a total heathen."

"I thought..." I stuttered. "Isn't it too soon?"

"To meet Anne? That's up to you." He exhaled, his hands falling to his sides. "I can't make that decision."

When Lanie and I had separated, I worried Anne would get attached to her mother's boyfriends. Not in a jealous way either. I didn't want a revolving door of people coming in and out of her life while Lanie and I tried to live our own lives. But Anne didn't have to know the specifics of my relationship with Parker. She was ten. And as long as Parker and I were appropriate, she'd think he was one of my friends.

"I'm not ready to come out to Anne," I said. "But, if you're okay with being in the friend zone while she's here, I'd love for you to meet her."

"I can handle that." Parker took the bottom hem of my shirt between his thumb and forefinger, his candid blue eyes searched mine. "Can I be honest?"

"Please."

"I love kids, don't get me wrong. But I'm nervous. What if I do something I shouldn't, like swear or—"

"I swear all the time. Lanie and I have never been PG-parents."

He laughed and leaned close enough I could feel his breath on my lips. "It's going to be hard not touching you tonight."

"It'll be good practice for tomorrow when we're in class."

"Can I kiss you again before we go inside?"

Pulling me into his strong arms, he pressed his chest against me as I nodded. My heart thundered, a shiver spreading over my skin as his mouth melded to mine. The kiss was messy and fast, and when he pulled away, I licked my lips, savoring the sweet taste he'd left behind.

"Do you like mushrooms?" I asked and he laughed, the deep rumble of it vibrated against me.

"Not particularly."

"What about waffles?"

"Who doesn't like waffles?"

I smiled, his answer lifting the weight off my shoulders.

"I think you and Anne will get along just fine."

Chapter 18

PARKER

little girl with dark hair and gray eyes, like her father's, blinked up at me as I walked into the kitchen. When I'd met Lanie at the door, I had to admit I'd been intimidated. I didn't have to be straight to acknowledge that she was fucking gorgeous. I had a moment where I doubted myself. She had all this history she shared with Van, this woman who'd stood next to him in the doorway looking like she fit into his life way more than I might ever be able. I was a confident guy. But right now, with this small, delicate version of Van sitting before me, I'd never been this damn nervous in my entire life. The kind of nervous that made my palms sweaty. Shoving my hands into my back pockets, I gave her a smile.

"Hi..." she said, wrinkling her nose at the mushroom she had in her hand. "Who are you?"

"Anne." Van gave her a look that reminded me of my

mom, and I had to hold back a laugh. "Where are your manners, little monster?"

"What did I say?" she asked, and a chuckle escaped past my lips.

Little monster.

Van smiled at me, and a heavy warmth filled my stomach. Apparently, I had a thing for dads.

"It's okay," I said, fighting a sudden urge to tug on one of her pigtails. "My name's Parker, I'm a... friend of your dad's."

"I'm Anne." She dropped the mushroom onto the cutting board with a bored expression. "Do we have to eat these?"

"No... I can save them for another day." Van's eyes slid in my direction as he walked around the counter. "Parker doesn't like mushrooms either."

Anne hopped down from her stool, and I thought she was tall for a ten-year-old. It was another trait she'd gotten from her father. But she stood in front of me with her hands on her hips, all balls and confidence, sizing me up in a way Van's shyness would have never allowed.

"What about waffles?" she asked.

"The best breakfast dish, in my opinion. Van says you're an expert waffle maker."

"Toppings expert," she said, grinning, and scooted past me toward the fridge.

Van watched us as he scooped the veggies he'd cut up earlier into a plastic container. His gray gaze smiling, and hell if I didn't feel some type of pride taking root in my chest. Like maybe I wouldn't fuck this up tonight and ruin whatever progress we'd made over the last couple of days.

"That sounds official," I said, holding Van's stare, and leaned my elbows on the counter. "How did you become a toppings expert?"

"Practice," she said, but it sounded more like, "duh."

Van let out a soft laugh as she set a carton of blueberries and strawberries onto the counter. Fuck, he was attractive, more casual than I'd ever seen him in loose-fitting jeans and a light gray t-shirt that stretched across his broad shoulders. His hair was messy from my fingers, his lips full from our kiss, and when I smiled at him, he blushed.

It was going to be a long night.

"Strawberries or blueberries?" Anne asked, her voice as serious as if she'd asked me about the purpose of life.

"Both."

She nodded satisfied. "Syrup or whipped cream?"

"Um..." I hesitated and any confidence she had in me evaporated as she narrowed her eyes. *Well, goddamn.* "Both?"

"I agree."

"This is a test, if you haven't noticed," Van warned, snapping the lid shut on the veggies.

"I'm sensing that." I smirked, and he grinned as he cleaned up what I assumed he'd originally planned on making us for dinner, leaving me to his daughter's inquisition.

"Nutella?" she asked with an anxious furrow of her brows.

Unfortunately, I had no idea what the hell Nutella was, and I cringed when I said as much. "I've never had it."

Her mouth popped open as she shared a look with her dad.

"Uh-oh..." He gently squeezed his daughter's shoulder as he placed a waffle iron on the counter. "Go easy on him... I'd kind of like it if he stuck around for a while."

Hiding my amusement, I rounded the counter and inched in beside him. Lowering my voice, I asked, "You want me around for a while, huh?"

Lightly touching my finger to his thumb, he turned to face me, both of us staring at each other, his slow smile so damn tempting. Maybe an adult would've keyed in on how close together we were, but his daughter didn't seem to notice.

"He has to try it, Dad." She placed a jar on the counter. "Like, he *has* to."

Van was the first to look away, shaking his head, he said, "Parker doesn't *have* to do anything. Be polite."

"But he has—"

"Hazelnut?" I asked and winked at her as I picked up the jar for a better look. "Is it like peanut butter?"

"No." She laughed. "Here..." She reached into a drawer and pulled out a spoon. "Just taste it. It's way better than peanut butter. Do you like chocolate?"

"Is that even a question?"

Van laughed and leaned his hip against the edge of the granite counter. "I'm not a fan."

"What?" I asked, adding as much mock horror to my voice as possible, and his daughter giggled. "That's... I don't even know what to say, Van. I'm not sure we're friends anymore, if I'm being honest."

"My mom isn't a big fan either. They're both weirdos." Anne handed me the spoon, the expectation in her eyes overwhelmed me, like this one thing could make or break my chance at becoming her waffle-loving soulmate. "I hope you like it."

"Wow," I said with a mouth full of epic. "This is fu—freaking amazing."

"Yes! It's the best." She pumped her fist and wiggled her hips. Probably the cutest thing I'd ever seen.

"Nice save." Van laughed, forgetting himself as he brushed his thumb over the bottom corner of my mouth. When my lips parted with a quiet exhale, his eyes widened and darted to his daughter. "Sorry, you had some chocolate—"

"Thanks," I interrupted him and tried to divert her attention since she'd started to stare at us like we had four heads. Or maybe I was paranoid. Either way, I needed to give myself some distance from Van before I mauled him in front of his daughter. "I think I want to try Nutella and strawberries on my waffle."

"That's my favorite, but you need whipped cream... oh, and cookie butter too," she said, turning toward the pantry. "I'll grab the waffle mix."

Moving to the other side of the counter, I grabbed a stool and sat down. Van mouthed the words "I'm sorry," and I whispered, "I'm not."

My smile grew as he exhaled and shook his head, a playful smirk spreading into a soft dimple on his left cheek that I'd never seen before. A wolfish gleam lightened his eyes, his easy confidence beaming back at me, and I wished he could see himself the way I did.

"Can I have two this time?" Anne asked.

"You have a hard time finishing one, sweetheart."

She scowled and crossed her arms. Van expertly ignored her, but I didn't miss the small smile on his lips as he started cutting the strawberries.

"Anything I can do to help?" I asked and he shook his head.

"I've got it," he said. "But thanks."

"I can eat two," Anne grumbled and slid onto the barstool next to me.

Coughing to hide my laugh, I admired her full-blown sulk-fest.

"You can watch *Twister* while I get everything ready." Van peered across the counter. "Maybe Parker would watch it with you."

"You like disaster movies?" I asked, surprised. "That's cool."

She rolled her eyes, lugging me by the hand as she jumped down from her stool. "It's a movie about tornadoes."

"I know."

"*Not* disasters."

I looked over my shoulder and caught Van staring at Anne's hand in mine. I almost let it go, thinking I'd overstepped, but when I met his gaze, I heard the silent thank you in his smile.

"Aren't tornadoes disasters, though?" I asked, foolishly continuing the argument, and took a seat on the couch.

She curled up on the opposite side, television remote in hand. "Tornadoes are a weather phenomenon. Scientists are still trying to figure out how they work."

"But they cause damage..."

She dropped her shoulders and tilted her head, glaring at me like I was the dumbest asshole on the planet. The girl was damn cute.

"I'm only saying... a movie about tornadoes is basically a disaster movie like... *Into the Storm*, or that one with the volcanoes."

"Those movies are so fake." She settled into the cushion of the couch and pressed play on the remote. "Just watch."

I chuckled but did as she asked, wanting to make a good impression. About thirty minutes later, Van called out that dinner was ready. Anne reluctantly switched off the television and I followed her over to the kitchen table. It had four chairs and sat in front of a large bay window. The sun hadn't set yet, the sky bruised with purple and a deep pink spanned across the horizon and over the large back yard.

Van said, "It's a great view, you should see it at night."

"I'd like to."

"That can be arranged."

I took the seat across from him, my pulse jumping at the subtle innuendo in his tone as he handed me a plate.

Reaching for the strawberries, Anne took the bowl from my hands. She didn't give me a chance to experiment on my own, directing me in the ways of proper waffle consumption, and by the time we'd finished with dinner, I'd eaten my weight in sugar. Luckily, Van let me help clean up, and I was able to burn off some of the excess Nutella and syrup energy. With the three of us, we'd been able to get the dirty work done quickly and ended up with enough time to finish *Twister* before Anne had to go to bed.

"I should probably get going," I said as I stood from the couch and stretched my arms behind my back.

Van's eyes snagged on the exposed skin above my waistband as my shirt lifted. "Give me a second and I'll walk you out. I just have to make sure she brushes her teeth."

"Sure," I said, and without thinking, pulled the end of one of Anne's braids. "It was nice to meet you."

"Maybe next time you can try the cookie butter," she said, and I nodded.

"Sounds like a good plan to me."

"It's time for bed, kiddo." Van started down the hall, turning he said, "I shouldn't be long."

I waited for him by the sliding glass doors that led to his backyard, stealing a peek of the sky. The stars disappeared behind thick clouds, the oak tree branches that lined the right side of his fence yawned and swayed in the breeze. I stepped outside to get a better look, walking out onto the porch. I leaned over the railing and the clouds parted, revealing thousands of tiny pinpoints of light as they broke through the cobalt blue veil.

Warm arms wrapped around my waist, and I hummed as Van pulled my back to his chest. "You don't have to leave yet."

I leaned my head to the side, shivering as his teeth nipped at my skin.

"What about Anne?"

"She's already asleep."

"That was fast," I said and turned to face him. "I'm guessing the massive amount of carbs she had for dinner helped?"

He rested his hands on my hips as he laughed. "I think that might've been a factor, plus the story I read to her, she's heard it a few times."

"I think it's cute you read her stories."

A light breeze rustled through his hair, and he looked up at the sky. "I think it might rain." Van stepped back and took my hand in his. "Come on, I want to show you something before it storms."

A twinge of excitement pinched inside my stomach as he led me to the center of his yard. Smiling, he kicked off his socks and shoes and I did the same, the cool blades of grass soft against my bare feet.

"What are we doing?" I asked, confused as he let go of my hand and sat down on the ground.

He patted the space next to him and I sat down too. "I bought this house for the backyard."

"It's huge."

"I thought about putting in a pool, but I didn't want to ruin this."

"Ruin what?"

He leaned back onto his elbows and looked up at the sky. "This."

I followed his line of sight and sucked in a breath as the panoramic view unfolded all around me. Those tiny points of light had expanded once we'd left the confines of the porch, surrounding us. The sky seemed almost close enough to touch, and all I could think about was a scene from *The Lost Boys*.

"This makes me think of Pan and Silas," I said and leaned back next to Van.

Our elbows touched, the heat of his skin drawing me closer until my thigh pressed against his too.

He looked at me, his lips curling up at the corners. "How so?"

"Remember, Pan rescued Silas from King Juno's dungeon, and—"

"That's right, and they barely escaped and hid from Wendy in that field."

"It was the first time they kissed." I pressed my lips together as his eyes fell to my mouth.

"*How easy it would be... to get lost inside the stars with you,*" he quoted one of the lines from the book, and a goofy-ass smile broke across my face.

"Damn. Pan was a smooth motherfucker."

Van's head tipped back as he laughed openly, and hell if I didn't want to bury my face in the hollow below his Adam's apple, feel the sting of his stubble on my lips. Like the weight of my stare had touched his cheek, his laughter subsided, and he turned his head. With only the dim light from the porch behind us, his gray eyes seemed silver. We both leaned in, slow and gradual, every inch closer, the pull between us beat like a drum. He rested his back in the grass, my body covering his. Van's hands fell to the curve of my ass, and I pressed our hips together as I tasted the maple syrup on his tongue. Holding myself up with my palms, I kissed him as he held onto me, his hard dick rutting against mine. He swore, shuddering below me, his fingers gripping the back pockets of my jeans, pleading for me to move faster. A cold drop of rain splashed against the heated skin of my neck, and then another, trickling down the side of my cheek.

Breathless, I rested my forehead to his shoulder. "Shit."

Van pushed his hands into my back pockets and lifted his hips, his voice rough and desperate as he spoke. "Don't stop."

I raised my head as the rain started to fall in earnest, his hair already damp, his eyes wild. My shirt stuck to my skin, the humid scent of dirt pulled into my lungs with every ragged breath. "What about—"

"Park..." His face flushed as small drops of rain beaded along the line of his upper lip. "Please."

Thunder rolled somewhere in the distance as I gave him my mouth. Licking the condensation from his lips, he opened for me, moaning as our cocks aligned, grinding together, trapped behind wet denim, the friction, the rhythmic pulse of our hips, the rain, the dirt, the smell of earth and lavender on his skin, and his hands, his strong hands grasping, holding me against him, it didn't take long for both of us to lose control. I dropped my head into the crook of his neck, my fingers twisting in the grass as I came too quickly. Van swore through his release, his hand on the back of my head, his chest rising and falling beneath me.

I rolled to my side and onto my back. Closing my eyes, the sky opened up with another clap of thunder. "Yeah... I might need to borrow a pair of shorts or something for my drive home."

Van's deep laugh made me turn my head and open my eyes. He stared back at me. A blade of grass stuck to his cheek, and as he smiled, I wiped it away.

"Or something..." He ran a thumb along my jaw, the storm soaking us through. "This is... you... you make me want to be impulsive."

"I'm sorry I—"

"No, Parker. It's a good thing."

"It is?"

"Yeah..." The rain slowed as his thumb traced another line along my jaw to my mouth and back again. "It is." He lifted onto his elbow and placed a soft kiss to the corner of my mouth.

"We should probably go inside before we end up like Marcos and get pneumonia."

Van pulled back, concern written in the stitch of his brow. "He has pneumonia?"

"Nah... just a virus, but the fucker acts like he's dying."

I captured his laugh with my lips, and at some point, it started to rain again.

Chapter 19

PARKER

Chilled to the bone, I stood next to Van in his giant bathroom staring at our mottled skin in the mirror. My teeth chattered, regardless of the effort I'd put forth to clench my jaw, and he laughed, his smile reflecting back at me through the glass. Rainwater dripped from my soggy shirt as I peeled it from my skin and pulled it over my head. Van's gaze traveled down my body and lingered on my abs a beat longer than I think he'd meant to. The pale color of his cheeks colored in my favorite way when he realized I'd caught him checking me out.

"You can use my dryer," he offered, swallowing thickly. "If you want."

"Thanks."

I wrung the fabric out over the sink, watching him as he pulled his shirt over his head. The lean muscles in his chest and stomach moved under the skin, guiding my stare to the dark trail of hair that disappeared below his waistline. The weight of the wet denim caused his jeans to fall low on his hips, and he was all torso and long, etched lines I wanted to trace with my fingers.

"I'll throw these in the dryer together," he said as I handed him my shirt. "And see if I can find you something to borrow in the meantime." He rubbed his palm over his wet hair, looking over at the shower. "I'll set whatever I find on my bed, feel free to use what you need."

"Van," I said, a flicker of uncertainty pulsed through me as he turned to leave. I didn't want to push him. This was only our second so-called date, and I was about to get in the man's shower. Alone. Which seemed entirely inappropriate seeing as how his daughter was down the hall. But he was right here, and I needed more. I hid my insecurity and gave him a crooked smile. "You could join me... I'm pretty sure you have grass in your hair."

His laugh was soft as he hesitated in the doorway. "God, I shouldn't be nervous, considering—"

"We came in our pants less than fifteen minutes ago?"

He nodded, his smile awkward.

"I want to be honest with you," he said, lowering his eyes and staring at our balled-up shirts in his hands. "I don't think... I'm not ready for—"

"Hey." I walked toward him, and he looked at me. "We don't have to do anything but shower. And if you'd rather not do that either... that's fine too. I can rinse off really quick, put on a pair of your sweats and kiss you goodnight. I don't expect anything from you... ever. Alright?"

"Okay." He dropped our shirts onto the floor, the loud slap echoing through the room, and unbuttoned his jeans.

"I thought—"

Van walked past me and opened the glass door to the shower, reaching in, he turned on the faucet.

Resigned, he scrubbed a palm down his face. "Being naked with you intimidates me. It makes me want things I know I'm not ready for. I've only ever had sex with Lanie."

"Sex?"

He met my gaze with a half cringe, half smile on his face. "Yeah."

"Sex and fucking are two different things." Christ, I didn't think his face could get any redder. "In my opinion, we've already had sex."

"Oh..."

I stepped toward him, bringing us chest to chest, and lightly grasped the back of his neck. "I've made you come, Van. More than once. The definition of sex doesn't have to fit neatly inside a box." Steam spilled through the open shower door as he breathed against my lips. "Sex can be whatever you want it to be."

"I want it to be everything just... not yet."

Everything.

His skin brushed against me with every deep breath he took, his lips grazing mine once before he reached between us and unclasped the button on my jeans. Our skin, no longer chilled, was damp from steam and sweat as we undressed each other. Hot water poured over us as we stepped into the shower, and Van tipped his head back under the spray. I took a second to admire him in this unguarded moment, admire his dick, heavy and hard between his legs.

"Still nervous?" I asked, resting my hands on his waist, he blinked at me through wet lashes.

"No." Van pressed a palm flat against my sternum and dragged it down my stomach. "Maybe."

"All we have to do is shower. I'll even wash your hair."

I grinned as an easy laugh relaxed his shoulders.

"Wash my hair?"

"Turn around," I said, and he raised his brows. "I'm serious."

I couldn't tell if he was curious or worried, but he did as I'd asked. The shampoo bottle sat on a small shelf behind me. I grabbed it and poured a decent amount into my hand. He groaned as I worked up a lather into his hair with my fingers and leaned into my touch.

"Jesus... you're good at this," he said, his muscles loose as I massaged his neck and shoulders with my soapy hands.

"You're welcome."

He dipped his head under the water again, washing away all the suds before he turned around. "It's your turn."

We switched spots, the hot water on my cool skin like needles, at first. I lowered my head once he had a handful of shampoo. His touch was cautious, but after a few seconds he found his confidence, his fingers gently scratching along my scalp and down the back of my neck. Glancing up, I smiled at his thoughtful expression.

"What's that look?"

He laughed, smearing the shampoo down my chest. "I was concentrating."

"Concentrating is just another word for thinking, you know." I reached past him for the body wash.

"I was thinking about how sweet you were with Anne tonight," he said and held out his hand like we did this every day. I filled it with soap, and he ran his palms over my chest and arms as he spoke. "You didn't have to listen to all of her weather facts, but you did."

"She's a cute kid."

"She likes you." Van's hand paused over my heart, and I wondered if he could feel the rapid rhythm beneath my skin.

"I wasn't sure how tonight would go," I admitted, and he smiled as I popped the soap bubble on his jaw. "It's a relief knowing I didn't fuck it up."

"I'm glad you stayed for dinner."

"Me too."

He grasped the nape of my neck, pulling me in for a quick kiss.

"I read what you sent me," he said and kissed the corner of my mouth. "The stories about your dad."

"Shit... you did?"

I dropped my forehead onto his shoulder, and he chuckled.

"Parker... your words are fucking brilliant."

I turned my head and kissed the side of his Adam's

apple, inhaling the damp scent of his clean skin as his hands found my waist. "Thank you."

"Would you mind if I showed them to my boss?"

"What?" I raised my head, thinking he was messing with me. "You're for real?"

"I wouldn't say it otherwise. The stories have potential."

"To be published?"

"I think so," he said. "With Anders's guidance I think we—you could turn them into a novel. I believe in your work, Parker." He stared at me, a few seconds passing in the silence, the water rinsing away the last traces of soap from our skin. He drew nervous circles on the edge of my hip with his finger. "Anders would look out for your best interests. Even if this doesn't work out between us."

"Are you going to tell him about us?" I asked, hoping for a yes.

I wanted someone to know, someone beyond this private bubble we'd created. It made it more real, made the thought of hiding this more bearable, made the *"even if this doesn't work out"* sound less daunting. I wanted to tell Marcos, tell my best friend about this amazing guy who believed in me even if we'd only just started.

"I think I might have to."

"But you don't want to?"

He searched my face, a deep crease forming between his brows.

"I want to."

The weight inside my chest shifted, making it easier to breathe.

"Are you worried about what he'll think?"

He exhaled a long sigh and nodded. "My reputation is important to his firm. But I've thought about it a lot, and if we're careful and make it through the semester, it should be okay. It's not like I'm a full-time professor. I'm hardly there. I doubt anyone would notice once you're no longer in my class."

"I'd like to tell Marcos. He's my best friend, and hiding it from him is—"

"Tell him." Van framed my face with his hands, his thumbs sweeping across my cheeks. "If you trust him, I trust you."

"He won't say anything," I said. "He's been fucking with me about having a crush on you since day one of the semester."

Van's smile stretched across his face as he draped his arms over my shoulders.

"You had a crush on me?"

"I was totally hot for teacher."

He hummed, his cheeks darkening again as he brought his lips to mine. We continued to explore each other under the guise of soap and water. Fingers and nails and skin. We touched and kissed until that tender pressure, that ache, boiled over.

"I need you to ..." he said, between kisses. "I need..."

"What do you need?"

"Make me come, Parker."

Slick and hard in my hand, Van watched with hooded eyes as I stroked his cock. I touched my lips to the hollow below his ear, kissing my way down his neck and shoulder. I moved lower, grazing his nipple with my teeth, and he threaded his fingers into my hair. Van rested his back against the shower wall, his grip tightening, the pinch of pain against my scalp made my mouth water.

Leaning down, I teased the head of his dick with my lips, his breath catching in his throat, I raised my eyes. "Is this okay?"

He nodded once, his desire evident in the rigid line of his jaw. But his uncertainty was there, too, storming inside his irises.

"I need you to say it."

"Yes," he gasped, the word sharp and gritty as I knelt down onto my haunches in front of him. Water trickling over my skin. I rubbed my nose into his groin, the dark hair of his inner thigh rough against my cheek. Van loosened his grip in my hair, his fingers trailing down my cheek, he held my chin. "It's more than okay."

The pad of his thumb caressed my bottom lip, following a straight line down my jaw to my shoulder. I licked the underside of his cock from the base to the tip, dipping my tongue into his slit, immersing myself in his salty taste. Van hissed, his fingers digging into my skin, while his other hand moved softly through my hair. The two contradicting sensations prickled at my flesh, sending a flood of goosebumps down my arms as he pushed into my mouth. My lips stretched around the heavy head, and I wanted nothing more than to swallow him whole, show him how good this could feel. How good *I* could make him feel. He swore as I worked him deeper into my mouth, making it only halfway, my lips meeting my hand as I stroked him. Inch by inch he took my mouth, fucking into my throat until my nose dusted the dark patch of hair covering his pubic bone.

Van groaned, bucking his hips as I gagged, his fingers curling sharply into my skin, and without warning, his release exploded down my throat. "Oh fuck," he panted as I struggled to swallow all of his load. "I'm sorry. I—"

"Don't be." I wiped my mouth with the back of my hand and stood to my full height, smiling at the way he wouldn't meet my eyes. "Look at me." He was breathless, his pupils dilated, his face splotched with red. "I'll take it as a compliment."

Resting his forehead against mine, he laughed. "God, that was—"

"The best head you've ever had." I grabbed the firm muscles of his ass, pulling him closer, shuddering as my dick rubbed against him. "I know I'm—"

Van crashed his lips into mine, his hand on the side of my face, and I stumbled back, dizzy with the taste of him still on my tongue, the pressure of his lips, and the urgent way he consumed me. Dropping his hand, he wrapped it around my shaft, jacking me slow—slow—so fucking slow.

"Van," I whispered, covering his hand with mine and grunted as he squeezed me tighter. "Fuck... that's good. Like that."

He was rough, every stroke hard and relentless, until he found his rhythm. His teeth on my neck, my chin, my lips, the breathless sound of my voice as I said his name, my low, quiet groans seemed louder as I chased my climax. Pushing my back into the wall, he covered my mouth with his, stealing my breath and muting the sounds I couldn't seem to control. My head tilted back, breaking away from his kiss as the familiar desperate burn spread from the bottom of my spine and my balls tightened. Van left a path of open-mouthed kisses on my overheated skin, from my neck to my navel, looking up at me with hesitation in his eyes. But before I had the chance to tell him I didn't expect him to blow me, that he didn't have to do anything he wasn't comfortable with, he leaned down and took the head of my dick into his mouth.

"*Jesus Christ*." The surprising wet heat of his tongue almost pushed me over the finish line as he bobbed his head again and again and again.

Sloppy and uncoordinated, it didn't fucking matter, I'd already been teetering on the edge, and I came with a string of expletives, my fingers buried in his hair. My body sagged against the tile as he stood, licking his lips. Neither of us said anything for what felt like minutes when, in reality, it was probably only a few seconds. I worried we'd gone too far, worried he'd felt forced to return the favor. The short high I'd been riding plummeted.

"You didn't have to—"

"I know," he said, raising his fingers to his mouth.

"If this is too much—if it's too fast... I don't ever want you to feel like you can't say no."

"I didn't want to say no," he said, a deep flush cascading down his neck. "I wanted to know what you tasted like too. What it would feel like?"

I reached for his hand, turning it palm up, and rubbed the waterlogged, pruned tips of his fingers with my own. Feeling vulnerable, I might've needed a reason to hide my eyes, or an excuse to touch him. "What did you think? Terrible? Strictly chicks from now on?"

I tried to joke, but he didn't laugh. "It was different... in a good way. I like the way you taste, Parker." When I lifted my eyes, he was smiling. "I thought I was the only one who blushed."

I exhaled a laugh and bit the corner of my lip as I palmed the juncture below my neck. "Only for you, professor."

It was well past eleven by the time I'd gotten home from Van's. The apartment was dark except for the grainy gray light flickering from the television. Marcos was sleeping on the couch, his mouth open, snoring like a goddamn bear. I debated on leaving him there, knowing in the morning I'd have to listen to him bitch about the crick in his neck. I nudged his knee and he grumbled something completely incoherent. Sighing, I picked up the half-eaten bowls of soup and brought them to the sink. I ran the water, rinsing them out, my mind somewhere else. With Van. Waffles and rain and books and blushes. Dirt and grass. Late-night showers and more firsts. I was still back at his house, the smell of his soap covering me. I lifted the collar of the t-shirt he'd let me borrow to my nose and inhaled the scent of his detergent.

"Are you sniffing yourself?" Marcos asked as he

trudged into the kitchen with his coffee mug. He set it into the sink, his hair sticking up in every direction. "That's fucking weird, *mijo*."

"Glad to see you've risen from the dead," I said and leaned against the counter as he grabbed another mug from the cabinet. "How are you feeling?"

Filling the cup with water, he shrugged. "Better, I think. I can actually taste the funk of my own mouth... that's a good sign."

"And it's disgusting."

"Fuck off." He plopped two tea bags into the mug and put it into the microwave. "Nice shirt, by the way." He looked over his shoulder, grinning like he had me all figured out. "Emory?"

I stared down at the University's emblem stretching across my chest.

"It's not mine."

He raised his brows and pursed his lips. "You don't say... Those aren't your pants either, lover boy... last time I checked, you couldn't afford designer clothes."

"They're just sweats."

He leaned over and snapped the waistband. "Those are not just *sweats*. They're Thom Browne, and I'm guessing your mystery man, aka sugar daddy, has money because those pants cost at least four-hundred dollars."

"What? That's insane."

"Quality, *carnal*... it'll cost you."

"They don't fit or feel any different than the cheap-ass sweats I wear to the gym." Four-hundred dollars. Fuck, now I was worried I'd ruin them. "I'll be right back."

I heard Marcos laugh as I shut my bedroom door.

I immediately stripped out of the pants that could have funded a month's worth of groceries at Pride House and folded them before I sent Van a text.

> **Me: You're probably sleeping. But why in the hell would you lend me $400 pants?**

Marcos pushed my bedroom door open and squealed. "*Dios mio*, why is your dick hanging out?"

"Fuck, can't you knock?"

"I mean... it's not like I haven't—"

"Out."

Of course, he didn't leave, leaning in the doorway, he didn't even have the decency to avert his eyes. I tossed my phone onto my bed and grabbed a pair of briefs and gym shorts from my dresser.

"What do you want?" I asked as I got dressed.

"You come home wearing designer pants, smelling your shirt, also not yours, all smitten and shit, and expect me not to ask questions?" He cocked his hip. "You know me better than that."

"Sit down," I said, and he balked at my stern tone. "Will you sit your ass on the bed so I can do this? Please."

"Since you said please..."

Marcos sat on the edge of my bed and my stomach knotted. I trusted him not to say anything. And even though he'd teased me about my crush, the truth was a boulder in my throat. The pull I felt for Van, how I couldn't stop thinking about him, how big all of this was already, how did I explain this to my best friend who literally took nothing seriously.

"You can't say a *word*, Marcos."

"Okay, okay."

"I'm not fucking around, not a word, alright?" I ran my hands over my hair and exhaled. "Sorry, I didn't mean to raise my voice."

"I'll forgive you if you kill the suspense and just spit it out already."

"I'm dating Donovan."

"Wait... Donovan, as in..." His eyes widened and he bounced on the bed. "No way, you're banging the teacher?"

"We are not banging." I rolled my eyes. "Please don't make me regret telling you."

"Does he know that I know?"

"Yes, I asked him if it was okay to talk to you about it."

He squealed again and started coughing. "Fuck, that hurts."

"You can't tell anyone. Not Tam. Not a soul. He could lose his job. He has a daughter... shit, please... you can't—"

"Don't offend me, Park. You're my family, I wouldn't say anything to anyone."

"You're a gossip."

"True... but I love you, *hermano*. Your secret is safe with me." His smile was more vibrant than I'd seen it in days. "Oh my God, was he the app guy?"

"Yeah."

"And you didn't know?"

"How could we?"

"This is like some soulmate shit. I'll have to do your cards before you leave for work in the morning."

"My cards?"

"Tam taught me tarot."

"I'm good, but thanks." I laughed and shoved him in the chest. "Cards? Come on, Marcos."

"They're scary accurate. You'll see."

I wouldn't but I didn't feel like arguing.

Exhausted, I dropped down onto my bed. "We've only been on two dates, but like I said on Friday, I really like him."

"It's more than two dates. The app. Class."

"You know what I mean. It's new and terrifying." I fidgeted with the hem of my pillowcase. "I met his daughter tonight. Her name's Anne."

"Meeting the kid... That's fast."

"It's fast, but it wasn't as intimidating as I thought it would be. Anne's cute as hell... smart. And besides, he hadn't planned for her to be there. His ex-wife dropped her off unexpectedly."

"Whoa. You met the ex too?"

"Briefly." I leaned into my pillows and covered my eyes with my arm. "She's beautiful."

"Well, she's an ex for a reason."

"They were high school sweethearts. He's never been with a guy before me."

"Stop it... you get to deflower Mr. Brody."

"Oh my God!" I kicked him with my foot. "Get out. I need to sleep, I have work tomorrow."

He stood up and the mattress shifted. "I want every detail tomorrow, *mijo*. Every. Single. One."

I didn't answer him, smiling when my door shut a little harder than necessary.

Chapter 20

DONOVAN

Parker: You're probably sleeping. But why in the hell would you lend me $400 pants?

Me: You needed something to wear.

I pressed send, leaning against the kitchen counter with a huge grin on my face and took a long sip of coffee. Everything that had happened last night left a vivid stamp on my memory, loud and hot. My God. Setting my phone on the counter, I closed my eyes and raised a hand to my lips, feeling the burn Parker had left behind. Inhaling, I could smell him, smell the humid scent of his rain-soaked hair, the hard touch of his hands on my face. My heart sped up and I grinned again, my eyes slowly opening to the morning sun as it spilled through the window. I stared out at the lawn, thinking about everything and nothing and I was full and happy. I was happy. Something I hadn't been in such a long time.

"Dad, we have to go soon." Anne gaped at me, her hand on her hip. "What are you doing?"

"Sorry," I said, taking a deep breath. "Zoned out. Did you brush your teeth?"

"Yeah."

"Get your bookbag, I'll be ready in a second."

My phone chirped and I picked it up, swiping my thumb across the screen.

Parker: Good morning.

I laughed at the sleeping emoji he sent.

Me: Did I wake you?

Parker: No, just getting out of the shower.

An image of him standing fully nude in my own shower assaulted me.

Me: Thank you for that visual.

Parker: Anytime... Question?

Parker: Did you really spend $400 on a pair of sweats?

I laughed again and my shoulders shook.

Me: No, they were a gift from my sister. She can be... excessive.

Parker: No shit.

"Dad," Anne whined, and I glanced at the clock.

"Aw, hell."

I had to leave in fifteen minutes if I wanted to get Anne to school and arrive to work on time. I gulped down my coffee, singeing the tip of my tongue. Slipping my phone into my pocket, I washed out my coffee mug and finished knotting the tie around my neck. I grabbed my keys and laptop bag before heading for the door.

"Let's go, little monster."

The morning air was cool, the heavy cloud bank overhead threatening more rain. I looked forward to fall every year, not that it got very brisk in Atlanta, but the change from the overbearing summer heat was nice. The rain I could do without. I unlocked the car as Anne complained about the weather.

"We have time, go grab a jacket," I offered as I opened the back door for her.

"It's not that cold," she grumbled, brushing past me, and slid into the back seat.

The radio host warned of a traffic jam on I-85 as the engine came to life.

"You're gonna be late." She flashed her gray eyes at me in the rearview mirror.

"Nah," I said, backing out of my driveway. "It'll be fine."

I wasn't fine. There'd been an accident a few blocks from Anne's school, and everything was gridlocked.

"Should have left earlier," she said.

"I know."

"Shouldn't have slept in so late."

"Anne," I warned. "I'm sorry, alright."

I'd hit snooze on my alarm clock one too many times this morning. In my sleep-hazed head, I had time. Which I would have had if I hadn't needed to take Anne to school. But it wasn't her fault I'd stayed up late. Nope. That was on me. Would I change a thing about last night? Absolutely not.

"It's okay," she said as the car in front of me inched ahead. "Mom is always late."

"She's not always—"

"*Dad.*"

"Okay." I chuckled. "She isn't very punctual, but being an adult is hard. And now we both have to do it on our own. We're trying."

"I wish..." She stopped talking and I glanced over my shoulder. Her hands were wringing in her lap. "I wish you guys didn't have to do it on your own."

She held my gaze in the rearview mirror.

"I miss our family too," I said, my voice cracking. "I love your mom, and she loves me, but we didn't work anymore, hon. It's better this way. We would have ended up fighting all the time."

"I know." She stared out the window. "It still sucks."

"It sucks."

She turned and smiled at me. The smallest of smiles. "I like when we make waffles."

"Me too."

"I liked your friend."

The traffic started to move again, and I focused on the road as I spoke. "He's nice."

"Will he have dinner with us again?" she asked as I pulled into the drop-off lane in front of her school.

"If that's okay with you?"

"Yeah." I put the car in park, and she unbuckled, leaning between the two front seats to kiss me on the cheek. "Bye, Dad."

She hustled out of the car and slammed the door, leaving me in a daze. The car behind me honked and I held up my hand. "Jesus, I'm moving."

I was thirty minutes late for work by the time I walked into the office lobby. Kris peered at me from her desk.

"Is he pissed?" I asked, my eyes fixing on Anders's closed office door.

"Probably, he'll get over it, though." She handed me a file. "Here's the info for your nine o'clock call."

"Thanks." I glanced at his door. "Maybe I should talk to—"

"I wouldn't," she shook her head. "Ethan's in there."

"Oh..." I said and then my eyes widened. "*Oh*."

She laughed. "Oh, indeed."

"You don't think..."

She shrugged, her grin a mile wide. "They remind me of how Cesar and I used to be. We couldn't keep our hands off each other..."

"And now?" I asked and she waved me off.

"We're fine... just a little harder when you have a toddler running around." Kris smiled. "Maybe you should knock on the door. I mean, if he can do... whatever he's doing in there, then you can be a little late from time to time."

"I think I'd rather hide in my office." I held up the file. "Thanks again."

"Not a problem."

Anders's door opened as I walked down the hall. His fiancé, Ethan, laughed about something and I ducked into my office. I switched on my computer and sat down, pretending to look busy. Setting my phone on my desk, I noticed I had a couple of notifications. Right as I unlocked the screen, Ethan stopped in front of my door.

"Hey, Van." His lips broke into a warm smile. "How's it going?"

"Good, and you?"

He ran a hand through his already messy hair. His cheeks splotched with pink stood out against the blue color of his scrubs. "Tired, long shift last night."

"Did you hit that traffic coming in?" Anders asked as he sidled in next to Ethan, and holy God, his hair was a mess too. His tie askew.

I tried not to smile.

"I did. I'm sorry I was late I—"

"Don't worry about it. It happens." Anders's face lit up with a smile as he stared down at Ethan. He wiped his thumb across Ethan's lips, and I looked away. "As long as it doesn't become a habit."

"Don't be such a hard ass," Ethan said, and I chanced a glimpse in their direction. "Ignore him, Van. He'd never fire you. He likes you too much."

Anders rolled his eyes and I laughed.

"Good to know, but I promise. It won't be a habit."

Anders pressed his lips to Ethan's forehead. "You better get home and get some sleep. I hate these night shifts."

"I have to start somewhere." Ethan waved at me before taking Anders's hand in his. He nodded his head toward the front of the office. "Walk me out?"

Anders nodded once and kissed him again.

"It was good to see you." Ethan gave me a small wave.

"You, too."

"I'll be back in a second," Anders said. "I want to go over something with you before your first meeting."

I nodded, and as they both walked away, my phone vibrated against my desk.

I had three missed texts.

Parker: Shit. Did I offend you?

Parker: I'm sure your sister is great. I mean, she'd have to be to buy you those sweats, right?

Parker: I'm going to assume you don't hate me. But if you want to put me out of my misery, text me when you can.

Smiling, I typed out a quick response.

Me: I don't hate you.

Three dots popped up at the bottom of my screen.

Parker: No?

Me: Not at all. I was late for work because I was up late, not hating you, and then I got stuck in traffic.

Parker: I'm being one of those weird, needy types... who I do hate, by the way.

Me: I think your worry was reasonable. I left you hanging. But I like that you worried. Is that bad?

Parker: No. It just makes you a sadist.

I laughed and cleared my throat as Claire walked by shooting me a dirty look.

"'Morning Claire."

She didn't respond.

Me: I do not enjoy people's pain. For the record.

Parker: Damn. I thought I might get to bump you up to lesson number five.

Me: Ha.

Parker: What, not a whips-and-chains kind of guy?

Me: I guess I can't say no since I've never tried it, but I'm going to go out on a limb and say probably not.

Parker: No whips and chains. Check.

I figured he was only joking, but I wondered if maybe he wasn't.

Me: Is that something you'd ever want?

Parker: No. Not that I'm judging those who like it. But it's not for me.

Relief slowed my pulse.

Me: I'm not judging either, but thank God.

Me: Off topic... Can I talk to Anders today about your work?

Parker: Can we talk about BDSM again?

Me: He's going to love it.

The dots at the bottom of my screen danced and disappeared four times.

Parker: You can show him.

Me: We can talk about what he thinks after class. Would you want to have dinner with me again tonight?

Parker: Yes.

Heat crawled up my neck, excitement fueling the fire as I stared at the screen.

Me: I'll see you this evening, then.

Parker: Text me if he hates it?

Me: He won't.

"Got a minute?" Anders asked as he walked into my office and shut the door.

"Of course." I set my phone on my desk. "What's up?"

He sat down across from me, his brows knitting together as he said, "I told my mom Ethan and I are getting married on a riverbank, most likely the Chattahoochee. She wasn't pleased."

I chuckled at his wounded expression. "Did she disown you?"

"Not this time. But I'm sure she thought about it." He laughed and rubbed his jaw. "I told her she could do the invitations. I think it was my saving grace. Anyway," he said. "The call this morning, Kris should have given you everything you need."

"She did. I appreciate it."

Anders started to stand. "Let me know if you need anything else. Blanding Production can be a pain to deal with. Ask for twenty percent, they'll bargain you down to ten, which is perfect."

"Before you go, can I..." My throat narrowed and I sucked in a breath. "Can I talk to you about something?"

Anders sat back, his light eyes assessing me. "Is there something wrong?"

"No... I mean, at least I hope you won't think so." I pulled at the tight knot of my tie. "There's this..." Student? Guy? God, this was awful. "I want to be honest."

"I always prefer honesty," Anders said, eyeing me warily.

"I want you to read something one of my students wrote. It's phenomenal, Anders. And I think he has so much potential, but I don't want you to think I'm being biased."

"Because he's your student?"

"Yes, and..." I swallowed, my tongue sour in my mouth. "And... we... well, I... It's new and I know it's unconventional and—"

"Van..." Anders stared at me, the soft lines around his eyes deepening as he smiled. "Take a breath."

I did. It was ridiculous. I counted to ten and then started over.

"I'm bisexual."

Anders blinked a few times. "Okay."

"I've never had a chance to explore it, you know. And I met a guy online. We've hung out a few times, and he's... he's..." I wiped my damp palms over my slacks. "He's amazing."

"That's great," Anders said, his smile stretching to his eyes. "Seriously, I'm happy for you. It has to be hard dating again, after everything."

"It was terrifying."

"I can only imagine."

I took another long, deep breath. "He's a student, Anders."

"Wait... the author or..." His smile fell.

"I didn't know. When I met him online, I had no idea. He's twenty-four. And shit, I shouldn't have gone through with it once I met him, but he's... he's—"

"Amazing."

"Yeah." I sank back in my chair. "Please don't fire me."

"Why would I fire you?" He cocked his head to the side, confused. "I would be more worried about losing your job at Winchester. What's their policy?"

"No fraternization whatsoever. If we get caught, I'll get fired. God, this is so unprofessional."

"He's an adult, it's not that scandalous." He smiled and I exhaled. "I'm assuming you don't want them to fire you, though."

"I doubt I'd be able to get a job teaching anywhere if they did." I rested my elbow on the table and pressed my fingers into my temple, trying to relieve the sudden ache in my head. "But he'll only be my student until December, right? After that I'm hoping it won't matter."

"Is he out... about his sexuality?"

"He is."

"And he's okay with hiding?"

"I mean, I think so. For now." I met his gaze. "You're not upset?"

"Van, I don't give a shit who you date as long as it's a consenting adult. I dated Wilder on and off for years. Total conflict of interest. And I'm marrying my ex-assistant. Who am I to judge?" He sat up. "If you like him, make it work. December isn't that far away."

"Thank you for not firing me."

His chuckle untied the last knot in my stomach as he stood. "Send me his work, I can't promise anything."

"It's once-in-a-lifetime writing."

"And you're thinking with the right head?"

"I am," I grinned as he tapped his knuckles on my desk.

"Send it, I'll read some of it on my lunch."

"Thanks."

He opened the door, but before he left, he said. "You're a good agent, a good friend. I know I can be... difficult, but if this does blow back on the agency for some reason, I want you to know I'll defend you to whoever will listen."

"Anders, I—"

"But try not to let it blow back, alright." The command in his voice was unmistakable.

"I won't," I said, and hoped like hell it wasn't a lie.

Tonight's class had been interesting, to say the least. Despite everything that happened between Parker and me over that last few days, and all the secret smiles he'd sent my way, I thought I'd kept up a professional appearance. But, after my long night last night, and my even longer day, I was exhausted. My head in Parker's lap, his hand running through my hair, I struggled to keep my eyes open. His other hand rested on my hip, his fingers drawing symbols and letters on my skin under my shirt. The movie on the television served as white noise, making it that much harder to stay awake. Occasionally he would laugh, and I'd smile. The scent of his soap and cologne, the warmth of his body, this easy intimacy, I almost liked it better than sex. Well... maybe.

"You awake?" he asked, and I hummed.

"A little."

"Do you want me to go?"

I opened my eyes and was met with a smile. "Not yet."

"You're tired," he said and laughed when I shook my head. "Van, you looked dead on your feet in class."

"Is that a nice way of saying I looked like shit?"

"I'm just glad Marcos was still sick, so I didn't have to hear his jokes about how I kept you up all night."

"I'm not looking forward to seeing him again," I said, and Parker grinned. "He's going to make it awkward."

"Only for me." His fingers trailed over my lips. "He's under strict orders to keep his mouth shut."

"And he'll listen?"

Parker's blue eyes stilled, serious and raw as he stared down at me. "He's an idiot, but he's an idiot who loves me and would do anything for me."

"Anything?" I asked, not fully convinced.

He looked at me, searching my face for something. His throat worked as he swallowed, his hand in my hair again, he said, "I've known Marcos since basic training. He's had my back. Always. Our first year at MacDill, I thought I could be out. There was no more '*don't ask don't tell*'. Marcos told me I was crazy. I didn't believe him." His voice was hoarse, the fingers on my hip trembled as he spoke. "I should have."

"Did something happen?" I asked, knowing the answer by the way his eyes had turned to glass.

"I met a guy, another airman. We talked online for a few weeks, decided to meet. He was nervous. He wasn't out. At least that's what he'd told me." Parker's chest stuttered as he exhaled, thinking of things I was terrified to know. "We met at a bar, and it seemed like things were going good. He wouldn't look me in the eye, which should have been a red flag, but I was dumb, and young, and wanted... shit... I—"

"Park." I sat up, curling my legs underneath me and faced him. "You don't have to tell me, if it's too difficult."

"I do." He wet his lips and picked at the hole in his jeans. "We walked to one of the nearby piers, I was buzzed, not thinking straight. I didn't see the other guy until it was too late."

"Oh God, Parker..."

His jaw clenched, his nostrils flaring as he tried to shore up whatever storm was building inside.

"They beat the shit out of me. Called me every slur you could think of. Told me I was worthless. Told me I didn't deserve to serve my country. I don't remember much after that, but I remember calling Marcos. I woke up in the hospital ER. Concussion. Broken ribs. Broken nose. I was broken. Marcos wanted to report them. I begged him not to. I was embarrassed and scared. The guy was an officer, his friend—I had no idea. Marcos never said a word. We told the police I'd been mugged. Told my CO the same thing. The closet was my home after that night. For four years."

A tear fell down my face and he wiped it away. I hadn't even realized I'd started to cry. There was a small scar that cut across his eyebrow, and I traced it with my thumb, and he closed his eyes.

"Marcos keeps my secrets and I keep his."

I cupped his face and he leaned into the touch. It didn't change anything, but I wasn't sure what else to say. "I'm sorry. I'm so fucking sorry."

"Me too." And God, he smiled, and my chest ached. "But they didn't win. Maybe they did for a while. But not anymore."

"And I've asked you to hide again," I said, the realization cutting me in two. "I can't... I shouldn't have—"

"It's not the same." He leaned in, the warmth of his breath on my lips. "It's not, so stop overthinking."

Parker kissed me soft and sleepy. Like he hadn't just opened an old wound, like he hadn't started to bleed all over again. His hands in my hair, his tongue parted my lips. It didn't last long, but this kiss was different from the previous kisses we'd shared. It tasted like trust and hope and something I couldn't name, something that was unique to him, something sweet and somber.

This man. I didn't know. I didn't know. Turns me to dust.

"The free association assignment," I said, and he nodded.

"It was about my last week in Florida. I met the guy at a bar. It was a one-time thing. But for some reason I'd told him everything, let him fuck me. All of it was my choice. I took back my freedom under the same pier where I'd almost lost everything."

Earlier we'd talked about his writing over boxes of lo-mein, talked about a future he didn't think he could have, but he'd said he'd given some thought about changing his major to creative writing next semester. He didn't get it, how rare his talent was, how special. He'd laughed when I told him Anders was interested in talking to him about working on a novel. He'd laughed like I'd been pulling his leg, like he wasn't good enough. I'd said, "I told you so." And he'd laughed again. I had no idea. No idea the scars he held. I should have told him he was worthy, like that stranger on the beach, who'd had him in a way that twisted me up inside. That he was this rare and special person. That he deserved this, that he never deserved to bleed. I wanted to say it now, but it felt like it was too late.

Instead, I said his name and kissed him until we couldn't breathe.

Chapter 21

PARKER

The drive to my mom's house in Marietta usually didn't take me longer than twenty-five minutes. Depending on traffic, I could get there in twenty, but today seemed to drag. It was only ten in the morning, and I was already tired. I'd stayed up too late, which had become my routine over the past six weeks. If I wasn't at work, or over at Van's, I was home trying to catch up on my classes. I yawned, trying to keep my eyes focused on the road, the fall foliage burning bright orange and yellow as the car sped by.

"Stop yawning, you're making me tired." Marcos leaned forward and turned down the volume on the stereo. "You need me to drive?"

"I'm fine, we're almost there."

"Most accidents happen when you're only a few miles from home."

I glared at him. "I'm fine."

"Someone's cranky today. Maybe if you would man up and deflower the professor already, you'd be a little less irritable."

"It's not like that, asshole." I laughed. "And would you please stop using the word deflower."

"He's an ass virgin... it fits. I mean, unless him and his ex-wife used to—"

"*Marcos.*"

"Calm down," he said, mumbling something in Spanish under his breath.

"We're not ready."

I kept my gaze fixed on the road even though I could feel him staring at me.

"He's not ready," he said.

"It's only been a month."

"It's been six weeks. You've fucked guys you've known for thirty minutes, Park." He turned in his seat to face me. "You're over there almost every night."

"Why are you so concerned about my sex life?" I asked, my aggravation leaking through my half-hearted smirk.

"Jesus." He held up his hands. "Forget I said a word."

He turned away and looked out his window. The guilt ate at me. He was nosy and intrusive, but it came from a place of concern. I'd known him long enough to have thought otherwise. He was my mother hen.

"It's different with him," I said. His glossy lips twitched, fighting to keep quiet and I smiled. "Say what you want to say."

"How is it different?" he asked, facing me again. "I swear to God, you never tell me anything anymore. Tell me all the romantic shit, *mijo*. I need it. My love life is nonexistent. I need to live vicariously through you."

Laughing, I pulled off the interstate and stopped at the red light. "I don't need more with him. I mean, we fuck around, and it's hot as hell, but I like just spending time with him too. I like being with him in any capacity. It feels easy, Marcos... we click. I don't need to fuck him to know that."

Being us was enough.

I liked how Van would always put his head in my lap on the nights we'd watch a movie. And how excited he'd get when Anne brought home art from school, hanging it on his fridge like my mom used to do for me. I'd only hung out with him and his daughter a few times, but each time, I'd gotten to see him without any guards up. When he was with his daughter, I got to see him—just him. And he was beautiful. After the night I'd opened up to him about my assault, something between us had changed. I'd never told anyone besides Marcos about what had happened to me. And I hadn't planned on telling Van either. At least not that soon. But he had a funny way of getting me to talk about all the things I'd locked up tight, of making me believe I was more than I thought I could be. Especially when it came to my writing, and when he'd kissed me that night, all I'd felt was relief. Relief and fire, and every time I had a chance to be in his orbit, I took it. I took it because I couldn't stop the pull, that tugging sensation that tied me to him in ways I'd never felt before. I'd spent a lot of time hiding from something serious, but when I looked at him, I thought maybe I'd just been waiting.

"I don't want to push him, Marcos. Yeah, it's been a little over a month, but we're still figuring everything out. And I... I think he's someone I could see myself ending up with."

"Like forever?"

"Hell... I don't know."

"Aww." Marcos raised his hand to his heart. "He gives you the butterflies."

"I can't tell if you're making fun of me."

"Oh... I'm totally making fun of you." He laughed when I playfully punched him in the shoulder. "Parker Mills with the heart eyes, I would have never thought."

"I do not have heart eyes."

"*Marcos, I think he could be the one.*" He spoke in a high-pitched voice and batted his lashes. "*I like spending time with him.*" He cracked up, barely containing his glee, and wiped his fingers under his eyes. "Haven't even gotten the ass, and you're whipped."

"Have you always been this immature?" I asked and chuckled when he nodded.

"Always." He inhaled, trying to catch his breath. "Fuck off, you love me. I keep you young."

"I guess."

"I do have a serious question."

"That terrifies me."

"Do you think he's going to let you top him?" He waggled his brows, and I shook my head.

"That's your serious question?" I ignored his incredulous look and made a left when the light turned green. "We haven't really talked about that yet, and I haven't even stayed an entire night there, man. Taking it slow is okay. Stop looking at me like that."

"Like what?"

"It *is* possible for two men to be together and not fuck."

"I know." He wrinkled his nose. "To each his own and everything. You do you."

"I hate you," I said, smiling when he gave me the middle finger. "I should have left you at home."

"Your momma loves my ass. Besides, you have no idea how to use a sewing machine."

"I can't believe you want to make all the costumes for this play."

"Why? I get to make clothes and do make-up, it's basically my dream job. Except for the whole not getting paid thing."

"You do realize that's the entire purpose of volunteering... service."

"Whatever. Pride House is lucky to have me."

As much as I wanted to tease him about his humble nature, he was kind of right. Every year, near the holidays, the shelter had an increase in their census. The nights were colder during the winter months, and the need for coats and more beds almost doubled. Throughout the year we survived on government funding and charitable donations, but every December, Pride House put on a play to help raise money for the influx during the holidays. The residents and staff all got involved. Everything was handmade or donated. Sponsors usually helped pay for the supplies, but for the most part, we did it all on our own. Maybe it was my relationship with Van, and how we'd met, or maybe it was my love for the book, but I'd offered to write an adaptation of *The Lost Boys,* and everyone loved the idea. At least we hoped everyone would love it. The new director and his staff were supposed to be here this week. Hopefully, the guy wasn't a total asshole.

"You should get Van to be one of the sponsors since you both get a hard-on for that book."

"Horrible idea," I said and turned onto the long, grass driveway that led up to my mother's house.

"Why?" He shrugged. "Get his agency to sponsor it. They like books, it makes sense."

I put the car in park and shut off the engine. Staring at the small trailer home that had seen better days, I asked, "You don't think that's rude of me to ask?"

"No. It's not like you're asking Van for money." He pulled down the visor and opened the mirror. He pressed his lips together and wiped a finger under his eye, removing the faint black smudge from his mascara. "They could probably use it as a tax write-off."

"Maybe."

He shut the mirror and stared at me. "If it makes you uncomfortable, then don't ask him, I was only—"

"I'll think about it."

"Parker." Marcos rested his hand on my shoulder, and I met his gaze. His smile was soft as he said, "He likes you. Not that I'm telling you to capitalize on that. But it's obvious. I mean, the students in our class are fucking idiots if they can't see the way that man looks at you. All I'm saying is, I bet he'd want to help you."

"I don't know, his boss is always busy. I have a meeting with him this Friday to go over some of my work, and even then, he had to fit me in. But... yeah, maybe you're right. I could pitch the idea to both of them, then."

"That could work," he said. "Or..." He held out his hand. "I could ask him."

"Hell no."

"Come on," he pouted. "You never let me tease him. I'm always on my best behavior. I can be an adult, you know."

"You can?" I asked and bit back my grin.

"Güey." He grumbled and opened his door.

"Do I want to know what that means?"

"No... I don't think you do," he said and stepped out of the car. He bent down, his arm on the frame. "You think your mom made those cookies I like?"

All traces of his previous annoyance had dissipated. The guy was a whirlwind, but he wouldn't be Marcos any other way.

She'd made two dozen.

We were in the kitchen going over Marcos's costume ideas when the oven timer went off.

"I'll get it," I said and leaned down to kiss my mom on the cheek.

"Thanks, baby."

I didn't understand Marcos's obsession with these cookies. Oatmeal and raisins, in my opinion, had no business calling themselves a cookie. Grabbing a rag off the counter, I pulled the tray out of the oven. The scent of cinnamon filled the room, and like always, I second-guessed myself thinking I might like them this time. Of course, I wouldn't. The smell was deceiving as fuck.

"Just set them on the stove, Park. They need to cool," she said, like she hadn't told me this a thousand times over the years.

I placed the hot tray on the stove and smiled as I caught her watching me. My mom liked things a certain way, and I couldn't say I didn't blame her. Raising two kids on your own had to be hard, setting limits, keeping the status quo. It's how she survived, how we all did. She had to be two people wrapped in one body. She'd worked as a teacher for most of my life. And when the rest of the teachers took off for the summer, she worked at the local diner for extra cash. She had worked hard for us, but I didn't truly grasp how much she'd done for us until recently. The situation wasn't the same, Van was divorced, not a widower, but I could see some similarities between him and my mom. Which I guess might be weird to some, but I found it comforting. Much like this house, Van's wasn't immaculate, definitely lived in, but everything had its place. Everything he did was to make sure Anne had a safe place, a home when she was with him.

"Thanks, sweetie." She shooed me out of the way, situating the tray how she liked it. Nostalgia filled my chest and I smiled. Scooping the cookies onto the wire rack she'd set out earlier, she asked, "Have you heard from your sister lately?"

"Not in a few weeks. Why, everything okay?"

"I'm not sure, she seemed down. She called me yesterday, said she might come home for Thanksgiving this year." Mom saved two cookies for Marcos and put them on a plate. He's always liked them fresh out of the oven, even if he ended up with a burnt tongue in the process. She glanced over at Marcos and lowered her voice. "I was thinking of doing the whole thing this year, bird and all...you think he'd come this time?"

"I could try, but you know how he is."

"I know it's not very Christ-like to say so, but his momma is an asshole, if you ask me. That boy is all light." Her blue eyes sparkled as she stared at my friend. "It's a shame, treating your blood that way."

"He has you."

"And you." She handed me the plate. "Go make him smile, alright."

Her chestnut hair was more gray than brown these days, her laugh lines more pronounced, but she looked the same to me. She was still the woman who'd given me everything. She was late nights when I couldn't sleep, and warm milk. She was bandaged knees and tissues that wiped away tears. She was acceptance and love when I'd brought home a boy from school and told her I liked him better than girls. She was worry and hope when I left for the Air Force. She was heart and happiness, and a second mother to my friend who had none of the things I'd been lucky enough to have.

"You like him better than me," I teased, and she swatted my arm.

"Well, when you say shit like that..."

"I told you she liked me better." Marcos grinned at my mom as he took the plate out of my hand. "It's okay, you can tell him, I'm much more fun."

"Shut up and eat your cookies." I gently smacked the back of his head, and he pinched my arm.

"You see how he treats me," Marcos said around a mouth full of oatmeal and raisins. "At least now that he has a boyfriend I don't have to—"

"Boyfriend?" Mom almost dropped the spatula in her hand. "Since when?"

"Shit." Marcos cringed, but I could see the smile he'd failed to hide.

"Yeah... shit," I said, giving him a murderous glare.

"Parker. What's he talking about? You have a boyfriend?"

I sighed as I sat down at the kitchen table. What the fuck was I supposed to tell her?

"I don't have a boyfriend," I said and when she raised an eyebrow I added, "Technically."

Her gaze bounced between Marcos and me. "What does that mean?"

"We're dating, we haven't labeled it. It's only been about a month."

"You never date anyone for a month. I mean, I have to say, I held hope you and Marcos one day..."

Marcos made a gagging sound and I kicked him under the table.

"Mom, he's like my brother, that's gross."

"But dating your professor is just fine," Marcos said under his breath and my eyes widened.

"Dating your what?" She was distracted, washing the cookie sheets, and I fucking hoped to God she hadn't heard him. I didn't feel like killing my best friend today.

"It's nothing, Mom. If we get serious, I'll let you know."

I exhaled the breath I'd been holding when she nodded. "He must be special if you've kept him around this long. I love you, son, but you're a bit of a player."

I laughed openly and Marcos did too. "A player?" I asked. "Where did you hear that?"

"I'm not as naïve as you all like to think. You and your sister, both. If these walls could talk." She raised her eyes to the ceiling.

"Oh..." Marcos dragged out the word. "Do tell, Mrs. Mills."

"Mom," I cut her off as she opened her mouth to speak, and she laughed. "Can we change the subject?"

"I'd like to meet this guy." She pointed the spatula at me. "It would be nice for once."

"Yeah, Mom... Like I said, if things work out."

That seemed to placate her, for now, but I knew I wouldn't hear the end of it until she'd actually met him. If that ever happened, I figured she never needed to know the details of how we'd met.

"They'll work out," Marcos said, stacking a few patterns together, he stuck them in his bag. "You're practically in love with the guy already."

"In love?" Mom asked, her tone filled with what could only be described as delight.

Fucking Marcos.

"I think it's time for you to move out," I said, and his head tipped back as he laughed.

"You wish, *mijo*."

Right then, I really did.

Chapter 22

DONOVAN

"Hey." Parker smiled at me from my office doorway, and I still couldn't get over how good he looked in his dark-washed jeans and steel gray button down. He'd had his appointment with Anders today, and I thought it was cute that he'd dressed up like it was a job interview. "You ready to get out of here?"

"How did it go?" I asked, closing my laptop.

He walked in and shut the door behind him. "I think it went well. Anders is fucking intense."

I laughed as I stood, wrapping my arms around his waist. He leaned on the edge of my desk as I pressed a quick kiss to the corner of his mouth, to his jaw, below his ear. "Did I tell you how much I like you in this shirt?"

He buried his nose in my neck and inhaled. "Yeah, about a dozen times since I got here."

Leaning back, I ran my hands up his chest. "We should go out to dinner to celebrate."

"You don't even know what Anders said." He bit the corner of his lip, his smile giving him away.

"I already know he wants to sign you, Park. You wouldn't be here otherwise."

"Then, I guess we should celebrate."

"You decided to sign?" I asked, and he nodded. "Parker, that's—"

"Fucking crazy." His smile fell and he lowered his head. "The shit I write... it's bits and pieces of the stuff I have in my head. What if I can't ever write an entire book?"

"He'll help you. Push you when you need it." I rested two fingers under his chin and lifted his head. "You can do this."

"I want to believe that."

"Anders is only a facilitator. Write what you want, Parker. You don't owe anyone anything. If you never write a book, or if you write twenty. Do it for you and no one else."

He cupped the back of my neck, his eyes falling to my mouth. "We don't *have* to go out."

"I want to take you out."

He kissed my bottom lip, the heat of his breath sweet against my skin as he spoke. "A real date, in public and everything?"

I rested my forehead against his. "I should have taken you out sooner."

"Van..." He framed my face in his hands, his blue eyes boring into mine. "We're midterm, soon it will be finals week, after that you can take me wherever the fuck you want. I don't care about where we eat food, as long as you're there, I'm happy."

"We can—"

Parker's mouth captured mine with a hungry kiss, a low groan rumbling in his chest as his hands threaded through my hair. His hold tugged at my scalp, and I pressed against him. I was already hard for him, my cock brushing his thigh. I thought about what it would be like to be on my knees for him, here, in my office, behind my desk. Heat gathered along my groin, my heart beating faster and faster, the voice in my head whispering, *ask him for it, ask him for it,* as his mouth opened and our tongues swept against each other. He tasted like mint, and Parker, and God, I loved the way he took what he wanted. I wanted to be that bold. I wanted to sink to my knees and—

There was a soft knock on my door, and I broke away from his mouth. His cheeks were red, his pupils dilated as he stared back at me.

"Just a second," I said, and Parker laughed, dropping his face to my shoulder.

He lowered his hand between us, cupping my erection, and I shuddered. "Better do something about this before you open that door."

He palmed me again and I squeezed his ass. "You're making it worse."

Parker raised his head, grinning. "I know."

"Just letting you know I'm heading out for the evening," Kris said, and I could have sworn there was a smile in her voice. "Let Parker know I'll send him the contract on Monday."

I cleared my throat, gripping Parker's waist as he stroked me through my pants. "I... um... Thanks, Kris."

"You two have a nice evening," she said, and my face flushed.

I exhaled a harsh breath and grabbed his wrist. "Anders is still here."

"You told me he and Ethan are always fucking around in his office."

"I mean... I don't know, but—"

Parker laughed again and it was soft and warm. "Still want to take me to dinner, or should we just get take-out?"

I kissed him deeply, ignoring the sharp ache he'd created. Breathless, I smiled as I shook my head. "We're going out."

"If we must," he teased, and I kissed the corner of his fake frown before I stepped away.

"I have to pick up Anne from her afterschool program and drop her off at Lanie's studio. Then we can grab whatever you want."

"She should come with us."

"On a date?" I asked, shoving my laptop into my bag.

Parker watched me, shrugging, he asked, "Why not? There's the Fall Festival at Centennial Park. They probably only have carnival food, but it could be fun."

Like a deer in the headlights, I stood silent and still, my throat tight as I counted away my nerves. His smile was crooked, his eyes a little shiny as he waited for my response. He'd been sweet to Anne the handful of times he'd been around her, but this—he wanted to include her, and I had no idea why it was hitting me as hard as it was, but this gesture settled something inside me. It felt permanent, and that had to be premature. It had to be. Because this was supposed to be *just* dating. It was supposed to be feeling out what I wanted, exploring my sexuality, but it had become more. Every free night I'd had I'd given to Parker, and I didn't mind it. I wanted it. Needed it. Needed him.

Raising my bag onto my shoulder, I leaned over and kissed him on the cheek. "She'd love that. I'll have to run it by Lanie first."

"Yeah, alright." He eyed me, curiosity blooming inside his irises. "Everything...okay?"

"Yeah... everything's okay." I laced our fingers together. "Ready to stuff yourself sick with greasy carnie food?"

"Lead the way."

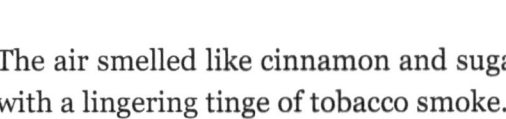

The air smelled like cinnamon and sugar and fried flour with a lingering tinge of tobacco smoke. Centennial Park was packed, which was expected for a Friday night. We were a long way from Winchester, and I didn't think anyone would recognize us, but it was good Anne was with us. I didn't get to do stuff like this with her very often, and it helped keep up appearances since I couldn't hold his hand or kiss him in front of her. We didn't look like a couple. Which shouldn't have bugged me, but it did. It would be nice to have his hand in mine, or to kiss him when he said something sweet to Anne. I almost did when he'd won her a stuffed elephant at one of the booths. This was a test in patience, and it made the sacrifice Parker had made for those four years he'd served that much more poignant.

"Look, Dad, I can win a fish," she said and tore her hand from mine. She ran toward a gleaming yellow booth with a red sign that had an orange goldfish painted on it.

"Should we tell her these fish are already half dead?" Parker asked in a whisper.

"I'll let you crush her dreams."

He bumped my shoulder, his fingertips grazing my arm. Goosebumps covered my skin, and it had nothing to do with the cool temperature outside.

"Parker," Anne called back at us. "You have to win me a fish."

"I've been replaced," I said, feigning offense. "Kids are so easily swayed. All it takes is a fluffy stuffed animal and it's all over."

He chuckled and held out his hand. "By all means, professor, win the girl a fish."

I bit the side of my cheek, knowing damn well I sucked at this stuff, but I accepted the challenge, ego be damned. I bought three rings for ten bucks, cringing at the price. But Anne held her toy elephant close to her chest and clapped furiously, her eyes wide with excitement. I guessed ten bucks wasn't much if it garnered that type of response.

"You can do it, Daddy."

Daddy.

My heart squeezed. She hadn't called me that in years.

How hard could it be? There were several tall, narrow glasses all stacked closely together. Each glass was filled with water and a single fish swimming circles inside of it. All I had to do was get a ring around one of the glasses and the fish was mine. Easy.

I made my first throw from behind the wooden barrier right as Parker poked me in the ribs. The ring clattered off several glasses and fell to the hay-covered floor.

"No cheating," I said, and he held up his hands with a wicked smirk on his handsome face. "Watch him, Anne."

She giggled but narrowed her eyes, not letting him leave her sight.

I tried again and missed.

Parker leaned in, his lips close to my ear, and I shivered. "Shoot for the middle glass, the rest are all too close together." He grinned at me as I looked at him over my shoulder. "You got this, *Daddy*."

I huffed out a laugh and turned back toward the game. Anne stared up at me, her eyes big, silently imploring me to win, win, win. Taking a deep breath, I aimed for the center glass and tossed it. Sailing through the air, the ring landed just short of center, and by some miracle or force of God, it flipped and circled around the center glass.

Anne screeched, jumping up and down before tackle-hugging me. "You did it!"

"Were you worried?" I asked and laughed when she nodded. "Ye of little faith."

"Huh?" she asked, and I shook my head.

"Never mind, go pick out your fish." I mussed up her hair with the palm of my hand as she turned toward the vendor.

"I would have totally bailed you out, you know, if you missed. I mean, the girl had to have a fish."

Parker reached for my hand, and without thinking I took it and pulled him close. I kissed him on the lips and his breath hitched. I realized what I'd done, and my stomach dropped. Anne was staring at us, plastic baggy in one hand, her elephant in the other. A fat goldfish swam around and around inside its new home while everything else had frozen in time. Everything except for the damn fish.

Instead of letting go of my hand, Parker held on tighter.

"Cool fish," he said, even and unruffled. Like this whole thing hadn't been turned upside down. Like my panicked heart wasn't trying to claw its way up my throat. "Check out its fat cheeks. What're you going to name it?"

Anne blinked once and then again, her smile slow and steady as it spread across her lips. "Tony."

"Tony?" Parker laughed and I remembered to breathe. "That's an interesting name."

She looked back at the booth. "It's his name. I thought it fit."

We all looked at the vendor and he waved. He had big cheeks and a handlebar mustache.

"Tony works," I said, and despite the fact my palm was sweating inside Parker's hold, my voice sounded normal. Unfazed.

"I think I'm going to get some fries. You guys want anything?" he asked.

"I'm good." I couldn't eat anything if I tried. "Anne?"

"No, thanks."

He smiled and gave my hand a short squeeze before letting go. "I'll meet you at the Ferris wheel?"

"Alright." I watched him walk away, wishing I could follow, or at least fall into a hole.

Anne held the bag close to her face, making fish lips. I wasn't sure if I should say anything. Maybe she thought that's what friends did. Friends could hold hands and kiss each other.

It was possible.

I was also delusional.

"Don't worry, Dad," she said, keeping her eyes on her new pet. "I think it's cool."

"What's cool?" I asked, my voice failing me as I swallowed.

"Parker... he's your boyfriend."

"Anne..."

She lowered the bag, her smile quiet. "Mr. Adair at school has a husband. He came to class to talk to us about what it was like to be a firefighter."

"Oh."

"It's okay. I kind of already figured it out," she said.

"You did?"

"I'm ten, almost eleven. I notice things."

Smiling, I rubbed the back of my neck. "You notice things?"

"You look at him like you used to look at Mom." Her smile dimmed enough I noticed. "You're happier."

"Hey... your mom made me happy for a long time, but—"

"I know... I'm not mad or anything." She gave me her elephant to hold and took my hand in hers. "Do you love him?"

"I like him a whole bunch."

"He's pretty cool..." She turned, her gaze scanning the festival, the lights glimmering in her gray eyes. "Do you think he'll be sad if we don't go on the Ferris wheel? I'm afraid of heights."

"We can skip it, then." I tugged on her hand. "Let's find Parker and maybe we can do the tilt-o-whirl again."

"No way, you guys squished me last time."

"But wouldn't it be funny to see Parker turn green again?"

A conspiratorial smile pulled her cheeks into dimples.

"Yeah... totally worth it."

We made our way through the crowd, my head spinning a mile a minute. I hadn't meant to come out to my daughter like this. I'd had this vision in my head where I would sit across from her at the kitchen table. We'd have waffles. I'd tell her and Lanie at the same time. Answer any questions as honestly as I was able. But I think the way it happened tonight was better. This wasn't about Lanie and me anymore. Anne and I, we were our own little unit. Her acceptance was all I wanted.

We found Parker sitting on a bench people watching, a small carton of fries in his hand. He'd rolled his sleeves to his elbows, and the slight breeze ruffled his hair. It was longer now, in need of a trim, but I liked it. In an overcrowded park, in a sea of people, he stood out like a beacon. I couldn't stop myself from smiling.

"I'm glad he makes you happy," Anne said, beaming up at me. "I missed your smiles."

I reached down and gently pinched her dimple. "I smile all the time."

"Not like this." She glanced over at Parker who'd caught sight of us. He stood and headed our way, throwing the rest of his fries in the trash can. "Can I tell Mom?"

"I'd like to be the one to tell her, if that's okay."

She hooked her pinky with mine. "She won't be mad."

"You don't think so?"

"No, she goes on dates with Matt."

Matt was new.

Well, then.

I waited for some type of reaction. Some feeling of jealousy or regret. There was none.

"Hey." Parker held my gaze. "All good?"

I nodded and he smiled at Anne, giving her his full attention. "Ready to go on the Ferris wheel?"

"Actually, we thought about going on the tilt-o-whirl," I said and laughed when he grimaced.

"You two go ahead, I might skip it, though. Had those fries and—"

"Nope, you have to go." Anne grabbed his hand and pulled him toward the rides.

"But who's going to hold Tony? I don't think he'd like the tilt-o-whirl very much."

286

"Dad can hold him, and you can ride with me."

Surprised, he looked over at me and mouthed the word *help*. Chuckling, I followed behind, feeling lighter than I had in years. The weight of my impromptu coming out had been temporarily lifted, and I focused on being in the moment and enjoying my time with my daughter—my daughter who had accepted me without any conditions. It wasn't until later, after I'd dropped off Anne at her mom's, and met Parker back at my place, that the heavy feeling returned. All the adrenaline from earlier came crashing down, and all I could do was overthink. What if Anne got too attached? What if Lanie wasn't okay with my sexuality? Would she stop me from seeing Anne? She wasn't like that. At least, I didn't think she was.

"Van," Parker wrapped his arms around me from behind, pulling my back to his chest, and kissed the curve of my neck. "Tell me what's going on inside your head."

"Anne called you my boyfriend."

Of all the things I could have said.

I turned in his arms and was met with his perfect, crooked grin. "Does that label make you uncomfortable?"

"No... but... does it make you uncomfortable?"

"Not at all. Maybe a few weeks ago I might've thought it was too soon for that." He ran his fingers through my hair and my eyes shuttered closed, opening again as he said, "I think about you all the time. And when I'm not here with you, I want to be. Marcos makes fun of me for it incessantly, but I don't give a fuck, because for the first time in my life I've actually found someone who makes me happy."

I kissed him in the middle of my living room, nothing I could say would match the way I felt. Showing him seemed more appropriate. Like always, it started off slow and soft. His hand in my hair, mine on the back of his neck. Lips and breath turned into tongue and teeth. Light touch to rough fingers. Skin and nails. Once we were both panting, his blue eyes fiery, I found the words I wanted to say.

"I can't stop thinking about you either. And every time you leave, I wish I would have asked you to stay."

"Ask me."

Breathe.

I counted to ten.

I wanted this.

Breathe. Breathe. Breathe.

"Van..."

"Stay... tonight. I want you to stay."

The pad of his thumb drifted over the line of my jaw. "Then, I'll stay."

Chapter 23

PARKER

*M*y boyfriend, I smiled at the word, stood in his bathroom doorway wearing nothing but the towel around his waist. His hair was wild and damp, sticking out every which way, a shy smile splitting his face. He watched me with his quiet eyes as I slipped out of my towel and tossed it into the hamper he had by his closet. The fine hairs on the back of my neck and shoulders prickled from the cold, but my chest was warm, heavy with the way he stared at me, like I might disappear at any moment, like he couldn't believe I was here.

"I...I have those sweats you borrowed, um... second drawer on the left." He pointed to his dresser, his eyes falling to my dick. We'd just messed around in the shower, but that didn't mean I wasn't game for more. When it came to Van, all I ever wanted was more. More kisses. More touches. Him. Every inch. "You know, the overpriced sweats."

He chuckled, and I grinned as I sat on the edge of his bed. "Or... And I think I like this idea better. We could forgo the clothes. I mean, it's my first sleepover. I think it's a rule we're supposed to be naked the whole night."

"Is that so?" he asked, loosening the knot on his towel, and letting it fall to the floor. He walked toward me, his confident stride something I'd yet to witness and Christ, did it work for me. My cock hardened, and his chest hitched as he stopped in front of me. He ran his fingers through my hair. "I'm not familiar with that rule."

"It's a thing," I said and peered up at him. Miles of silky skin and lean muscle on display. I reached up and flattened my palm on his stomach. "Or at least, it needs to be."

"I think I could get on board with that."

"Mmm," I hummed, lowering my palm, and gripping his shaft.

He was thick and hot in my hand. A ragged breath caught in his throat as I leaned in and licked the head. Van's eyes never left mine as I took him into my mouth. I worked him to the back of my throat, groaning when he thrust his hips. I cupped his balls, and his fingers twisted in my hair. I pulled back, stroking him as I buried my nose in his groin, licking a line down to his sack, wanting to taste him, wanting to give him everything.

"Lie down," I said, my voice husky and more demanding than I'd meant.

But he didn't hesitate.

Van sat on the bed and situated himself onto his back, his head on his pillows. I crawled over his body, leaving soft kisses on his hip, his abs, his chest, his neck, his cheek, the corner of his mouth. It was the first time we'd ever been like this. Every time we'd had a chance to be with each other, besides the two times we'd showered, it had been fast and messy and half-dressed. Hands and mouths, never skin on skin like this, laid out with the weight of my body over his.

"This okay?" I asked, resting my hands on either side of his head.

"Yes." He raised his head and we kissed for what felt like hours.

Wet and deep, his stubble burning my chin and jaw, our cocks leaking against our stomachs, and every time I moved my hips, we'd shudder, a silent plea for more. I didn't want to rush him, didn't want to make him feel like I needed anything other than this, him beneath me, kissing me like I was his entire world. I wanted him to pace this, ask me, and when he finally did, it was like the first sip of water after a long run under the midday sun.

"Parker," he panted against my lips. Lifting his hips, he grunted as I rocked against him, our cocks rutting together. "Please."

I straddled his thighs, taking us both in hand, and he let out a desperate moan. Van pierced me with his gaze as I jacked us both, his bottom lip pinned between his teeth. I pushed us to the edge and stopped when we were both close to falling.

"Do you trust me?" I asked and his pupils eclipsed his irises.

"Yeah... I do." He sat up on his elbows as I moved.

I spread his legs a little, keeping my eyes on his, making sure I wasn't taking too much or pushing him for more than he was willing to give. He showed no signs of reluctance as I pressed his knees back almost to his chest.

"I'm not going to do anything you don't want. If you don't like something, tell me and I'll stop. Alright?"

He nodded, his cheeks and chest flushing with color. "What are you going to do?"

"Taste you." He was fully exposed, and I ran the pad of my thumb over his tight hole. "Here."

He shivered as he closed his eyes.

When he didn't say no, I leaned down and licked the length of his dick, sucking the head into my mouth. I teased his ass some more with my thumb, rubbing slow circles over the sensitive skin. My saliva trickled down his shaft, and I groaned when he reached for his thighs and pulled his legs back even farther.

"Fuck... look at you," I said and sat up, wanting to see his face. He stared back at me through hooded eyes, chest rising and falling with weighted breaths. "Van..."

I let his name hang in the air between us as I leaned over and kissed his stomach, his hip, his inner thigh. I took my first taste and he fucking whimpered. The sound was ringing in my ears, it made me lightheaded, and I wanted to hear it again and again. I worked him open with my tongue until he was writhing, a fist in my hair, and one tangled in the blanket. He kept saying my name, and I wondered if he realized it. Like a chant over and over. Parker, Parker, Parker. I wanted nothing more than to bury my fingers inside him, fuck him until my name was more than a whisper, and scratched at his throat when he cried out in relief. I let the tip of my thumb slip inside him, and he stopped breathing.

"Parker, I—" I sat back, and he lowered his legs, framing my hips. "I don't have any condoms."

"That's okay... we don't have to—"

"I've only been with one person, and I... if you want me to get tested, I—"

"Van..." I massaged the muscles of his thighs and he exhaled. "I don't think you need to be tested if you've only been with Lanie. Unless you think she cheated on you before the yoga guy."

"No... it was only that one time, but we were over after that." He lifted himself up onto his elbows. His hair still wild. It made me smile. "What about you? Have you been tested?"

"Yes... right after we started dating, actually. I get tested every three months or so if I'm... active." I squeezed his thigh when he lowered his eyes. "Hey... what are you thinking?"

"That I ruined the moment. I have no idea what I'm doing, and you're experienced, and I feel out of my depth. What you just did, it felt..." He fell back onto the pillow and covered his eyes with his arm. "It felt fucking amazing, and all I could think was, God, I want this, I want more, but then—"

"I had to go and slip my thumb up your ass?"

He started to laugh, his entire body shaking with it.

"Yeah," he said, lowering his arm, he caught his breath. Van sat up, resting his hands on my hips and dusted his thumbs over my skin as he spoke. "I want to... with you, and I know you like being the top, and I think I could, but I—"

"Do I prefer the top? Sure. But what I prefer the most is for you to be comfortable in what we do. You didn't ruin the moment, I'm always hot for you." I grinned as I held his face between my palms. "I want to kiss you, though. But if you'd rather me not because I—"

"Kiss me."

And I did.

I kissed him until his breathing evened out, until his lips were swollen when I pulled away.

"When you say prefer..."

I chuckled as I lowered my hands to his neck. "I like getting fucked too. I'm versatile like that."

Hell, his cheeks turned fire engine red. "Oh..."

"In fact, if you wanted, you could have all of this..." I waved my hand along the length of my chest to my dick. "Right now, if you asked me nicely."

His fingers pressed into my hips as a crooked smile lifted his lips. "Tonight?"

"Yup, all you have to do is ask, Van."

He brushed his mouth over mine, his tongue licking the seam of my lips, and I opened for him. Blood rushed to my groin again, filling me, bringing me right back to the flash point. The thought of giving myself to him, without any barriers, no condoms, I'd never done that before, it made my heart gallop.

"I want you," he whispered into the curve of my neck, kissing his way to my shoulder and back to the spot below my ear. "I just... I don't know how to—"

"I do."

I stole another kiss before I crawled off the bed. I'd left my jeans hanging over his desk chair. I dug into my back pocket, feeling his eyes on my skin as I pulled out my wallet. I opened it and smiled as I found the small packet of lube I'd stashed behind my insurance card last Pride. I'd gotten it at one of the booths, it was supposed to taste like donuts or something equally ridiculous. I didn't care. It only needed to serve one purpose. I made my way back to the bed, packet in hand, and laughed at the wide-eyed look on Van's face.

"What's that?" he asked as he rested his back against the headboard.

I straddled him again and grinned when his hands immediately went for my hips, his thumbs making those familiar passes over my flesh.

"Lube."

He swallowed.

"I see."

I kissed his cheek and then tore open the packet with my teeth. "Don't look so worried."

"You remember the whole I've never been with a guy thing, right?"

"I think I can recall you mentioning something about that," I said and placed another soft kiss on his lips.

Squirting the lube into my hand, I reached between us. Slick and easy, I glided my palm up and down his shaft, coating every inch of him until he was breathing hard against my lips. His hands fell to the cheeks of my ass, spreading them as he pulled me closer. His finger grazed my crack, and I moaned into his mouth.

Breaking our kiss, he found my eyes, and said, "I want to know what it feels like to be inside you."

"I want to feel you too."

I reached back, slipping a finger inside myself, and held onto his shoulder with my other hand for balance. My head tipped forward, my mouth opening on a silent gasp as I prepped myself for him. His curious fingers followed mine, and when I looked up again, I pulled out, letting him fuck me with his finger. I dropped my mouth to his, hungry for the taste of his tongue as he unknowingly brushed against my prostate.

"Ahh... fuck," I panted. "Right there, Van."

He pressed against it again, and now I was the one whimpering. One finger became two, then three. My entire body thrummed with need as he stretched me. I had to grab his wrist, stopping him before I came too soon.

"I think I'm ready," I said and dragged my teeth across his lower lip.

He moved his hands back to his favorite spot on my hips, his eyes hazy with lust. I kept my hold on his shoulder as I positioned myself over him. Van dropped one of his hands and wrapped it around the base of his cock. His jaw pulsed as I lowered my body, his gaze fixed between us as he guided himself inside me. I breathed through the initial sting, until he broke past the first ring of muscle. He grit his teeth, his gray eyes dark and hungry as our bodies melded together. Fully seated inside me, he reached up, caressing my jaw with his thumb, the pressure of it almost bruising as he claimed my mouth with a forceful kiss. I tried to move my hips, needing to feel him, but he held me in place with a firm grip.

"Wait." He rested his forehead on mine. "Or I'll come."

I breathed, a laugh itching at my lips. "I'm that good?"

"Too fucking good."

"I've never done this before," I admitted. "Without a condom."

He met my gaze. "No?" I shook my head, loving the smile forming on his lips. "A first for both of us, then."

I started to move, and his nails dug into the flesh of my ass. I hoped I'd still be able to feel the sharp bite of it in the morning.

"Slow," he whispered, and I held his shoulders as his mouth met mine.

I pushed all my desire into this kiss, trying to pace my body, focus on his tongue and how it danced with mine, how each breath he took became one of mine. How his skin was silk under my fingertips, how the heat of his body, like his breath, was my heat too. Van snapped his hips, driving into me again and again, and I grunted as I held on with everything I had. He lifted me, pushing me down onto my back. The whole "taking it slow concept" no longer applied, apparently. I was okay with that. Van teased my hole with the head of his dick, painting it, marking it with his pre-come before sinking back into me. He grabbed my thighs, pushing in at the perfect angle, and I arched my back. My toes tingled as he pounded into me, every loud groan I elicited egged him on. Van leaned down, a single drop of sweat dripped down his cheek to his lips, the salty taste of him bursting over my tongue as he kissed me. I bucked my hips, getting closer, my dick pinned to my stomach as he rocked into me. His mouth was savage, showing me a side of him I didn't think existed. He bit my neck, and my shoulder as I told him I needed more, told him how close I was, how I wanted him to fill me up.

"Fuck," he groaned, pulling out, only to fill me up again.

A needy moan poured past my lips, and I tried to reach for my dick.

He leaned back, granting me access, and fucked into me harder and faster as he watched me jack myself off. I came first, crying out, my neck straining as my head fell onto the mattress. My orgasm seemed to never end. It splashed hot against my skin, my legs shaking as Van's eyes locked on mine. I raised my head, wanting to watch him while he fucked me. He said my name, Parker, Parker, Parker, his head lulling backward as he groaned. His hips jerked, uncoordinated as he flooded my body with the heat of his release.

"Van. Look at me."

He raised his eyes, emptying inside me, taking up a space that only belonged to him. His face marked with pink, his wild hair, his stormy eyes, his tight jaw, his swollen lips, his strong hands, all of it, I wanted to keep it inside of me too. Out of breath, he tried to slide over to the mattress.

"Not yet." I raised my hand and he leaned down. With my palm on the back of his neck, I pulled him to my chest. His cock half soft inside me, I kissed him. It was sloppy and sated, and we both laughed when I licked his nose. "I think I could get used to bottoming."

Our slick skin stuck together as he pressed against me, mess and all. After a couple of seconds, his smile faded into something more serious and bewildered. "Sex has never been... I mean, it's been..." He sighed, exasperated. "It's never felt like this."

"Like what?" I asked and hid my wince as he pulled out.

Van rested on his side, and I turned to face him. He touched my cheek, and I pushed the sweaty strands of hair off his forehead. "This was different."

"Because I'm a guy?"

"That," he said and smiled. "And it was... I can't think of how to explain it."

"Because I'm the best. You're never fucking a woman again. Parker is the god of all things dick?" I bit back a smile when he blushed and scrubbed a palm over his face. "Is any of that fitting the bill?"

His shoulders shook as he chuckled. "You're so humble."

"I try."

"This is the most vulnerable I've ever been," he said, and the urge I had to tease him vanished. "Even with Lanie, when we first started dating, it didn't feel like this. Maybe it was because we were just kids, and the gravity of it all wasn't there. And over time, things changed... faded. But every time I'm with you I feel like I'm chasing this feeling, and it's big, Parker. And tonight... I finally caught up to it. I've never felt this good. Ever."

I wanted to make another joke. Tell him he was dick drunk. Make it seem like what happened wasn't that big of a deal. But it would be a lie. Because I'd never felt this good either.

When I didn't immediately respond, Van fell onto his back and stared at the ceiling. "Did I say too much? I said too much. I do that and—"

I scooted closer, resting my cheek on his chest. My hand splayed over his abs, my load drying on our skin. "You didn't say too much. I'm processing."

"That doesn't sound good."

I gently slapped his stomach and he laughed. "Let me think. My brain is all fuzzy. I just came harder than I ever have in my life."

"Really?"

I pinched him this time and he swore. "Yes, really." It was quiet and I would have bet money if I sat up, I might've seen Van's first-ever smug smile. I took a deep breath and tried to assemble everything I wanted to say. "That big feeling..." His fingers trailed over my skin and along my spine. Back and forth. Lulling me into a place of contentment, a place of safety I'd never had before. "I have it too. In so many ways."

"How do you mean?"

"I've never really had a serious boyfriend before. A serious anything. You've given me that. All of it. Today, when I met with Anders, you know what he said?"

"What did he say?"

The tips of his fingers continued to move, mapping every line, every sharp edge as I spoke. It made it easier to be honest. "He told me I was too green. That my prose was all over the place, and that at times I could be over the top."

"Shit. Parker, I—"

"No... listen. He told me I had a lot of growing to do, but underneath all the chaos... I was a shining light." *A shining light.* My throat felt thick. "He told me I had more talent in one sentence than some authors have in an entire novel, but I had to learn how to craft a story. He told me..." I inhaled the scent of Van's skin, loving how it mixed with the smell of our sex. "He told me... You believe in me... and that it was rare for you to put yourself on the line like you have for me. He told me that he trusts you. And that he wants to help me meet my potential."

"He said that?"

I raised up onto my elbow and stared down at him. I cataloged the curve of his lip, the dip of his nose. "He did. And it terrifies me. I want to be everything you think I am, Van. I want to be worthy of your trust. And it might sound stupid, because it's just sex, but it felt like you trusted me. It was more than a promise of words."

"You *are* worthy." He cupped my cheek, and I leaned into the touch.

"Am I? Everything since I've met you feels unreal."

"You are... When I told Anne about you, she said she's never seen me this happy. She's a kid, but she sees it, sees us."

"Anne is pretty smart," I said, smiling like an idiot.

"The smartest." He touched and traced my lips. "You don't have to be everything, Parker. You're already amazing. You're enough, as you are."

"As I am."

"Yeah." He sat up, holding his weight with his palm as he kissed me.

It was tender and rough and overwhelming. Everything between us spun, all the pieces we'd handed to each other. It was immense and surreal, but underneath all the chaos there was a shining light. Me and him. And I was enough. I was enough.

Chapter 24

DONOVAN

We both smiled at each other in the mirror, toothpaste covering our lips as we brushed our teeth. The morning sun filtered in through the bathroom window, muted by the opaque glass. Getting to wake up next to Parker after last night had made for one of the best mornings of my life. His warm skin under my palm, the soft golden hair on his arms beneath my fingertips. I'd thought I'd been dreaming, thought everything that had happened, everything we'd shared had been something I'd conjured up. But he was here. Here with me in my bed, his smell on my sheets. Here with me in this bathroom, his blue eyes sparkling with mischief as we both stood there unapologetically nude. Our reflections explicit. His skin marked by my teeth, mine by his nails. We'd fucked again this morning, half-awake and groggy in the shower. Parker had given himself to me, given me his trust and his patience, and God, I was falling. Falling for him. For this. The idea of sunny mornings, and eager lips, and shared glances. I wanted this. I wanted to give myself to him, even if it scared me, even if I wasn't sure if I could take it. I wanted to try. For him.

"Stop it," he said, his voice muffled around his toothbrush. He leaned down and spit into the sink. Raising his eyes, he stared at me through the mirror as he turned on the faucet. "Stop thinking so hard or you'll ruin our postcoital buzz."

"Our what?" I asked, leaning down. I spit into my own sink, chuckling as I turned on the faucet. "I swear, some of the things you say…"

We both rinsed and spit again. It was all very domesticated. It made me smile.

He rested his hip against the counter and faced me. I tried, unsuccessfully, not to look at his dick. When I lifted my gaze, I was met with a self-assured smile. He ran his hand over his abs, his stomach muscles contracting, and if he didn't have things to do today, I'd never let him leave this house. Or get dressed. His body was art.

"Now I *have* to know what you're thinking," he said, and I rubbed the back of my neck.

Of course, my face flushed.

"I wish you didn't have to leave so soon." I took a step toward him. "If I could, I'd figure out a way to keep you here all day." One more step and my hand was on his hip. I couldn't get enough of the way his skin seemed to make my own tingle. Smiling, I said, "I liked waking up next to you."

He raked his fingers through my hair, his eyes falling to my mouth. "Is that all you were thinking about?"

My knuckles dusted the ridges of his abs. "I might've been thinking about how nice it would be to have you naked all day too."

"Mm. I could be into that." His lips were wet and minty as he kissed me. Parker pressed his fingers into the nape of my neck, and my tongue slipped into his mouth. After a minute or two, we were both breathing heavy, our chests together, our bodies ready for more. "Hell," he groaned, resting his forehead against mine. "I could stay. I could—"

"You have to go. You have a play to write."

He exhaled, his hot breath tickling my lips. "I don't think I can."

Leaning back, I said, "You know you can."

"Because I write scripts all the time."

I tugged him close, ignoring his sarcasm. "I'll help you. We can make it smaller. Focus on Silas and Pan. Your play doesn't have to be a perfect adaptation of *The Lost Boys*. Make it your own."

"You'll help me?" he asked, and Jesus, the look on his face.

It made my heart trip all over itself. He stared at me like I was something to be revered.

"Park... I would love to help. Every night, if you want."

His crooked grin was back in full swing. "Every night? Do I have to be naked?"

"It's not a requirement, but..."

Parker pinched my ass, and I swore, leaning down I bit his shoulder.

"Ow," he groaned, and I laughed.

"Stop fucking pinching me, then."

We were teenagers.

I cupped the side of his cheek. The pad of my thumb grazing his lower lip. "I could lower the number of assignments I give you in class. Lighten your burden."

"No way. No special treatment," he said, his smile gone. "I'm serious, Van. That's when shit gets messy. Alright?"

I nodded, knowing he was right, hating myself a little for doing the one thing I promised myself I wouldn't.

He covered my hand with his. "I don't want you to have a reason to regret us. If things don't—"

"Yeah, I get it." I stepped back, the light and easy feeling of the morning drifting away.

Reality was a much heavier weight to carry.

The truth was Parker was my student. He was the first guy I'd ever been with, and he was much younger than me. We'd only been together a short while.

The truth was things might not work out.

That truth hurt me the most, because if I were being honest with myself, I might've already fallen for him. Not fallen in love. Not yet, at least. But shit, I could see it. It could be waking up with him and toothpaste kisses. It could be watching him grow as an author. It could be waffles with Anne on the weekends, and late-night movies with my head in his lap. The possibility of us was what made me force a smile when he called my name.

"Van..." he said as I walked toward the bathroom door. "What just happened?"

"Nothing." My smile held, but he wasn't buying it. I stood in the doorway and wished I hadn't put that worried look on his face. "The thought of us not working out, of having regrets. It's not a great feeling. Especially after..." He opened his mouth to say something, and I held up my hand. My smile was real this time. "But that's how this works, right? Dating? Boyfriends. We see how it goes, and if we're lucky, we find the person we've been looking for."

"Am I that person for you?" he asked, prowling toward me with a cocky smirk, but his voice had vacillated enough, I noticed.

I kissed his cheek and chuckled, wrapping my arms around him. "I don't know. But I can't lie and say I don't hope that it's you."

His forehead rested on my shoulder, the heat of his body stealing away any lingering chill from the air. "It feels too soon to think it, but I hope it's you too."

We stood like that, breathing each other in, neither of us ready for that fucking reality pulling the hands on the clock.

"Can I make you breakfast before you go?" I asked, and he lifted his head with a dopey grin.

"I will always say yes to food."

Laughing, I let go of his waist and turned into the bedroom. "Do you have time?"

"No, and yes. Rachel won't care if I'm late. I'm not technically working today anyway."

I pulled out a pair of underwear from my dresser drawer and slipped them on. "And the new director will be there?"

"Chance," he said, slipping into his pants. He didn't have on underwear. And now I'd be thinking about that all day. Perfect. "I met him on Thursday, seems decent enough. He's worried about the cost of the play, even though we told him we'll get sponsors."

He sniffed his shirt and wrinkled his nose.

"Want to borrow one of mine?" I asked, opening another drawer, I pulled out a simple blue cotton t-shirt and held it up.

"Thanks. I'm already having to go commando all day. Which is weird as fuck."

Or sexy as fuck.

"I could lend you a pair of—"

"That's okay," he laughed. "I draw the line at wearing another man's underpants."

"But you're okay with what you did with your tongue last night."

"Hey... I have standards." He took the shirt from my hands. "And don't act like you didn't like what I did to your ass last night." Parker leaned in for a kiss. Once, twice and he sighed. "I can't think about that, or I'll never leave, and I really want you to cook me breakfast."

His laugh made my stomach warm.

"Get dressed, I'll make you eggs."

"Of all the dirty talk, you picked my favorite kind."

"If that's true, what would you say if I asked to make you dinner tonight?"

"I'll be back at seven."

I pulled into the driveway of my parents' house. I hadn't planned on coming over today, but after Parker left, my brother had called and invited me over to their place for lunch. Apparently, Owen had some news he wanted to share with our family. I'd immediately called my gossipy-as-hell sister to see if she had any intel on said news. I'd hope it wasn't that he was moving away for a job. I hardly saw him as it was. If he left Atlanta, I didn't think we'd ever see him again.

Depressed by the thought, I stared at the red brick house we grew up in. It was one of the older homes in Milton, on the smaller side, but I loved it. I'd hoped to find something like it when I'd looked for houses after my divorce. This place, my family, they'd always be my home. On my way over, I'd thought about sharing my own news, and decided that I would. I wanted them to know about Parker. Maybe not all the details, but that I was finding myself, dating a great guy whom I hoped they wanted to maybe meet someday. Deep down, way below all my nervous anxiety, I knew my parents. I knew this house and its cluttered shelves and dusty family photos. Dad's books and Mom's old French romances. She'd been a stay-at-home, peanut-butter-and-jelly kind of mom, and my dad, he'd always wanted to make sure we understood how important it was to learn, teaching us like we were one of his pupils at Emory. They'd accept me. The words rang true in my head, and as I was about to open the door, my sister knocked on the window.

I almost jumped out of my skin.

"Shit, Olive."

"Are you hiding?" she asked, grinning. "Can I hide with you?"

She stood back as I opened the door. "You really have no idea what Owen has up his sleeve? The whole twin-to-twin thing isn't ringing any bells?"

"Nothing. It's unnerving." She linked her arm through mine as we made our way to the front door. "Do you think he's moving?"

"Shit, that's what I thought too."

We stopped, staring at his car parked in the drive. "He can't move. Mom and Dad would be devastated."

"Just Mom and Dad?" I asked, knowing her answer.

She glared at me with glassy eyes.

"He's a bastard most of the time, and he makes me crazy, but he's my second half, Vannie."

"Hey... don't call me that."

"I'm feeling sentimental, fuck off."

I huffed out a laugh and kissed her cheek. "He's not moving."

She sucked in a breath, and nodded, her hope palpable. "And what about you? Are you going to tell the parents about your boy toy?"

"Way to make it sound sleazy," I said as we started back toward the house again. "He's not my boy toy. He's my boyfriend."

She stopped suddenly, all wide-eyed and expectant. At this rate we'd never make it inside.

"Since fucking when. Last time you called me, you said it was casual. Why was I not informed the minute this label was created... unless. Wait, were you both in bed when—"

"Jesus, Liv. Can we not."

"Okay, okay." She pressed her lips together.

"I can't believe you sometimes," I said, and she was giddy.

I broke down and told her about what happened at the festival. About Anne and how she'd figured out that Parker and I were more than friends.

"She's such an observant kid, Van."

"I know. It's scary sometimes."

Olive shoved me in the shoulder. "Did you ask him to be your boyfriend after that?"

"Why does that sound childish?" I asked and she shrugged. "Yeah, Liv... basically. We talked about it last night."

"When he stayed over?"

"When he stayed over."

She crooned and mussed up my hair. "Aw... I can't wait to meet him."

God help us all.

When we finally made our way inside, we were greeted by the heavy scent of spice and peaches. I hadn't been over here in what felt like forever, but was instantly at ease as we walked through the house. Nothing ever changed around here. The same old wallpaper, and couches, with their ugly floral pattern and worn seat cushions that sat in the den. It doubled as my father's office, and as always, he was hiding away inside. Olive let go of my arm and headed for the kitchen as I popped my head in to say hello.

"What are you working on?" I asked and he lifted his head, his glasses sliding down his nose. A nose I swore got bigger every time I saw him.

"Oh, you know, this and that." I smiled at his familiar words. "No little monster today?"

"She's with Lanie."

"I see." He took off his glasses and set them on his cluttered desk. "Maybe bring her by next weekend? We need to finish that tornado puzzle she just had to have."

"I can make that happen," I said and loved the way his eyes lit up.

"Don't see her enough. After this semester, I'll be an old retiree. I need her to keep me young."

"Sixty-five is the new fifty."

He snorted, his bushy eyebrows dancing as he laughed. "Is that so?"

"It's the word on the street."

He clapped his hand on my shoulder. "Don't tell your mom, she might think I'm capable of renovating the guest bathroom after all."

"I could help."

He eyed me and I held back my laugh. "Let's go see what your brother has to say. All this fuss. He better not tell us he's moving, your mother will be—"

"Devastated. We all will be."

I followed him through the living room, and as the kitchen came into view, I smiled. Olive was sitting on the counter, her legs dangling like she was ten and not forty. Mom laughed at Owen, gripping his arm, she pulled him close. She was nervous too.

312

"What if he's gay," I said before I thought better of it, hoping like hell my dad's response wouldn't break my heart. It was a selfish thing to do. But I had to know.

"Lord, that's what your mother said to me last night. She always thought he and Shane were closer than they let on."

"What?" I asked, incredulous. "She thinks Owen and Shane..."

"Who knows. You know your mom. She loves her romances."

"You guys would be okay with that?"

Dad turned to face me, a flash of something I couldn't decipher passed over his expression. "He's our son, Van. And your brother. Family. It doesn't matter to us, and it sure as hell shouldn't matter to you who he—"

"Dad..." I interrupted, wanting to tell him right then and there about Parker. But I hesitated. This was something I had to tell them both at the same time. My mother would never forgive me if I told my dad first. "I don't care if he's gay. Not at all. As long as he's happy."

"That's all we want for our kids."

My eyes stung as he watched me. He'd probably kick my ass for dating a student, and maybe I deserved it, but he wanted me to be happy. And God, happy wasn't a sufficient-enough word for how I felt about Parker.

"I'll remind you of that when you're bitching at us about something." I gave him a lopsided smile as he elbowed me in the ribs. He reminded me so much of Olive.

"Come on, let's get this show on the road. I'm hungry."

Fortunately, for all of us, he didn't have to wait long. My dad could be a bear when he was hungry. Every time we got together as a family, we all had our roles. It was efficient. Olive had always overseen the drinks, Owen plates and cutlery, and I'd helped my mom with whatever loose ends she had. Which had turned out to be nothing too serious today. I'd helped her make ham and cheese sandwiches, and when the peach pie was ready, we all sat down to eat. It was quiet at first as we stuffed our faces, my mom throwing glances in Owen's direction every ten seconds. Olive kicked my foot under the table and nodded toward her brother. She'd never been very subtle.

I swallowed my food and wiped my mouth before I asked, "What's the big news? You're not moving, are you?"

Owen's face paled as he took a deep breath. I couldn't remember a time he'd ever been this anxious. Fuck. Maybe he was moving.

"No... I'm not going anywhere." He set his napkin down and cleared his throat. I noticed his hand was shaking. "I should have said something sooner, and fuck, I—"

"Owen," my mom gasped. "Please don't swear at the table."

Olive choked on a laugh, and I stepped on her foot.

"Sorry, Mom." He rubbed his brow and shifted his gaze, staring at me when he spoke. "I should have said something, and believe me, I've always wanted to, but I was... scared as hell." He held up his hand and my mother closed her mouth.

"Hell isn't even a swear word," Olive muttered under her breath and Owen rolled his eyes.

"Figures I couldn't get through this without messing it up. I'm just going to say it." He took a deep breath, his eyes never leaving mine. "Shane and I are engaged."

Our day at the zoo. Everything he'd said. It all clicked into place. I was an idiot. He'd tried to tell me.

"I knew it," Mom crowed, her smile stretching wide across her face. You'd think she'd found out we won a million dollars. "I told you, James."

"Wait...what?" Olive stared at her twin. "Why didn't you ever say anything to me?"

Owen's throat bobbed and he rubbed his eyes with the heel of his hands. "Shit... Liv. I didn't know what you'd think, or if—"

"You know me better than that."

"May I remind you, my lovely daughter, that this is not about you." Mom gave my sister a sad smile. "It might hurt that he kept this from us, but imagine how he must feel, thinking he had to hide this from us for all these years. Owen..."

"I'm sorry, Mom." His voice cracked and she leaned over to hug him.

A tear ran down Olive's cheek, and my dad just smiled. I was stunned silent. Did I tell everybody now? Did that steal my brother's thunder? Holy shit, how hard had it been for him all these years?

"I still wish you would have told me. Our twin connection.... This whole time it was a big fat lie." She laughed and it was wet. "I love you. You know that."

"I know."

"You're getting married," she said, and he nodded.

The whole table stared back at him.

"Owen, I—" I swallowed, and he exhaled a shaky breath. "Congrats...This is... this is amazing news."

"Thanks, little brother." His smile was small, the secret between us connecting us in a way I would have never imagined. He gave me a private nod, a silent, *you can do this, too.* I wasn't surprised when he said, "You know, you never told me how that date went."

I laughed and mouthed the word fucker as my mom whipped her head in my direction. Owen hated attention. I should have known this would be a shared experience. There was no thunder to steal.

"Date? What is he talking about, honey? You're dating already?"

"Already? Mom, it's been over six months, the woman cheated on him. He's entitled to a little—"

"Thanks, Olive... for your support." I rubbed the back of my neck. "But I think I got it from here."

"What are you all going on about," Dad grumbled. "Why is everything such a goddamn secret?"

"I have a boyfriend," I said, and the collective gasp I'd expected from my parents never came. "His name is Parker. We've been dating a little over six weeks."

"They met online," Olive said, proud of herself.

"Online?" my mom asked. "Is that safe?"

"It went well, then?" Owen asked, his crooked smile back in place as he lifted his glass of water to his lips.

"Yeah..." I swallowed again, hating all the eyes on me. "It went well."

"He's a good guy?" The concern on Mom's face made my heart squeeze.

"So far, yeah. We're figuring it all out."

"But Lanie?" she asked.

"I'm bi-sexual."

She looked at my brother and he held up his hands. "What? I had nothing to do with this."

"I was going to ask you if you were bi-sexual too." If we weren't at the table, she would have added dumbass.

"Nope, gay as fu..."

"Don't finish that sentence, young man." Mom pointed her fork in his direction, and he pretended to zip his lips like a child.

"I'm still single and pathetic, if anyone cares," Olive added, and reached for the pie.

"God, you're not sleeping with your loser ex-husband again, are you?" Owen asked and she glared at him.

"No... I'm not."

"For now," I said, and she flipped me off.

"Do none of my children have manners anymore?" My mom threw up her hands, and my dad started to snicker.

He couldn't stop. Laughing so hard his cheeks got redder by the second.

"James," my mom admonished. "Have you lost your mind?"

He waved her off and caught his breath. Coughing a few times, he sputtered, "No, darling... but I have to say, this has been the best family meal I think we've ever had. Wouldn't you agree, Van?"

I couldn't stop the laugh from bubbling up my throat. I couldn't believe Owen, or I, ever doubted our parents. The love they had for us, it smelled like peaches and cinnamon and laughter and smiles, and it wrapped around all of us like a warm blanket.

Definitely the best meal.

The best morning.

The best day.

Chapter 25

PARKER

"What if we leave Wendy out completely?" Rachel suggested as she slid my notebook across the table. She scratched red ink over the outline I'd been working on all morning, and I might've wanted to murder her. "The play is shorter this way, and will fit the ninety-minute window we've been given. I mean, she's important, but Juno is a villain, too, let's stick to a less-complicated storyline."

I picked up my notebook and stared at the page, feeling overwhelmed again. The local high school was hosting the play this year, giving Pride House the biggest theater they'd ever worked in. "What if we just use the *Peter Pan* script you found online. The one all the schools use."

Rachel was not impressed. Her disappointment was heavyset in the furrow between her brows. "You pitched this idea. And I know you have a lot on your plate, but you love this book. Don't give up. Isn't that what we preach to these kids every day?"

I looked over to the other table in the common room where Marcos, Jake, Denny, and Makayla were sewing costumes. Marcos was yammering, and Denny had a cautious smile. Makayla looked frustrated, but Jake was right there helping them. The other kids were out back with Chance and the two guys he'd brought with him from Florida, building props from the sketches we'd found online. Hell. If I didn't believe in myself, how could I ever expect these kids to take what I said seriously.

"You're right." I sighed.

"About Wendy, or you being a whiny baby?" Rachel grinned, and I tore out the page with the outline on it. "What the hell, Park?"

"We'll start over. No Wendy."

"Wait... No Wendy?" Marcos glared at us. "Then, why the fu..." He stopped himself, his eyes darting around the table full of kids. Makayla giggled. "Why am I over here making a dress?"

"The Wendy arc takes up too much of the story." Rachel stood and walked over to the other table. "But I'm sure the dress can be utilized in some way." She lifted the sleeve and rubbed her thumb over the velvet material. "This is really pretty."

"Thank you." Marcos puffed out his chest with a dramatic flair only he possessed. "Your flattery will get you everywhere."

She laughed and shot me a look. "I'm going to head out back, see how it's going."

With Rachel out of the room and Marcos occupied, I had a moment to focus. Keeping in mind what Van had said to me about the play not having to be a perfect adaptation, I scribbled out a rough outline, and was happy with what I'd come up with. I pulled my laptop out of my bag, popped in my ear buds, and lost myself inside the words on the page. I didn't allow the negative thoughts to break through. All thoughts of inadequacy and fear were sequestered. I didn't think about formatting, and how I had no clue about stage directions. Instead, I thought about stars and kissing in the rain, lavender, and hot hands. My head was filled with ships and magic, Pan and Silas, and at times, I pictured myself as Silas and Donavan as Pan. An hour had passed, and I hadn't realized it until Marcos sat next to me and waved his hand in front of my face. I saved the document and pulled out my ear buds.

"You're kind of creepy when you write," he said. "You have this faraway look, and your lips move like you're talking but there's no sound. It's like you're in a trance or something."

I shut my laptop and yawned. "I zone out and lose track of time. I can't help it. Did you get a lot done?"

"We did." He ruffled his fingers through his curls and smiled. "Now I'm waiting on your slow ass to see what other costumes we need to make."

"You can write the play if you want."

"Sure... I'll get right on that. And you can slave away, hand sewing a dress for a character that no longer exists."

"Still feeling bitchy about that, huh?"

He stared at the pile of fabric on the other table. "A little. It's a great dress."

I chuckled and bumped my shoulder into his. "I'll make sure we use it. Thanks, Marcos, for all your help."

"You're welcome. I'll never admit to saying this... but it's fun. I wish there'd been a place like this when I was growing up. Maybe those teen years wouldn't have been so difficult.

"Things could have been different for so many kids."

"I mean, maybe there was something like this and I didn't know," he said. "Resources were shit back then. I'm glad Pride House is expanding."

"Sorry to interrupt," Chance stood in the doorway covered in sawdust. "Rachel sent me in to tell you both, if you want food, you better get your asses in the kitchen." He held up his hands when Marcos narrowed his eyes, and a small smile cracked through his rugged features. His sun-aged skin crinkled around his eyes. "Her words, not mine."

"Thanks, man, we'll be right there," I said, and he nodded.

Chance rubbed his thick, dark beard, a habit I noticed he had, and sawdust sprinkled onto the floor. "We could use your help after lunch. The kids want to start building the ship."

"As lovely as that sounds... I have... uh... a thing. Things, many things to do."

Marcos flicked my knee under the table when I barked out a laugh.

"Marcos isn't a fan of manual labor."

"Bullshit, *mijo*. I can build shit just as good as this overgrown tree hugger over here. But I just got my nails done." He wiggled his fingers. "Not wasting a perfectly good manicure."

Jesus Christ.

"Overgrown tree hugger?" Chance asked, and by his deadpan expression, I had no idea if he was insulted.

"Sorry, my friend forgets social cues sometimes." I stared at Marcos telepathically trying to tell him he's dead to me if I get fired. "He doesn't actually work here, he's just a volunteer, we could throw him out."

To my surprise, Chance chuckled, and I let out a relieved breath.

"It's okay," he said, pushing his hands into the pockets of his cargo shorts. "I'm not offended."

"See," Marcos waved his hand in Chance's general direction. "He's not offended."

"What about you?" Chance flashed his dark blue eyes in my direction. "Feel like pitching in?"

"Yeah... I can."

His assessing gaze shifted back to Marcos, and then drifted to the table where the costumes were laid out. "We all have our talents," he said almost to himself. The guy was kind of quiet, in a contemplative way. Not weird, but definitely an island unto himself. "Thanks for volunteering your time. I'm sure you have other things you could be doing on a Saturday morning."

"It's nothing." Marcos attempted a bored expression, but I could see the pride in the way he held himself. Shoulders back, legs crossed. "I'm glad to donate my services for the greater good."

Chance hummed and rubbed his beard again, his eyes trailing from Marcos's cream-colored sweater down to his heeled feet. He pointed a thumb over his shoulder. "Don't wait too long or the pizza will get cold."

He turned to head back to the kitchen, and once he was out of ear shot, Marcos said, "Don't look at me like that. That man looks like a bear, and not the fun, gay kind."

"What if he fires me? You know he brought those two guys with him to work here. We're overstaffed now."

"He's not going to fire you."

"He could."

Marcos flicked me again, this time on my nose, and I swatted at his hand. "He's not going to fire you, drama queen. You told me the man traveled all over the world building houses for homeless people. He doesn't have it in him to fire people."

"Can you please just behave like a normal fucking human being for once and not be an asshole."

"He's wearing cargo shorts, Park. Cargo. Shorts."

"You're such a snob. He's building a set, using power tools, what's he supposed to wear?"

"I bet his closet is filled with torn jeans and flannel. Or worse, cargo shorts and old tye-dyed shirts that say stuff like *Earth is our friend*." He wrinkled his nose. "He had dirt under his fingernails."

"Oh my God, he's been outside all day." I shoved him in the shoulder as I stood. "Don't be a dick. You know he's kind of hot under all that sawdust. He's tall... built... big blue eyes..."

Marcos gasped. "Not even."

"Please," I said. "He's totally your type."

"Now I'm insulted." Marcos stood, his oversized sweater slipping off his right shoulder. "Enjoy your pizza."

"Come on... don't go." I held back my laugh, my smile as apologetic as possible. "The kids will be sad."

"They know I have to go, I told them earlier. I have plans."

"You don't have plans. You're bailing."

"Okay, fine, I don't have plans, but I'm tired and I need a nap."

"A nap sounds good right about now," I said. "You think I could sneak out with you?"

"Even if you could, you wouldn't."

I groaned, hating that he was right. "I'll see you back at the apartment later?"

"Not staying at Van's again?" The smirk on his face was a warning. I wasn't going to like what he was about to say. "Please tell me you finally..."

"If you say deflower," I whispered. "I swear to God, Marcos."

He looked back at the door before leaning in. "Well... did you?"

"No. Not really."

"What the hell does that mean? Wait... maybe I don't want to know."

"I let him..." I scrubbed my hand over my face, wishing I wasn't having this conversation in the middle of my place of employment. "He fucked me."

"Really..." His smile grew. "Was it all romantic and fabulous?"

"Shut up." I started to walk away, but he followed me like an overzealous cat.

"Did he cuddle with you after?"

I didn't make it but a few steps into the hall before I stopped. Marcos gave me shit, but this was his way of checking in, his way of making sure I was okay. It was overbearing, but I would have done the same for him. I rubbed the top of my head and faced him.

"His daughter knows about us, she found out at the carnival last night. He accidently kissed me in front of her."

"No way."

"Yeah. And then she called me his boyfriend, I guess."

"Is he your boyfriend?"

"He is." My body betrayed me, and the goofy smile I'd tried to hide broke through anyway. I lowered my voice, my stomach all tied up as I told him the truth. "When I'm with him, hell, I don't know. It's crazy, but I can see this future, it's all there in front of me. In front of us. And I know what you're going to say."

"What am I going to say?"

"It's too soon, too fast. I'm being impulsive. That there's a difference between lust and love, and I know... I'm not in love with him, Marcos. But—"

"You're in love with him."

"Marcos."

"Park." He said my name and it was gentle. His usual snark was absent. "I *know* you. And it takes you forever to realize shit. And that's fine. Process your little heart out. But I see what I see. And I'm always right."

"Always?" I asked, grinning when he lifted his hand to his heart.

"Always, motherfucker. Now listen. I'm not saying you need to go and declare anything. You're right. It's too fast, and you're infatuated, and you may see this future, but love isn't a race. It's a steady climb."

"*A steady climb?* Christ, did you just make that up?"

"No... I remembered it from my daily affirmations app."

I dropped my head into my hands and laughed.

"Take it slow, *hermano*. You always rush through everything. It was true back in basic, and it's true now."

I raised my head and met his eyes. "I thought I was supposed to be the smart one."

"Um... No, that's me. You're the... no... I'm the hot one too."

I laughed, but then the silence stretched out between us.

"He sees me... you know."

"I know."

"It's a lot," I said. "I didn't think I'd care about him this fast."

Marcos draped his arm over my shoulder and smiled at me. "Just take it slow."

"A steady climb... got it."

"You never said if you were hanging with your man tonight." He lowered his arm. "If not, Davis and Alex invited us over."

"Thanks, but—"

He started to walk away, waving over his shoulder as he went. "Have fun at Van's."

I chuckled, turning toward the kitchen when my phone chirped.

I pulled it out of my pocket, and was glad Marcos wasn't here to witness my reaction when I saw Van's name on my screen. Fuck, I was smitten.

> **Van: *I tried not to text you like five times. My sister says I have no game.***

Cracking up, I typed out a reply.

> **Me: *Text me as much as you want.***

> **Van: *I'm supposed to give you space.***

> **Me: *According to your sister?***

> **Van: *No, my brother. I'm over at my folks.***

My pulse accelerated.

> **Me: *And you're talking about me?***

> **Van: *I came out to my parents today.***

"Holy shit."

I pressed the call button next to his name and the phone rang once.

"Hi," he said, and the sound of his voice sent a twist of warmth through my gut.

"You came out to your parents?"

His laugh rumbled through the speaker. "It's not that exciting. My brother came out first. He's engaged to his roommate."

"You're joking."

"I'm serious. He told them today, and then casually asked me about you in front of them. I figured since they didn't freak out about Owen, I might as well be honest."

"Damn. You seem okay? I'm guessing they took it well."

"Yeah" he said, and I thought I heard his voice break a little. "They did. It was good. God, I feel... at peace. I know for some the outcome is very different. I'm grateful."

I sagged against the wall in the hallway, wishing I was there with him. I wanted to tell him how proud I was of him in person.

"Hell, I want to kiss you right now."

"You can kiss me as much as you want tonight." In the background, I heard a female voice shout the word *gross*. There was a rustling sound, then laughter, and maybe a squeal. I laughed too. "Jesus Christ." He was breathless. "You'd think my sister was the baby of the family. I'm sorry about that."

"It's okay." I hoped he could hear the smile in my voice. "I'm just happy everything went like you hoped."

"It was better. I'll have to tell you more tonight because I have an audience now."

"Hi, Parker." A chorus of voices rattled through the phone, and my boyfriend groaned.

"I would like you to know that my siblings are both forty years old, but have evidently forgotten what it means to be an adult."

Marcos had told me to take it slow. And it was good advice. But my mouth opened, and my heart spoke. "I hope I get to meet them."

"My family?"

"Yeah. They seem fun."

"I'd like that," he said with a quiet laugh. "Though, I think you'd all gang up on me. So maybe not."

"I would never."

"I have a hard time believing that."

"I've kept Marcos in check this whole time. Give me some credit," I teased.

"Park." Rachel stepped into the hall. "Shit, sorry. There's like two slices left."

I lowered the phone. "I'll be there in a sec. Save them for me?"

"Only if you save me. Chance is talking sponsors again." She rolled her eyes. "Hurry up."

I raised the phone back to my ear. "Sorry, Van, I have to go. The new boss is stressing about sponsors again. Rachel won't feed me lunch if I don't divert his attention."

She stuck her tongue out at me and headed back into the kitchen.

"Yeah, of course."

"I'll see you tonight."

"Tonight," he said, and I heard him exhale. "And hey, Park. If you're short a sponsor, I can talk to Anders about having Lowe Literary pitch in."

"You don't have to do that."

"I know. But I want to, and Anders would want to, as well. He picks a charity every year to donate to anyway. Why not this?"

I'd thought about asking Van for help, but like I'd told him this morning when he'd mentioned my assignments, I didn't want to take advantage of him, or our relationship.

"Thank you... I mean it. But we should talk about it more when I come over."

"You're stubborn."

"You have no idea."

"We'll talk later, then," he said.

But before I could respond, I heard the chorus of voices again in the background singing, "Bye, Parker."

I didn't know my cheeks could ache from smiling.

Chapter 26

DONOVAN

The crisp November air clung to my cheeks as I stepped inside the classroom and switched on the lights. My heart skipped a beat as the room illuminated. The lecture notes from the professor who'd used the classroom earlier were still scribbled across the white board. I thought after my first class, maybe even the first week, the sensation, the excitement would have died out, but it never did. Every class started the same. My hands would get clammy as the students started to roll in. I'd worry my assignment or lesson plan would be boring and not well received, or worse, someone would fall asleep during my lecture. I'd only had a couple of students drop the class at the beginning, and I tried to remember that every time I got nervous. And as much as it shouldn't have, it always helped having Parker in the room. The secret smiles he'd send my way had given me the confidence to continue without missing a step whenever I stuttered over something, or when I'd get overly excited about one of the books a student had chosen for their paper. He believed in me as much as I believed in him.

When I signed up for the dating app at the end of August, I never thought I'd find something serious. I'd thought I would go on a few dates, be single for once, figure out what I wanted next, figure out who I was beyond Lanie, beyond being a dad, and maybe, if I was lucky, I'd find someone. Someone to let me figure things out on my own, someone to let me discover myself at a pace I could handle, someone who wouldn't rush me into something I wasn't ready for. Parker had done all of that and more. He helped me see myself through a clear lens, and when I opened my eyes every morning, I no longer questioned what I wanted. Parker was my next step, my new beginning, and tonight I was ready to give him everything, all of me. He never pressured me, never asked me for what I knew he wanted, and maybe it was kind of terrifying, the idea of giving him my body the way he had given me his so many times, but it also gave me solace.

I was distracted by my thoughts and missed it when the classroom door opened.

"Donovan..." Vivian Decker, the dean of the English department, smiled at me as she walked toward the front of the room. "Do you have a moment? I know it's poor timing." She checked her watch as I finished hooking up my laptop to the overhead projector. "I should have emailed you, but you know how it is... busy, busy. I'm glad I caught you, though, before the deluge of students arrive."

She held out her hand and I shook it, praying to whoever would listen she hadn't seen the way my fingers trembled. Paranoia spiked my pulse as my gaze flicked back to the door. Parker was always early on Mondays.

"Vivian... it's good to see you." My voice sounded steady enough, if only I could get my smile to work. I cleared my throat. "With the evening classes, I don't get to check in very often."

She lowered her hand, her ice blue gaze skated around the room before landing back on me. "I'm afraid that's one of the downsides of being an adjunct professor, but after this semester you won't have to worry about that."

"I won't?" My late lunch churned in my gut.

Did she somehow find out about Parker? Was she here to fire me? Jesus, fuck. She was here to fire me.

"I hope not." She smiled again. That was a good sign, right? "I'm going to observe you tonight. I've received excellent feedback on your midterm review from your students, and it's customary for new staff to have at least one or two of their classes audited, especially if we're thinking of offering a full-time position."

"I'm sorry, what? A full-time position?" I stammered, switching from worry to utter surprise. "Are you serious?"

Full time? I couldn't afford to leave Lowe, and hadn't I promised Anders I wouldn't leave? What about Parker? Full time meant more hours on campus. No more evenings only. It meant more interaction with administration, and when Parker changed his major to creative writing next semester, it would all be too close, too risky. If they found out about our relationship, even if Parker was no longer my student, they'd fire me anyway. Or at least open an investigation as to when our relationship started. And I wasn't going to ask him to hide any longer than I already had.

Shit, why was I even thinking about this?

Because teaching had always been something I wanted, and never thought I'd have a chance to do. Deep down, I knew I could make the salary work if I truly wanted it to, and the only reason I had to turn down the offer was about to walk in the door any second.

"It's rare to have a professor with such high marks on their first survey, and..." She hesitated, her smile turning apologetic. "We're losing two professors after the semester, and to be honest—"

"You're desperate," I said, but my smile didn't fall.

"A little." She cringed. "But I can assure you, you would have been one of our first candidates, in fact, I haven't asked anyone else yet."

"Vivian, I—"

The door opened, and Parker walked in, his wide smile, usually a breath of fresh air, had sweat breaking out across my forehead. He stopped abruptly as she turned to look over her shoulder, and I watched as his Adam's apple bobbed in his throat.

"Have a seat... Mr. Mills. We can go over your assignment in just a moment."

The authority in my voice came out of nowhere, and I swear to God his lips twitched.

335

"Sure thing, Mr. Brody." He gave me a lopsided smile, and my collar became a noose.

I pulled open the top button on my shirt as Vivian turned to face me again. Pushing a strand of her black hair behind her ear, she said, "I'll take a seat in the back, but please, pretend like I'm not here."

"Easier said than done," I muttered under my breath as she walked away.

She chose the very back row, but even once the room was filled with students, she wouldn't be hard to miss. Parker waited until she was seated before he approached my desk with his notebook tucked under his arm. To make my life more miserable, he had on a black sweater that hugged every ridge of muscle in his arms and chest. His hair was damp, and I could smell his shampoo. He'd kept the sides trimmed short but hadn't touched the length on top since we'd started dating. When I asked him about the change, he'd said it was because he liked the way I ran my fingers through it when he gave me head. And holy shit, I couldn't think about that right now.

"Mr. Brody," he said, his smooth voice, his cocky smile, there was nothing I could do to stop my cheeks from filling with that familiar shade of pink. "Who's the chick?"

"That would be the dean of the English department," I whispered, and his smile died. "Did you finish the paper?" I asked, this time loud enough anyone in the room could have heard.

"Um... shit."

I heard her soft laugh, and Parker opened his notebook to a random page with equations and math notes.

"I think I want to change the ending," he said, and I knew he was talking about his play. On the nights he stayed over, we'd work on it together, and sometimes on the nights Anne was there too. Sometimes she'd chime in with ideas, and I loved that he'd listened to her as intently as he would have if she were an adult. "Everyone pretty much has their roles nailed down, but I don't want Silas to die."

"He doesn't die. Tink sacrifices herself so Pan can have his happily ever after."

"I know, but... what if Pan saves Silas, instead." His lips parted into one of my favorite smiles. It was the same smile he'd given me the first morning we'd woken up together, or whenever Anne told him some amazing fact about the weather, or when his best friend said something outlandish in class. It was one-hundred-percent real and unfiltered. "What if Pan sacrifices himself. Tink will still give up her magic and sacrifice her life, but it will be for both of them, which makes more sense anyway."

"One last grand gesture to show Silas how much he loves him," I said. Parker wet his lips, and God, I wanted to reach up and brush my thumb over the curve of his mouth. "I think that's very romantic, Mr. Mills."

"Maybe we can talk about it some more after class?" he asked as a couple of students walked in.

"I think that's possible." I lifted my head and noticed Vivian had her phone in her hand, her attention glued to the screen. "I have something I want to go over with you as well."

"Oh?" Parker took a step toward me as another group of students walked in. "What's that?"

His spiced soapy scent was thick in the heated air between us. My body reacted to him, not giving one single shit that the room had begun to fill with students, or that my boss was only a few rows away. Half hard, I took a step back and moved behind my desk.

"I'll see you after class, Mr. Mills."

He rapped his knuckles on the desk before making his way to his usual seat. I tried, unsuccessfully, to pretend Vivian wasn't there as I pulled up my lesson on the laptop. A few minutes passed as I read over my notes and wiped down the whiteboard. When I turned around, the seat next to Parker was no longer empty. Marcos had shown up, and already had Parker laughing about something. I hadn't had a chance to spend any time with Parker's friend, and I thought maybe that was a shitty boyfriend thing to do. Anders and Ethan were having dinner with us tonight at my place, maybe I should invite Marcos too. I had a few minutes to spare before class started, plenty of time to shoot off a quick text.

Me: Do you think Marcos would want to have dinner with us tonight?

Parker: Are you sure?

Me: I wouldn't have asked otherwise. I want to know your friends.

I pressed send and glanced up in time to catch his small smile.

Parker: He said sure.

Parker: He also said he's not into threesomes.

Me: Did you actually ask him?

Parker: No. Not yet.

I coughed to cover my laugh, even though the room was buzzing with conversation.

Parker: But he'll be there.

I set my phone on my desk and counted backward from ten. The class quieted down as I lifted my gaze and surveyed the room. Vivian watched me intently, but I gathered my nerves and pushed them aside.

"Should we get started." And all eyes were on me. "*The Colossus* by Sylvia Plath..." I blinked, trying to remember what I was about to say, when Parker raised his hand.

"Yes, Mr. Mills."

"It's depressing," he said, and the class laughed.

"Why is it depressing?" I asked, eager for his interpretation, hopefully Vivian Decker couldn't see just how eager.

"I think she's talking about herself," he said.

"I think she's talking about her father," Lydia, one of my less-vocal students argued, and I leaned against my desk, thrilled she'd decided to engage in the discussion.

"I think it was her husband," another student said.

I took a chance and gave Parker a soft smile. He nodded, rubbing the back of his neck as he spoke. "Maybe it's about all of them. *'The sun rises under the pillar of your tongue. My hours are married to shadow.'* Maybe she doesn't feel seen. She talks about being put back together in the beginning. Maybe she thinks she can't be whole because of all these things in her life that hover over her?"

"Maybe," I said. "Poetry is unique, in that only the author will ever know it's true meaning, yet we can try to reflect inside the words, see what we see in ourselves, make it what we want it to be. Lydia, however, is correct. *The Colossus* was written about Plath's father after his death."

I paced in front of my desk, asking students to tell me about their favorite lines from the poem, asking them to interpret them, to tell me what they loved, what they hated, did they even like it. And as time ticked by and the class neared its end, I forgot about Vivian, forgot about the full-time position I wasn't sure I wanted. Parker gave me all of his secret smiles, and I tried not to blush a thousand times.

Marcos actually jumped into the conversation, too, but mostly had negative things to say about Plath's work. "It was boring, I mean, what the hell is she even talking about? Was it about a farm? She lost me when she started talking about the barnyard."

"You're such an idiot," Parker teased him, but he grinned anyway.

"Be nice, Parker."

"I'm very nice, Mr. Brody." Parker leaned back in his chair and stared at me with a smirk on his face that would make a nun blush.

Jesus Christ.

I lowered my eyes to my laptop, choosing to ignore him. It was the safest thing to do. "Now... for Wednesday's assignment." The sound of papers rustling made me smile as the students prepared to take notes. It was much better than the groaning I'd started off with in August. "I want you to write a six-stanza, free-verse poem about a person you know. It can be anyone. It doesn't have to be a loved one. You can make assumptions about the barista at Starbucks if you like. As long as it's six stanzas long, I'm happy." The students started to put away their notebooks, and I raised my voice over the rising sound. "Also, your third book review is due before Thanksgiving break. That's two weeks, people."

I picked up my phone as everyone started to file out of the classroom and sent Parker a text.

Me: I'll finish up here and meet you at my place.

Parker: I can wait.

Me: Probably better if you don't.

Parker: Sure. See you later.

Vivian made her way toward the front of the room as I slipped my phone in my pocket and started to pack up my things. Parker turned to leave without meeting my eyes, and I assumed it was his way of being covert, but something about the look on his face gave me pause.

"Mr. Mills," I called out. "If you could wait a minute... we can go over the play like we discussed."

He hooked his thumbs under the straps of his bag and nodded. "Yeah, I can wait."

"I won't keep you," Vivian said. "But I wanted to tell you, the job is yours if you want it. I'll have my secretary send over the offer tomorrow."

"That soon."

"Don't worry. You have time to think it over," she said. "Enjoy the rest of your evening."

Parker passed her on her way out of the classroom. Once the door shut behind her, I relaxed.

"What job was she talking about?" he asked.

"She was here auditing the class. She wants me to take a full-time position."

"Why don't you sound thrilled?" Parker stared at me with the same unsettling look on his face from earlier. "Is that because of us... because of me?"

"No..." I lied and took his hand in mine. The room had emptied, leaving Parker and me alone. There wasn't another class after this, lowering the chance that anyone would catch us. "A professor's salary is nice, but not that nice. And who knows about benefits, and I only have a masters, I'd never get tenure. And maybe I want to look at other schools first."

He gently squeezed my hand before letting it go. "Van, you love teaching, and this offer could be everything you've wanted." *No, that's you.* "Don't leave Winchester for me."

"I'm not."

"You can't lie to me, professor." He leaned in and kissed my cheek. "Though, I do love a grand gesture, I don't expect you to give up on something you've always wanted. We'll figure it out. Stop thinking so hard. Look at the offer."

"You're bossy tonight."

"I get that way when I'm starving." He pressed a quick kiss to my lips. "Look at the offer."

"Yeah, okay. I will." I grabbed my bag off the desk, and decided we needed a change in subject. I didn't want to think about jobs and choices I didn't want to make anymore. "Is Marcos actually going to come?"

"He is. I texted him your address. He said he wanted to run home and take a quick shower. By quick, he means he'll be at least thirty-minutes late, and you should probably also know, he loves to overstay his welcome."

"I'll kick him out," I said. "I have plans."

"Are they sexy plans?"

"Perhaps."

Parker laughed and reached for my hand but caught himself as I opened the classroom door. A few students lingered outside. He pushed his hand into the back pocket of his jeans and smiled. But again, there was something else, an undercurrent of disappointment he'd failed to hide, and despite what he'd said, it made me want to email Vivian first thing in the morning to decline her offer before she even had a chance to send it.

Chapter 27

DONOVAN

"How come you never use the dining room when Anne is here?" Parker asked as he walked into the kitchen. "You guys should have tea parties and shit in there."

"Tea parties?" Smiling, I asked, "Does she seem like a tea-party type of girl to you?"

He shrugged, pulling open a cabinet and grabbing plates. "No, but I mean, how do you know if you've never had one? My sister used to dress me up in her princess dresses and make me have tea parties with her. It wasn't terrible. The cookies were decent enough." I laughed and he grinned at me as he set the plates on the counter. Wrapping his arms around my waist, he said, "I even wore a tiara."

"I think I need to see pictures."

"No pictures, unfortunately, but if you ever want me to get dressed up in something frilly..." He leaned in and whispered in my ear, his five-o'clock shadow scraping against my cheek as he spoke. "I could probably borrow something from Marcos."

"Mmm, as fun as that sounds, I prefer you naked." I curled my fingers into his sweater and pulled him in for another kiss.

"Careful, professor. We have company."

Ethan's voice carried into the kitchen from the small dining area next to the living room. If Parker and I moved a few feet to the right, we'd be able to see him from where we stood.

"Then, it's probably not a good time to tell you I want you to fuck me tonight?"

"Van..." His pupils were wide as he leaned back. "You can't say something like that to me and not expect me to throw everyone out, like right now."

"It's my house."

"And?"

I laughed and rested my forehead against his.

"Are you sure that's something you want?" he asked. His hand was on my neck, his thumb pressed against my pulse, and I wondered if he could feel how sure I was.

"I'm sure," I said and pulled back as I took a breath. "I trust you. Trust us. I want you, Parker. In every way."

I drew my thumb along the smooth curve of his smile, and he closed his eyes. "I don't know why, but I'm nervous."

"For you or for me?"

"Both," he said and opened his eyes. "What if you hate it, or I hurt you and—"

"Can we help with anything?" Anders leaned against the opposite side of the breakfast bar with Ethan at his side.

I dropped my hands from Parker's waist, wishing he could have finished what he was about to say. "I mean, if you want to help me open up these take-out boxes... I'm not sure I can handle it."

Ethan chuckled and walked into the kitchen. "I think I can help with that."

"Should we wait for your friend, Parker?" Anders asked.

"Nah... he's always late. He won't mind if we start without him."

"Help yourselves," I said. "I got a little bit of everything. Hope you like Indian."

"I don't think Ethan's ever had it before," Anders said, and smiled when Ethan's nose wrinkled.

"Nope, can't say that I have."

"He's not a very adventurous eater." Anders's eyes sparkled with mirth as he stared at his soon-to-be husband. "I took him to this restaurant in New York once. It was the first time he had sushi. I tried to get him to eat octopus."

"Fuck that," Parker said, and Ethan high fived him like they were old buddies and hadn't met only twenty minutes ago.

"There is no reason in the world to eat something with eight goddamn legs. Not unless it's the apocalypse and it means survival." Ethan grinned at Anders as he sighed.

"It's actually quite good," I said, and Parker raised his brows with a disgusted look on his face. "I'll have to take you out for sushi, see what you think."

"I'm going to have to pass on that date night, babe," he said with a lopsided smile. It was the first time he'd ever called me babe, and it caught me off guard. Like he could read my mind, he leaned over and kissed me on the cheek. The affection in front of my friends made my cheeks burn. We rarely got to be open like this in front of others, and God, I liked it. "The babe kind of slipped out." He spoke low enough that only I could hear him.

"I liked it."

"...think it's weird to eat something that's in the same family as a spider," Ethan said, oblivious to our side conversation.

"You eat crab." Anders' smile was triumphant.

"Fuck, I hate it when you're right." Ethan attempted a scowl, but Anders placed a kiss on his forehead.

"Love you, too."

The four of us dug in, scooping rice, tikka masala, and curry onto our plates. Ethan seemed skittish, at first, but when Anders fed him a piece of chicken, he added another scoop onto his dish. Once we were settled around my small dining room table, I poured the wine I'd opened earlier into my glass, and passed the bottle to Anders right as the doorbell rang.

"See... he's always late," Parker grumbled as he stood. "Sorry."

"It's fine, we've barely started," I said. "Sit down, I can let him in."

"It's okay. I'm going to give him shit." Parker leaned down and placed a chaste kiss to my lips.

As he walked away, Ethan chuckled.

"What?" I asked, and he covered his smile with his fist as he chewed.

He swallowed and took a sip of his wine. "It's different seeing you with him. You seem... I can't think of the word."

"Content," Anders cut in. "I've only seen you two at the office a couple of times together, but watching you two tonight... you seem lighter, less burdened. I'm happy for you, Van."

"Thanks..."

I didn't know what else to say. Since the beginning of September, Parker and I had been hidden away inside my house except for a few occasions we chanced going out together, or when we had class. Our relationship felt surreal sometimes, like we were trapped inside the top of an hourglass, and the time we had together was the sand sifting away into another reality, one that might not belong to us outside the bubble we'd locked ourselves in. Having everyone here, kissing Parker in front of my friends, we'd started to intertwine our lives. We hadn't shattered the glass, but we were getting there.

"Sorry I'm late, Mr. B. Traffic was ridiculous." Marcos smiled as everyone stared at him.

His hair was a tangle of curls and spilled over his forehead. He had on a crop top gray sweater and high-waisted jeans. The boots he wore added a few inches to his height, and instead of the usual dark eye make-up I was used to seeing him wear to class, his face was clean except for the pink gloss on his lips.

"This is Anders and Ethan, and you know Van. Everyone, this is my friend Marcos. He likes to be fashionably late because he's a giant attention whore."

"Like that's a bad thing?" Marcos pulled out a chair and sat down. "Besides, it takes time to look this good."

"Shit…" Ethan choked on a laugh. "He's worse than Wild."

"I noticed," Anders said, but his smile was amiable. "We have a friend who—"

"Wilder Welles," Parker interrupted as he sat down. "He's one of my favorite authors."

"Wait… are they talking about that twink author Mr. B invited to class at the beginning of the semester."

"Please, call me Van."

Marcos smirked. "I like Mr. B better. It makes you blush."

"Marcos, don't be a dick."

"Like I could be anything else, *mijo*." He blew Parker a kiss, and Ethan cracked up.

"Holy shit, I think I love you." Ethan wiped his mouth with a napkin. "I can't wait to tell Wild you called him a twink."

"Please don't," Anders said. "It's been quiet around the office. It's… tranquil."

"Nice word," Ethan said, and they both shared a private smile.

"One day I want to pick Wilder's brain, and if my best friend insults him, I'll never get the chance." Parker's gaze landed on Anders. "I still can't believe you want to represent me when you have clients like him."

"Parker..." Anders's brows dipped into his familiar, stern agent face. "Your talent is your own. And what I've seen so far rivals Wilder Welles's best work, you just have to learn your craft."

I rested my hand above Parker's knee and gave it a soft squeeze. "He's right. I can already see how much you've worked on your craft every time you send me something new to read. I mean...you wrote an entire play."

And like we weren't sitting at a table with several sets of eyes watching us, I brushed my lips over his. It wasn't chaste like earlier, or quick. Parker reached up, grabbing the back of my neck with his big hand, and opened for me. It might've only lasted a few seconds, or maybe it was longer, but when I pulled away, all I saw was him.

Someone cleared their throat, but it wasn't until Marcos spoke that the spell was fully broken. "Damn, Mr. B... that was hot."

"Jesus Christ," Parker whispered, but he was all smiles as everyone laughed. He shoved his friend in the shoulder. "Just call him, Van. Okay, asshole?"

Marcos held up his hands. "Whatever you want." He pushed the bottle of wine toward Parker. "Here, drink this and stop being a bitch."

"And how do you two know each other?" Anders asked.

"We served in the Air Force together," Marcos said. "I know... I don't look like the type, but a girl's gotta do what a girl's gotta do, speaking of which, who do I have to blow around here to get some curry?"

"It's not that kind of dinner party," Parker said, resting his hand on my shoulder as he stood. "Come on, I'll make you a plate if you behave."

As they both headed into the kitchen, I thought Anders was going to choke to death. He coughed, or laughed, I couldn't tell. Either way, I couldn't stop myself from smiling.

"Wow," Ethan said. "Can we keep him, Daddy?"

"Ha-ha." Anders shook his head. "I already have one drama queen in my life. We'll let Van keep this one."

Parker pulled back the blanket on my bed as I watched him from the bathroom doorway. Chilled, I rubbed my towel over my damp skin one last time before tossing it in my hamper. We'd taken a shower after everyone left about an hour ago. He'd already ditched his towel, standing naked, the muscled globes of his ass flexed as he moved. His back was chiseled, his broad shoulders carved to perfection. He was power and strength personified, and I was about to give him my body.

"What are you doing way over there?" he asked, giving me a crooked grin as he sat on the bed. "You look cold."

"Are you saying my dick looks small?"

Laughing, he said, "There is nothing small about your dick. And if you get your ass over here, I'll show you just how much I like it."

I hummed and made my way over to the bed, trying to ignore the lube sitting on the nightstand. Parker's warm hands cupped my ass as he nuzzled his nose into my groin. I threaded my fingers through his hair, and he leaned back.

"You don't have to," he said. "What we already have... it's good, Van. I'm good."

"I want to." I ran my knuckles across the arch of his cheek. "I want to at least try."

"And you swear to fucking God you'll tell me to stop if you don't like it?"

"I swear to fucking God," I said, his honest concern making me smile. "If it's too much I'll tell you."

His fingertips tickled the backs of my thighs as he spoke. "Consent is important to me."

"I know."

"And I never want to hurt you."

"I know."

"And—"

"Parker. I want you to fuck me."

He bit the corner of his lip, his blue eyes fixed on mine. I waited for him to say something, but all he gave me was a quiet nod of his head. He moved to the other side of the bed, leaving enough room for me to lie next to him. He propped himself up onto his elbow, a strand of his dirty blond hair falling into his eyes as he looked down at me.

"I meant it when I said what we already have is enough." I started to speak but he covered my mouth with his hand, and I chuckled. "Listen. I know what you want, and believe me, I'm fucking ready for it, but what you're giving me, what you've already given me, it means something to me." He raised his hand, tracing my lips with his finger. "And I wanted you to know that."

I took his wrist in my hand and kissed his palm. "It means something to me too."

It means I think I've fallen for you. It means I think I love you. It means have me. It means I'm yours.

Parker sat up and leaned over me, his hands on either side of my head. The weight and heat of his body covered me, and I was no longer cold. His lips pressed against mine, a low moan rumbling in his chest as I raised my hips, rutting against him. Wet kisses marked my neck, my chest, and my stomach. With one hand he hooked my right leg over his shoulder. He'd seen me like this before, but tonight his slow perusal of my body was more intense. Like kindling to a fire, heat ignited low in my stomach, rising with his gaze, it colored my chest and neck. Parker licked his thumb, his eyes never leaving mine as he rubbed it against my hole. I shuddered, desperate to close my eyes but wanting to keep them open too. He held my gaze as he lowered his head, as his tongue swirled around the tip of my cock, as he took me to the back of his throat.

"God," I gasped, my fingers twisting into his hair, my voice breaking as he swallowed. "Park."

He sat up and took a breath, pushing my legs to my chest. I gripped the backs of my thighs and gave in to the urge to close my eyes as the tip of his nose trailed through the hair on my legs to my groin. He licked a line down the length of my shaft, taking my balls into his mouth, and I moaned his name again. I almost dropped my legs, wanting to bury my hands in his hair, but when the hot pressure of his tongue pushed into my ass, I forgot to care about anything else.

"I love that sound," he said, and I realized I'd started to whimper.

He fucked me with his tongue, the soft intrusion almost too much to take. It wasn't enough, and I found myself muttering the words *more* and *please* the longer he tasted me, teased me.

"You want more?" he asked and crawled over my body.

I dropped my aching legs as he stroked my cock, pre-come leaking onto my stomach, and said, "Yes. Please... yes."

He reached toward the nightstand for the lube, and my heart gave two unsteady beats before finding its rhythm again. Parker bent down and kissed me, deep and sweet, but when I heard the click of the bottle opening, I froze.

"It's okay," he whispered the words into the corner of my mouth before he kissed me again. "Tell me to stop, Van. Tell me if you can't take it."

He kissed me and kissed me, his hand stroking me slow and slow and—I was on the edge. Parker moved in small increments of time and touch, and one second my lips were raw from his rough kisses, and the next my thighs and balls felt the burn of his stubble too. He tasted me again, this time with more aggression, until I was pulling at the sheets, until a cool, slippery finger pushed inside of me, and I cried out when it brushed against my prostate. He took his time stretching me, one finger, then two. I thought about all the times I'd done this for him, tasted him, filled him, and marked him as mine. I wanted it. Wanted to be his, marked and full and...

"Ahh..." My eyes slammed shut as he slipped in a third finger. "God, I..."

"I can stop."

"No, don't..." I took a few deep breaths as his other hand slid up and down the length of my dick. "Feels good."

He gave me time to adjust, sucking my cock, slow and slow and—I was on the edge again. When he finally pulled out, I spread my legs for him, and he knelt between them.

"Do you want me like this?" I asked.

"If that's okay with you?" He leaned down and I wrapped my legs around his hips, his lips grazing mine. I nipped his chin and he smiled. "I want to see your face."

"That's okay with me."

Parker reached down and grabbed the base of his cock, the head nudging against me, he said, "Promise... if I hurt you—"

"I promise."

He visibly swallowed, his jaw pulsing as he pushed his way inside my body. A spike of hot pain made me cringe and he stopped. "You good?"

"Yeah, keep going."

I breathed him in, inch by inch, the pain slowly giving way to something more, something overwhelming and full, and when he was buried inside me, his chest rising and falling with restraint, I finally understood what it meant to feel whole.

"Van..." he said, but it was more of a rasped whisper. "Can I move?"

"Yes... I need you to."

He gripped my hips, lifting me as he pulled out and pushed in, sweat breaking out across my temple and forehead as he found his rhythm. His eyes remained soft as he fucked into me, my moans filling the room as the head of his cock hit the exact spot I needed over and over again. Parker grunted, the low sound mixed with the slapping echo of our bodies, uncensored and uninhibited, as it surrounded me. My fingers dug into the muscles of his back as he leaned down, his mouth striking against my lips like a match. I held onto him, my dick trapped between us, the friction, his skin, my skin, and Jesus, I thought I might come without having to touch myself at all. Sloppy and hungry, my tongue pushed past his lips, and with my grip on the back of his neck, I thrust my hips, matching his pace as the edge he'd had me dangling from became harder and harder to hold.

"That's good," he said, "Fuck... Van... you feel so good."

He sat back and grabbed my thighs, slamming into me, stealing my breath. His pulse pounded under his skin near his throat, and I wanted to feel it against my lips when he came. I grabbed my dick, stroking it from root to tip, my climax building faster and more pronounced every time our bodies came together.

"Park... I need..." I groaned, my breath catching again in my throat. "I need you to kiss me."

He fell forward, holding himself up with his hands, leaving me room to get myself off as his mouth crashed into mine. I kissed his lips, his jaw, my teeth sinking into his shoulder as my orgasm ripped through me, spilling over my fingers and onto my stomach, and coating his chest. It kept coming, my moan just as drawn out and loud, my whole body trembled with it. Panting, I brought my lips to his pulse, my sticky hands on his hips as he came inside me. Parker's heat was my heat, he'd marked me like I'd marked him. Firsts and more kisses and sweat and more kisses, until he collapsed next to me, tucking his nose into my neck, and inhaled.

A few minutes passed, our legs intertwined, and every breath we shared brought us back down to Earth.

"I didn't hurt you, right?" he asked, and I turned onto my side.

Almost nose to nose, I smiled when he pushed my damp hair off my forehead. "I'll be sore tomorrow, but it was worth it."

Parker reached between us, ignoring the mess, and ran his hand down my chest to my hip. He tugged me closer, until my body was flush with his. My mess was his mess.

"Is it bad I kind of want you to be a little sore. At the risk of sounding cliché, I want you to think about this, think about us all day tomorrow."

"I think about you all day regardless."

He smiled, and it was the kind of smile I would package if I could. I'd open it whenever I started to doubt myself, or us, or anything, for that matter. It was sunlight breaking through a heavy cloud bank.

"You do?"

"Parker. At the risk of sounding cliché..." I held my breath and counted backward from five to one. "I... I'm crazy about you."

It means I think I've fallen for you.

"Yeah?" He leaned in, his gaze falling to my mouth.

"Completely."

It means I think I love you.

"Good, because I'm pretty fucking crazy about you, too."

It means have me.

"Good, are you going to kiss me now?"

"I always want to kiss you," he said and pushed me onto my back.

It means I'm yours.

Chapter 28

PARKER

The aquarium parking lot was almost completely full. When I'd finally found a parking spot, it was already thirty minutes past the time I was supposed to meet Van and his daughter. Anne's birthday was this past Monday, but since it had also been the week of Thanksgiving, Van wanted to wait until after the holiday to celebrate. If I hadn't had to take my mom and sister to the airport, I would have been on time. The fall breeze seeped through my thin sweater as I jogged toward the entrance. The last thing I wanted to do was ruin Van's birthday date with his daughter. Yesterday, when I'd stayed the night at his place, he'd invited me to tag along. It had been kind of a surprise that he wanted me to come. We'd been a lot more careful about how often we were in public after he'd gotten the full-time job offer two weeks ago. He'd tried to say he didn't want the position, but I'd told him he should take his time to consider it. The dean had emailed him the official offer, and as he'd predicted, the pay hadn't been comparable, but the college did offer an extensive benefits package. With my encouragement, he'd talked to Anders, and they'd both worked out a plan where, if Van decided to take the job, he could still work for Lowe, but with a smaller client list. He'd have the best of both worlds. He could do what he'd always wanted and supplement his income. The only thing holding him back was me, and the longer he went without giving the dean an answer, the guiltier I felt.

There was a small group of people milling around outside, and as I made my way around all the eager families, I spotted Van. My chest tightened as I stared at him. He stood out in his dark jeans and black sweater, his smile wide for his daughter. His cheeks and nose were pink from the cold, his hair a little wind swept. The only word I could think of at the moment was breathtaking. If I wasn't worried about the influence it would have on his decision about the job, I would have told him already how hard I'd fallen for him. For us. For Anne. I didn't care if we had to be careful or hide longer than we'd originally anticipated. I graduated in two years. Things between us might not last that long, but if they did, two years seemed like nothing after all I'd already been through. He was worth the two years.

"Park!" Anne practically tackled me as I approached them. "You're late."

Van's gaze was soft as I bent down and gave his daughter a hug.

"I'm sorry, little monster. I had to take my family to the airport," I said. "If I give you a piggyback ride, will you forgive me?"

"I think so," she said, and as she wriggled her way onto my back, she dug her heels into my stomach.

I might've grunted.

"You're getting too big for piggyback rides, sweetheart." Van laughed. "Park, you don't have to do that."

"I'm not too big," she pouted.

"Are you doubting my strength?" I asked him, a private smile curving my lips. "I'm pretty sure I could lift you if I wanted."

Like I did last night.

But I kept that to myself.

He blushed, stuffing his hands into his pockets, he said, "Should we head inside?"

"Can we see the whales first?" Anne asked. "Or the penguins."

"Penguins, we should save the whales for last," I said, and she rested her chin on my shoulder. "They're the best."

"Good plan."

The inside of the aquarium was packed wall to wall with large groups of people: families, moms and dads, and shrieking children.

"I thought everyone went shopping the Saturday after Thanksgiving," Van said as he scanned the crowded plaza. "I didn't think this many people would be here today."

"My sister and my mom went shopping for deals yesterday. Spent all day fighting for some rare toy for my nephew." I laughed. "Mandi said Mom almost got into a fight."

"Which toy?" Anne asked.

"Some robot thing, I don't know, kiddo. Definitely nothing worth getting into a fight over."

"Was your sister sad to leave?" Van asked me and I nodded.

"Yeah. But at least my mom flew back with her to help her pack everything up," I said. "They'll be back here with my nephew after the new year."

"I don't think I could have gotten through my divor—" He stopped mid-sentence, his gaze landing on his daughter. "I couldn't have gotten through everything without my family."

"She should have come home a long time ago. I'm just upset it took him leaving her to do it."

After his last business trip, my sister's shithead husband had come home and asked for a divorce. Guess he found some other chick he could manipulate.

"Who knows? Maybe she'll find someone new, someone who can change her life for the better."

A lump formed in my throat, and I swallowed past it, smiling as my stomach did a somersault. "Maybe."

Anne wiggled and I let go of her legs as she slid off my back. "*Look*, cuttlefish," she said and ran toward one of the display tanks.

"Thanks for inviting me along today." I leaned into him, watching as Anne set her hands against the glass. A squid-type fish swam by, and she turned to smile at her dad. "I like getting to spend time with you both."

His smile wavered. "I'm sorry we don't get to go out as often as we should."

"That's not what I meant."

"I know, but it's true. You shouldn't have to hide away in my house, Park."

I exhaled a sigh, wishing I wouldn't have said anything.

Wrapping my arm around his waist, I pulled him closer and tried to lighten his mood. "I don't know," I whispered, my lips brushing against the shell of his ear. "I kind of like getting you all to myself. In your bed, against the wall... and that was just last night. You've become quite the needy bottom."

He pressed his lips together as I pulled away, his skin flushing all the way to the tips of his ears.

"Parker." He breathed my name with a quiet laugh. "The shit you say."

"You love it."

His gaze flicked to my mouth and back up to my eyes. Van didn't have to say anything, the tether between us, that invisible, tangible thing that linked him to me and me to him, it was there, vibrating like a guitar string. I thought I heard it hum three unspoken words in the way his gray eyes lightened when they met mine. *I love you.*

"Parker, come on." Anne grabbed my hand. "Let's go into the tunnel."

Van released his hold on my hand, his grin slowly spreading as he watched me get dragged away. He was behind us when I saw her. She was at the entrance of the tunnel with two small children at her side. I tried to move Anne in the opposite direction before Van caught sight of her, too, but Dean Decker turned our way the exact moment he sidled in next to me.

"Oh shit," he said, and Anne giggled.

"*Dad.*" She tried to let go of my hand, but I held on tight.

"Hey, kiddo, let's... let's..." I watched in horror as the dean approached us, but her eyes were fixed on Van. "I want to buy you one of those giant stuffed whales."

"What?" Anne looked up at me confused.

"Um... I saw one, in the plaza. Come on, let's grab it before it's gone."

"But what about the—"

"We'll come right back. I don't want someone else to buy it." I started to move as the dean smiled at Van.

"Donovan," she said, and I turned away, practically dragging Anne like she'd done to me only a few minutes ago. "How funny, I was just thinking about you."

Out of the corner of my eye, I saw Van rub the back of his neck. "Vivian..."

"Come on," I said and forced myself not to look back.

"Why are you whispering?" Anne asked.

"I... I don't know."

She giggled again, looking over her shoulder. "Who's that lady?"

"That's your dad's boss at the college." I kept my eyes straight ahead. "Did you want the beluga whale or the whale shark?"

"The beluga whale," she said.

"Big, weird looking white whale for the win."

"They're cute," she argued, and when I looked down at her, I grinned.

The tension in my shoulders remained, but once we got to the store, the more at ease I felt. Maybe the dean hadn't seen me. And even if she had, I'd walked away. It wouldn't have looked like we were together. I could have just as easily run into Van like she had.

"That's a big stuffed animal," I said, and cringed when I looked at the price tag. But Anne blinked up at me with those big gray eyes and I was helpless. "Think it will fit in the trunk?"

"I hope so."

If not, I could always shove the fucker into my back seat.

One-hundred-and-twenty dollars later, Anne was the proud owner of Bobbie the beluga whale. We walked back out into the plaza and set the large toy on one of the benches. I was about to text Van, but he found us first.

"Hey," he said, avoiding my eyes. "What do we have here?"

"It's a beluga whale. Parker got it for me."

"Oh?" He lifted his gaze, but he seemed off. "That was nice of him."

I rubbed the top of my head, inundated with anxiety. I couldn't stay. I couldn't take the chance of her seeing us together. "I... wanted to get her something since I can't stay."

Van's chest deflated as he nodded. "That's right, I forgot you had—"

"I have to go over the lines with some of the cast at Pride House. The play is only a couple of weeks away. We still have a lot to nail down," I said, hating the crestfallen look on Anne's face.

Van was distracted, looking around the room.

"But you just got here," she said. "What about the whales and the penguins?"

"I know, and I'm sorry I have to leave. I wanted to make sure you got your present," I lied. "But I guess I should get going now."

Van finally looked at me. "Okay."

"Will I see you later?"

"Yeah... I'm taking Anne to Waffle Love for dinner, but you can come over for cake after. If you want." He spoke, but his voice sounded miles away.

"Call me when you're back at the house?"

"I will."

"Happy birthday, little monster." I reached down and hugged Anne. "Hope you can fit this thing in your car."

Van gave me a small but real smile. "I'll make it work."

I stepped toward him unconsciously and he stepped back, taking Anne's hand. It was stupid, he was only being careful, but I hadn't expected it to hurt as much as it did.

"See you tonight," I said, and reluctantly walked away.

I'd had the whole rest of the day to stew about the run-in

with Dean Decker. To wonder what was said. If she knew. If Van was in trouble. If I was making a bigger deal out of all of this than I needed to. If she hadn't audited the class, would she have even known I was one of his students? I mean, who checked that shit anyway? I wasn't about to text Van and interrupt his time with Anne just so he could talk me down. My only saving grace was that Marcos had been at work the entire time. I didn't have it in me to fake my way through the afternoon. But it was close to seven-thirty, and I knew he'd be home any minute. I stared at the ceiling, thinking over the past few months. I'd never thought I would fall in love with Van this soon. But I had. I'd told myself I didn't mind if our relationship had to remain a secret for now, and it had been an easy thing to believe because when we were together, it never felt like hiding. Today was the first time I'd gotten a taste of what it would be like if we stayed together long term while we were both at Winchester. It fucking sucked. I hated walking away from him, hated having to leave because he could lose his job, lose an opportunity he'd wanted for so long. But I hated the idea of not being with him even more.

I rolled out of bed and grabbed my phone and wallet. I wasn't going to let Van overthink this. It was reckless, and maybe a little selfish, but as I picked up my keys, I decided I didn't care. I wanted to be there when Van got home. I wanted him to know I wasn't going anywhere. Twenty minutes later, I pulled into his driveway, and when I saw his car, my confidence waned. He'd said he'd call me, and he hadn't. I stared at his front door, my heart pounding out fast, erratic beats.

I'm crazy about you.

I sucked in a breath remembering the words he'd told me the night he'd given himself to me. He wanted me here.

I got out of the car, wiping my hands on my jeans as I stepped up onto the porch. Knocking twice, I waited, my stomach twisting and turning until he opened the door, until he smiled at me softly, until he tilted his head and said, "Hi."

"You didn't call."

His throat bobbed, his grip on the door handle tightening as he spoke. "I was about to."

"Oh." I wet my lips. "I was worried about... everything."

He stepped outside and closed the door. "Park..." Running a hand through his hair, he said, "Vivian didn't see you. At least, I don't think she did."

I exhaled the breath I'd been holding since I walked out of that fucking aquarium. "That's good?"

He didn't speak right away, and I swore I could hear the wheels turning inside his head. "That's how it would be for us, Parker. Every damn time. The college policy is clear cut. We aren't supposed to be together, and if I take this job—"

"Van, stop."

"Let me finish what I want to say." The irritation in his voice was unexpected.

"I'm sorry."

He pushed his fingers through his hair again. "I can't have both. I can't have you and work at Winchester."

"Why?"

"You know why."

"I don't care about hiding. I can handle it."

"You shouldn't have to handle it," he said, throwing up his hands. "I can't have both. If I stay at WSC, I can't see another way around it. We'll both end up getting hurt."

"I'm twenty-four years old, I think I can decide for myself what's best for me. You have to stop worrying about me."

"I never meant for any of this to happen. I never meant to fall for you." He blinked a few times, and my heart was on fire. "If I had known who you were when I met you online, I would have never pursued this, and maybe I should have walked away. But getting to know you... being with you has been one of the best things to ever happen to me."

I took a step toward him, and when he didn't back away, I closed the distance. My fingers clutched the sides of his sweater. "I care about you. About us. About Anne. My past... hiding... it isn't an issue. What we have, it's not like anything I've had before. Take the job, Van. I don't need you to protect me. It's my life."

"Your life is my life too." He raised his voice, and I dropped my hands as he stepped away from me. "And I won't let you do that, I won't let you hide again, not for me. It's not fair to either of us."

"Daddy." Anne stared at her father, the door barely cracked open. "Why are you yelling?"

"I..." He closed his eyes for a brief second, trembling as he exhaled. "It's nothing, sweetheart. I'll be inside in a second."

Her eyes bounced between the both of us. "But I thought Parker was having cake too."

"Anne... go inside, alright? Give me a few minutes."

It was the sharpest I'd ever heard him speak to her.

She shut the door, and the stillness that descended was unbearable.

Your life is my life too.

"Van..." The ache in my throat tried to render me silent. "If this is about you losing your job, losing a chance at what you've always wanted, regardless of how I feel, I'll walk away. I'd never take that from you. But if you turn that job down, to protect me, then you're an idiot. I don't need you to sacrifice this job for me. I just need you. I know what I want, and it's you. I'm not ready to let you go."

His gray eyes were silver, shining under the moonlight as he stared at me. "And I can't ask you to sacrifice two years of your life for me."

"I'd sacrifice more... for you."

"I could look at other schools."

"What if you can't find another permanent position? You'll resent me."

"I won't," he said and reached out, grazing my wrist with his fingertips.

"You will. Take the job, Van." My legs like lead, I struggled to do what I had to. I backed away from him and stepped off the porch. "We've only been together since September, what is a few months compared to a lifelong ambition? I'm not worth that."

"That's not—"

"This," I interrupted and motioned between us, loading the lie to the tip of my tongue. "Is not worth all of that."

"Parker..."

"You don't want me to sacrifice two years, and I don't want you to throw away an opportunity you might not get again. You know how I feel. You know what I want. When you figure out what *you* want, let me know."

I turned to leave, hoping like hell he'd stop me, like I had the night we first met. I wanted him to say, you're right, I'll take the job, I want this, I want you. But when I got to my car and looked back at the porch, he was gone.

Chapter 29

DONOVAN

Three days.

Seventy-two hours.

Four-thousand-three-hundred-and-twenty minutes.

And I was miserable.

"Dad." Anne stared at me from across the breakfast bar. "You're sad."

I shook my head trying to remember what I'd been doing. "I'm okay..." Anne's math homework was spread out in front her, and I exhaled. "What problem were we working on?"

"You're sad," she said again, and this time I noticed the quiet strain in her voice. "Is it because you and Parker had a fight? Mom had a fight with Matt a few weeks ago and he bought her flowers. Maybe Parker likes flowers."

I forced a tired smile. I hadn't slept well since Saturday. I'd argued with myself so many times. *Call him. Don't call him. Text him. Give him space. I'll talk to him in class.*

He hadn't shown up.

He wasn't there.

Fuck, my chest hurt.

"I don't think flowers are Park's thing, little monster."

"You could invite him over. Tell him you're sorry for yelling."

"Sometimes saying I'm sorry isn't enough."

"Why?"

"Anne... you shouldn't be worrying about this. It's adult stuff, okay?"

Her brows knitted together as she set her pencil down harder than I thought was necessary. "I'm worried. You were happy and now you're sad. And I really like Parker." Her voice cracked and my eyes started to burn. "Is this like what happened with Mom? Did you guys break up?"

"I don't know."

"Can you fix it?"

"I don't know," I said and rubbed the bridge of my nose.

I hadn't spoken to Parker since he walked away from me on Saturday. He'd said what we had together wasn't worth it. He and Marcos hadn't shown up for class on Monday. Those facts alone led me to think maybe we had broken up. That wasn't true either. He'd told me I had to figure out what I wanted, but I'd known what I wanted for a while now. Him. It was an easy choice. All it would take was a phone call and I could fix this, fix this fucking crack in my chest that pinched and split every time I took a breath. But I couldn't do it. I couldn't call him because it would turn into another argument about who should sacrifice what. He'd say I'd resent him, and I'd say he'd resent me, and round and fucking round we'd go. No. I had to fix this another way.

Anne didn't say anything more, but her watchful gaze never wavered as I moved through the motions of making dinner. Tuesdays she usually stayed with me, but she had a dentist appointment in the morning. I had an early meeting, or I would've taken her myself. Lanie would be here to pick her up in an hour, and I didn't want to be a broody asshole for the rest of the night. My time with my daughter was limited enough already. I put the pot on the stove to boil and plastered on a smile.

"You know... Mom said *The Day After Tomorrow* is playing at the old dollar theater we used to go to."

"No way." She practically bounced off her stool. "Can we go?"

"I don't see why not. Maybe Friday."

"Yes." She pumped her fist, all traces of worry gone from her eyes. "Yes, yes, yes."

I laughed as I opened up the box of penne pasta. "I'll even let you put butter on the popcorn."

She cracked up, her head falling forward. "And salt."

"All the salt," I said, and for the moment it didn't hurt to breathe.

With Anne here, eagerly chatting away about snowstorms and ice ages, it was easier to forget how shitty the last three days had been. It was easier to forget about the choices I had to make. But once dinner had been cooked, and cleaned up, and the doorbell rang, an old but familiar loneliness had begun to settle in for the night.

"Sorry I'm late," Lanie said as she walked into the kitchen. "I had to drop Matt at work." She mussed her fingers through Anne's hair and bent down to kiss her cheek. "Ready to go?"

"Yeah." Anne slid off her stool, and I laughed at the dejected glare she sent in her mother's direction. "I have to go to the bathroom first."

Lanie stared at her as she walked away. "She's grumpy."

"She hates it when you mess up her hair."

"She does?"

"Oh yeah," I said and set the pot I'd finished washing onto the rack next to the sink to dry.

"Well, shit." Lanie plopped down onto one of the stools. "How was your day?"

"Like every other day."

"Uh-oh."

"What?"

"Something happen at work?" she asked.

The pinch returned, deeper this time with everything I wasn't sure how to say.

"Van." She reached across the counter and covered my hand with hers. "You can talk to me. We're divorced, but you were my best friend once too."

"We were." I lowered my head. "I miss that."

"Then, talk to me."

"I've been seeing someone," I admitted, but kept my eyes on the counter. "It's getting serious... and I think..."

I swallowed through my hesitation. "I love him, Lanie. And I don't know what to do. I messed up."

"Him?"

"His name is Parker." I lifted my head and was met with glassy eyes and wet lashes. "Lanie, I—"

She wiped at her eyes, her smile trembling as she said, "I'm happy for you, Van. Truly. I just wish... You could have told me. I would have understood. I should be shocked, but I'm not... you've always been, I don't know. Like maybe, not all there? But you found it." She squeezed my hand before letting go. "The thing you were missing."

"You're wrong, though. It doesn't work like that," I said, my voice almost too thick to speak. "I never missed a thing when I was with you. I loved you, Lanie. With everything that I was. I might've not had a chance to know this other side of myself, but when we were good, I never needed anything else. It's different with him, but it doesn't diminish what we had."

"You've always been good at knowing what to say," she said and sniffled.

"I wish I knew what to say to him."

"You love him?"

"I do."

"Does he know?"

"I don't think he does."

Her laugh was light as she wiped at her eyes again. "Hell, Van. Have you told him?"

"No."

"There's you're answer," she said, looking at me like I was an idiot. Maybe I was. "You have to tell him that you love him. Whatever happened, maybe he'd be more understanding if he knew."

"Yeah... It's complicated."

"Isn't it always," she said as she fidgeted with her car keys. "Has Anne met him."

"She has. He's the one who bought her that big ass whale."

"I like him already... he's good with her?"

"Yeah, he is."

She set her keys to the side and leveled me with a look I knew all too well. "Just tell him how you feel. And if that doesn't work, then he doesn't deserve you."

"You don't know what I did."

"I don't. But I know you, Donovan, and whatever it is... you'll make it work."

Three days had turned into nine, and when he hadn't shown up last Wednesday for class, I'd thought for sure I'd fucked everything up beyond repair. But as I stood by my desk, summarizing the final assignment, he walked into the room. He kept his head down, his hat low enough I couldn't see his eyes. It wasn't until one of the students in the front row turned to look over their shoulder that I realized I'd stopped talking.

"Uh..." I couldn't do this. Fuck... I couldn't do this. Each breath I took was marked as I tried to collect my thoughts. "Um... what... what was I saying?"

"The final..." someone said, and I ran a clammy hand through my hair.

"Yes. Thank you... The final."

Parker flipped his hat backward, his blue gaze penetrating. His chest rising and falling in quick succession as he stared at me. The dark circles under his eyes made me wonder if his nights had been as restless as mine.

I counted to five in my head before he looked away.

"When did you say it was due?" another student asked, and I remembered where the hell I was.

"Friday," I said, and tore my eyes away from him. "The final assignment is due on Friday, but you have all of next week to turn in any late work since we don't have an actual final exam."

I did my best, going over the assignment while stealing glances at Parker. The handful of times he'd caught me, he'd look away. It was torture having him here, missing his secret smiles, his loaded, inappropriate looks. I was standing in the front of the classroom, but his scent was everywhere. Soap and spice in my lungs and on my hands, and I heard him in my head. He said, *figure out what you want*, and *you know how I feel*. Instead of walking up the aisle to pass out the outline, I handed it to the first row and asked them to pass it back. I didn't trust myself not to say something to him if I got that close. The hour dragged by as everyone worked on their paper. While most of the students had tapped away on their laptops, Parker scribbled into his notebook, ignoring me. As class ended and everyone started to pack up, my heart rate increased. He stood to leave, and despite the number of students remaining in the room, I called out his name.

"Parker, can you stay a minute?"

Parker.

Not Mr. Mills.

I didn't give a shit anymore. I was done hiding.

He looped his thumbs under the straps of his backpack. "Not really."

"It..." I stammered, my nerves bundling up in knots. "It won't take long."

His shoulders sagged and he clenched his jaw.

"Please."

He made his way down the aisle as the room emptied, and keeping a few feet between us, he said, "I'll make sure all my missed assignments are in on time."

"That's not what I wanted to talk about."

His jaw pulsed again, and God, I wanted to reach out and touch him.

"I don't have a lot of time. I have to get back to Pride House." He glanced at the door. "The play is this weekend."

"I know."

He exhaled a long breath. "What do you want, Van?"

"I... I don't know," I said, and his posture stiffened. "But I'm figuring it out."

"It's been over a week." His bright blue eyes vulnerable, he asked, "Why didn't you call?"

"I didn't want to argue," I said as the last student left the room.

"You could have texted... something. You left me fucking hanging."

"You're the one who walked away. You left."

He'd told me I needed to decide, he'd put the ball in my court. And the longer I'd tried to figure out what the hell to do, the more my insecurity took root. Each agonizing day that passed, each class he missed made it that much harder to reach out to him. The more time I'd put between us, the more I'd worried I couldn't fix this. It didn't help that we were both trying to be martyrs.

"I'm not doing this." He turned to leave, and as I grabbed his arm, goosebumps scattered across his skin.

"Wait, okay... just... wait a second." It was harder to let go of his arm than I thought it would be. The heat of his body lingered on the tips of my fingers. "I'm not taking the job."

"Van... I don't want do this again."

"Christ, you're a stubborn ass."

His lips twitched as he faced me. "I'm stubborn?"

"Full time, part time... If I stay here, we can't be public. And before you say anything, it doesn't matter that you're not going to be my student after the semester. You were, and the dean knows it. When you change your major to creative writing next semester, Vivian, the entire English department, they'll eventually know who you are, and if I'm faculty, that's not going to fly. I can't take the job, and I can't stay here. I'm going to put in my notice."

"No... You can't."

"I can. You told me to figure out what I wanted. And I have."

"You can't quit because of me."

"I'm not."

"That's bullshit, Van."

I heard the exhaustion in his voice. He was breaking too.

Stepping toward him, I said, "I know what I want."

"Van..."

I closed the distance he'd put between us and set my hand on the curve of his neck. He closed his eyes as my thumb trailed along the length of his jaw.

"There will always be another job. As much as my pride hates the idea, I could probably work at Emory if I asked my dad to pull some strings. But I want *you*, Parker." I leaned down and rested my forehead against his. "I love teaching, but I love you more."

He tipped his head back, his mouth meeting mine in a soft surrender.

"I love you..." he whispered, his hands in my hair, the tips of our noses brushing together. "And Anne... so much."

"I shouldn't have let you walk away. We should have had this conversation nine days ago."

"I can agree with that." He framed my face with his hands. "But I shouldn't have walked away in the first place."

"Maybe." I leaned into the rough skin of his palm, and I was home. "It was our first fight... we were bound to fuck it up."

"Can it be our last fight, because these last nine days were a nightmare. And I'm pretty sure Marcos is done with my mopey ass. He might actually throw me out."

I laughed and wrapped my arms around his neck. "I have a spare bedroom."

"Don't tempt me," he said, but his smile dimmed. "I don't want you to resent me."

"I want to hold your hand in public without worrying who might see. I want to kiss you and meet you for lunch. If I worked here, that couldn't ever happen. This is about me as much as it's about you. I choose this." I placed my hand in the center of his chest. "I want more than three months, Parker. I want as much time as I can have with you."

"I'm here for whatever you want," he said, and I remembered. "This is all for you."

He'd sent those words to me, what felt like ages ago, but even though the meaning had changed, my heart responded with those same quick and clumsy beats. I kissed him, letting the heat of his breath fully heal the crack in my chest. My hands dropped to his waist, my fingers gripping his shirt, holding him close, and I didn't worry about anyone catching us. All I wanted was to show him I was here, too, and it didn't matter if it was three months or three years, I'd choose this. I'd choose us every time.

Chapter 30

PARKER

Frantic was the only way I could describe it. Backstage, the kids from Pride House rushed around, getting dressed in their costumes and moving props. Marcos was frazzled, too, and I heard him trying his best to be polite to one of our younger cast members who wouldn't sit still long enough for him to glue on her fake lashes. Even Chance, our cool and collected director seemed nervous. He asked me about a thousand times if I needed anything and if everything was ready. I got the impression he didn't like it when he had nothing to contribute. Me, on the other hand, I was one-hundred-percent freaked the fuck out. I peeked out from behind the curtain again and started to sweat. The place was almost full. The crowd was at least double the size from last year. But last year I hadn't written the play, and the responsibility of everything made me nauseous.

"We have a problem," Rachel said in her too-calm-shit-is-about-to-hit-the-fan tone. "Denny... is... Parker, he's having a full-blown panic attack in the bathroom and just threw up all over himself."

"What?" The room started to spin. "He's Silas."

"I know."

"We start in like twenty minutes."

"I'm aware of that little tidbit as well."

"Rach..." Jesus Christ. "I mean, we can figure out the costume, but he's going on, right?"

She pressed her lips together and winced. "No... he said he can't do it."

"Shit." A tiny part of me wanted to march over to the bathroom and tell him to suck it the fuck up. That he wasn't a quitter. That he could do this. That we were depending on him, but he didn't deserve the guilt trip. He worked hard, and I know he was scared from the beginning, but like the rest of these kids, they'd been forced in roles they never wanted their whole lives, and I wasn't about to add to that trauma over a stupid play. "What are we supposed to do?"

"I heard Denny isn't going on?" Chance asked, and Rachel and I both deflated.

"He's going to fire us," she said under her breath.

"Will you quit it with that."

Chance stared at us both. "What's the back-up plan?"

I didn't have one. "Let me think."

I paced back and forth a few times and Marcos noticed. "What's going on?"

"Denny isn't going on," Rachel said, and my stomach clenched again.

"Fuck." Marcos didn't even try to lower his voice, and I think Chance might've actually glared at him. I couldn't tell. The man was impassive as hell. "Oh my God, Park. You can be Silas."

"What? No."

"Why not?" Rachel asked. "You wrote the damn play. You know the lines."

"It could work," Chance added, and I wanted to scream. I think Marcos's drama had started to wear off on me after all these years.

"For one, I have no costume," I said. "And I'm not kissing a fourteen-year-old."

"Nix the kissing scene and we're good," Marcos said. "I got the costume under control. Chance, give me your pants."

"Ah..." His thick brows dipped into a severe line. "Why?"

"You're the only one around here close to Parker's size." Marcos held out his hands and the silent "duh" hung between us all. "Besides, those jeans have seen better days, it fits the whole homeless lost boy look perfectly."

Rachel covered her smile with her hand.

"Marcos..." I warned and he shrugged. "It won't work."

"It will," he insisted and called one of the kids over. "Can you grab me a few of those ivy garlands off the cottage prop. I think two or three will be enough."

"I'll look ridiculous standing next to Jake. I'm a grown-ass man. I can't be a lost boy."

385

I wrote the play. I wasn't a goddamn actor. My gut churned, and the empathy I had for Denny increased threefold.

"Park, what else can we do?" Rachel pleaded and Christ, this was happening.

"Fine. But I want a raise, and you have to promise to never fire Rachel," I pointed at Chance, and he actually laughed.

"Sure."

"And I'm not kissing Jake. I'll just... rest my cheek against his when the time comes."

"Sounds good," Rachel said, setting her hands on my shoulder. "Now hurry the hell up, the curtain is supposed to open in ten minutes."

"Wait a minute," Marcos said as Chance started to walk away. "I wasn't joking. I need those pants."

"I can wear my own jeans."

"No... they're too nice."

"There's holes in the knees." Chance pushed his hands in his pockets, looking Marcos up and down. "I think I'll keep my pants on... for now."

When he walked away Rachel asked, "Did he just hit on Marcos, or am I high?"

"He did no such thing." Marcos made a fake gagging noise, and I was too nervous to laugh.

"You're on the clock, Basulto, make me pretty."

Back in the dressing room, Marcos quickly turned my jeans into shorts. He cut out a jagged line around my legs, and I was surprised at how well they turned out. Instead of a shirt, Marcos wrapped the ivy from the cottage around my waist and chest.

"I don't look half-bad."

"Sit," he said. "I only have three minutes, I can't promise you anything fabulous, but close your eyes."

"Um..."

"Don't give me shit, *mijo*." He snapped his fingers and I sat in the chair. "Thank you."

"You're scary sometimes," I said and closed my eyes.

"Yeah... well, you're an idiot all the time so..."

I couldn't see his face, but I knew him well enough to know he was smiling.

"You're enjoying this."

"You have no idea," he said and applied something to my eyelids with a featherlight touch. "Almost done. One more thing."

"Can I open my eyes?"

"Not yet. Pucker your lips."

"Fuck that."

"It's only gloss, stop being a baby." He rolled the sticky substance on my lips, and I sighed.

"I hate you."

"If you hated me, you wouldn't have helped me finish the assignments I missed in your boyfriend's class. Which I only missed because I'm a loyal motherfucker."

"You're not supposed to mention that."

"Shut up and open your eyes."

I blinked at him, and the smile on his face was next-level smug.

"Do I look dumb?"

"You look hot, and it's freaking me out. I can't have incestuous thoughts about you, Park. We've made it this far."

I shoved him out of the way, and I didn't recognize myself in the mirror. "Holy shit."

"I'm that good."

I pressed my lips together, the slick gloss shined under the lights. My cheeks were flushed, my eyes ringed in a dark black liner, and he'd smudged some gray on my lids, with a little bit of blue flaring out from the corners.

"I'm kind of pretty."

"No shit." Marcos admired his work and my reflection in the mirror. "Van is going to come in his pants."

"You can't say shit like that when there are kids around."

"I'm sure they hear worse at school." He smacked my shoulder. "You better hurry, I think everyone is getting in first position."

I jumped up and took my phone out of my pocket, but before I set it on the vanity, I shot Van a quick text.

Me: I have a surprise for you.

The heat from the stage lights had sweat beading on my forehead for the majority of the play, but I was grateful they'd made it next to impossible for me to see the audience. I'd only stumbled on a few lines in the First Act. The Second Act I'd found my stride, and by the third, I was truly feeling it. I didn't think acting was in my future, but it was incredible to have this opportunity, to have the chance to be one of my all-time favorite characters, even if I'd wanted to puke for at least the first twenty minutes.

Knowing Van was here with his daughter, my own real-life Pan, helped to steady me.

The stage darkened as I walked across it. The entire room was immersed in silence as the spotlight lit up Tink's grave. It was fiction, but as I stood staring down at the tombstone the kids had painted, my throat ached. I thought about last Wednesday, about those terrible nine days when I thought I'd pushed Van away, when I thought I'd lost the chance to tell him how much I wanted him in my life. I thought about all of it, and my lashes brimmed with tears. I told myself it was the emotion of the day, the panic, the weight of all this responsibility crashing down, but it was relief. Pure fucking relief, and when Jake, aka Pan, walked out from the right side of the stage to take my hand, I exhaled a wet breath.

"She's gone," he said, and I nodded, wiping carefully under my eyes. Marcos would kick my ass if I messed up his make-up.

"She did this for us," I said and turned to him. I rested my cheek to his like we'd planned, no reason it needed to get weird, and I felt Jake's quiet chuckle against my skin. I took two breaths, remembering my lines, and faced the audience. I pointed at the ceiling. "You see that cluster of stars, Pan? The three just below the moon."

He made a show of looking up at the ceiling in wonder. "I can see them."

"The bright one, it's Tink." I smiled one small smile. "She sacrificed herself for us, and now she will always be remembered."

"We've all sacrificed," he said, threading his fingers through my other hand. "But we're lost boys, do you think we'll be remembered too?"

"I do... The other two stars, Pan... One day they'll belong to me and you."

"They'll belong to us," he said and rested his temple against my arm.

"And every night the world will know how much I love you."

The lights shut off and the crowd erupted with applause. I laughed, and Jake jumped up in the air, banging into me like a maniac. "Holy crap, we did it!"

I high fived him as the lights switched back on and the entire cast came out onto the stage. We all linked hands and bowed to the standing ovation. I found Van sitting three rows back, beaming up at me. He bit his lip and shook his head as I blew him a kiss. Adrenaline rushed through my veins, and I had to tell myself not to jump off the stage and maul him with my mouth. He'd put in his notice yesterday, and after finals week, we would be in the clear. I didn't think I'd ever not feel guilty for the choice he'd made, but as Anne waved at me, and Van laughed again, it was difficult for me to focus on anything other than the love I could see in his eyes.

After we exited the stage, the crew and cast hugged and cheered, and Chance gathered us all into a huddle. Marcos wiggled in next to me and held my hand.

"I might be a little in love with you, but it'll pass, just give it an hour." He grinned and set his head on my shoulder. "You were marvelous...in case you're in your head about everything."

"Thanks." I wrapped my arm around his waist as Chance cleared his throat.

"I know we've had a lot of changes recently," he said, his eyes settling on Rachel. "But I think the future of Pride House has always been in your hands. What you have here. What you've all accomplished, it's astounding. You should be proud of yourselves." The kids whooped and Rachel smiled. "With ticket sales and two very generous donations from Lowe Literary and St. Benedicts Hospital, we raised a little over fifteen-thousand dollars."

"Holy shit," Marcos gasped.

Rachel looked at me and started to cry. All the kids, kind of awestruck, stared at Chance.

"I've been a lot of places. Worked with a lot of organizations. But what I've seen here... I'm grateful to be a part of this. *'Fairy tales are more than true: not because they tell us that dragons exist, but because they tell us that dragons can be beaten.'*"

"He just quoted Neil Gaiman," I whispered, and Marcos lifted his head.

"Who?"

"I did," Chance said and gave me an actual smile. "What Gaiman said has always stuck with me. We all have dragons we have to slay, and tonight you did it. You worked hard and it showed."

All the kids cheered again, and I'd never seen them this happy before. After a few more hugs and tears from Rachel, we made our way to the dressing rooms. Marcos packed up his make-up and I pulled on my shirt.

"Hey, Park." Denny approached me with a weary smile. "I'm sorry, man."

I clapped him on the shoulder and pulled him into a side hug. "Don't be. Everything worked out."

"I guess it did." He hung his head. "Not 'cause of me, though."

"You worked hard on this, Denny, and I would've loved to see you on that stage. But only you can set your limits. And tonight, you hit one, and that's okay."

"Yeah?"

"Yeah." I squeezed his shoulder. "Don't worry about it, okay... go celebrate with everyone. We all deserve a little fun after all our hard work."

"You coming to the pizza place?" he asked.

"I can't. My boyfriend is taking me out to dinner."

"Oh," he said, dragging out the vowel with a smirk on his face. "Have fun."

He lightly punched me in my arm before he walked away.

"Listen," Marcos said, as he pulled his bag over his shoulder. "I have to take off, but..." He swallowed and exhaled a sharp breath. "Look, I know I don't say it enough, but I think you're fucking amazing. I hope you get that."

"You *are* in love with me," I said and grinned when he narrowed his eyes. "What will I tell Van?"

"Fuck you, Mills. This is why I can never say nice things to you." He waved his fingers at me. "You always get a big head about it."

"Thank you." I kissed his cheek and he nodded. "For all your help."

He started to walk away as he said, "You know, I asked Rachel about becoming a full-time volunteer."

"Oh... does a certain tree hugger have anything to do with that?"

"Don't offend me." He waved over his shoulder. "See you tomorrow."

I grabbed my phone off the vanity, and as I headed for the auditorium door, I checked my messages. I laughed when I saw I had a notification from the Pegasus app.

@MeAndMyShadow33: I have a surprise for you too.

@MeAndMyShadow33: I think you forgot to teach me a very important lesson.

I pinned my bottom lip between my teeth as I typed.

@TheLOstBOy: You have my attention.

I was about to open the stairwell door when my phone pinged.

@MeAndMyShadow33: Role playing. Is there any way you can take that ivy home with you tonight?

@TheLOstBOy: You'd like that?

@MeAndMyShadow33: More than I should.

@TheLOstBOy: I might be able to make that happen.

@MeAndMyShadow33: Right now, I just want you in my arms.

@TheLOstBOy: On my way.

Eager to find him, I jogged down the stairs. The crowd had thinned, and I spotted Van talking with Ethan and Anders and...

I almost tripped over my own feet. Pen Aster, the author of *The Lost Boys* was here, standing next to my boyfriend and his daughter. Van turned his head and smiled when he saw me. I didn't, couldn't move. He let go of Anne's hand and walked toward me.

"What did you do?" I asked, and Christ, my voice shook.

"Anders made it happen, I just asked him if he could."

"He's here. Pen Aster is here. And... Oh shit... Was it terrible?"

Van pulled me into his warm arms. "He loved it."

Fuck it all, I got choked up and let him wrap me up in his embrace. My hands flat on his back, I buried my nose in the crook of his neck, and it was all earthy and lavender, and I might've almost cried. Almost.

"I can't believe you did this for me." I pressed my lips to his skin. "How are you not freaking out?"

He laughed as I lowered my arms and looked into his eyes. "Believe me, when he showed up, I had a moment. I forgot the word hello."

My shoulders shook as I laughed. "You did?

"Anders will probably remind me of it daily for the next month."

"Parker." Anne let go of Ethan's hand and ran toward me. "That was so cool."

"You liked it?" I asked and leaned down to hug her.

394

"My favorite part was when you stabbed King Juno, the blood looked wicked."

"It was the perfect adaptation." Pen Aster held out his hand and I shook it. His bones felt fragile. His skin as thin as paper. "I liked the twist you had at the end."

I stared at his white hair, the wrinkles on his face all smiling back at me. "I, uh... I..."

"Parker and I are huge fans," Van said, and I leaned into him. "I think he's a little starstruck."

"Like you were," Pen said, his voice wobbling as he laughed. "I didn't think anyone knew who I was anymore."

"You gave me something to hope for," I said, and I had no idea how I found the words. "When I was a kid. Reading about someone like me. It made me feel like I wasn't alone."

His hand trembled as he raised it to my shoulder. I didn't know if he was nervous, or if it was from age. He had to be over ninety years old.

"I'm glad I was a light for you."

"For so many," Van said.

"Tonight, you all were a light for me. You sure know how to make an old man feel special."

I had about hundred questions for him. But instead, I said, "It was an honor to have you here."

A younger woman I didn't recognize looped her arm through his. "We better get going, Uncle Pen. I don't want you to wear yourself out."

"Don't fuss over me, I used to change your diapers," he grumbled, but it didn't have much of a bite.

"Thank you for inviting him," she said to Van. "It meant the world to him."

He shook all of our hands again and pinched Anne's cheek before he turned to me one last time. "Good job, son."

My jaw pulsed as I tried to breathe through the sudden onslaught of nostalgia. Homesick for my father.

"Th... Thank you."

"We'll walk out with you, if that's okay?" Ethan asked, and Pen nodded.

"Anne, sweetheart, go outside with Anders, okay? I need a minute with Parker, then we'll go to dinner."

She took Anders's hand as he said, "I want to talk about the play next week. I think we could do something with it. I'll have Kris call you."

"Yeah, okay... that would be great," I said stunned, and he gave me a quiet smile before he walked away.

The room was almost empty as Van cupped my cheek, his thumb passing softly over my skin. "You looked beautiful up there." He nodded toward the stage. "I felt it in the end. It was real for you."

"It was."

His familiar lips were warm as they enveloped mine. He held my face, kissing me like I might break.

"When you walked out on the stage... Parker. I can't explain it, but it didn't surprise me. It should have been you."

"I thought about you the whole time." I placed my hand on the back of his neck pulling him in. "Every line..." I kissed his jaw, his chin, finding my way to the soft dip above is upper lip. "Belongs to you, to us."

"And every night," he said. "I'll make sure you know how much I love you."

Epilogue

DONOVAN

Four Months Later

Thunder clouds hovered over the trees, the wind picking up enough I worried the small tent where the grooms stood would blow over, or worse, Anders's mom would have a heart attack. She'd fretted over the pale purple ribbons she'd strewn in the tree branches and glared at the three rows of chairs all unprotected from the elements. Her lips contorted into a frown as another ribbon blew away into the river. If I'd read her lips correctly, she'd just dropped the f-bomb.

"Why is that woman even trying to salvage this shit show?" Marcos asked and Parker nudged him with his shoulder.

"Hey, be nice," he said, and I laced my fingers through his. "You promised Ethan you wouldn't whine about the weather."

"That was your first mistake." Wilder bounced his daughter Sam on his leg. "Never, and I mean ever promise

Ethan anything when it comes to the great outdoors, especially fishing. You'll end up in humidity hell with gnats biting your ankles."

Jax lifted Sam from his husband's lap and tucked her under his arm. Her big eyes turned up to the sky as a couple of rain drops fell. "I told Ethan they should have gotten married in January. Less rain."

Marcos gasped as he held out his hand. "Oh, hell no. Nope. I'm waiting in the car, *mijo*."

"Christ, Basulto, it's just rain. How the hell did you ever make it through basic?" Parker gave him a pointed look, and Marcos flipped him off.

"I didn't have on two-hundred-dollar pants when I was in basic."

"Thank God," Parker said. "Spending that much money on pants is out of control."

"Amen." Jax grinned at Parker. "I've been telling Wild that for years."

Wilder snuggled into his husband's side. "We can't all look as sexy as you do in jeans and a t-shirt. Some of us need accessories."

"You're sexy without any of that stuff." Jax kissed his cheek and I smiled at the way Wilder preened.

"You two are adorable," I said.

"You and Parker look pretty cozy." Wilder tapped me on the knee. "I want credit for your little duo... I called it that night we went to dinner."

"You did?"

"Yup, I said he had a crush on you. Oh..." His eyes lit up. "And I told you about Pegasus."

"Babe, leave the man alone, you can't take credit for his relationship."

"I sure can."

I laughed. "No, it's okay. I guess I sort of owe you a thank you."

"Sort of—"

"Thank you, Wilder."

"You're welcome."

More rain trickled down from the sky, and a few umbrellas popped up among the small gathering. Anders and Ethan had only invited close friends and family. Nora, the agent I'd replaced two years ago, flew in from Seattle with her brother Luka. Overall, there was less than twenty-five people here. It was intimate, like Ethan and Anders had wanted, and as they both smiled at each other, it was safe to say they didn't give a shit about the rain, or the wayward ribbons. Ethan's hair blew wild in the wind, his cream-colored linen button-up whipping at his sides as he reached out for his soon-to-be husband's hand. Anders held his gaze, dressed in a similar-style shirt except his was gray. They both had on loose-fitting slacks and sandals, and I had to smile at how laidback my boss looked. I didn't think I'd ever witness such a feat.

"When is this thing going to start?" Marcos asked and Parker shrugged.

"We're waiting on my brother and his girlfriend," Jax said. "My mom had to pick them up and she's—"

"The slowest driver on Earth," Wilder interrupted. "What? Don't look at me like that. You know I love your mother."

June and Gwen, a couple I'd met at Wilder's last release party, turned around in their seats.

"Don't start with me, June, it's hot and wet," he said, and she rolled her eyes.

She reached back and handed him her umbrella. "Will this shut you up?"

"Yes. Thank you."

Parker chuckled at my side, and I laid my arm across the back of his chair. I leaned in and whispered, "Are you having fun yet?"

Eventually the rest of the guest list showed up, and by some sort of miracle the rain stopped long enough for the ceremony to start. Ethan's cheeks were flushed as Anders leaned down to kiss him, their hands together, he said, "You ready to do this?"

"I think I was ready the day I watched you sleep on the plane." Anders pushed a strand of hair from Ethan's forehead and nodded at the officiator. "We're ready."

The woman held up her hand and the small crowd went silent. Even the wind stopped. The only sound came from the river, the white noise muted as she spoke. "Anders and Ethan asked me to be here today, but only to bear witness to their union. They have written their own vows and asked you all here to share in this special day. And if I may," she said, and Parker rested his hand on my thigh. "I'd like to say thank you for allowing us all to be here with you as you embark on this new journey together."

"I'm getting married on a cruise," Marcos whispered, and Parker lightly kicked him in the leg.

"Word of the day," Anders said. "Ours, defined as which belongs to me and you."

"Love." Ethan let go of Anders's hand and reached into his pocket. "Defined as a deep affection for someone."

He slid a ring on Anders's finger. Anders did the same for Ethan as he spoke. "Commitment... defined as a pledge... a dedication."

"Forever," Ethan said, staring down at their joined hands. "Defined as an infinite number of days, for always."

Anders lifted his chin with two fingers and bent down, pressing a kiss to Ethan's lips. My face heated, the moment too private for all of these prying eyes. When he pulled away, Ethan spoke low enough that I didn't think anyone could hear what he'd said. Anders nodded, his throat bobbing as he swallowed, and when they turned to face us, Anders's lashes were wet.

The officiator stood at their side, a huge smile on her face. "Please welcome, for the first time, Anders and Ethan Lowe."

Everyone clapped and cheered in celebration. Anders lifted their raised hands, his smile sheepish, his cheeks pink. People started to stand, hurrying over to congratulate the happy couple. I didn't know when, or if, I wanted to get married again. But seeing the smiling faces before me, the joy radiating from the two men under the tent, I couldn't rule it out.

As if he could read my mind, Parker asked, "You think you'll ever be ready for picket fences again, professor?"

"I don't know," I said, my eyes landing on his mouth.

Our lips met and the rain fell harder. Marcos squealed, or maybe it was Wilder. I couldn't be sure. I slid my hand into Parker's hair, and his hand slid to the back of my neck. Movement flickered in my peripheral vision, and I should have been worried that we were being rude, but after last semester ended, any time I had a chance to kiss my boyfriend in public, I took it. I didn't know how Parker would have ever been okay with hiding. Getting to have him like this meant everything. Having him meet my family, meeting his, watching him flourish in his new classes this spring, getting to read all of his work, and watch how much he'd grown as a writer in such a short time, I didn't think we'd be here if I'd stayed at Winchester.

Parker breathed and I breathed, and I bathed in the heat of his touch.

"Mhm." He broke away from my lips. "I think it's raining."

Little rivulets of water dripped from his hair. "We should probably get under the tent."

"Probably," he said, but neither of us moved. "I don't need any of this, you know."

"Marriage?"

"Yeah..."

"It's not so bad," I said. "But I might have to settle for a kiss, and a dog named Chuck."

"And a fish named Tony."

"I could get on board with that," I said and gripped the wet fabric of his shirt, kissing him without worrying who was watching.

The End

Acknowledgements

My heart is so full.

I don't have the words to explain how grateful I am for all of you! So far this year I've been the closest I've ever gotten to reaching my goal of being a full time writer, though I'm not there yet, I'm so lucky because every year I'm only successful because I have the best freaking readers! You've stuck with me through all of my ups and downs, my genre hops and continue to trust me with your time and love.

I could never achieve my dream of being a writer without each and every one of you. Thank you for being there for me, for believing in me. It's a privilege to do what I do.

Thank you to my editing team. Elaine and Kathleen. You two amazing women! I couldn't do this without you.

Thank you to my PA and my BFFL Ari. May Marcos hold your namesake dear to his mother fucking heart. Love you! I can't imagine how the hell I'd survive without you.

Thank you to my Biscuits! Gah! I can't tell you how much your hard work means to me! THANK YOU THANK YOU!

Special thanks to Beth for all the side work and graphics and therapy you give me. And Jodi for managing my ARC Team, being a typo finding queen, and all the ledge dodging chats hahaha! Kelly and Heather for being a support and a shoulder to cry on. To Linda at Foreword and everyone at GRR, and to all my friends in the author community I'm so grateful!

Thank you to my beta team and heart! Anna, Kristy, Sammie, Cornelia, Ari, Emma, Elle, Jodi, Beth, Braxton, Azeely, Alissa, Saxon, Layla, Sarah, Cass, and Taylor! Y'all are the heart and soul of this process and I love you immensely!

To my friends book world and "in person" thank you for being there for me. I know at times I can be MIA, say and do the wrong things sometimes, being human is hard y'all, but it's an honor to have you in my life, to be able to call y'all friends.

To my family and my kiddos. I'm sorry for the missed movie/game nights and the late hours, but I think I've finally got it all figured out! We have lots of snuggle bunches and magic movies headed our way. I love you Wolf, Kell Bell, G and MJ more than you'll ever know.

These are always the hardest to write because inevitably I will forget something. But please know, if you are in my life, you mean the world to me!

Lastly, I want to say thank you to all of my fellow healthcare workers out there, the social justice warriors, and folx that are fighting the fight for equality in any way they can. May you find peace in your work!

Much love and side hugs,
Amanda

Other Books

Forever Still Series:
Still Life
Still Water
Still Surviving

Avenues Ink Series:
Possession
Kingdom
Poet

Twin Hearts Series:
Let There Be Light
Seven Shades of You

For Him Series:
Love Always, Wild
Not So Sincerely, Yours
Dear Mr. Brody

The Rulebook Collection
Breakaway

Stand Alone Novels:
Sacred Hart

Erotica:
Beneath the Vine